THE REEDSMITH OF ZENDAR

BOOKS BY DANIEL SIDE

A Lesson in Revenge
The Reedsmith of Zendar
A Change of Heart*

*forthcoming

THE REEDSMITH OF ZENDAR

DANIEL SIDE

CreateSpace Independent Publishing Platform
A Daniel Side Publication
Binbrook ON

The Reedsmith of Zendar
Copyright 2014 by Daniel Side

All rights reserved. No part of this book may be used or reproduced in any manner whatsoever including Internet usage, without written permission of the author.

This is a work of fiction. The names, characters, places, or events used in this book are the product of the author's imagination or used fictitiously. Any resemblance to actual people, alive or deceased, events or locales is completely coincidental.

Book design by Maureen Cutajar
www.gopublished.com

ISBN: 1499688806

This one too is for Lynda.

Acknowledgements

I would like to thank the following people who helped improve this novel. Duane was relentless with his efforts to help me take the novel out of Sarnia Ontario and transpose it to Zendar. Many thanks for all your observations and suggestions. Thank you Andrea, Linda, Emily and Leann for venturing into the fantasy world for the first time and providing constructive feedback. Thank you Erica for proof reading. And as always, thank you Lynda for your patience, cover photography, the final proof reading - and for supporting all aspects of the Zendar experience.

That being said, any mistakes or shortcomings are, of course, mine.

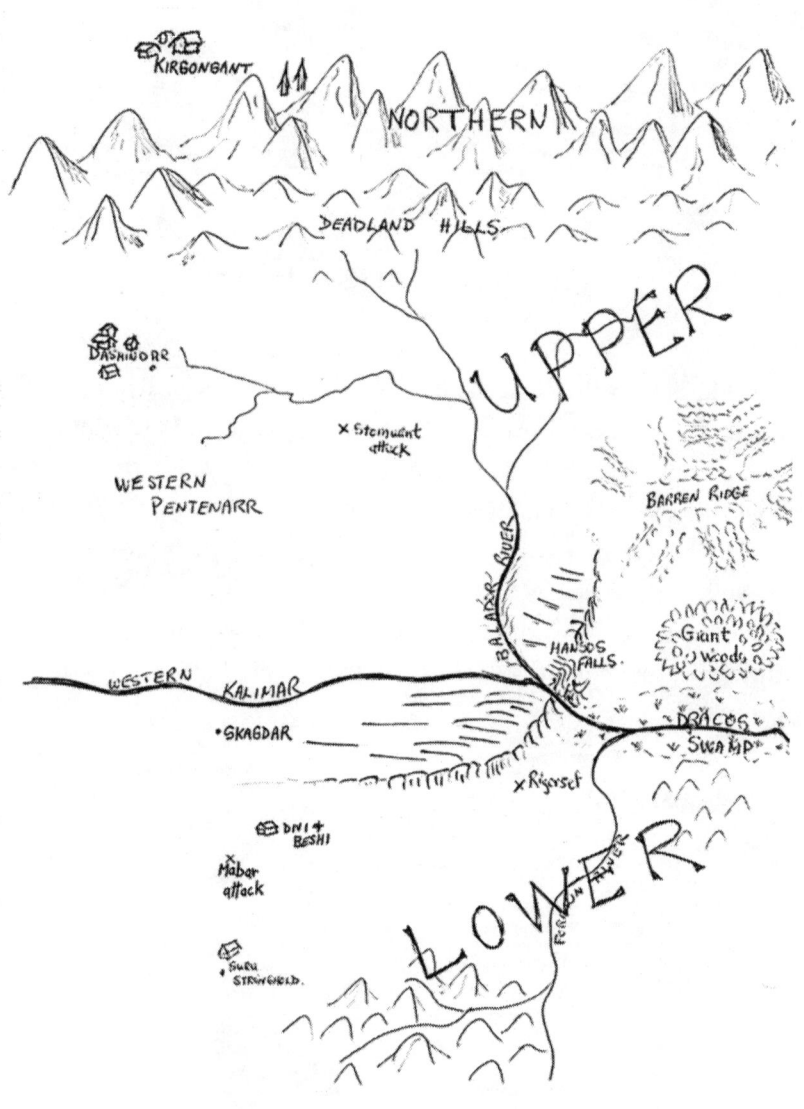

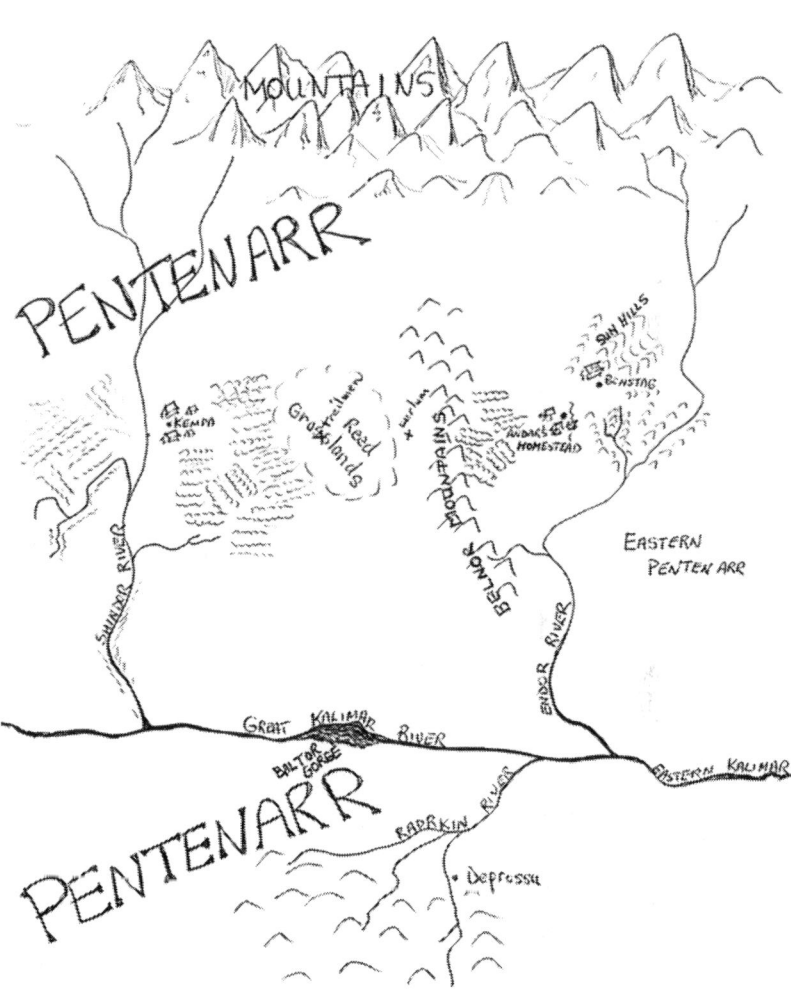

Contents

Prologue 1

Part One 3
A GENTLE ROAR OF WHISPERS

Part Two 105
SURU STRONGHOLD

Part Three 209
BEYOND THE NORTHERN MOUNTAINS

Part Four 307
RELEASE FROM THE HUNGER

Epilogue 358

THE
Reedsmith
of Zendar

PROLOGUE

John finished the last of another mug of warm, flat beer, wiped is lips, and set it on the picnic table. The kids, still full of enthusiasm, were in the house donning capes and helmets, grabbing swords. His brother, sitting beside him, smirked with pleasure.

"My night off this year, big guy," said Mark.

"I know, I know. Christ, after all this sun, not to mention the beer, all I want to do is crash."

"Yeah, I know how you feel. But you love the sun, and this damned heat, and wouldn't want it any other way. And as for the beer, without it we would have strangled one or two of the kids by now."

"Yeah, you're right. Come on guys, hurry it up! It's getting dark and the mosquitoes will be out soon."

The back door exploded outwards and two of John's children, capes flying, helmets askew, made their presence known.

"Dad, Mike said that he was going to tell the story this year. How come he gets to do it?" asked John's youngest son Gordon. "I want a turn."

John looked at Gordon and sighed. "Mike does not get to tell the story this year, and when you're old enough you can tell it, but not this year. I am. Now go sit."

John and Mark's wives emerged from the back door, ushering the remaining three children out and over to the circle of wood blocks that surrounded a small fire.

"Sit!" Donna said. "John, it's getting late and it has been a *long* day. Can we get on with this?"

"What's the matter, hun? Not enough Zendarian ale?"

"*Now*, John."

"Okay, okay." He moved to the fire and sat. "Listen up every one. Did you all have a good time?" A chorus of cheers answered him, bringing a smile to his lips. "Great. What did you like most?"

"The King's Message!" shouted Mike. "I got there the fastest."

"No you didn't," said Susan. "I liked shooting the arrows. It was fun."

"I liked climbing the Dragon, but the steps should have been closer together. I couldn't get to them all."

"Sorry, we'll have to fix that next year," said John. "Okay, now it's time for the closing fire and a legend of Zendar to go with it."

"What's it about, Dad?" Gordon asked.

"Well, I think you're ready for one of the longer tales of Zendar."

"All right!" said Susan.

"You're going to have to sit still and listen carefully because it is long." John could see his wife's eyes start to smoulder and looked away quickly.

"Wrap your cloaks around you and get comfortable. The story starts near a small village. Its night time and we're just outside the reedsmith's shop."

Part One

A Gentle Roar of Whispers

Chapter One

One with the shadows, the assassin stalked his prey beneath Zendar's two moons. The reed trees cast tumbling shadows on the green mist floating above the forest floor as the Suru, clad in green, slipped between two tree trunks. Humid night air muffled the sound of a scaled watralermis that scurried from his path. Now close to the young woman, the Suru could see the pale red sheen of moonlight on her hair. He assessed the lichen and rock ahead. Careful to keep his aura close so that she would not sense his presence, he lowered his taut frame and crept through the roiling mist, skirting the gnarled roots of the aged trees as he tightened the distance between them.

Ahead, the light evening cloak chased Dreanna as she walked in nervous haste towards the shop. All around her the throbbing drone of bark bugs filled the air. From the windows of the building, an amber glow pushed back the night. She hesitated at the door, gathered her nerve and eased the latch free. The sound of thudding blows greeted her as she slipped inside. Round reed log walls and heavy ceiling beams made the smith shop appear smaller than it actually was. A raised hearth, one side completed by the striking plate, sat in the center of the hardened dirt floor. The light from hanging crystal torches danced and flickered, coaxing shadows into a gentle dance across the storage racks and shelves that filled the walls.

Dreanna pursed her lips and twisted the plait of brown hair that hung over her shoulder. Her young face was strong, but the hazel eyes were marred with doubt. She took a deep breath and closed them when she saw the polished stone pendant around her father's neck. Her mother had always worn it. Sadness weakened the control of her aura and it seeped outwards. She was still learning how to control it. She strengthened her defence, drawing it in closer to hide it from her father. She wanted to watch him, gauge his mood, before making her request. Dreanna opened her eyes and stared across the dimly lit room.

Her father, clad in knee-length breeches, his worn smith's apron and gauntlets, worked at the hearth, the red glow from it lighting his tall frame. Self-consciously she studied his muscled shoulders, her eyes sliding down the brown chest to the sweat-stained apron. Around his neck the azure pendant swayed gently with the jump and roll of his lean muscles as he worked the reed. The hammer swept down smoothly, bounced once then leapt up over his shoulder again. It hurtled down, time after time, creating the rhythm that Dreanna knew so well from childhood. She saw the motion of his legs, felt the pulsing beat in the air, and knew it was good. She drew a deep breath and stood straight and tall.

"Father, it's time that someone teaches me how to make love."

Andar winced in surprise, the burnished hammer awkwardly striking the reed he had been flattening for a sword blade. He grunted, annoyance streaking his face. He had sensed her presence; it was the demand that caught him off guard. Andar looked to his daughter standing in the shadows.

"Father, I'm old enough now."

"Dreanna, I-"

"It wouldn't be hard for you to find a young man from the village." She moved towards him, drawing strength from her frustration, fierce in her commitment to win this battle. "It's not far, and I'm sure there is *someone* in the village that would do this for you, for me. It's been many days now since the change, and I've tried to tell you, tried to let you know that, that I'm ready, that it happened, and, and..." In the hearth's glow, Dreanna's tanned face was uncertain, yet her shining eyes implored him. Then they hardened in challenge and refused to falter.

Andar scowled his annoyance again, trying to bully her, but he knew he must acknowledge the woman in her, not the girl. He *had* noticed the tell-tale signs: her fuller, womanly body, the musky scent when the sun warmed her as she worked in the yard, the greening of her eyes; the obvious strengthening of her aura. He had known of her coming of age and ignored it, and that he knew was wrong. Andar shook his head in self-reproach. She took his action for resistance.

"Father, I need a real lover, not an imaginary one!"

He stared at her, taking in the wide stance, hands balled into fists jammed firmly on her hips. The jut of her jaw spoke of her defiance and her desire. Andar gazed at her and saw the vision of his wife, and she was beautiful. Stepping forward, he cupped her cheeks in his callused hands.

"By the Landsite, you *are* your mother's daughter." His laughter, the first in many rains, sounded strange, even to his ears. "Yes, Dreanna, yes. You need not worry. There are many young men in Bonstag, thousands throughout Pentenarr, who would be honoured. I know you're ready, and soon we'll release this passion of yours upon those in the village." He smiled and pinched her nose. "Forgive me, I've been foolish." He hugged her. "But it's late. Tomorrow we'll talk and make decisions. No, no more. Tomorrow."

Dreanna heard the finality in his tone, saw the stern cast of his face. Her frown turned to a mischievous grin. "Thank you, Father. Thank you!" She reached up and kissed him, a long, full kiss upon the mouth, and it caught him unawares. He stuttered, cursing her half heartedly, but hugged her tightly again before letting go. Dreanna laughed and skipped to the door, whirling in pleasure to watch him.

Neither saw nor sensed the Suru climb silently through a window to crouch in the darkness.

Andar was embarrassed; by her kiss, by his avoidance of Dreanna's needs, by his sudden show of affection after so long. She had surprised him, and in doing so had driven a wedge into the cold sadness that gripped him so tenuously. His mood was lighter than it had been since the accident. Suddenly he felt that perhaps the worst was over. He raised the hammer and began again, the muffled cadence filling the temperate air of the shop. The torches above him flickered as he hardened the mottled green and yellow reed, hammering the fibers closer together, drying it slowly over the hearth. He encouraged the rhythmic motion, feeling the warmth of the pulsing coal shards nestled in the ashes. The turning of the blade, the rocking back and forth as the hammer rose and fell set his mind at ease.

As he worked his brow relaxed, easing the lines of age. Green eyes set in a bed of sun creased wrinkles focused on each blow of the hammer. Taller than most and lean muscled, Andar didn't fit the image of the barrel-chested smiths of Zendar. Although gray streaked the brown hair, except for a gradually thickening waist, years of smithing had kept the former council guard fit. With marriage and children, he had abandoned the turmoil of the early years, retreating to the solitude of the country and becoming content with a life of hard work and simple pleasures near the village.

Dreanna's eyes widened when a shadow detached itself from the darkness and glided silently towards her father. The eyes of the Suru were demanding, preventing her from warning of the danger. Terror stricken, she reached for the door. Finally she screamed when the Suru hurled the dagger accurately towards her and drew a short-bladed sword.

Dreanna's shrill scream startled Andar, draining the blood from his face. Turning, his eyes met those of the shadow. Instinctively, he brought the hammer down, deflected the slash aimed at his throat, then let the hammer rotate in an arc and hurled it at the chest of the Suru. Without pausing he sprang to his left and seized a tall reed from a stack leaning against the wall. He risked a glance and took in the dagger imbedded in the door, Dreanna frozen in terror.

"Run to the house Dreanna!"

Andar's heart thudded wildly, his mouth dry as he sought his attacker's eyes again. The assassin had nimbly dodged the hammer, but Andar saw the subtle change of confidence as the eyes became wary. Andar lunged forward, jabbing with the reed at the man's cowled face. The assassin's blade flicked effortlessly, cutting off the end, a grim, threadlike smile of satisfaction tracing his lips. Andar launched the now crudely sharpened spear then hurled himself low at the Suru's waist. The assassin avoided the staff with a fluid twist of his body, but Andar's shoulder jarred him, his arms closing around sinewy thighs. He reached upwards, searching for the sword arm and the descending pommel, but the blow thudded at the base of his neck. Pain surged, blurred his vision and rocked his head back as his grip on the Suru weakened. Again the pommel fell, showering pain and darkness. As in years gone by, Andar felt the fear. Felt the rush of panic as death closed on him.

Desperately he grasped at the dark tunic. With a surge of strength and scrambling legs he pulled and pushed himself upwards. His hands found the corded neck and his legs locked around the wriggling torso. Now with his remaining strength, he dug his thumbs into the assassin's throat. The Suru abandoned his sword and tore at the hands of the smith. Andar exerted pressure, was rolled beneath his foe, then lifted from the floor and smashed into the hearth. His grip loosened and fell free when hot coals burned into his back. Numbed and reeling from the shock he watched the assassin stagger back, violent gasps racking the Suru's body.

"Andar!" His father's voice came from outside.

Through blurry eyes he saw Dreanna on the path, his father and son behind her.

"Grandfather! Doros! Hurry!" she yelled.

Andar lurched upright, his bruised ribs and the coal burns bringing a curtain of darkness. He fought it, shaking his head. Air still rasping in his throat, the assassin's eyes flicked to the doorway and the approaching figures. He grabbed a firing clamp from a post and hurled it at the smith. Andar blocked it, bearing the blow on his forearm, but he breathed a sigh of relief as he watched the Suru spring head first into the black void of the open window and disappear. Pain was everywhere as he slumped, sitting in a daze against the warm hearth.

Then they were at his side. Swords in hand, his father Lanos, and son Doros stood shocked and breathless. Crying, Dreanna clutched at him, adding to his pain. His arms enfolded her with a fierceness that belied his exhausted state.

"I'm all right, I'm fine," he whispered.

"Who was..." but for the second time that night he cut Dreanna off. It was as if he was in a dream, his speech thick and halting.

"No, not now. Doros, take the lead. Father, take Dreanna to the house. I'll follow and see you safely there."

"Come, Dreanna," urged Lanos. "Do as your father says." His wrinkled hand took her arm. In the seamed face she saw his eyes were moist. "Yes, Grandfather," she finally acknowledged, but her eyes returned to her father.

They eased through the beamed doorway and moved along the path under the amber sliver of Capci. To the east, distant Kunic, hung red and swollen among countless stars. In single file they crept forward, the leaves of the soaring reed trees motionless in the night air. A gila weasel, orange and blue scales glinting, darted across their path, its sweet, pungent odour clinging to them. Eyes searching everywhere, probing with his sense, Andar followed them to the house. Met at the door by their atogg, Lanos pushed the animal aside and entered. He calmed Dreanna and her younger brother, while Andar and Doros ensured the fortress-like safety of the barkin, checking each room, barring each window. The atogg, sensing the tension, trotted after Andar, sharp claws clicking on the floorboards. Despite arguments from his family, Andar took the pet and opened the front door.

"Bar it, Doros. I'll see to the shop." When the door closed, he looked at the atogg who sat at his feet, large eyes intent on him. With his fist he gave the signal to seek. The atogg's hairless body tensed, it's long, lean form still as it searched the night. Although deaf, its sense of smell and eyesight were acute. Andar followed the animal, searching in vain with his sense for the aura of the attacker. He didn't care about the shop, but wouldn't rest until he was sure the attacker was gone. The two circled the house following the path until it brought them to the shop once more. He signed for the atogg to guard the door and entered.

Andar went through the motions of closing the shop, still focused on his sense, reaching out into the night, searching. *Nothing.* With a sigh of resignation, he moved about the shop, trying to calm his thoughts and emotions. The flickering torches threw fearsome shadows into his path, only to dance harmlessly away the next moment. He shuffled to another timbered window, probing out into the night before closing the shutter and dropping the thick crossbar into place. Wincing in pain, he stooped and picked up the assassin's sword. Unconsciously he ran a hand down the side of the blade, the artisan in him evaluating the maker. It was straight and true to the tapered needle point without the undulating curves that were often a mark of lesser smiths. He grasped the end and tested the temper, anger for the craftsman flaring within him, as if he too had been a part of the attack on his life.

Andar wiped the sweat from his forehead. He had sent the others to the house in case the assassin was still close, but as the moments passed it appeared he was not. But that meant nothing. Even with his strong sense, he hadn't been aware of the assassin's presence until the moment of the attack. *Why should I be able to sense him now?*

"Father?" The call from the house had a worried lilt to it.

Pulling the dagger from the door, Andar eased it closed and acknowledged his daughter with a wave of his arm. Pain raced along his shoulder and he drew his breath sharply. He sighed again, and with the atogg in the lead, trudged down the sloping path to face questions he could not answer.

Chapter Two

Light flickered on the vaulted ceiling in the common room. The flames in the fireplace curled lazily around the wood. Only the faint chirp and crackle from the stone hearth disturbed the silence of the room. Like the smith shop, the formidable log reeds, notched and stacked, gave the room a sense of security. A feeling Andar didn't share tonight.

He sat contemplating his golden, flickering companions, melancholy after two tankards of reed ale, sipping a third, as his mind wandered aimlessly over the events of the evening. The ale had helped to numb the pain from his wounds, but like the Suru, had undermined his confidence. As he slouched in his chair, the fire revealed what he felt he had become; a small and insignificant man, just like the little fires he built. No longer did he heap the wood on high, goad the flames to leap and twist with unbridled energy. Andar poked it irritably, creating a shower of sparks, winking red, fading black. Pain in his shoulder rewarded his effort. He brought the tankard back to his lips, eyes closed.

Dreanna had clung to him, crying at first as the two other children listened, wide-eyed and fearful, unable to believe that someone would come to their home and attack Father. After many hugs, reassuring words, and making light of a bungling attempt at stealing some half-finished swords, they had been ordered to bed, accompanied by Lanos. Andar had remained in the common room and had just finished his first ale when Lanos, moving slowly on bowed legs, had returned.

"Are you all right?" his father had inquired, speaking for the first time to his son, worry lines freshly etched around gray eyes.

"I'm going to be a little sore tomorrow." Andar looked down at the floor boards. "But it's better than being a little dead," he added with a forced grin.

"You were almost killed," Lanos hissed, his graveled voice rising. "Save your humour for your drinking mates." Their eyes locked and the old man's anger waned as he read the pain and worry in his son's face. "Fetch us both an ale." He averted his eyes and turned to leave. "I'll see to some salve for your burn."

Andar shuffled to the eating area beneath the loft at the other end of the common room, ducked under some hanging herbs, and slid two tankards from an open shelf. He filled them from the keg that squatted on the end of the table. When Lanos rejoined him, Andar they stood in silence, drinking and staring at the murky brown liquid in the tankards. The doughy fragrance and brackish taste went unnoticed as Andar emptied the contents. Finally, grim smiles lessened the tension between them and Andar lowered himself onto one of the benches, setting his tankard upon the table's worn surface.

Lanos examined the wound. The burn wasn't deep, but covered a large area of flesh, the raw, red tissue blotched with black soot. It had oozed tears of blood and fluid in long spider fingers down Andar's back to the waist. As Lanos worked they talked.

"You sensed no one," Lanos began, more a statement of fact than question.

"No, nothing. It was as if he wasn't there. Even after when I reached out, nothing."

"He must be well trained in closure. *Very* well if you could not detect his aura. But why would anyone...want to kill you?" Lanos' voice was thick, his lips barely able to form the question.

Andar had thought of denying the suggestion, but knew it would be useless. "It was...it was Suru."

"What?" The old man froze, his face a mask of disbelief. "No, tell me you jest." But he knew his son, and there was no humour in his voice.

"It was Suru," Andar said softly. "But who? Who would do this?"

"Yes, yes. Who would do this?" Lanos asked. Despite his forced calm, his hand trembled as he scratched his thinning gray hair. "A displeased customer?"

"No. Why would anyone go to the trouble and expense to hire Suru if they were displeased with the work of a local reedsmith?"

"True." Lanos dabbed at the burns some more. "Andar, you don't think the Ancient Order has anything to do with this? Surely it couldn't be."

"I had thought of that, but I don't think so. I can't believe they feel threatened by me."

"Then who? Who could possibly-"

"I don't know," Andar growled, frustration boiling over.

"Enough. Enough for now," the old man soothed. Tenderly he spread the salve on the cleansed wound, wincing when Andar did. "You handled yourself very well, son."

"I was lucky." Andar rose and Lanos followed him back to the far end of the common room.

"No one survives a Suru attack because they are lucky," Lanos said. Despite himself, his eyes shone. "Blessed be our Ancestors but you make me proud. Farsnor told me that once, on a Northern Campaign against the Stomuants, he saw a Suru in action. It was before Damour took the throne. When being Granleeder meant more than fancy clothes and words." He mimed his displeasure. "Old Sordon, bless his soul, at least tried to prevent the deformed ones from raiding us." Lanos finished the last of his reed ale, his eyes distant on past events. "Farsnor was with them. The cold and the mountains drove them back. Never did see any Stomuants. But Farnsnor said they encountered a Suru who wounded two of the guards and killed a third before he escaped. Said he had never seen such deadly speed." Lanos stared proudly at Andar. "Wait until I tell Farnsnor how you chased a Suru away!"

"Please, it was only because you and Doros came to my aid that he left." Andar turned to Lanos. "Make no mention of this to anyone. No harm was done. Perhaps it was a mistake."

"No harm done?" Lanos stared incredulously at his son. "Are you serious?

It was only through good fortune, your skill, that you weren't killed, and perhaps Dreanna too."

"I know, I know!" Andar's voice was angry. "But what can be done now? The town council will be sympathetic, but can do nothing. The Ancient Order won't care. Will even be pleased. It will only draw unneeded attention to us by others curious for a tale. No, let's keep this to ourselves."

"Fair enough, son," Lanos agreed quietly, his weathered face tightening. "But what if he comes back?" It was the question that had already begun to torment Andar.

"It must have been a mistake. A terrible mistake that is over now."

That had been the end of it. Lanos had grudgingly retired while Andar remained on the pretense of numbing his shoulder with another ale. He had poured it and sat in front of the fire, staring upwards into the darkness, the beams and trusses above hidden in shadows. When his mind had become exhausted, after a final check of the house, he entered the side hall and entered the first of his children's rooms.

On the left side of the small room, Colonar, his youngest, lay sprawled on his back, the sleep of youth heavy upon him. He had his mother's nose and delicate chin, and many of her practical ways. Andar checked the barred shutters yet again and with a grim smile noticed the small sword lying next to his son. He eased himself onto the edge of the bed, pain momentarily pulling his breath away. Bending, he brushed the bangs back and kissed him lightly on the forehead. He levered himself upright and turned to the other bed.

Doros was a year younger than Dreanna. The thin angular face was partially hidden by the mane of black shoulder length hair, the lanky body, in sleep's repose, still young and unmarked. His son's breathing was deep as Andar bent above him resting his hand on the pommel of the sword Doros had driven into the floor near the head of his bed. Anguish over their stormy relationship assailed Andar. He chanced a touch and reached out to gently lay his hand on Doros' shoulder.

In the hall, he stopped out of habit to look at one of the many wall ornaments that adorned the length of the corridor. All had been made either for, or by one of his children. Each held a memory. His fingers glided over the crudely carved figure of a head that was supposed to be him. Doros had cut himself twice in the process of making it. Both times he had come running to Andar. Although he hadn't cried, neither had he shied away from the comforting hugs of his father. But Doros had been young then. He entered the second room.

Dreanna lay still in her bed but opened her eyes as he entered. They studied him pensively as he folded slowly onto the bed beside her. She had remained the closest to him. She seemed to understand his pain, his moods. His loss.

"I was so frightened, Father, so afraid. I didn't sense him. I couldn't warn you. I tried but..." Her voice cracked and her eyes filled with tears.

Andar took her head on his shoulder, stroking her hair gently. "It's all right, Dreanna. It's all right now. It can happen. It's all right."

She shuddered, her head bobbing up, and although her eyes were still wet, she no longer cried. She ran a thin forearm under her nose. "You were wonderful, Father, so completely wonderful! I never knew you could do anything like that. I will never forget it. Never." With that, she put her arms around him and they held each other. Andar stared woodenly over her shoulder, embarrassed by the pride she felt for his actions, and by the fear he had felt while doing them. She lay back, retrieving the dagger from the bed and held its thin stiletto blade fiercely in front of her. "The next time I will not freeze like a child," she said. Her voice was firm, and he saw the hardness in her eyes. He reassured her there wouldn't be a next time, but understood that she knew better.

In the common room, Andar climbed the hewn stairs to the loft above the eating area. He sank onto the bed, the borders of sleep encroaching upon his battered body. The pain from his shoulder forced him to roll inwards. One half the width of the bed lay silent and empty before him, as it had done for many rains. He still slept on his side, unable to move towards the center, as if to do so would acknowledge Katrena's absence. Tonight the emptiness was a hollow ache. His arm reached out to lie across the smooth expanse as his other hand reached up to hold the pendant that had been hers. Finally his eyes closed and exhaustion overwhelmed him.

It loomed large in front of him, intangible but overwhelming and oppressive. Every way he turned it was there, blocking his attempts to move, but never touching him. Smooth like highly polished reed wood, large and spherical, it was a terrifying barrier that closed in on him. It weighed him down with an enormous burden that slowed his arms and legs until he couldn't move. And now the fear started to build with the feeling of helplessness that grew as his efforts to fight proved more and more futile.

The shape elongated and towered over him, the brown mass changing to blue-black hues punctuated with slashes of white, pin-points of yellow. It moved against him and the fetid odour assaulted him. He gagged and tried to turn away, but could not. He was helpless, bound by some invisible force that held him as those terrifying white slashes moved closer to his face.

With a startled lurch Andar awoke, his heart pounding, his body soaked in sweat. As his breathing stilled, he sank back and stared at the roof, oblivious to the ache of his shoulder and ribs.

It had been his nightmare as a boy. It had faded as he had reached manhood but started again when Katrena had died. For many rains his grief and sense of loss had triggered the old nightmare, until finally, with his acceptance of her death, it had become infrequent. And now it was back, more threatening and terrifying than ever. And different. It had never been able to hold him before. Never pulled him close. So close that he could smell its stench. With a shiver, Andar realized that before it had always been an intangible force confining him. Now it had become something alive, something powerful and more frightening than that of his youth. More real than a simple dream.

Andar rolled from the bed, the pain of his shoulder already less intense as the salve did its work. Awake now, he knew sleep would not come easily. He moved to the window, unbarred it and pushed the shutters outwards.

The night was silent except for the bark bugs. Capci's amber crescent had all but disappeared, chased through the night sky by full bodied Kunic, the larger red orb colouring the languid clouds. Green mist from the lichen swirled upwards falling again as it cooled. From the top of trees, the call of a drenn broke the silence, the long note eerily human. Staring into the darkness, Andar fought to suppress the fear that gripped him. The close encounter with death stirred long forgotten memories when death was always at the forefront of his life.

As a young man he had been caught up by the colour and adventure of those who lived by the sword. Enthralled by their stories in the taverns and captured by their commanding presence, he was fascinated by their weapons and how effortlessly they used them. And thus it was that he pursued such a life. However, all too soon he found that earning a living by the sword was not the same as the training and the games that he mastered so easily. The carnage he witnessed, in the alleyways of the city and the desolate trails of the caravans, took its toll. The cruelty and bloodshed, the callous self-serving acts of so many destroyed his respect for his fellow man. The continual violence was an awakening, each and every confrontation life-threatening. He wrestled with his own mortality, until he felt he would burst from the conflict of introspection and duty commitment.

Andar shook his head willing the thoughts away. His breathing was deep, his face flushed as he relived that painful time in his life. Pulling the shutters tight, he returned to his bed. He stared at the ceiling, sleep a fleeing captive beyond his reach. For so many nights he had studied those few square feet above his head when Katrena died.

At first it had been a means of holding on to her, for together they had studied the planks before or after making love. Katrena would point out the old man with the big nose, or the baby pippula that Andar never thought looked like a baby pippula, but said it did anyways. He would lie there and try to remember exactly how she had discovered each particular marking, how she had sounded, or pointed, or nudged him. He would remember the excitement in her voice with each of her discoveries, and how he praised her for her clear eyesight and clever imagination. And then she would turn on him, knowing he was humouring her, and she would punch and pinch him, tickling him until he begged her to stop, or he stopped her, as the mood suited them.

Although not always, they would then make love. But now they were just markings, smudges of color on color without Katrena to breathe life into them.

It had been an exuberant, wide-eyed zest for life, tempered with gentleness that had attracted Andar to her. With her competing for his attention, the adventure of the guard, already in a state of disillusionment, soon became a burden. It wasn't a long courtship, and in even less time the two of them had planned Andar's retirement from the Council Guard.

Disappointed by the self serving motives of many, wary of the violence, they built a homestead far from the village. By choosing smithing he could still be in contact, in a remote way, with the life that had fascinated him. Together they had raised children, his business had grown, and life had been good.

Andar tightened his hand around the sword that lay beside him, drawing little comfort from the familiar feel of the smooth, worn grip. He closed his eyes, aware that the night would be long. There was no fooling himself. Life had been good, but Katrena was gone, and now someone wanted him dead. The Suru would return.

Chapter Three

Bonara, First Merchant of Deprossa, paused in anticipation at the entrance to the chamber and savoured that first thrill of excitement. He inhaled the familiar musty scent, thousands of years old. It was the magic elixir that strengthened his will, that stoked the fires of his ambition. The knowledge that the cavern promised still filled his mind with awe. And he alone knew of its existence.

Fingers combed his graying beard as he held the torch aloft and marched inside. The dark tunnel behind him was an ever present reminder of the past. It was twenty long years since that first frightening passage down the tunnel to the unknown. He had been a young man then. Images of that day flickered before him; images that recorded the watershed of his life.

That day, like all the others, had been long and empty, but had ended worse than most. In the tiny shop, a customer, swathed in the gaudy finery of distant Krowden held him captive behind a low counter. He leaned on the counter pointing a heavily ringed finger. His large jowls jumped as he berated Bonara.

"You promised the delivery, you little erront."

Bonara squirmed beneath the patron's glare and tried to explain. "Most honourable, Buitris. The matter is beyond my control. Within the next day, two at the most, the caravan-"

"Silence, you miserable shakir! I wish what was promised today, not tomorrow or the next. I do not care to hear excuses. You, Bonara will never be other than what you are, a petty merchant selling cheap wares. I should have known better. I don't want them now. You can keep them."

Bonara lowered his eyes, his face turning white beneath the close-cropped black beard.

The man withdrew his bulk from the counter and waved a beefy hand to a waiting servant. "Come, Partris. This bores me."

Alone in the shop, the intimidation gone, Bonara's fear had turned to anger as he beat upon the counter. "It's not my fault. The caravan is late. It's not my fault!"

At closing time, Bonara locked the door to his shop and trod homeward through a small ravine, belittled and defeated by fate once again. A thousand times he had walked the ravine bottom seeking quiet at the day's end, escape from a life that frustrated him. Some evenings he would walk furiously to purge himself, cursing customers and village life alike. Other evenings, he would sit by the stream bed, unsatisfied with life, but melancholy and accepting.

Chance, fate, destiny: all words that Bonara applied to the event on that one, extraordinary evening. Even today, after all these years, he marveled that if the course chosen had been slightly different his life might never have changed. The rock had given way under foot, and he had sprawled face down peering into a small black opening. He struggled to his feet, the mishap another irritant to his tiresome existence. He tried to ignore the head-sized opening, but the air that seeped out, stale and pungent, caught in his throat. Bonara bent, and peered cautiously within, but nothing was visible. The rocks on either side fell away under his hands and soon, to his consternation, he knew that he had found something strange. Something that he could not explain.

I don't need this to disturb my life. However, the mystery of the hole, the scent of age, and its promise of the Ancient Ones kept him near.

At the lip of his find, Bonara's shadow, broken and twisted by the rocks, darkened the opening. He reached down and felt the sloping interior of a rock pile. *What if there is something in there?* Fearfully he eased one leg over the edge of the opening. *It's too late. There's not enough light.* He moved the other leg inside, arms in a vise-like grip upon the entrance.

Tomorrow. I can come back tomorrow with a torch. But Bonara lowered his head until he stared into the black abyss. It was too dark, for his head and shoulders screened the dying light. He moved his right arm inside and hooked the crook of his left one carefully over a rock at the entrance. For a moment the light streamed in over his head as he leaned forward. Then the entrance boulder fell inwards, his teeth flashed in a grimace of white and he tumbled headlong into the black void below.

His hands clutched his head as he tried to protect himself. After the first sickening lurch his tumble ended. He had fallen only a short distance and lay sprawled among small rocks and boulders. From the opening above, pale light flooded the cave. He fought to keep the fear from his heart as he struggled to his feet. Somehow he had known it wasn't just a cave. In front of him a man-made tunnel disappeared into the darkness. There was no mistake. The walls were parallel, the ceiling evenly rounded, and the floor flat and smooth. *It must have been fashioned by the Ancient Ones!* There could be no other answer. He climbed towards the beacon of light at the top of the mound of rubble. Then he was out. Out and free, and still frightened and hurrying home.

Bonar stepped into the cavernous chamber, smiling ruefully as he recalled his moment of discovery. He remembered the scared little man who had scurried back to his home. He marvelled at what he had been like. *How sad and desperate I had become. Yet to be so frightened and still return.*

The next day, armed with torches, unable to put the discovery from his mind, he had returned. Early from his shop he had set out. At the black mouth of the hole, the sun warm on his back, he looked down weak in his resolve for there would be no excuses today. He knew it was not far to the bottom. He had the torches to chase away the fears of the dark. Yet still he was afraid. *Always afraid. Afraid of this discovery. Afraid to stand up to the customers. Afraid to demand fair payment.*

"May the Ancient Ones forgive me. Is there not anything that doesn't frighten me? I must do this!"

Anger flared and consumed his fear. It was a chance to change, to break free of the cursed mould that life had fashioned for him. It was, perhaps, a chance to discover some remnant of his first forefathers, The

Ancient Ones. At last, with shaking hands, he lit the torch and slid feet first into the opening.

The heavy musk of long disuse assailed his nostrils as, with the torch held aloft, he inched forward. Bonara entered the tunnel that soon rose gently. He turned to look back towards the entrance, seeking reassurance from the opening. The dust of thousands of years puffed beneath his feet, rising to tickle his nose. A deep breath, several more steps, and he reached the crest of the gentle incline. Continuing would take him down. Down and out of sight of the opening. Bonara started to retrace his steps but stopped.

He shook, the urge to break into an uncontrolled run for the surface held in check by some new and powerful force. His stomach churned, threatening to empty as he staggered against the tunnel wall. Bonara closed his eyes, gripping the rock as he felt the battle sway within him. Though frightened and unable to understand what was happening, he viewed the raging conflict with awe.

His lips twisted into a grim smile as he stared down the dimly lit tunnel. Bonara pushed away from the wall, his body stiff, movement awkward. He walked further along the tunnel again, paused at the top of the incline, and continued, out of sight of the entrance. Now he trembled, but with an excitement he had never known. Something had happened within him. He was disoriented in his thinking, but revelled in the new sense of power and strength that coursed through him.

The excitement of that distant event rekindled itself in him again today. Bonara strode through the dimly lit chamber, towards the center, and seated himself in the huge chair which sat upon the raised platform. His hands caressed the smooth, silver surface of the arms as he studied the multitude of coloured lights that glowed and pulsed from above. His eyes burned with a fierce pleasure. *Yes! That had been the exact moment! Before I had even discovered all of this, I had changed.* He threw his head back and his laughter echoed quietly through the chamber. It faded away, all sounds absorbed by the thick rock walls and the quiet whir of machinery.

On that day, in the feeble light of the torch, through the monotony of the unchanging tunnel, it had seemed like time had stood still. It was evident that it led downwards and Bonara sensed that he was constantly moving left. After a time it came to him that the tunnel must form a giant corkscrew that spiralled downwards. The air was stale and musty, but breathable, the temperature dropping slowly. His confidence grew.

Without warning, the wall to his right vanished in the torch light. He froze, willing himself to calm, calling upon his strange newfound strength. The walls and ceiling of the tunnel had disappeared, but on lowering the torch, he saw that the floor was still intact ahead. Bonara eased forward, to the very edge of the disappearing wall. He held the torch out, moving it to the right and left and saw that it was just a corner. The rock wall continued unchanged to his right.

He realized it must be a room. To enter a tunnel with only one course to follow had been easy. The prospect of becoming lost in the room caused a new trickle of fear to slide down his throat. But it was not the fear he had lived with for so long. The fear that had immobilized him. *I must be cautious, and at the first sign of confusion, stop and turn back.* Holding the torch high, and drawing a deep breath, he began again, his one hand tracing a track in the dusty wall to the right as he entered the room.

A structure loomed out of the darkness on his left, the light from the torch dancing weakly over its surface. Bonara froze again, the sweat breaking out over his body despite the coolness of the room. He stood staring, rooted to the spot, the torch in his hand beginning to shake. Light and shadow jumped over the surface of his find, distorting it, and adding to its unearthly nature. Bonara closed his eyes tightly and fought to control his breathing. He fought the fear that clawed at his insides. Time passed and nothing happened. It gave Bonara the strength he needed and slowly he opened his eyes. The tall smooth object stood silently, gray-brown dust covering its undulating curves. It offered no threat, other than its ancient nature. He ventured a hand forward, cautiously touching the dusty surface, finding it cool to the touch.

Bonara plucked nervously at his beard as he shuffled past the structure to find another identical object, and another after that. Beyond in the dark he could discern more hulking shapes. The light danced faintly off their surfaces. He dared not leave the safety of the wall, but lit another torch and threw it to his left. It struck one, ringing off the hard surface, echoing in the darkness. He drew in his breath, and gazed, awestruck at the myriad of objects standing silently, row upon row in the shadows. He crept along the wall, lighting torch after torch. The light steadily grew creating a tomb like setting.

Mid-breath Bonara's breathing ceased and his body grew still. His ears strained to hear. Nerves frayed to the point of breaking, his feet refused to move as he held his breath. From ahead came the sound of... something. On the verge of flight, he listened. The sound did not grow louder or appear to be approaching him. He began to breathe again, controlling it with great effort as he shuffled forward. The noise grew until it filled his senses. The wall he followed ended at another black void that was the source of the sound. He came abreast of the entrance, directly exposed to the constant, humming throb. An intangible cloak of sound, it no longer grew in volume, but wrapped around him. Then in the center of the room he saw the green light shining softly.

Bonara smiled at the memory and looked down at the green orb glowing in front of him. He reached out and caressed its convex surface with a finger. *My light. My guiding light.* Whenever he wanted to think, to recharge his energy and sense of purpose, he would sit here, and stare hypnotically at it as his mind worked.

He had been irresistibly drawn towards the light, eyes wide in terror as the noise enveloped him further. He inched past the throne-like chair to stand mute in front of it and, with a shaking hand, reached out to rub the dust of thousands of years from the bubble glowing in the center of the sloped table. Freed from time's dusty veil, he watched it grow brighter with each cleansing stroke. Then he sat. Sat on the impossibly large chair and remained still. For hours, he listened to the whirl of sound coming from the many objects around and above him. The sound seemed to gradually subside as his fear did, until it became a soothing companion. Then he had retraced his steps homeward. He knew that his life's work lay before him.

A life's work like no other. When he discovered that first cavern, his life had changed. He had changed, grown confident and strong with each new visit. And wealthy with his new found abilities. It had nurtured him. He had toiled at it for many years, exploring the mystery of his planet's earlier inhabitants, of a race that had arrived on Zendar before his own Ancient Ones. The first years had been so painfully slow, but with each disappointment, with each simple success, he had moved closer to his ultimate goal. Here beneath the surface, a stone's throw from his village of Deprossa, he had spent twenty years of investigation. Twenty years of looking for them.

Once again Bonara said a silent prayer to the Ancients, thanking them and requesting their help and blessing, for the location of the final cavern had been discovered.

Chapter Four

It wasn't until mid-morning that Andar sat at the eating table. He was sore and stiff, his mood foul as he leaned on the marred surface, nodding and grunting to the continuous flow of talk that issued from his father and daughter. Mercifully, the youngest two had already eaten and been dispatched to their chores. He pushed upright, his oath quelling the morning's banter as he lurched towards the door.

"I've checked already and found nothing," said Lanos. "I saw Doros and Colonar to the barn and told them to lock the doors. Tonsut is inside guarding them. They are to stay there until either you or I give the word. No adventures today."

Andar glanced at his father then looked away cursing himself. "I'm glad someone has their head about them this morning," he muttered, but it never passed unheard, and rekindled the morning's painful conversations.

"You know I'm up early, and after the night you had..." Lanos trailed off.

"May Kaptan Dukor forgive me, but that's all the more reason why I should have checked early this morning for any other traces of,., him." Andar fought to control his anger and disgust, having little success.

"Father, after last night we all knew you needed to rest," Dreanna said, bringing him a warm loaf of leavened reebread, a knife and sweet cornut spread. "Now, take your time waking up." With that she leaned forward and brushed his forehead with a kiss. "But don't forget, you promised we could talk about it today." The press of one of her firm breasts on his arm did nothing to quell his mood. She left the room as Andar cradled his face in his hands, elbows propped on the table.

"It's not right, son," Lanos remarked. He set two steaming rees on the table and eased himself onto the other bench.

"What isn't?" Andar sullenly tore at his loaf, face reddening with annoyance.

"Not letting a woman her age *be* a woman. You know she's ready. Has been for some time now. Not to teach her to use her new urgings is only going to frustrate her."

"I know, I know." He looked at Lanos who sat patiently waiting. "I've just been too busy," but he knew Lanos wouldn't accept the feeble excuse, for his father knew him better than he knew himself. Andar picked up the ree, walked to the window, and looked out as he sipped the hot, green liquid.

"With every day she looks, acts more and more like Katrena. She's all I have left of her. She helps me remember so much of what was, of what we had. It will be gone."

"She is gone, son." Lanos said it softly then sipped his ree, waiting for Andar. The silence stretched on.

Images and memories of Katrena crowded in on him as he moved unconsciously to the Ancestral Cup that sat alone on the Shelf of Indebtedness. He stared at the cup, his eyes tracing the delicate, impossibly detailed carvings that adorned its surface. It had been in his family for generations, a physical reminder of their ancestors who had loved and fought and carved a life from their new world. It symbolized the gratitude that all knew they owned; respect given in thought and deed, back even to the original Ancient Ones. Until a year ago it had been a simple, unadorned cup. The day he had buried Katrena, Andar had taken it down and started carving. It became his final gift to her and, after days of toiling, he had kissed it and wept as he replaced it upon the shelf. Then he had returned to the shop to wield his hammer until he could no longer stand. When the clang of hammer on striking plate was silenced, his mourning ended. But not his sadness or the memories. Those tempered his moods until he was not the same. He knew this, but was powerless to fight it. He also knew that Lanos was right. He must gather strength from her memory, from those who had gone before her, and do what was needed, what was right. After kissing his fingers, he reached up to touch the cup.

"A trip to the village has been necessary for some days now. I've finished that piece for Dabar, and we have to go to Gartonnar's Collecting. I'll tell Dreanna this morning that she should come with us."

"Don't forget to tell her why."

"Yes, tell her why," but his voice was pensive and distant.

"Son, we must talk about last night."

It came back to him in a rush, his face growing hot as his stomach knotted. "Not now." His eyes found his father. "We will, but not now. I need time. Time to think."

The rest of the day was spent in the shop where he felt most comfortable, most at ease. He immersed himself in the unnecessary production of basic weapons to take to the village. They were quickly fashioned, yet still bore the unmistakable mark of a skilled craftsman. The dagger he had just finished was well formed, giving it balance and a pleasing appearance. Both edges were sharp and true, and despite the exaggerated speed at which he had worked, Andar knew it would withstand all but the most extreme blows. He placed it on the workbench beside the others and searched for a reed among the stacks stored vertically between the windows in shallow, water-filled troughs.

From a mere shoot, the reeds grew quickly, many washed away by the regular torrential downpours which shaped the way of life for all. Those spared continued to grow rapidly, eventually becoming immense, soaring trees. When freshly cut, soft and malleable, the wood could be shaped and carved and bent to any form or purpose. Allowed to dry, it lightened, hardened and would support many times its weight. It could be used to make a morning ree or shredded and woven to fashion a protective rain cloak. The reeds had proven to be the Zendarians' miracle, revered by all.

Andar chose one and using a small knife quickly carved the end into a point. Standing them in water kept the green and yellow mottled reeds soft, and it yielded effortlessly to his tool. Next he fastened the reed to the work bench and began to shape the circular stalk with long strokes of a drawknife. When satisfied, he moved to the striking plate and his favorite stage of production, the hearth and hammer.

In the centre of the room the hearth stood waist high, thick vertical reeds bound together that held the earth in place upon which the fires were built. Here a cherry-red glow pulsed from the middle of the charred fire blocks. The large bellows, that fed the fire with air, was secured a foot above the floor, controlled by the long levered pull that was at arm's reach.

He chose a hammer, heated the reed in the coals and moved it to the striking plate, hammering it with an unconscious rhythm that encompassed his body. It was a deceivingly simple skill, to gradually heat, beat, shrink, and harden the fibers of the reed together until the texture of it changed to an altogether new material, so unlike its original as still to cause Andar to marvel at the transformation. Only through countless years of smithing had he learned how long to leave it in the coals each time, when to turn the blade, where and how hard to strike it. The ability to create tools and weapons such as these distinguished Andar and others as true reedsmiths, capable of demanding respect and goodly sums for their work.

Time passed and the hammering continued ceaselessly long into the warm afternoon. Doros called him for the mid-day meal, but was sent gruffly away. He left without question. It was again like when his mother had died.

Andar was making the extra items to set his mind at rest, to relax his body, tight from the night's encounter, but it crystallized reality, causing a new wave of terror to settle upon him. The Suru would return; it was only a matter of time. Although unsuccessful the night before, Suru honor and reputation would ensure that he did. There would be no second chances for him the next time. The assassin, alerted to his skill, would not be so casual with the next attack.

The hammer paused momentarily at the end of its strike, thudded awkwardly, and left a blemishing mark on the blade. The marred surface triggered his anger. He smashed the mark, again and again, beating at it until he was exhausted and could no longer raise the hammer. Andar's shoulders slumped forward and he bowed his head, staring at his protruding stomach as if seeing it for the first time; a threat to the image of himself; growing old and slow and fat, not the father, warrior, lover that he always aspired to be, and sometimes felt he was. It was suddenly gone, brought to an end in one night, by a man whom he knew nothing about, for a reason he knew nothing of. And it wasn't over, and he knew he wouldn't survive the next attack, and he knew he didn't know what to do.

He sat alone in the smith shop for a long time, feeling small and helpless, angry and afraid.

Chapter Five

Baron Grenfeld moved casually along the boardwalks through the cluttered streets of Dashindar, savouring the confrontation ahead. He noted again, with a mixture of contempt and pride, how the villagers, beggars and merchants alike, averted their eyes or disappeared quietly from the street as he advanced. All knew the purpose of his venture beyond the walls of his estate.

His guards in tow, he swayed towards one establishment then another, toying with the fear of the owners, enjoying the stricken look of panic on the faces of those who had daughters. Under the close cropped hair his black eyes glittered at fumbling, stuttering fathers. With a warm smile, he would bid them good afternoon, and turn on his heel, but always slowly enough to catch the look of relief and shame that spread across their features.

The game played to boredom, Grenfeld hurried through the streets and alleys towards his destination. His guards, unneeded today, were hard-pressed to keep up with him as his excitement grew, anticipation reddening his hairless face and quickening his breath. The woman, chosen by his chief advisor, could have simply been fetched by the guards, but Grenfeld enjoyed the march through the village to remind them of his power. And he enjoyed the excitement of that moment when he would see her reaction to having been chosen.

That would happen now, for he had arrived.

Shadows from the torches flickered on the timbered walls of the sleeping quarters. The silence was complete except for the moans of the girl and Grenfeld's heavy breathing. The light glistened on his face as he raised his head from between her thighs. He held her by the ankles, knees bent, exposing her to his probing eyes and tongue. His breathing slowed as he raised himself and knelt between her legs. The young woman's compliant moans turned to sobs as her hands unclenched and travelled to her bruised and swollen face. A thick, blunt hand slapped them away.

"Look at me!" Sobbing uncontrollably, she stared at him. "That's better." Bending, he wiped his face on her stomach, then caught one of her nipples in his mouth and bit down until she cried out. "Now, we continue," and he lowered himself upon her.

Grenfeld sat and toyed with the dagger at the table in the dining hall of his home. The girl had been a disappointment. Although young and full-bodied, her spirit had been broken from the moment they had met. Already he had sent her back with his guards, a pouch of coins clutched in trembling hands.

His house in the village, one of the few three stories high, overlooked the courtyard below. In homage to the reed logs and tradition, on the outside they had been left round, but Grenfeld had directed, at great expense, that they be flattened inside. Tapestries and paintings covered the walls, several woven carpets softening the floorboards. He pushed away from the banquet table and ambled to the window, viewing the dusty courtyard below.

Countless years ago he had envisioned gardens, with paths and a brook, to which he would bring a new love. At first he had been obsessed with the need to find someone. Someone to replace her. Daily he would haunt the city taverns, the shops and pleasure dens. Searching. Never could one be found to measure up to his memory of her, and eventually he settled for less, married, and had a son. His wealth had grown, as had his power, and today there was nothing in the city that did not yield to his influence. It mattered little to him that only money and fear ensured his position of power. With the death of his wife, he had begun looking again and they were always young women, as young as his first love had been so many, many years ago. None refused his advances. None would dare. Eventually he stopped looking again and had grown content to have any woman he wanted. Content until now.

Grenfeld returned to the table and slouched on the bench. He had met Bonara, and that cursed merchant had thrown his life into turmoil by unknowingly dredging up the past. His talk of Bonstag had returned haunting images of her, for long ago he had been her teacher, her mentor. She had always been the source of his passion and lust, but even now, he could hear her laughter, her scorn, as she rejected his advances on that final day. His arm jerked back and drove the dagger's point deeply into the table. Thick forearms and shoulders trembled with the effort of controlling his remembered anger. He pressed his forehead against the pommel of the weapon then pushed away from the table, a trapped liggarat, pacing its cage.

When he found out about her death from Bonara it had given him cause to celebrate. Yet his mood had soured and quickly gone cold. She had been taken from him those many years ago and now again with her death. There was a new finality to losing her. Always there had been the dream, the option of using his wealth and power to return and reclaim her. Take her, like he did everything else. His anger at her, at him, grew, festering inside, until he thought of little else. The need to replace her drove him time and again to the village, to those as young as she had been. To those who resembled her. But now she was gone and the women could not distract him. Today had been a waste of time. But he would try again, tomorrow.

Chapter Six

The sun shining down on Andar and his family had already burned away the morning's green mist. The day had dawned fresh and cool, but now the heat as it pierced the clear dry air was intense. To fight it, all were clad around their waists in traditional short wraps, loose-sleeved tunics protecting their shoulders and arms. Weapon harnesses and trail bags were the only other articles encumbering them. They walked a meandering trail along the crests of the valleys which fell away on either side. Many of the smaller ravines were dry, but in some, small streams still carved delicate paths into the flood plains at the bottom of the steep chasms. In the wider rivers, which served as silent highways for the narrow, planked boats, the water churned slowly southwards to eventually enter the Great Kaliman River.

It had been another long night of restless sleep and waiting. Nothing had happened and Andar was now convinced an attack would take place on the trail. Only Lanos remained at home pleading tired legs and the ability to take care of himself. The children's company worried him but he wouldn't leave them behind.

On the path but half an hour, they were joined by others also village bound. Their addition relieved Andar's tension somewhat, for he hoped for safety in numbers. Many were families, much like his own, most farmers who tilled the terraced slopes. Clad in rough-woven tunics with the occasional splash of color from some finer material, they carried what produce they could upon their backs, head straps stretched tight.

Narrow boardwalks and suspended bridges over countless ravines made the traditional, two-wheeled carts impractical in the Belnor Region. As others in still greater numbers continued to join the trek to Bonstag, Andar remembered that the Light Festival was in progress. Most from the surrounding area would converge at Bonstag for part or all of the three day celebration of "The Telling".

Dreanna bounded lightly to him, grabbing his arm in excitement. Ever since he had told her of the visit to the village, and its purpose, she had been a mixture of thinly controlled girlish excitement and womanly demureness. It seemed to Andar that overnight she had blossomed with the knowledge of the purpose of the trip. Perhaps it was only his imagination, but the dark hazel eyes seemed older. At this moment though she clung to his arm and was again his little girl, eyes glistening, teeth flashing as she revealed her latest gem of information.

"You'll never guess who's coming to the Festival!" she said.

"Just about everyone, it would seem."

"No, no. Someone special! Someone we would like to see. No, I suppose that's not true. Someone we would like to hear."

"Your grandfather."

"No! Tonata," she said, relinquishing the information with a dramatic pause.

Andar was impressed, for Tonata, a Friend of the Ancients, was widely known as one of the greater tellers of stories, an historical orator who was welcomed to any village or city. "The Telling", traditionally told at every Light Festival, was known by all, but to hear it related in depth and detail with dramatic flair by a truly gifted teller would be something to remember always. Although he never relished trips to the village, Andar felt a rush of excitement at the prospect of being a part of it.

"I'm not going anywhere, Father."

Distracted from his thoughts, Andar studied his daughter. "Of course you are. The village awaits."

Dreanna put her hand on his arm and squeezed it gently. "I'm not going anywhere, Father. My coming of age won't change anything. I'm not going anywhere."

Andar fought the lump in his throat as he accepted her naive sincerity. "Again, so much like your mother. She too always took care of me."

"Well someone must!" she teased and skipped ahead once more to walk with Doros.

The journey continued, uneventful as they passed through endless dark, soaring forests of reed trees and over countless rope bridges spanning rain cut gorges. Yet even here, on the near vertical walls, young reeds flourished vainly until the next deluge would wash them away. Gradually the ravines yielded to rolling hills of forest and, as the time passed and they approached the village, Andar found some of the tension draining from him. At last, topping the final hillock, the village lay before them, nestled in the valley below.

Already the terraced slopes surrounding it were crowded with the traditional white tents of visiting merchants. Set in rows, one above the other, a brightly colored marker topped each peak, indicating the city or town they were from. They tripled the size of the village, something Andar had not seen before. The Festival of Light always drew the largest crowd of merchants each year, but Andar realized that it must be the presence of Tonata that had created such an influx. Again the desire to be a part of that celebration pulled at him. Everyone would feast and celebrate tonight, tomorrow evening, the third day of celebrations, being reserved for "The Telling" and the prayer offering. He thought of returning already knowing that if it was at all possible he would.

With their approach to the village outskirts, the cries of the barkers carried over the air, tempting some, luring others. During the Festival, every village business, from tailor to tavern owner extended into the streets to take advantage of the once a year opportunity that made half of the yearly profit for many of the merchants. The noise and tumult of the village grew and swirled around them as they entered the main street. Gaudily garbed merchants, unable to set up their wares within the village, juggled an armful of goods, approaching everyone with their good-natured pitch. The aroma of exotic foods from distant Cordance, strangely colored and spiced, hung heavy in the air, redolent and tempting to prospective customers. Here a Friend of the Ancients, surrounded by villagers, held court as he entertained them with The

Saga of Nalistar, a seldom heard legend, while beside him a group of musicians sang and played one of many traditional songs. Behind them, two competitors with swords hacked at reeds firmly secured in the ground.

The crowd pressed about them and Andar yelled for his children to stay close. Shouldering his way slowly to the center of the village, he halted as he realized the danger. It would take nothing for the Suru, in this jumbled confusion, to end his foolish life. Sweat beaded his forehead as he stared vainly into the strange faces about him. He felt an arm on his wrist and jumped, reaching instinctively for his dagger.

"Father, is something wrong?"

Relieved, he smiled at Colonar. "No, of course not," he said, grabbing his son's hand, eager now to escape the crowd. "Come, everyone. We're almost there."

The inn was on the edge of the village at the far side of town. Like all the villages of Pentenarr, the workmanship and mismatched architecture of the small shops and homes on the narrow streets of Bonstag lent the village a jumbled quaintness. The old center of town was composed mainly of ancient buildings, the reed logs, darkened with age, beautiful for their history and often touched with reverence by visitors. Although Bonstag was not one of the early villages, even these buildings, hundreds of years old, were a link to the past, as close as many would ever get to The Ancient Ones unless they were able to make the pilgrimage to Orrdamoor. Some of the newer shops and stores were of hewn wood, each thick plank lapping another, the trim surrounding doors and windows carved with designs. Massive rain troughs, made from halved and hollowed reeds, hung heavy on the porches of each building, an intricate system of drain pipes carefully constructed to disperse the rains.

At the tavern many drinking patrons sat outside the inn, the good-natured din mixing with that of the street. Usually one of the quieter eating and lodging quarters, such was not the case today. They climbed the porch and entered. At the end of the low-beamed ceiling, the fireplace threw capering shadows on the walls. The odour of roasted sleerak mingled with the pale smoke floating beneath the ceiling floorboards. In front of the flames, a sweating cook's helper turned the dripping roast, while at the tables and benches that scattered the floor, festive merrymakers shouted and cavorted.

Andar acknowledged several welcoming shouts and wound his way to a table at the back. He didn't miss the gossip and noise. Both Katrena and he had needed the peace of the countryside. They hadn't been seated more than a moment when the owner's daughter spied them and approached, her tray expertly balanced despite the fluid sway of her hips. The upswept hair was a whirlwind of coppery chestnut above an alluring smile. Gray eyes sparkled with pleasure as they alighted on Andar.

"Why if it isn't the master reedsmith himself come to our humble tavern," she bawled, feigning a look of wonderment. "And with all the family in tow. We are truly blessed!" She bent over and around Andar, pressed her full, loosely bound breasts on his shoulder, and planted an affectionate kiss on his cheek. Andar saw it didn't escape Dreanna's notice, her eyes studious as she smiled at Jadosa. Doros and Colonar nodded greetings.

"Father will be so pleased to see you," said Jadosa. "You've been away from the village too long. Far too long," she whispered into his ear.

"It is good to see you again, Jadossa."

She smiled mischievously at Andar. "The Light Festival has brought you to us?" she asked.

"Yes. That, some products here," he said indicating the sack of weapons, "and Gartonnar's Gathering." Andar watched Dreanna as he spoke, smiling at the nervous relief on her face.

"Father is going to the Gathering as well. I wish I could, but someone must stay and mind the tavern. But I'm talking too much. I'll fetch him for you."

"No. Let me go back and surprise him. He must be in the back with his hand in every pot driving the rest of the help crazy."

"You know Father," she said with a grin. "Go and talk to him and I'll fetch the children some ale."

He saw Dreanna and Doros stiffen and redden at being mentioned as such, and quickly took his leave.

When Andar entered the kitchen, Rakosur's back was to him. He stirred the contents of a pot of thick berddon stew, deep in concentration.

Sweat ran from the bald crown down into the fringe of thinning brown hair. The air was thick with moisture, the scent of a dozen spices and herbs rising from a pot that boiled on a bed of coals near an open window. There, a half dozen tiny capcits bobbed their feathered heads, shuffling back and forth, hungry for handouts. One was bold enough to land on the handle of the pot. Rakosur waved them all away with a beefy arm. He was a dozen years older than Andar and had run caravans in his younger days, bringing salted fish, and spices back from the port of Terestar on the Regor Sea. Andar had often been assigned to protect them and they had been friends ever since. Three quick steps and his arm encircled Rakosur's neck.

"You keep your lusting daughter away from me or you just might have a grandson to feed in this miserable hovel."

Rakosur's momentary silence ended in a bellowing guffaw that resembled Andar's name. "Ah, my young protector! You have returned to us. By the Landsite, but it's good to see you again!" and with that he threw his arm about Andar's shoulders. "What brings you at last to my humble tavern? You have been away far too long."

"So Jadosa has already told me,"

Rakosur smiled broadly. "I should worry if I were you. She'll not let you escape without some serious conversation. For old times sake," and he clapped Andar heavily upon the shoulder.

"I've brought some weapons to sell, but more importantly, it's Dreanna's time. I would be honored if Sarta would lead her."

Rakosur's eyes widened until they threatened to pop out of their sockets. His grin lit up the room. He sobered quickly and answered with the gravity that suited the request.

"It is Sarta and I who are honored by your request. The answer shall be divined this very afternoon, my friend."

Over the bubbling pot, stories were reminisced and arrangements made between the two for Sarta and Dreanna to meet later in the day. Arm in arm they left the kitchen and joined the others. Conversation was brisk and the laughter frequent and, after enjoying a simple but filling mid-day meal of sleerak strips and fresh reebread, they took their leave.

Andar left his children at Sotenar's, a merchant friend, one of the few families in the village that Katrena and he had visited. He strode through the village and grudgingly stopped at the table where the representatives of the Ancient Keepers were collecting the traditional contributions for the Ancient Order's temple in Orrdamoor. He said little, avoiding any confrontation with the two who took his stipend and checked off his name in their records. Soon he found himself on the path that led to the terraced slope of Bonstag's Field of Life.

Each village had one, a sacred patch of ground where one could begin his journey to join The Ancient Ones. Tended by members of the village contingent of the Ancient Order, the reed shoots were clipped daily, allowing only the yellow Dallipons to flourish among the waist high, tangerine grass. A dozen villagers were scattered about the field, picking the yellow flowers that gently swayed on the ends of the stalks. Andar spied Gartonnar. Plucking one of the multi-petal flowers from the sea of coarse grass, he approached the old man.

Gartonnar rested on a low-backed bench, his gnarled hands clutching a tankard of reed ale as he watched his friends and companions gather flowers. His legs, thin and bowed, rested on a keg of ale. Beside him, various breads and fruits lay spread on a small table. In a semi-circle in front of him was an array of woven baskets filled to various stages with flowers the same as the one that Andar held.

"I acknowledge and honor your decision to partake of the Flowers of Dallipon."

The old man turned awkwardly at hearing Andar's voice, genuine pleasure in his eyes. "Andar, you came. It pleases me greatly that you do so."

"I wouldn't dishonor you or myself by missing this day, Gartonnar." The two clasped hands tightly, the old man's eyes shining wetly for a moment.

"Some reed ale, Andar? One last time, for an old warrior's sake?" They drank slowly, enjoying each other's company and the warmth of the day.

Years gone by, Gartonnar had been the stiff and demanding master trainer of The Council Guard. He had been old then, but not in spirit or energy and had understood the challenge before him when Andar had arrived. He had understood Andar's personal turmoil, and when Andar left The Guard, Gartonnar resigned himself to the departure with grudging acceptance. "You have more natural skill than any man I know, but you don't have the heart for the violence and killing. It's a wise choice you've made."

The real friendship and respect came later. A chance meeting, a sword requested by Gartonnar in those first early struggling days; Katrena's liking for this gruff old warrior and his inability to dislike the woman who had helped to take away his best pupil. The friendship grew, the lessons renewed, and now in retrospect, standing here on the warm flower strewn hill, Andar realized his survival the day before was a direct result of this tired comrade.

Rakosur arrived in his sleeveless food-stained tunic, a woven, broad-brimmed hat protecting his balding head. Soon the two were in the field with the others, filling baskets with the aromatic flowers. The heat of the day grew, the sun drying the earth.

"Rakosur, you've probably traveled as much in your youth as Gartonnar," Andar said.

"Aye, Andy. Damn site more I wouldn't doubt," he answered, the familiar worldly swagger coming immediately to his voice and stance as he raised his head, chewing absently on the stalk of a Dallipon.

"Well, you won't do much of anything else if you continue doing that," said Andar, motioning towards the flower stalk bobbing up and down in his friend's mouth.

Rakosur's eyes narrowed on the inviting, yet deadly vegetation hanging from his lips. He spat profusely, cursing it, himself, and these "damned collecting parties" in general for several moments. When the show had ended for, if nothing else, Rakosur was a performer, Andar broached his subject.

"What do you know, about...Suru?" The words struggled to escape as he consciously looked around. His manner did not go unnoticed.

"This be a casual question you're askin', Andy?" He stood eyeing his friend, all traces of humour and good nature set aside.

Andar stood upright, trying hard to set his face, but abandoning it as their eyes met.

"No one mentions them casually, do they?"

"No, that's the truth."

"One tried to kill me two days ago."

"What! Here in Bonstag? Where did this happen? Are you sure?" His questions were a harsh whisper, intense and disbelieving.

Andar related the incident quickly, leaving nothing out. At the finish, Rakosur stood silent and sullen. Finally he spoke.

"Andar, lad, what is it you've done? What could he possibly want with killing you?"

"I've asked myself a hundred times the same question, but there is no answer that makes sense. I've not enough money to matter to anyone. I was once very good with a sword, but no Suru needs prove himself on me. I don't know. By the Landsite I wish I did."

"He'll be back, Andy. You know that, don't you?"

"Yes. I thought by now, on the way to the village, in the crowded streets. I can hardly talk to anyone without my mind being on it. What about the children? Dreanna was almost killed. She thinks I'm wonderful, because by some good fortune I was able to stop him. What can I do? What? Tell me!"

Andar saw that he was shaking and turned his head away to stare at the quiet figure of Gartonnar sitting peacefully. For him, it would soon be over, his long voyage come to an end. Embarrassed, he turned to Rakosur.

"There's no shame in fear, Andy. It's healthy. Keeps one alert and ready for... whatever."

"Yes, but it's impossible to live with. I know. I've seen it before." They were both quiet for a spell.

"I don't know that I can add anything that you don't already know. They have been around since who knows when. Men, some women, trained from youth, their only purpose to kill. They're for hire but no one seems to know how to contact them. I suppose they have their own methods of choosing victims, missions, call it contracts. They don't stop until finished, Andy."

Andar nodded silently. "Well it would seem then that my fate is sealed," he said, forcing himself to smile grimly once more. It occurred to him that these grim smiles could very much become a part of his life, as short or long as that might be.

They emptied their baskets into the others surrounding Gartonnar and said their farewells. Andar felt Gartonnar sensed the turmoil within him. Clasping hands for the last time, he studied Andar's eyes, leaning in close to him.

"A man can shape and control the destiny of his life. You did so when you left The Guard. You know this, my young friend. Now believe it once more." His brow relaxed, his tone lightening. "May you hold the Landsite in reverence always, and may the spirit of The Telling touch your heart and that of your children." The words were little different than those expressed to him twenty years before in parting. Unsettled by the memory, he repeated the answering phrase.

"May the Ancient Ones bless you with the same fortune, Gartonnar." Then Rakosur and he were walking down the hill without looking back, Andar's mind a jumble of frightening thoughts and fears.

Although they sought out a neighboring tavern for ale and conversation, neither Rakosur nor Andar were any longer in the mood for bantering. They talked of the rains that both knew would be returning soon despite the silence of the reedcrystal shards that hung motionless and quiet outside Rakosur's inn. A "Stone Sleeper", the first in many years, had been born to a couple several weeks ago. It had been discovered and reported to The Council. The deformed infant had been killed and quietly buried in the hills, leaving the parents distraught and grieving. After several ales, Rakosur returned to his tavern, while Andar visited Sotenar and then, leaving the two boys there, returned with Dreanna to the tavern. As they arrived, Rakosur was in heated conversation with his son, Sarta.

"We *will* need them before the week is out, and, as things seem to have settled down somewhat at present, you *will* gather some more lanket for the next stew."

The thinner, taller version of Rakosur rolled his eyes in frustration. "We have some in the back, Father. And anyways, it will take too long for me to-"

"We need them, Sarta. No arguing. Look, here is Andar and Dreanna. Andar, let Dreanna go with Sarta." The sarcasm dripped from his tongue as he leaned in toward Sarta. "We need more lanket and the poor lad is so worried about returning in time to help out at dinner." Sarta's gaze travelled to Dreanna and his eyes studied her with interest.

"Of course," said Andar. "Dreanna could you help Sarta with this important task? I thought that you might help Jadossa in the kitchen, but if Sarta needs the help."

Dreanna's eyes slid from Andar to Sarta and back again. "Yes, Father." She returned her gaze to Sarta. "I would be pleased to help him."

"Good, then its settled." Rakosur said. "Grab some baskets from the kitchen and go. But quickly. Don't waste any time." He looked at Andar and fought the smirk on his lips. "We need those lankets."

Dreanna and Sarta looked at Rakosur and then each other. Dreanna smiled shyly at Sarta for the first time. Slowly she straightened her posture, her womanly curves further enhanced by a deep breath. "Please lead the way, Sarta. I don't know anything about lankets, but I am eager to learn."

Sarta looked from Andar to his father as his smile broadened to a grin. "Come, Dreanna. It's been some time since we've seen each other. We have much catching up to do." Together the two made their way between tables to the kitchen. Andar's eyes never left Dreanna's form until it disappeared behind the door.

And so the day passed. Andar finished his business, selling the hastily made weapons with little trouble. Dreanna and Sarta returned with a basket pitifully empty of lankets. She heartily approved of Sarta as her teacher, eager to know when they could meet again. Soon, except for Colonar, who chose to remain behind and visit with Sotenar's children, they were on their way home.

Without Colonar to slow them down, the journey took less time and it was with a sigh of relief that they arrived home before darkness set in. Apprehensively, Andar looked for Lanos who was nowhere in sight, but his father appeared heading from the shop, his face strained as he greeted Andar. As the shadows lengthened and the green mist started to form near the ground, Andar closed and barred the door.

Concealed within the foliage, the Suru settled himself and waited patiently.

Chapter Seven

Sitting on the long porch under the overhang in front of the house, Andar looked towards the garden where Dreanna and Doros tilled the soil. That morning he had worked in the shop, his children confined to the house. He had cursed as he stared out the window for, caught up in the swinging of his hammer, he had forgotten the event of two days before. Only for a moment, but it frightened him, for it reinforced what he knew. He couldn't keep a constant vigilance, moment to moment, day after day.

After the midday meal, he had moved to the front of the house and set up on the porch, his sword beside him. He had allowed them to venture to the garden where he could watch them as they worked. He knew he couldn't lock them up in the house forever, but the fear that they might inadvertently get in the way of the Suru again, as Dreanna had in the shop, was ever on his mind. He closed his eyes, feeling sick at the memory of pulling the dagger from the door where she had stood.

He glanced down at the intricate carving on the face of a ceremonial shield. As tall as he was and half that wide, it was one of many he had produced over the years, used by The Council Guard for The Light Festival. He blew on the surface, chasing away the shavings, and inspected the symbolic torch he had finished. The shields were time consuming and he was chastised by Lanos each and every time he began a new one. But it was something Andar felt compelled to do. They were always purchased by the council guards and provided another link to that former life. Perhaps a strange penance for leaving, he wasn't sure.

Andar set the shield aside, and stepped off the porch. It was impossible to do the work with his eyes and thoughts on his two children. "Dreanna, Doros, come here."

The two looked up, leaned their tools against a tree trunk and walked towards him. "Dreanna, time to start the evening meal. Give your grandfather some help. Doros, in the barkin by my chair are several knives. Stain them for me. Use the inach for the handles, a light coating of reast on the blades. Make sure you let it soak in before you polish it."

"I know how to stain them," Doros said, stalking off before Andar was finished. "Yes, Father," said Dreanna turning and heading for the barkin.

"Make sure you bar the door." Neither acknowledged his call.

With a sigh, Andar picked up his sword and the belt with its dagger, and sought out the pond behind the house. He hoped a cooling swim would combat the ugly mood that would not leave him.

It had been a favorite spot for him and Katrena; a warm, relaxing, sun-drenched niche within the forest that surrounded the house. Escaping from the children, with threats that they were not to be disturbed, they would lose themselves in the sun and water and themselves; a special time each day for the two of them.

Andar descended the incline to the pool of water, leaping from boulder to boulder. With weeks of effort, he had diverted the nearby stream into the naturally funnel-shaped cleft. Twenty feet deep at the neck, the rock-filled depression widened to fifty feet at a length of a hundred, where it once again met the natural grade. He had created a second channel leading from the shallow end back to the original stream bed and the job was complete. It had taken longer for the depression to fill than he had expected, but when it had, their private pond was complete. The gentle flow of river water kept the pond fresh and clean. Only when the rains came did it become a boiling, churning froth that overran the bouldered banks. The channel created to empty the overflow was soon carved deeper by flood waters necessitating a make-shift dam, but it was little more work and functioned admirably.

Although he felt it useless to try, on a flat rock by the water's edge, Andar searched with his sense again for any aura that might be close by.

Finding nothing, he unwound his wrap, plucked the dagger from its scabbard, and dove cleanly into the pool. He surfaced, then jackknifed his body, stroking downwards. The sensual freedom of his nakedness in the cool water brought their swimming ritual back in a rush. It had been the same for Katrena, and when they had dragged themselves, dripping with water into the sun, both found the moment difficult to resist. It was only recently that he had learned to welcome the memories of those days that had kept him from the pool for many rains. Andar clamped the dagger in his teeth and stroked back to the rock. With a fluid motion, he pulled himself from the water onto a flat boulder.

The warmth of the stone on his buttocks and thighs felt good. He ran his hands through his shaggy hair then leaned back on his arms, his head turned to the sun. The face, no longer young, was striking rather than handsome, more so now that age and experience had shaped it with character. But it was the emerald green eyes that separated him from others. They said they were the eyes of the "Ancient Ones".

His sense picked up Dreanna's aura and a glance revealed her carefully navigating the steep incline. Anger flared because she had not stayed in the house, but he watched her with a sense of pride and adoration as she neared; a lithe, statuesque beauty growing into a woman. He caught his breath and swallowed. Reaching the bottom, she looked up to find him watching her with smiling eyes.

"Don't be angry. Grandfather said he didn't want my help. When he saw you head towards the water, he told me to join you. He brought me to the ridge. He made sure I was safe."

"It's all right. I'm glad you're here," he said turning back to the pool so that she wouldn't see his face and his annoyance at Lanos.

"Finished already?" she asked. "The water too cold for someone your age?"

"Watch who you are calling old, child," he grumbled.

Dropping her drying cloth, she came up behind him, resting her hands on his shoulders.

"Thank you for arranging tomorrow. I'm ready, you know that don't you? I have been for some time now."

"Yes, I know, Dreanna. I'm sorry you've had to wait so long. It has been... difficult for me."

"I know. Grandfather talked to me this morning. I understand now."

He put his hand on hers. "I guess you are impatient to get to the village," he said.

Her eyes unconsciously moved to his penis, lying soft and warm in the sun. "Impatient isn't the word, Father," she grinned.

"What have I spawned?" he said in mock horror, seeing her smile. Grabbing her by the shoulders, he caught her by surprise and with one swift motion heaved her over his head into the pool. Her shriek was cut short by a mouthful of water.

"Look at me," she yelled.

"Yes, you're just as you wanted to be. Wet. That will teach you to look at you father in such a manner."

"You're far too old!" she screamed, sputtering with laughter in the water.

"You have a lot to learn, young one."

As she swam back to the edge, he rose to his feet, looped his dagger belt over his shoulder and, gathering his wrap and sword, made his way back up the bouldered incline. Half way up, he turned and watched as she swam to the water's edge.

"I'll call for your brother and watch the two of you while you swim." She waved back at him nodding her head. He crested the incline and climbed downwards over couple of boulders until the house came into view.

For the first time since Katrena's death he felt comfortable with Dreanna and her maturing sexuality. He had allowed his loss to colour his relationships with everyone close to him. Turning, he started back up. *She should know that things will be better.*

At the top of the rise Andar looked down, fear tearing out the bottom of his stomach. He started downwards, leaping from boulder to boulder, gaining speed as his bare feet silently gripped the warm rocks. He launched from a boulder half way down the incline, out towards the Suru who at the pool's edge had draped Dreanna over his shoulder. As he hurled through the air, the dagger belt he held encircled the Suru's head and Andar felt the tug of their weight as his body passed above them. The belt was ripped from his hand as it dragged the Suru and Dreanna into the pool. Without surfacing, Andar righted himself underwater and found Dreanna close to him, moving her legs weakly. Clad in dark green, his face hidden behind the cowl, the Suru in the water at the shore's edge pirouetted in their direction and pulled a dagger. Andar surfaced, encircled Dreanna's neck and pulled for the opposite side of the pool. Still disoriented, her weak struggles hindered his best efforts.

"Dreanna! Kick your feet! Kick your feet!"

She sputtered and gasped, but her feet began to move feebly through the water.

"Good! Kick!" But as he snatched a backwards glance, Andar saw her feet were dangerously close to the approaching Suru. He pulled harder, kicking violently beneath her, dragging her away from the assassin. The pull became heavy, impossible, and he realized that the Suru had grasped one of her feet.

Andar spun in the water. Dreanna was stretched between the two of them, hands fighting weakly to keep her head afloat as the Suru pulled himself along her body towards him. Dreanna's legs slowly curled up around the Suru as her arms floated towards him. Andar sensed her purpose, let go of her hair and submerged when she grasped the Suru. Her weight bore him under.

Andar's hand darted out and fastened on the wrist holding the dagger. He pushed Dreanna away with one foot and wrapped his own legs around the trunk of the assassin. Their bodies bucked and thrashed as they spun, churning the water about them. Working his grip towards the dagger, he felt a groping hand on his waist and with a panicked chill realized the goal was his genitals. Andar held his grip on the knife hand, twisted and kicked free. He pulled close again, using the suppleness of his nudity to attach himself to the back of the Suru. Now, his groin protected, he leaned forward onto the assassin's neck and shoulders, forcing him under the water. The Suru's violent struggles quickly brought them both to the surface. Andar rocked forward again, forcing him under. The Suru's free hand reached up to grasp Andar's arm in an iron grip and then he became motionless. Sensing his purpose, Andar tightened his grasp on the hand that held the dagger.

Time passed. The urge to expel the air in his lungs became intolerable. He swallowed to keep it down, heat seeping up his neck to burn his face. Andar knew that any moment he would have to release his grip to break the surface. He felt the body beneath him tremble with the same demands as they teetered, bobbing lazily below the surface of the water.

The Suru beneath him exploded, arms and legs clawing and pumping upwards. On top, Andar broke the surface first, his lungs sucking in air. Doggedly he held onto the Suru's wrist and with his other hand kept his enemy's head under the water. Berserk with the need for air, the assassin thrashed the water, his only goal the surface. Gone was the knowledge of Andar on his back, of the dagger clenched.

As the dagger flailed about, Andar pulled it to them using the last of his fading strength. It found its mark and the body below him jerked violently as blood stained the water and the struggling combatants. The turmoil lessened and then all became still. Slowly Andar was pulled under. With muddled thought, he realized his legs were still wrapped around the corpse. He released and caught a glimpse of it sliding to the bottom.

Andar's head broke the surface and he rolled onto his back, sucking in a great lung-full of air, too tired to move, until he remembered Dreanna. A weak jerk brought his head forward, and he peered over the surface of the water in search of her.

"Father! Father! I'm here!" She was swimming strongly toward him. The last of his strength disappeared with the knowledge of her safety, and his head dipped below the surface. Coughing and sputtering, he resurfaced, leaden arms fighting to keep him afloat.

Then Dreanna was beside him, supporting and pulling him as the two inched their way to the shallow end. Not until his hands and knees struck the rocks did he dare let go of her, and even then she had to drag him ashore. He lay awkwardly in a crumpled heap on his chest, unable to move. Yet his eyes never wavered from her as she knelt at his side, tears streaming down her face. For now he knew, and the fear he had felt before was nothing.

They didn't want him dead. They wanted Dreanna.

The Reedsmith of Zendar

The danger was past, yet his nerves tingled with an expectation that reason told him was unwarranted. *Recover the body and bury of it. There's nothing to fear.* Yet, in the shadows of the amber moon and its red cousin, the sword was there in his hand, every muscle on his sweating frame taut with tension and strain.

He reached the shallow end of the pond and sheathed his sword. Unbuckling the waist and shoulder belts that held his dagger, sword and pouch, he layed it on the ground. Removing his sandals and wrap, Andar waded into the tepid water. It was unrefreshing against the coolness of his perspiring body and lapped questioningly at his mouth, exploring who it was that dared disturb its calm. He swam to where he felt the current would carry the body, and made the first cursory dive without any success. The inky depths were impenetrable so that it took many more before he encountered it with a surprised start that sent him kicking upwards. He knifed the surface again, found the body and closed a hand around an ankle, stroking upwards, the body a heavy weight in tow. Andar broke the surface with a small gasp, rolled onto his side, and swam for the water's edge, awkwardly dragging the body with him. His feet scraped the rocks, he stumbled, caught himself, and with a last heave, dropped the corpse onto the shore.

The night's serpentine coils of green mist floated and twisted about him as he buckled his weapons belt over his wrap, then grappled with the body, hoisting the inert mass onto his shoulder. He began the arduous climb up the bouldered slope, the weight of the dead man increasing with each step. On the path the low rubbery leaves of the reed trees threatened to dislodge the body. Clouds obscured the moons, the blackness of the night pressing in close until at last the door materialized out of the mist. He raised the latch, entered the shop, and lowered the corpse, gentler than necessary. As Andar barred the door, his hand passed over the scar from the dagger. He should have known. The Suru would have never missed his target at that distance, even in the dark. Unless he had wanted to. The Suru had wanted to delay her until he had been dispatched. He had wanted her alive. At the pond the

Suru had stunned her and was going to carry her off. Angry green eyes hardened.

"Let's see what you look like, droxeur," he said, all revulsion and hesitation gone, replaced with cold hatred.

Andar yanked the green cowl from the head and peered at the pallid face. Clean-shaven, the face was unremarkable in death. The narrow cheek bones suggested the Suru was from the East. He remembered looking into the cold, impassionate eyes when they had fought. The face, now inanimate, could have been the face of any visitor in the village. Perhaps he had been there, watching.

Methodically, he stripped the body, examining each article, intent in his search. The pouches and hidden interior pockets revealed little of importance as he shredded the garments, cutting them away with his dagger. He had not expected to find anything. He turned to the body.

The ashen skin was stretched over the frame, gases already beginning to bloat the stomach and lungs. In death, it suggested none of the whipcord toughness that Andar had felt. Although pale from lack of blood, Andar realized that the skin had never seen the sun. The knife wound, tinged bluish around the edges, splayed open. The testicles were missing, a rough scar replacing them, a sacrifice for more effective fighting, a symbol of his dedication. Andar searched slowly, from the short-cropped yellow hair to the toughened soles of the feet. The only thing of significance he found was a black marking under the right arm. Many lines within a circle curved inwards to unite in the middle. There was nothing else.

Disappointed, he wrapped everything in the tunic then tied it to the body. Wrestling it onto his shoulder again, he extinguished the torches. Outside, the clouds had started to clear and he made his way by Capci's light to a distant hill. With much effort, he buried the body deeply in the heavy soil and covered all traces of his presence. Here there would be no danger of the heavy rains uncovering it, and access to the hill was difficult enough to discourage interest in the reed trees.

Mottled with sweat and dirt, Andar wearily retraced his steps to the pool, cleaned himself with a short, ungratifying swim, and returned to the house.

The Reedsmith of Zendar

The hardened mass rolled and tumbled against him, jarring him, so that he staggered and fell. Andar struggled blindly to his feet and spun about to face it, but his efforts were laboured and clumsy. It retreated so that the looming shape was shrouded in mist, two yellow points searing him in hostile silence. It wavered and dissolved into the mist and then was about him again, on both sides now, crowding and crushing him. As his terror grew, he fought back, pushing and shoving, trying to break free. When he touched it, parts of it crumbled, breaking off and flaking away, a stench soiling the air. His hands were lumped and crusted with pieces of it, and as he shook them from him, they fell away to lay writhing and pulsing on the forest floor. Something touched him on the shoulder and he spun to stare into the gnarled face of an impossibly old woman. In the seamed and wrinkled face, her eyes were a green phosphorescent fire that consumed him. He knew he was dying, layers of his body peeling off, caught in the updraft of her inferno. He was dissolving, dying, disappearing...

Alone in the dark, Andar awoke, the horror of the night leaving him weak and frightened.

Chapter Eight

The sky was cloudless, the heat at its peak. It was late afternoon the next day when Andar, dressed in his best sleeveless tunic, wrap and weapons harness, walked in silence beside Lanos. Headed to the village with his family, Andar's eyes were upon the rangy, sloping shoulders of Doros who was deep in animated conversation with Dreanna. Bristling with self-assurance, his swagger made Andar both annoyed and envious at the same time. Ready to enjoy the fruits of life, Doros was still unwilling to work for them. Was today to be arrogance, laziness, or brooding disrespect? Dreanna had never passed through this maze of debilitating moods. Beside Doros, dressed in a finely woven azure top from Krowden, Dreanna chattered to him beneath the sun shade she carried. Her excitement was almost palatable. For the tenth time that morning, Andar questioned why Dreanna was the target. The death of the Suru was of little consolation. Another would come when the first failed to return. All he had bought was some time. Perhaps if he could talk to Gartonnar before he partook of the Flowers of Dallipon.

Shouting a warning cry, Doros pointed to the three malbar that wheeled out of the reed forest ahead of them. Their disproportionately large wings silently beat the air in great caressing strokes, the heavy, rounded bodies hanging like grotesque, overripe fruit. With instinctive fury, venomuous jaws extended, they gathered speed as they hurtled towards their prey.

Four blades leapt from scabbards as they backed into a ragged square. The creatures closed on them, the foremost malbar targeting

Lanos, its yellow, human-like eyes fixed on the old man's. His sword arced over his right shoulder in an invisible blur, and sliced between the two yellow beacons. The body leapt apart, spewing fluids onto him. On either side of Lanos, the impact of blade on bone and sinew followed as the remaining two malbar attacked. Dreanna's blade cut through the gray translucent wing of one of them. It shrieked and tumbled at her feet, then began an awkward, dragging shuffle towards her. She nimbly leapt backwards and slashed at the head. It grimaced horribly, and snapped at the sword, meeting it open-mouthed. The blade smashed through the fangs and severed the top of the head. Doros' aim was better, catching the head of the third one slightly off center. The strike failed to drive the blade through the body, and he held onto the hilt, warily watching the malbar as it jerked in a death throe.

"I've told you before, Doros!" Andar yelled. "If you don't have the size or strength, then you must make up for it with speed!" Cautiously he walked closer and held his foot against the body as Doros, red-faced, tugged his blade from the malbar. "What if you had been alone? With your blade stuck in the first one, how would you deal with the others?"

Angrily Doros grabbed one of the wings, dragged and threw the creature from the path, and stalked off ahead. Dreanna hurried to join him. Andar sheathed his sword and let out a sigh as he watched them.

Lanos clapped him on the shoulder. "Come. We shouldn't let them get too far ahead." After a spell, he spoke again. "He did stop the malbar."

"Yes, but look at the position he left himself in," said Andar. "He could have been killed if we weren't here."

"But we were here. He didn't get killed."

"Not this time."

"The only thing he didn't do was drive the blade completely through," Lanos said. "Could you or I have done that every time at his age?" Andar remained silent. "I know he is getting older, son, but don't expect too much. No matter how much you want him to do everything right, to be prepared for all things, he won't be. He's going to get his share of scars. The best you can do is help and encourage him."

"That's what I was doing."

"I noticed you didn't say anything to Dreanna. Her aim was a drox sight worse." Again, Andar didn't reply. "Tell him he did well then remind him about the speed. Don't lose him, son, not this way." He paused, squinting into the sun. "There are too many other ways."

On their arrival in Bonstag, they proceeded to Rakosur's. He had cleared a niche at the back of the tavern for Andar and his family. Rakosur, his wife Junsa, and Sarta joined them for the evening's meal. When finished, Rakosur refused payment.

"Andar, you wish to shame me, yes? You honour me by choosing my son as a mentor for Dreanna then expect me to charge you for the celebratory meal? Sometimes I wonder about you, my young friend."

"You're right, Rakosur. The food wasn't that good anyway."

Dreanna and Sarta sat enjoying the show, stealing nervous glances at each other, saying little.

"What a perfect day for it!" gushed Jadosa, as she breezed by, bringing more ale. "And how special that it is to be on the Telling Day." She looked at Sarta. "You make sure you take your time and do a proper job, Sarta," she teased addressing her younger brother, who despite himself, blushed furiously.

"Jadosa, stop it. Leave the boy alone," Rakosur admonished.

"Sorry, Father. I just hope Sarta is half the teacher that Andar was." She smiled impishly at Andar, wheeling away before her father could swat her.

"Sometimes I don't know what to do with her." He sighed in mock exasperation, shaking his head with a grin.

"Father, I keep discovering so many new skills that you have kept hidden," Dreanna said.

"Don't you start," Andar replied.

Sarta and Dreanna looked at each other, laughing, relaxed in each other's presence for the first time that evening. Looking over Rakosur's shoulder, Andar saw Jadosa smile as she watched the two. She winked at Andar and he mouthed a silent thank you. Spirits high, the ale continued to flow.

As dusk approached, the four of them took two gourds of reedale and sought out the small cabin that Rakosur had reserved. It was near the Field of Life, on the edge of the village, apart from the much traveled paths. The two young ones walked ahead, holding hands, laughing often as the two fathers trailed them at a respectable distance.

Arriving, Andar beckoned Dreanna aside and held her hands, speechless as he gently rubbed them with his thumbs. Finally, he studied her face, alight with joy and anticipation. She shook her hair back, and a lump rose in Andar's throat, threatening to stop his blessing.

"With every day you look more like you mother, especially tonight. You make me very proud, Dreanna. May tonight be as special for you as it is for me." Bending he kissed her on the forehead. She started to reply, but he pressed a finger to her lips. "Go now. Go."

Dreanna saw his tenuous control and her eyes moistened in turn. She smiled and touched his face, then turned and walked toward Sarta who waited by the door. He held out his hand, and together they entered the cabin.

"A strange time, isn't it, my young friend?" murmured Rakosur, as he approached and threw an arm over Andar's shoulders. "That's why we have a gourd as well. Let's not waste it, Andy."

Distant from the cabin, they sat and talked of times and events that had cemented their friendship, of the births of their children, of loved ones, alive and dead. And when conversation waned, they grew still and watched night settle upon the village.

On the surrounding hillside, row upon row of merchant tents flickered into light as lanterns within each were lit. Their white, ethereal skins shone transparent in the green darkness, transforming the usually serene village hillside into a magical landscape. They ringed the flat grassy plain, where The Telling was to take place, creating a rising amphitheater of lights flickering bright and low in the mist.

Andar's eyes glistened. Heady with ale, filled with the grandeur of the scene below, overwhelmed with the emotion of Dreanna's night, he sat silently with Rakosur and together they emptied the gourd.

Between sips of ale, the two young ones undressed each other, savoring the experience; Sarta the pleasure of leading someone for the first time, Dreanna, burning it into her memory as a keepsake. When their firm bodies touched, it was over in a mad lusting rush, both of them clutching and pulling each other close. Soon they lay spent and panting, wrapped in each other's arms.

"That," he whispered, still breathless, "is how not to do it." He pushed some strands of hair from her face, kissing her on the nose and lips.

"No? Are you serious, Sarta? I quite enjoyed it. What more could there possibly be?" Her eyes were wide in surprise and inquiry.

"There is much, much more, Dreanna. We shall sip some more ale and then..." He caught the small smile on her face. Sarta rolled over on top of her, pinning her arms, pressing his face close to hers.

"Ah, such a clever little girl."

"Not so little," she replied, struggling in his grasp for a moment, head turned up. Their eyes met and held. "Teach me, Sarta. Show me." Her voice was soft, reaching out to him, exposing the loneliness she felt.

"Yes. Now we will go slowly. Now we will learn." He bent, lowering his lips to hers as her arms encircled his head.

Chapter Nine

Andar and his family wound their way between the glowing tents on the terraced slope towards the grassy incline below. Despite the crowd of people amassing, the atmosphere was one of silent reverence as anticipation leapt from one villager to another. Farmers and tradesmen nodded in greeting, their simple tunics and cloaks a background for the mosaic of color and finery draped on prosperous merchants, Council members, and the Ancient Order. All were drawn to the base of the broad valley, to the platform surrounded by the Council's Guard who stood resplendent in their burnished armor and red cloaks.

Seated midway up the incline, Andar wrapped his arms around his youngest as Colonar settled between his bent knees, and rested his head upon his father's chest. Dreanna sat to Andar's right, quiet and serene, studying the crowd, stealing glances at Sarta. Doros, silent and somber, gazed with intent upon the raised platform and the guards below. Andar remembered when, as one of them, he had stood there proudly during the Festival of Light. Now, as he watched them, he realized again that he had made the right decision those many years ago. His eyes travelled to the procession of the Ancient Order who solemnly walked to the front of the crowd and sat on low benches before the guards. Andar looked away, refusing to let them taint his mood on this special day.

The humid air clung to them as the cool of night sifted down from an indigo sky. Smoke rose from small pot fires that encircled the stage, its cloying fragrance permeating the shallow valley. In the twilight, the heat of the fires, here and throughout the awaiting villagers pulled the wisps of green mist inwards, clearing the view for all to see.

Three cloaked figures rose near the platform, sat on its edge, and began to play the traditional March of the Innocents. The reeflute's haunting melody caressed the air, carrying softly to the surrounding audience as the reedrum and shakeree set a hypnotic rhythm. The music wove a seductive spell, drawing everyone's senses to the moment. A fourth figure stepped forward and sat upon the solitary stool in the center of the dais. Dropping the hood of his cloak, he waited until the last strains of music faded into the night. He raised his face to the heavens and the deep baritone voice cut the air, the familiar words soaring above all who gathered there.

"Driven from our home planet by those who remain nameless, faceless, we found a new world to call our own." The crowd, as if one, murmured their acquiescence; a gentle roar of whispers that bespoke their commitment. And so their history began to unfold, as it did, once each year. The orator, Tonata, a master storyteller, a Friend of the Ancients, wove wonder into the history that all knew so well, making each event seem like a new revelation, as if heard for the first time.

Once again the great ship, mortally wounded, tore into the earth, breaking apart, spilling its living and dead upon the ground. Of the thousands it held, a bare two hundred and forty-three bleeding and battered survivors stood and watched the remains of their civilization burn. The ordeal for survival began; a slow, unrelenting struggle for life that saw many die, many change.

Impressions of an idyllic, garden-like planet were quickly altered. The malbar provided the first burst of reality, twenty-five of their number succumbing to the poisonous bites, and a race began to find a cure. Finally it had been done by the wisest and most skilled. In recognition of their efforts and leadership, they were named the Ancient Order. Individually they became the first "majiks".

The beginning notes of Rain's Lament reached out to the crowd. Upon the onset of the rains, the survivors rejoiced as the dusty world was anointed by the first drops. But joy turned to horror as, caught unaware, the planet released its watery death upon them. Fortunate were those who did not drown or who were not pummeled to death by the onslaught during that first lengthy, torrential downpour. Disaster after disaster continued, their numbers slowly dwindling, as each new obstacle took its toll.

Little had survived from the crash. They were now sophisticates with little or no technology and few resources. A civilized and cultured society, of those who had survived, few were "Majiks", trained to invent, to create. Out of necessity, the need to survive fashioned an ideology of cooperation. Everything became the property of all, with every man's door open to anyone in need. Women and men shared each other, and everyone rejoiced when that first blessed child was born.

The reed trees became their salvation. On a world bereft of minerals, they were the planet's gift to a helpless, tool-less society. With their intelligence and perseverance, they learned to do wonders with the reeds, and the crystals within them, fashioning the necessities of life to stave off the elements of nature and survive.

The music, playing quietly in the background, saddened as the first notes of Droxeur's Judgement braced all for the next chapter in their history. An outcrop of unique stone had been discovered. It was the first of such, holding a promise of things to come, for unlike other rock found at the bottom of valleys in river beds, it sparkled with the glint of minerals. A small band moved to explore and experiment with it, its importance uppermost on everyone's mind. And slowly, insidiously, it began to change them. Against the wishes of the Order, the leader of the group, Droxeur, refused to bring the group home, killing the Elder of the Ancient Order and fleeing. They turned violent, attacking others who approached to encourage their return. Then the physical deformities began. To kill them was unthinkable at the time. If only they had. They accepted the loss of their comrades and moved south, traveling far from the crash site, taking with them the remnants of their former life. A new settlement was established at Orrdamoor.

It had been the first split of the survivors. For thousands of years the Stomuants, now deformed past recognition, had been content to stay where they were, but as their numbers grew, so did their need for more of the damning substance. The mutants eventually disappeared, traveling northwards into the mountains in their search for more precious stone. As time passed, they sometimes ranged south from their mountain homeland, raiding remote settlements and taking villagers who were never seen again. It happened more often now, reawakening the horror of that chapter of their history.

It was the "Stone Sleepers" who were the saddest legacy from that early discovery. As if a cruel reminder of their early mistake, sometimes a child was born, mutated and disfigured, although the parents were normal. It was a cross they had to bear; an unspoken fear, that every time someone had a child, it might be a Stone Sleeper.

The survivors of Zendar grew strong, adapting to their new environment. Warily at first, they explored, creating new villages and towns. The temple at Orrdamoor kept the artifacts and precious few books. The Ancient Order wrote new ones, recording memories of their former heritage, recording the new developing history. In every town and village representatives of the Ancient Order were assigned by the Order's Royal Preceptors to collect monies to sustain the Temple at Orrdamoor and ensure that each new generation understood the debt and respect owed to Kaptin Dukor and the original Ancient Ones. "Friends of the Ancient Ones" traveled the paths and rivers of Zendar, bringing news, singing songs and reciting its history. Over time, different cultures developed, but their heritage was kept alive, the stories passed down from parent to sibling, and by the "Telling". There were many factions now upon Zendar who loved and quarreled and made war upon each other, but upon this day they were as one.

Tonata had finished, and mirroring him, the thousand carpeting the hillside shed their night cloaks and drew their swords. Beneath Capci, and its distant smoldering cousin, Kunic, in unison the citizens of Zendar executed the ritual strokes, parries and thrusts of the ceremonial drill that each had been taught since they were old enough to stand; the drill that symbolized their commitment to Zendar, The Ancient Ones and each other. The sound of a thousand blades, stroke after stroke, filled the night air.

Andar struck again and again as the timeless music of Unity of the Ages bound him to all. The rhythm of their sources became entwined, nurturing him, bonding him to his kindred who moved with him. Then his sword was driven skywards, the cry of "Zendar" bursting from him, to unite with the others: a roar filling the valley.

It took him several moments to control his breathing and surface from the trance that had enveloped him. As he sheathed his sword, he became aware that his family stood watching him in silence. He smiled at young Colonar who came forward and hugged him. Andar held him close, burying his face in his son's neck as he squeezed tightly for many long seconds.

Andar gazed down upon the mass of people slowly dispersing. All were quiet and subdued. They nodded to each other, clasped hands and embraced, instinctively renewing their kinship. Such was the power of "The Telling" and the ceremonial sword drill. This night, both had affected Andar deeply. He had made his decision.

Gartonnar's home was small and simple, as unpretentious as the man himself. A low cottage of time-aged timbers, it sat on a crooked side street among others of similar age and character. As he approached the door, Andar chased away a nearby wild atogg from the porch, its snout dusty from prowling for scraps. After knocking, it took some time for the bent, hobbling figure of the old warrior to appear in the doorway.

"Andar. I didn't expect to see you again. Come in." The welcoming pleasure of the old man's voice was so genuine that Andar felt a pang of guilt for all the visits not kept. He returned the greeting, motioning Gartonnar forward, closing the door behind them.

As he followed the gnarled body, Andar was taken back by the slow cumbersome shuffle and heaving breath, interspersed with small grunts of pain, as the old man inched his way towards the gently burning fire. A grimace of teeth, and an exhausted sigh, accompanied Gartonnar as he fell back into the chair. On the small round table beside him sat a tankard, half-filled with a pale yellowish liquid. Andar sat opposite. Gartonnar smiled, looking at the fire, then at Andar.

"It took me forever to set and light the fire. Forever," he repeated incredulously, the smile coming to his lips again as he shook his head slowly in disbelief. He raised his eyes and Andar saw the sadness, but only for a moment. Then the eyes were bright once more, focused on him questioningly. "What brings you to me, Andar?"

Andar's glance shuttled to the tankard and back to the old man. "I didn't mean to interrupt."

"Nonsense. It's a good thing you did, or else I wouldn't be of much use, would I? Now speak up. What's on your mind that you take an old man from his final journey?" and he grinned and was, for a moment, the same old warrior that had cursed and cussed Andar so many times years before.

Andar told his story carefully, leaving nothing out. When finished, Gartonnar said nothing, but sat, alternately studying the fire and Andar.

"You have decided to act upon the matter?" he asked.

"I have little choice."

"There is always a choice. Many simply make the wrong one, make it too late, or don't make it at all, which *is* their choice. Where will you start?"

"My only path is to find out who sent the Suru. I can't wait hoping no one else will come. They will, and then what? Dare I hope to be so lucky again?"

"Luck is what you call it? You stop a Suru twice and you call it luck?" The tone of the old man was a mixture of sarcasm and bewilderment.

"Lanos and Doros came to my rescue. If we had not fought in the pond I am sure I would be dead." He shook his head. "The mark on his arm. I need to find someone who has knowledge of this. I was hoping you might know of such a person."

Gartonnar was silent again for a time, his eyes focused somewhere beyond the room, misted over and distant. "Yes, I know of someone who may be of help, if he is still alive. To the west. In the town of Kempa there was a man, Josharat, who knew much of the Suru and their clans. From him you might get some answers regarding the marking. He may not be there any longer. He may be dead. He may not have or give you what you seek."

"Yes, but I must start. I must do something."

"Yes, I agree, you must. Who will accompany you?"

The question caught Andar off guard. He had not thought that far ahead. "There is no one. Lanos is too old, Doros too young. I'm not sure of anything. I would not risk their lives. That's why I am going. To stop the Suru, to keep them away from my family." Andar silenced himself, letting his face cool, his anger dissipate. Finally, "There is no one else that I could honourably ask. I go alone."

"If only I could go with you." The statement vexed Gartonnar and he stared at the cup beside him before turning to Andar again. "And you are afraid?"

Andar's eyes flashed angrily, the green hardening in hostile silence.

"At least you are wise enough to be afraid. It will make you cautious, alert you to danger," the old man soothed. He was all business again. "Daily. You must begin tomorrow and practice daily. Use Doros. Use Lanos. Both of them together. Enlist some of the council guards. Bring back those skills. And," he paused, painfully shifting in the chair, "you must also visit Maudausa."

Andar raised his brow in surprise, studying the quick, soft smile that touched Gartonnar's lips. "The Majik that lives in the Sun Hills?"

Gartonnar nodded. "Not only must your sword arm be strong, but your source as well. Yours has always been exceptional. But like others, you have never developed it. On a journey such as this, it would not hurt to know some of the secrets of The Order, despite what we think of them."

"But she's a Herm Majik," Andar said.

"Yes, she is now, but many years ago she was one of them. She withdrew through choice to become one of the Faithful."

"She won't see me," said Andar.

"When she senses your aura, she will speak with you. Mention my name," and the old warrior smiled again.

"How will I find her? The Sun Hills are many."

"You will find her. Or she you. Either way trust your source and the two of you will meet."

Gartonnar sat and toyed with the tankard, rubbing his withered fingers over its polished surface. Andar sat and watched him do so.

"Are you afraid, Gartonnar? Of leaving to join the Ancients?"

Gartonnar's faded gray eyes studied Andar and he adjusted his body carefully in the chair. "Afraid? No. Saddened is perhaps a more fitting word. Tired perhaps most accurate."

"What if my fear," and Andar snorted derisively, "my wise and cautious fear gets in the way? What if it stops me from acting, or making the right decision? What -"

"Andar." Gartonnar spoke firmly. "I believe in you. Your fear did not stop you when the Suru attacked. It did not defeat you. Believe in yourself."

They both sat listening to the gentle crackle of the flames.

Andar gazed into the fire, the pulsing, amber light softening the lines of his face.

"The Telling today was the best I have ever heard. It moved me, helped me to reach my decision. I was filled with the power of it. My source and my sense of purpose were so strong. If only I can hold on to it."

"It's there, Andar. Your source lies inside of you as it does in all of us to different degrees. In you, it is strong. It lies resting, much of it dormant but ready to be developed and used whenever it is needed. It won't let you down."

"I hope you're right, Gartonnar. I hope you're right."

"I'm older than you, and therefore wiser. Now throw some wood on that fire. Make it roar! If I'm going to drink this, I need a warrior's fire, not that of an old maid."

Andar's words were slow and halting, laden with emotion. "I will drink often from the Ancestral Cup to honour your memory. Like our first ancestors, you will be a source of wisdom and assurance on my journey. You will travel with me."

"You honour us both with your words."

And so Andar sat with his old friend as he drank. Gartonnar rested, peacefully watching the flames lick hungrily at the reeds. Near the end, he tiredly turned his head to Andar, the same quick, soft smile gracing his lips. Then he closed his eyes, and his breath slowed until he exhaled a last time. His jaw relaxed and his body, shrunken with age, settled in the chair and became still. The room seemed to grow quieter and Andar bowed his head, letting the sadness wash over him.

Chapter Ten

Breakfast was impossible, the noise, banter, and taunting endless. Crowded into their usual corner, spirits soared as a result of The Telling the evening before. Rakosur, in fine form, told one of the many adventures of his youth. Doros threw teasing barbs at Dreanna and Sarta and ate non-stop, adding another slice of roasted berddon and a third reed cake to his plate. As if challenged, Rakosur's wife, Lunsa, piled the planked table with more of the morning's fare.

"Look at this woman, Andar!" Rakosur bellowed, grabbing his rotund wife around the waist. "Have you ever seen such a prize! What I didn't have to do to win her!" She slapped him good-naturedly and made her way back to the kitchen, but Rakosur was off again, describing how he had made his conquest.

As Lunsa passed her daughter, Andar watched Jadosa turn from a stout, red-faced merchant, the teasing sway of her hips garnering the patron's full attention. She glanced in Andar's direction and smiled, caught in the act. Andar smiled back as she winked and ran her tongue sensuously over her lips.

She had always been a woman of physical emotion who differed little from Rakosur. He lived his adventures over the table with a mug of ale, she over the bed, with or without the ale. Indeed, she was hotly pursued throughout the village, but despite the pleasure she dispensed and collected, no man had been able to capture her heart.

He had gone to her last night, finally accepting the need of a woman, of intimate human contact. Not a comrade to drink with and exchange ribald stories. Not someone to listen to his woes, or give him advice, but a woman to hold him in his sleep and make him feel warm and safe. After an evening drink with Rakosur, he had climbed the narrow stairs to the simple sleeping quarters above. As he came to her partially open door, she looked up from her bed where she sat in the torchlight, knees drawn up, arms wrapped around them, waiting for him. Somehow she had known. Andar entered and closed the door behind him. She drew him down beside her, and when he had started to speak, she silenced him with a hand over his mouth.

"Talk is not what you need, Andar." Her lips closed gently on his and the longing and loneliness for someone escaped his tight control. It was over quickly, both of them uninhibited and unrestrained. His release came quickly, and Jadosa held him tightly then eased him down with gentle, firm strokes until she felt the tension drain from his body and he was still. For a long time they lay together, neither wishing to speak, comfortable in each other's arms, holding, touching, caring for each other until Andar rose to leave.

"It has been too long, Andar. Don't try to live in the past."

He had said nothing, but kissed her gently, then had returned to the main hall to think and plan.

Sitting with the others at breakfast, Andar drank deeply of the ree as he watched Dreanna experiment with her newfound sensuality. Sarta had departed and it had not taken her long to discover a youth about her own age sitting on the opposite side of the tavern. His gaze traveled often in Dreanna's direction, a result of her obvious stare. Whenever he looked in her direction, she would look away, only to repeat her focused assault. In spite of himself, Andar shook his head, repressing a smile as he recalled a time when he had tumbled into the world of adulthood and the physical pleasure it provided.

He knew that he was not ready to begin his journey. He needed to gather more information about the route to Kempa, never having journeyed far in that direction. His physical condition and fighting skills were no longer adequate for such a venture. And then there was the rains. The reed crystal shards on his porch hadn't moved yet, but it certainly couldn't be long now. He wouldn't travel in the rains by choice, no one would, yet time was critical. The longer he waited before leaving, the more time for a runner to take word to his enemy. There was also the matter of visiting the Majik. He would have to trust Gartonnar's word that he would find her. The Sun Hills were not far, so perhaps today, before they returned home. Andar glanced up from his tankard to find the young man Dreanna had been flirting with approaching their table.

"Excuse me," he said, a slight nodding bow directed towards Dreanna. "Could it be that we know each other, and this empty head of mine has forgotten such a beautiful face? If so, I wish to apologize for such an oversight." He nodded and held out a single flower for Dreanna, a beguiling smile on his lips.

Dreanna blushed and was momentarily speechless. Quickly, she regained her composure. "I'm sorry sir, but I believe you are mistaken. We have never met."

Andar could see from the young man's manner that he was having some fun at Dreanna's expense.

"Then please forgive my intrusion and accept this flower as an apology."

Her eyes held his, and she refused to be intimidated. "Thank you sir," she said, and accepted the flower. "Good day to you."

He bowed a third time, and still smiling, took his leave. Silence had overtaken the table, all eyes upon the two, but as the stranger stepped from the room, laughter burst forth. From across the table Rakosur grinned.

"Oh, Andar, I think you have more problems than you know!"

Andar looked at his daughter who gazed back at him innocently.

Smelling the flower, she smiled. "He *was* very good looking."

Andar stood at the foot of the Sun Hills having left the trail that continued east. The reed forest had thinned, and the undergrowth of foliage was gnarled and sparse. Many jagged rocks and boulders poked through the earth, their gray surfaces pockmarked and filled by clumps of soil in which tiny reed shoots vainly grew. The sun beat on him as he pushed deeper into the hills, trusting to Gartonnar's word that Maudasa would find him. Travelling instinctively, although sometimes faltering, he sensed the direction that seemed right, becoming sure of his route as if he were traveling homewards.

He rested, taking a drink from the gourd at his side. Andar slipped the strap of his harness from his shoulder and pulled the sleeveless tunic over his head, drapping it on top of his trail bag. Sliding the strap back onto his shoulder, he ensured the small throwing knife sheathed in the front was still in place then started moving east again. He sprang for a boulder, leapt upwards to another, then leaned into a steep grade, his legs driving into the climb. Scrambling up and over the surface of several rocks, he froze in mid stride as the figure of an old woman came into view not fifty feet in front of him. Seated on a small boulder, she pulled upon a long stemmed pipe, a wreath of smoke encircling her graying head. A magnificent multi-colored robe hung from small, squared shoulders. At her feet was a simple trail bag. With the staff in her right hand she was idly boring a hole in the soil.

Her eyes peered questioningly towards Andar. She removed the pipe from her mouth and motioned with it for him to approach. He did so cautiously, unsettled by the old woman despite her unthreatening appearance for he hadn't sensed her presence at all. When he neared, her eyes widened as she studied him.

"Such eyes as yours, traveler, I have not seen in many years. You have the eyes of a disciple. But I do not think that is why you have come. Your aura speaks plainly of that. Such turmoil. What it is you wish, I cannot perceive. Very good closure, when you are focused." Her own green eyes glistened beneath drooping lids as she leaned her chin upon a pink-skinned palm.

"I was told of you," Andar started. "Sent to you, that you might be of help. Someone wants my daughter. He said I should seek you out. I need your help. He said that I needed your help." Andar trailed off, embarrassed by his awkward speech. His face flushed, anger streaking along his legs and arms until he was trembling. As if she had been struck an invisible blow, the old woman winced then sat upright, eyeing Andar more intensely.

"So strong. Your aura is so strong. And uncontrolled. It leaps from you, but has no purpose. There is no focus to all this source energy you wield." She rubbed her wrinkled jaw then pulled on the pipe, coaxing the dying embers back to life, eyes focused intently upon him. "I cannot read your thoughts. Yes, good closure. Who takes it upon themselve to send you to me with offerings of my help?" The voice bristled with sarcasm, the question a challenge.

"His name was Gartonnar. He said I must see you."

Maudasa's countenance softened, her eyes abandoning Andar for the boulder strewn slopes beyond. They returned to him, somehow less guarded, the brittle edge gone. With grace that belied her age, she rose to her feet and motioned with the staff.

"This way. It is not far."

They sat within a tiny cabin, the reed logs small but expertly fit. The peaked ceiling was low and festooned with a multitude of dried plants and animals hanging from tapered beams. Covering the walls were shelves of all kinds, some skillfully crafted, others crudely fashioned. Upon all were countless rolls of reed parch, bound with cord, sealed with reegum. Other scrolls, bowls, and an assortment of strange implements and devices cluttered tables. The bowls were half filled with oddly colored powders, or overflowing with the shredded strands of plants that Andar did not recognize. In others, the dried remains of mixtures lay hardened in the bottom. A tiny fire and several torches provided light for the two as they huddled together in chairs by the fireside.

"Tell me of Gartonnar. Is he well?" Her manner was now informal, but Andar sensed that the question was more than casual.

"Gartonnar has taken leave to journey with our ancestors. He drank of the Flowers of Dallipon yesterday."

Maudasa stared at Andar, then rose quickly, moved to a shelf and lifted a cup from the rest of the clutter. She cradled it gently in her arms, pulled it to her breast and silently rocked back and forth before returning to Andar. Her cheeks were flushed, her eyes moist, as she poured some reed ale into the cup. She lifted it reverently in both hands.

"Gartonnar, with this cup we honour your memory. Sit at the side of our ancestors that you may add your wisdom in guiding our path." Maudasa took a drink and passed it to Andar who did the same, then returned the cup to her. Carefully, she poured the remainder of the ale into the fire, wiped the cup, and replaced it upon the shelf. As she settled once more, their eyes met across the fire, and Andar dared to ask.

"How is it that you came to know Gartonnar?"

Maudasa's eyes shone and her face lit as with the first touch of dawn. "Gartonnar was my husband."

Sitting across from Maudasa, Andar sucked on the end of the drenn bone then tossed it into the fire. The meal had been simple but good; some freshly baked reebread, the drenn that Maudasa had trapped yesterday and the boiled bulbs of cresstars.

Maudasa relit her pipe and pulled on it thoughtfully then blew the smoke into the air. Absently, she studied the cloud. A hole appeared in the middle of it and the smoke, now a ring, began to turn slowly, gradually turning faster, the edges spinning off, the ring of smoke gradually disappearing. Her eyes turned to Andar who sat watching her. "It was not to impress you. Many of the Friends of the Ancients can do tricks to entertain the crowds. I did it without thought. You could call it a habit."

Andar's eyes widened imperceptibly at her statement, for it was exactly what he was thinking about at that very moment.

"Yes, I can sense your thoughts when your guard is down," she said causing his eyes to widen more. "At least the essence of what you are thinking. Now you want to know about me. Gartonnar and me." She smiled at him, green eyes shining in a sun-creased face. "Ah, now I can not. That is a rarity. As I said before, your aura, your closure, both very strong. That is good. It will come in handy. But first about my Gartonnar." She leaned back and was silent, finally tapping the ashes from her pipe over the fire.

"To tell the tale of our lives would take more time than you have to give, so I will shorten it. I was one of those chosen to represent the Ancient Order in Bonstag, Gartonnar a young and very dashing guard. We fell in love, but because members of the Ancient Order may not commit to another, we had to live apart. It was hard but when I was summoned to Orrdamoor it became impossible. He would secretly visit whenever he could, but it was seldom. He moved to Orrdamoor, to be a guard there, advancing in the ranks. As my skills grew, more and more I was cloistered away, to avoid outside contact, to devote my time to the Order. Sad, how they've changed from that first Ancient Order. As I suspect you know, then as now, we have a "new" Order. They refused to let Gartonnar see me. He tried to reason with them. He stood before the Royal Preceptors, but all to no avail. Bitter, unable to remain in Orrdamoor and not see me, he returned to Bonstag." She raised a gray eyebrow as Andar opened his mouth to speak. "So how is it that I am here, so close to Bonstag but was not with Gartonnar? Over the years I learned firsthand of the self-serving nature of those in control of the Ancient Order in Orrdamoor. Unlike the common people, those supposed guardians of our past have lost the essence of who we are. Forgot, that we are a part of all who have gone before us. For them it wasn't about holding onto our past, about helping the people to grow and develop the source within them. It was about keeping the secrets of the source for themselves. It was about impressing and controlling others so that they might maintain their life of leisure and power." She smiled. "As you know from experience."

Andar had listened to the sadness grow as she spoke. He now understood the wistfulness in the eyes of Gartonnar whenever they had talked of days gone by. When she paused, he interrupted. "You said that there is-"

"...a secret to the source? I'm sorry, I must stop doing that, interrupting you. It must make me seem to be showing off." A reproaching smile touched her lips. "Not really a secret. Only a secret because it had fallen into disuse and then was hidden, and hence forgotten. The early records have even been changed to hide the true nature of its use, of its power. Not that those of the Order would allow, never mind encourage any to read them." She leaned forward, wrinkled elbows on her knees, her eyes intense on Andar's. "The secret, my talented young friend, is that the source, that everyone on Zendar has, could be much more than it is. Through lack of use during the ages it has wizened. Yes, some have a stronger sense and aura than others, ones such as you, but even they are but a shadow of what they should be. Of what our first ancestors were. And that is how the Order would have it, for the leaders have become tainted. They use the source, practise it, for it is how they maintain control, how they maintain their self-serving position."

" And you and Gartonnar never..."

"No. Too many years had passed. By the time I left the Order, I knew my path was no longer my own. I found a group of the Faithful, those truly devoted to preserving and teaching the past and its skills. I have trained many others who show the inclination to truly serve the people and the Ancients. My life...has been meaningful, if not by choice."

The conversation that he had had with Gartonnar flashed into his mind and he saw Maudasa inhale and let out a long sigh.

"Yes, my dear Gartonnar told me the same thing. There is always a choice, he would say. Then he would level his stare at me and tell me that not making a choice, even that was a choice, and he was right." She grinned a twisted smile. "He always was smarter than he took credit for. What a waste, all that smashing of swords." She straightened her back, twisting from side to side and her reverie passed as she focused on Andar once more.

"You are right, Andar, to call upon the members of the Ancient Order is a waste of time. Those in the village are merely scribes putting payment to record. The Council is hardly better in a situation such as this. *If* they believe you, they will sympathize, but can do little more. Being able to deal with the organization of the village and the petty squabbles does not qualify them to organize a search. The guards themselves are to protect the Ancient Order, the Council, and caravans. They are not trained to track down Suru. It has never been done."

Andar studied her for long moments before he spoke. "Gartonnar sent me here for your help. He would not have done so unless he was sure you could."

Maudasa reached for the pouch on the bench beside her and began filling her pipe. "There really is only one way that I can assist you in your quest to protect your family, and I think you know what that is."

It was now a rare day that Andar did not visit the village. The two hour walk became an hour's march and then a half hour's run. The trips, combined with the extra hours he spent at the hearth, swinging a heavier than usual hammer, began to diminish the sedentary layer around his waist. He ate voraciously, fueling himself to maintain his rigorous training. There were daily weapons drills with any number of different Council Guards. After meeting three of them in the popular tavern often frequented by the Guard, he sought their help in protecting his family, offering his smithing skills in exchange. Several followed him home that day and it wasn't long before others began showing up so that there was always two or three present. When they pushed away his offer of free weapons, he realized the bond among them had always been there.

Late in the evening, as Maudasa had instructed, Andar would reach within, gathering what strength he had left from the day's grueling routine, and use his source. Sitting weary in the loft, he would empty his mind of all thoughts and let his source flood his consciousness. At first little happened, but as the days passed, he became aware of his source expanding, thoughts and feelings dancing gently on the outskirts of his mind. Within him, he could feel the heat of the dying fire in the hearth, sense the odours of the evening's meal hanging in the air. Although he had always been able to sense the presence of others, now he was acutely aware of Colonar's deep slumber, felt the restlessness of Dreanna's broken sleep. Finally, Andar would turn his source inward to his aching muscles, soothing them with his will, encouraging them to stretch and grow.

Soon after he had begun encouraging his source to strengthen, the unsettling dreams were back with a clarity and ferocity that threatened to undermine his resolution. At day's end, battered and exhausted, sleep would claim him and pull him down into the depths of death-like slumber. Nothing could awaken him until, near dawn, the taloned claws of his nightmare image would click on polished stone beneath its feet. The creature's hard body would press against him, so intense that he couldn't breathe and he would awaken with a start, soaked in sweat. To fight it he would stumble to Dreanna's doorway and listen to her soft murmuring sleep in the early hours of the morning. He would see the shadow of her small form, remember the terror on her face and his own fear would be crushed and thrown aside. His conviction, stronger than the day before, would infuse him with a sudden hot rush, and he would steal from her room to begin training again so that he might grow stronger, willing to face another day of penance for being old, for having children, for being singled out for no reason he could fathom.

Day after day he labored, and gradually the strength, endurance and skills of a soldier began to return. Yet with each passing day, the time of the rains grew nearer.

The sandaled feet of the soldier danced in a feint, sending clouds of dust knee high into the air as the two combatants circled each other. Although taller than his adversary, the soldier found himself driven back by the sheer ferocity of Grenfeld as the thick arms and powerful shoulders of the baron struck crashing blows against his weapon. Time and time again he recovered at the last moment, barely able to deflect the rushing blade and avoid a serious wound.

The pleasure Grenfeld felt showed plainly in his cold, compressed smile. He lunged again, keeping the younger man off balance, then slidestepped his solid frame forward, pressing the attack further, unrelenting in his punishment, for each sword drill, was an opportunity to reinforce his superiority and control.

He pressed on, harder, willing the image of the young warrior to blur and change. His enemy was older, tall and lean, with dark hair. He was the one he fought each day here in his courtyard. Grenfeld redoubled his blows. One last powerful slash sent the sword spinning from the young warrior's hand. The soldier saw the blind fury on the face and knew his death was but a moment away.

"Grenfeld!" he screamed, as the sword began to fall, its deadly arc spinning for his head. At the last moment it veered to the left, the blade turning on the flat, as it whisked past, the edge barely grazing his skull. The blow stunned the warrior who stood dazed and frightened in defeat. A barking laugh rang loud in his ears: Grenfeld enjoying his game. The other men encircled the two. There was much shifting of feet, accompanied by sidelong glances. Most had experienced belittlement at his hands. It was the price one paid to serve the most powerful man in Dashindar.

Grenfeld strolled towards the house as he watched his shaken sparring partner retrieve his sword and return to the group of men. He saw the welcoming gestures, words of encouragement, and turned away, cold and detached once more. He could control them, but he would never be one of them. Nor did he wish to be.

A commotion at the yard gate and Grenfeld paused at the house entrance. He turned, eyes shuttered against the sun, studying the figure. "It's Titarius," he whispered to himself as recognition occurred. "It's Titarius!" the excitement growing in his voice as he stepped out quickly, powerful strides propelling him towards the approaching messenger. Before the distance closed he was shouting the question. "What word, Titarius? What word?" The warrior had reached him now, his face impassive. "Speak up, man! What word?"

Titarius was almost apologetic. "He was not successful. All have been seen in the village, so we can only assume he is dead. The body has not been found. We feared to venture too close, but there can be no other explanation." He lowered his eyes, not wishing to view the effect of his news.

Silence hung in the air. The messenger ventured a look at Grenfeld who stood locked in thought, his face emotionless. The eyes darted here and there, but saw nothing.

"The fool! I told him that it would not work. Of course the Suru is dead." He kicked the earth in anger. "It's good we prepared." He looked to Titarius. "Well done. A day's rest then you shall return." Grenfeld turned and strode back to the house. "Enough of this waste of time. Now we will do it my way!"

Chapter Eleven

"Watch what you are doing, Doros," shouted Dreanna as she spit out some soil that hit her in the face.

"Then move out of the way. Go work over there," said Doros. He stood upright and leaned on the handle of the duggip that he had been using to loosen the dirt around the base of the cresstars.

"Malshead, but you are miserable. Today, and everyday," Dreanna said staring back at him.

"Shut up, you're no better. If I hear you complain once more about father keeping you at his side, I think I'll be sick. At least since he has started going to the village again, you get to go with him. He just keeps me here, working." He glared at her. "You're just happy because you're going to get to rut with Rothus tonight. Most of the time you are as miserable as an old wrinkled berddon." He looked down at the soil between the rows of cresstars and angrily chopped at the dry earth.

Dreanna glanced in the direction of the path that would bring Rothus to her from Bonstag then turned to study Doros. "You're just jealous, because your time hasn't come yet. Ha! That's it! You're jealous, and you should be."

He stopped, smouldering at her teasing barb.

She smiled back, pleased with the effect of her attack. "There is nothing like it. The excitement, the anticipation, and when Rothus finally-"

"Shut-up!" Doros chopped harder and faster at the earth, ignoring her. After a few moments he stopped and took off his tunic. The sweat gleamed on his lean form. For him the change was a year away and although the shoulders were wide, his frame hadn't begun to fill out yet. He set back to work and Dreanna watched him for a moment, the pleasure quickly leaving her. She started turning over the earth. They worked in silence, only the dull thudding as they chopped into the earth and the nearby sound of swordplay as their father practiced with two of the guards.

"I'm sorry," she said finally. When he looked up she continued. "I'm worried. About father. What will he do? What can he do?"

"I want to help," said Dorus, jamming the duggip into the ground, "but...he won't let me. He treats me like a child. I can't go to the village with the two of you. He won't even practise with me any more. I hate it here!" His face was red with anger and frustration."

"He's afraid, Doros. For me, for you. Ever since Mother died you know what he's been like. Lost. He would never go to the village. Hardly ever talk to us, and never about Mother. And now someone has threatened me, perhaps you too if you had been there. He's afraid he may not be able to protect us, and that scares him more than anything. Have you watched him? I have. Sometimes he stands and stares out into the reed forest and his face... his face is sad, empty and small, if that makes any sense."

"I wish he would talk to us," said Doros. Tell us what he is going to do. What he thinks we-"

"That's the problem, Doros. He doesn't know what to do."

Despite the constant worry and fear, Andar welcomed the arrival of customers, the busy traffic seeming to offer a level of vigilance and protection. Several nearby farmers needed repairs, the village butcher wanted a new cleaver, and again one of the Council Guard arrived with crude drawings for a ceremonial shield. Juros, a carpenter from the village, wanted a saw. Andar hated making them. The time it took to flatten the blade so evenly and to cut and sharpen all the teeth took forever. He knew, as did Juros, that no one else in the village could make one, and so Andar felt obligated to do so.

As the days passed, he distracted himself with his training, convinced that he was not ready. He took to sleeping outdoors on the ground, adjusting his body once again to the life of a soldier. Although he knew he should begin his journey, the sense of foreboding that assailed him each time he entertained the idea drove it from his thoughts. Trusting Dreanna's safety to to the Council guards, Lanos and Doros, terrified him, but taking her with him was unrealistic. He had no idea how long he might be gone or what dangers he might encounter.

He knew that keeping Dreanna close to home with the guards made her feel a prisoner. She complained bitterly at being a slave, when he forced her to stay at his side as he worked. It was only the many excursions to the village with her father that she welcomed. The relationship she developed with a handsome youth, recently met in Rakosur's tavern, had helped. Rothus had traveled west from Kindarin seeking adventure, not uncommon for someone his age. Dreanna brought him home with them after their third meeting. He stayed for the evening meal, but not the night, much to her annoyance. When Andar enlisted Rothus in his training it pleased her greatly and strengthened her interest. After that, visits were frequent, and it wasn't long before he was spending the night, sharing her room. Like most of the young, after her first learning experience, Dreanna had chosen Rothus to develop her skills in the comfort of one lover. There was no commitment, only education for her, pleasure for both. Andar heard from Rakosur of the disappointment of his son at not being able to continue the instruction. It was only his young pride and self doubt that made him suffer and Andar knew Sarta would get over it.

Although the homestead had a new life and vitality that before had not existed, the noise and lack of work that accompanied it was unexpected. Dreanna would chase Rothus with endless energy, tearing through Andar's shop in hot pursuit. Their constant overt affection irritated him, and when he finally realized it was envy, shame burned his face and he cursed himself to think that he would deny his daughter the pleasures that he and Katrena had shared. And so he fought his reawakened loneliness with his training, keeping to himself.

Daniel Side

Rothus dipped a chunk of reebread into the stew and looked at Dreanna before taking a bite. He chewed, stopped and then grimaced, grabbing his throat, agony clearly on his face. Dreanna, who had been holding her breath as she waited for the verdict on her cooking, leaned forward and slapped his arm.

"Stop it! You know it's good. You are a nasty man!"

He raised his arms warding off her next blow. "You're right," he said still grimacing. It's delicious." He fell face down onto the table and he went still.

In the silence Dreanna started to giggle then smacked him again. "A nasty, nasty, man."

Rothus sat up grinning. "It is delicious. Truly."

"Good," Dreanna said, smiling. "Now make sure you eat all of it."

As they ate the midday meal in the kitchen, the sound of Andar's hammer carried from the smithshop through the open window adding to the banter of Doros and the two guards who were debating which type of arrow head was best.

"What's it like in Kindarin?" Dreanna asked.

Rothus looked up over his spoon. "Nice, you would like it. It's much larger than Bonstag of course, but still nice. Not too old."

"Then why did you leave if it's so nice."

"Because you weren't there."

"Oh you are a dangerous one," she said laughing. "Really, why did you leave?"

"When my father died it was up to my mother and my three brothers and me to run the tavern. We had helped for years. We all knew what to do. But it wasn't what I wanted to do." He pushed the empty bowl aside and wiped his mouth with the back of his hand. "My mother knew that. She always knew it. She encouraged me to travel, to strike out on my own and find what it was that I wanted to do."

"She sounds like a wonderful mother." Dreanna went quiet for a moment, her mind elsewhere. "I'm sorry about your father. How did...how did he die?"

"He stepped in to stop a man who had been beating his wife. He ended up getting stabbed."

Dreanna reached out and took one of his hands in hers. "I'm so sorry, Rothus. What a wonderful man he too must have been."

Rothus looked away, his eyes focused somewhere outside. When he returned his gaze he smiled sadly. "The Annals of Being say that the acceptance of an outcome of events is a matter of choosing. I have accepted it for what it is. But enough of this. What should we do today? Is your father taking us to the village, or must we amuse ourselves?"

Dreanna bent over the table and kissed him. "First we have to work the garden some more, otherwise I won't hear the end of it from Doros. Then, if you have done a really good job, I think I can find a way to pass the rest of the day."

Andar stood outside of Rakosur's tavern. Again he felt moody discontent for not beginning his journey today. Every day gave the enemy one more day to regroup and come after Dreanna. He didn't want to leave his family but wondered if he was simply afraid of this unknown quest. He shook his head angrily and stepped from the porch onto the dusty street as the shards of the reed crystals hanging outside each tavern and store started to move, tinkling chime-like, heralding the approaching rains.

The wind arrived. It lasted mere seconds, a great shuddering of nature, and then the calm set in, a silence as striking as the swirling madness moments before. Like everyone else in the street, Andar turned his face to the heavens.

The rains began. A few small drops struck the dry earth, raising tiny puffs of dust on the street. Andar welcomed the patter of the first drops on his face, tiny rivulets of pleasure trickling down his neck. Quickly the drops increased in size and intensity, spheres of crystal falling faster and faster, one after another.

The rains' rhythm grew. It gathered in small pools, the surfaces leaping and tumbling in time with each other. Every roof, walkway, porch and tree resounded with the impact of hundreds of thousands of watery beats. Reed troughs and pipes sang, quivering with nature's energy. Into the gutters it tumbled, leaping and splashing as it poured out the bottom to course along the streets and alleyways. Children ran in glee, chasing it, splashing each other in play, while the village watched and smiled, for in this watery embrace, life on Zendar would carry on.

The rhythm of Andar's feet on the wet path was faster than that of his hammer in the shop, but soothing in the same way. He ran, his sheathed sword in one hand, a wrapped loaf of fresh baked reebread under his other arm. His legs churned tirelessly as he approached home. The trail pouch bounced on one hip, countered by the cloak, tightly wrapped and slung over the opposite shoulder. Although it would only be a day or two before the rain's intensity made the cloak and head protection necessary, now the warm, bitter-sweet rain pelting his body, running down his trunk and legs, exhilarated him. The unfocused sense of euphoria was his undoing.

The blur of the Suru caught him unprepared. As he ran, Andar's sheathed sword swung forward blocking the Suru's strike, saving him from decapitation. Momentum carried him past the assassin who reversed his slash with a low, wide backhand, cutting smoothly through the layers of Andar's bundled cloak. Andar twisted around and drew his sword from the scabbard, back-peddling away as he tried to escape the dragging folds of his sodden cloak. His foot slipped from the compacted path and he sank ankle deep in the mud beside it. With powerful strokes the Suru drove him backwards, further from the path. Fouled by the cloak and ooze beneath him, Andar stumbled, rain sluicing into his eyes. Somehow he countered the second and third murderous thrusts.

The Suru stepped upon the dragging cloak and slashed again. The blow caught Andar's sword close to the guard, disarming him. Through the curtain of rain, he saw the Suru's blade weave back and forth then leap forward. Calf deep in muck, Andar staggered back, but the point of the sword caught him in the chest as he fell. His body slapped into the dancing quagmire and, like a thousand fingers, it grasped him. The Suru's sword tip was at his throat as his foot forced Andar under, mud creeping higher around his face. Andar peered upwards, the rain beating on his eyes, blinding him as the muck sucked him under. He tried to rise, but the sharp point was already drawing blood. The Suru's words, barely audible above the drumming splatter of the rain, held disdain.

"You are nothing, reedsmith. When I take your daugh-" The arrow caught him in his side, plowing through both lungs, the tip breaking the surface on the left side of his chest. He froze, jerked, and froze again, the pain, awe and puzzlement of death playing in his eyes. The strangled scream built inside him, unable to escape. Without realizing what had killed him, he toppled to the ground.

Andar dragged himself from the sucking embrace, clawed his way to the path as the rain washed the mud from him. Rothus, bow still in hand, followed closely by Dreanna, ran towards him.

"Why? Why did you kill him?" Andar screamed through the rain, unable to hide his anger, knowing he was wrong, but unable to stop himself. Rothus and Dreanna slowed their pace then stopped. Rain bounced from their heads and shoulders. Wet hair and tunics clung to their bodies. Bewildered, Dreanna approached.

"Why? Father, he saved your life. The Suru was going to kill you!"

Andar's eyes were riveted upon the Suru, his voice burdened with fear and frustration. "I'm sorry, Rothus. I wanted to question him. Get information from him."

"Information? He was going to kill you!" she shouted again, coming close, staring into his face.

"Yes. Yes he was." Andar looked away and shook his head trying to shake the stupor that bound him. "Rothus, you have my thanks."

Rothus paused uncomfortably. "The two Council guards are dead. We went to the barn to find Doros. Both of them were inside."

Andar's face tightened. "Doros?" was all he could get out.

"Doros is all right."

"Lanos and Colonar?"

"Grandfather took Colonar with him to visit Alashis," said Dreanna. "Doros was in the shop organizing the ropes." She stopped, her voice quivering. "He was organizing the ropes for the paths to link the buildings. Revlar and Armstra stayed with him. Rothus has been with me."

Rothus motioned towards the Suru. "He had dropped the bar on the door locking Doros inside. He's there now." Rothus looked with annoyance at Dreanna. "This one wouldn't stay there. She insisted on following me to the front porch. "It's lucky that I was there. That the two of us were on the porch." He was shouting to be heard over the rain. "He may have been preparing to attack us and you surprised him. It was only yesterday that Dreanna told me of the other attacks upon you and her."

Andar glanced at Dreanna and then at the dead assassin. The rain beat down upon the open eyes, filling the gaping mouth till it overflowed with traces of pink from pierced lungs. Andar climbed unsteadily to his feet. "Rothus, take his feet. We'll carry him to the shop. Dreanna, check that nothing is left here, that there are no traces of this.

As she bent to pick up his sword Dreanna saw the blood running down Andar's chest. "Father, you're bleeding!" The puncture in his chest wasn't long and not very deep. Staggering backwards had saved him. The rain constantly washed the wound clean so that it had gone unnoticed.

"We'll see to it as soon as we move this inside," he said, motioning to the corpse.

Together they carried the body down the path to the smith shop. Doros whirled with a start as the door flew open from Andar's kick. Shaking, Doros stared, his eyes wide as the bleeding body was carried through the doorway. He caught the wash of blood now running down his father's chest.

"Help your sister then close the door. Be quick."

Frightened, Doros bolted through the doorway almost colliding with Dreanna. They entered carrying Andar's cloak and pouch and the weapons.

"Dreanna. Go to the house and fetch something to bind my wound."

Dreanna's glance summoned Rothus and together they hurried through the doorway.

Andar looked grimily at his son then sank to his haunches beside the two Council Guards. Armsta lay with his throat cut, his sword still in its sheath. Andar gently closed the guard's eyes and moved to Revlar. His severed hand still clutched his sword. He had been run through the chest.

"They didn't have a chance, Father. He was suddenly there. It was over before..." His voice faltered then he looked at Andar. "I didn't have my sword. He looked at me then turned away and closed the door, locking me in." Tears rolled down Doros' cheeks. "Why? Why didn't he kill me?"

Andar stood and embraced Doros, holding him tightly. "I don't know, Doros, but thank the Ancestors he didn't."

Doros wiped his eyes angrily.

Andar turned from his son and knelt at the Suru and searched the body. Doros watched the blood run down his father's chest and legs, staining the Suru and the floor. Unable to stand it any longer, Doros tore off his tunic and held it to his father's chest. Andar's face wrinkled disapproval at the interference, but Doros stared back in hostile silence, holding the cloth firmly in place. When finished, all that Andar found was the same mark under the arm. When she returned with Rothus, Dreanna cleaned and treated Andar's wound with salve. As she bound it tightly across his shoulder, Andar spoke to Rothus who stood silently leaning on his bow.

"That was an excellent shot, in the rain, at that distance. Both lungs."

"It's what I do best. With the sword I am adequate. Much better with the bow." He said it as a matter of fact.

"Dreanna, you and Doros go to the house. Tomorrow we will return Revlar and Armsta to Bonstag. Rothus and I will get rid of this tonight before the rains begin in earnest."

"No. I'll help you." Doros said at his side, waiting, his face set. Andar studied him silently.

"Yes, it is our job."

As Dreanna and Rothus left, Andar shouldered the body. Doros brought the tools, and they buried the Suru on the same rise as the other.

Already streams and rivers were forming from the steadily increasing rain. It compounded their task, the soil quickly becoming muddy and unworkable. Finally finished, covered in mud, they looked at each other. The rain ran mud down their tired faces, washing them clean. Andar recognized the man's job his son had completed and smiled at Doros who stood somber and quiet before him. He didn't smile back.

"We'll stop these people, won't we Father?" Doros asked. It was half question, half statement of fact, but in his son's voice Andar heard the request for reassurance.

"Yes we will, son." He put his hands on Doros' shoulders and summoned up the last of his confidence. "No one is going to take Dreanna away. No one. Not while you and I still breathe." Through the dark and the rain, Doros stared back at him. At last, he nodded his head in acceptance of the promise and his face relaxed. He turned and together the two struggled through the rain and mud towards home.

That evening, after bidding the children good night, still shaken and upset from the attack, Andar returned to the smith shop knowing sleep would not come easily. He needed to do something. Slipping on his apron, he picked up a reed that had been shaped earlier for a sword blade. He poked the dying coals with it then found the hammer. The first blow was tentative, but each succesive one became faster and harder. The energy coursed down his arm as he smashed the reed time and time again. He needed to drain the anger and fear and this was the only way he knew how. The wound in his chest began to bleed again, but he ignored it and beat the reed, heated it and beat it again and again, until finally his energy waned. The rythm of the years took over and he continued long into the night, a purpose slowly replacing the anger. Tonight he would find out. He toiled, refusing to stop, reheating and hammering it, determined to find out if it was only a legend. Finally, at the very tip, ever so slightly, the colour began to change. In fear that it might disappear, he increased his speed, feverishly hammering the point. The tip began to vibrate. Shocked, he thrust it back into the fire, the vibrations travelling up the blade. Gradually they stopped and he examined the tip by the torch light, awed as he realized the Legend of the Purple blade was true. He stood staring at the blade, the reality of what he had done finally accepted. He had reached out and created a link to his ancestors. Somehow it was a sign of their support. Slowly now, he worked up and down the length, comfortable with the vibrations, until the entire blade shone a pale purple in the hearth's light. He held it as it cooled, still shocked at what he had done, then swung the unfinished blade, trying a traditional sword drill. The differences in weight and flexibility were small, but changed the sword's handling completely. It almost felt alive in his hand. When sharpened, the guard attached and the hilt wrapped, it would be an exceptional sword. He laid it gently on the striking plate and snuffed out the torches. Sleep would come easier now.

Chapter Twelve

By the morning after the attack the rains had increased in intensity. Now vertical columns of water thundered down to explode upwards. It pummeled the land, stripped and shredded the leaves from the reed trees, and changed the lush green world to a naked, alien landscape. As high as their calves, the dancing fury carpeted everything. It formed streams which united in larger rivulets that raced down the ravine walls to feed the white-water rivers that raged through the valleys.

Andar stood in the frothy run-off as the rain thudded on his head, neck and shoulders. While Rothus stayed inside with Dreanna, he and Doros had made preparations to link the barkin, smith shop and other buildings with the ropes, for at the height of the rains, visibility was non-existent, the most familiar of surroundings, strange and foreign. The attack by the Suru had postponed the rigging. Although it was still possible to do, it would be difficult. He readjusted the hand-carved face protector. Protruding outwards from his forehead, running down the sides of his face to the jaw, it directed the rain from his eyes, nose and mouth, enabling him to see and breathe. The hood of his cloak, woven thick with many layers, protected against the hammering blows of the rain which roared in his ears. Even so, the falling, silver sheen made visibility almost impossible. Only the intimate knowledge of his homestead and his sense enabled him to find his way.

As he lumbered through the din, Andar played out the thick rope that was securely tied to the house. For safety, a thinner rope, held by

Doros at the house, was tied to his waist. Andar anchored the heavier rope to the first building then pulled on the waist cord to signal Doros who made his way along the thick guideline to his new position. They linked the buildings together silently, for conversation, except from a foot away, was impossible. Gradually they created the limits of what would be their world for the days to come.

After the mid-day meal, all four donned their protective rain wear to start the arduous journey to Bonstag with the bodies of the guards. Loaded onto a small, two-wheeled cart, they struggled along the sodden paths until reaching the first bridge rendered the cart useless. Andar and Rothus each shouldered one of the guards and the exhausting journey continued until the village appeared just before night. The Council Guards accepted their brethren in mute silence, asking few questions, aware of the danger that Revlar and Armstra had accepted. Two more voiced their promise to accompany Andar and his family home the next morning. Honour for their fallen comrades demanded it.

They spent the night at Rakosur's tavern. Much to Dreanna's disappointment, Rothus decided to remain in the village. Andar accepted the decision gratefully. All knew the rains would soon be at their full force and last for countless more. He didn't know if he could have tolerated the antics of Dreanna and Rothus in close quarters for that long. The journey home was solemn, the mood and din of the rain effectively muting all.

Time passed slowly, the necessary work around the homestead slowing down as they were confined to the house. Dreanna grew restless, wishing to see Rothus. Andar worked in the smith shop and trained indoors, waiting nervously to leave on his journey. Doros and Colonar played and fought and were moody, and all the while Lanos, calm and unchanging, sat at the fire with the atogg, sipping his reed ale, watching over them all as the days slipped by.

One day, mid-morning, the rains stopped. As if a lever had been pulled, it ceased with the usual abruptness that rivaled the starting. As one, they hurried outside, greeted by the rush of stream and river. They willingly slogged ankle deep through the muck, soaking up the first rays of the sun as it warmed their upturned faces. In celebration, the ropes were taken down and stored, the pond, still overflowing its banks with gray-brown water, ceremonially inspected. A sense of rebirth raised their spirits.

The visiting began. A neighbour and his young son were the first. Colonar and his welcomed playmate chased each other in circles under the watchful eyes of their fathers. A farmer came to collect a new axe and Andar accepted a half cart of cresstars in payment. The council guard arrived and, pleased with the ceremonial shield, paid him an extra finn for the work. Rothus soon showed up, flashing a grin at Andar as he excused himself to seek out Dreanna. Andar had taken a liking to him. Older than Dreanna by a year or two, his handsome looks had captivated his daughter. Full of the same sense of adventure as Andar in his youth, Rothus seemed equally taken with Dreanna. That evening, on the pretense of needing his help, Andar busied Dreanna with a task and led Rothus to the smith shop. Inside, he closed the door and stared at Rothus, aware of the request he was about to make of a relative stranger. In the silence, Rothus shifted from foot to foot as he waited for Andar to say something.

"Now that the rains have ended, I must leave. I haven't known you long, but I've seen the way Dreanna looks at you. I believe that you have feelings for her as well." When Rothus made to answer, Andar held up his hand. "No, let me finish, for what I am about to ask is less than fair, but I'm her father, that is my excuse." Rothus nodded, but said nothing. "I don't know what your plans are. These first infatuations are oft short lived, perhaps not by those newly arrived to their time, but by those reaping their enthusiasm. Perhaps you may soon tire of Dreanna's attention, perhaps not. If you care at all for my daughter, I ask that you stay here, close to her while I'm gone. It is dangerous, and I do not ask it lightly. I'll understand if your journey must continue."

Rothus stood still, his face pale as Andar finished. "This is a dangerous matter," he said, "but what you ask is not hard for me to answer. I will do whatever I can to keep Dreanna from harm."

"You honour me and the Ancient Ones," Andar said, his voice tight with emotion.

Now it was Lanos' time for moodiness, for he knew that soon Andar would leave. Three days later, not even a visit and news from a passing Friend of the Ancients could cheer him up. Lanos welcomed the hooded old man with less good cheer than was proper. It was Andar who finally invited him in for a noon meal, and stories in payment. He gladly related the legend of creating Orrdamoor, the oldest and most sacred of cities, founded after the original group of survivors travelled south to abandon the Stomuants. Gray-bearded and pale-faced, the teller of stories and legends had journeyed from the north. It seemed there was little news from that direction. A raiding party of Stomuants had attacked a small northern village, carrying off a child. No, he had never been to Kempa, but had heard it was large and probably wouldn't suit country folk. Yes, he sometimes had the urge to settle in one spot and wander no longer. He admired Andar's home and property and asked if he would sell it. Such a homestead, he assured them, would sorely tempt him to settle. He left with many thanks, admiring the quickly clearing pool, offering to double the unmentioned price then slipped on the bank, falling headfirst into the drying muck. With a laugh and a curse he allowed himself to be pulled free. No, perhaps he would be safer to settle in a village.

Two new Council guards arrived to replace the others who left with the promise to return. Besides his request of Rothus, six had been enlisted to take days in guarding over his family while he was gone. Neither Dreanna nor Doros were enthralled with the idea, but Lanos nodded his approval at the arrangement.

Andar stood outside in the early morning mist. His worn weapon harness from the early years was familiar and comfortable, yet unsettling, for it signaled his departure. He was alone, although he knew Lanos was awake and moving around inside. He had said his good-byes the night before, the hardest thing that he had ever done, except for losing Katrena.

Colonar had not understood but knew something was wrong and had cried. He had clung to Andar, burying his face, wet with tears, against his father's neck.

"I don't want you to go. Please stay. Please!" Andar held his young son's face with both hands and used his thumbs to wipe the trail of tears from his eyes.

"I must go, Colonar. I know you don't like it, but I must. It's important. Important for all of us. I'll be back just as soon as I can. I promise."

"Who will take care of me?"

"You know I will, Colonar," Lanos said softly from the doorway. "Kiss your Father now, and tell him you love him and hurry home."

"I love you. Please hurry home."

Andar hugged him fiercely. "Good night, son. Have sweet dreams. I love you. See you soon."

Dreanna had cried as well, her self-imposed guilt coming to the surface. "I'm sorry, Father. I don't know what I've done. I-"

"You've done nothing. Nothing. Do you understand that?"

"Yes, but if anything happens to you-"

"Nothing will happen. You must believe that. You must be strong and believe that. Promise me." And so sobbing in his arms, she promised.

Doros had been grave, insisting, yet again, that he too should go. Andar hugged him tightly, choked with pride, and explained again how much he was needed here. With Lanos and Rothus, and the guards, he must protect Dreanna.

Lanos had said little, his heart heavy. He held his son's shoulders, and studied his face for the longest time, and then hugged him, and Andar felt him tremble. The old man offered to prepare the morning's meal, but Andar declined. He wished to travel in the early hours and would eat later.

So now he stood alone, outside of his barkin, close to everything that was precious, afraid to leave, afraid not to. His mouth was dry, and inside he felt as if he would burst. He slung his cloak and trail bag over his shoulders. Finally he took the first fateful step, then another, and soon his home passed from sight. It had begun.

The days passed slowly as Andar's family struggled to carry on. Doros handled it the best, taking charge of his father's many tasks. Lanos and Dreanna were the worst, each moving moodily through the day, caught up in their worry. Colonar often questioned when Father would return, but he accepted the answers at face value.

From across the pond, Rothus stroked towards Dreanna. As he neared, he dove under the surface and came up behind her, wrapping his arms around her. Dreanna struggled momentarily to escape his grasp, then turned in his arms and kissed him. He loosened his grasp and she pushed his head under as she broke free. Before he surfaced she swam to the water's edge, her naked body gliding under the sparkling surface. Rothus surfaced and spotted her.

"Hey, where are you going?"

She climbed out and, looking over her shoulder, saw him grinning at her. Guilt set in again. "Swim. I'm going to sit for a while. Warm up." She turned away from him looking for her drying cloth.

The constant presence of the guards was an annoying intrusion. Her time spent with Rothus was no longer what it had been. Today, like yesterday, she cared little for his playful banter and teasing, just as the joy, the sensual freedom of the water went unnoticed. Nothing she could do, nothing she tried, would take her mind from her father's absence. She worried about him constantly. It had only been a few days, and he would be gone for so much longer.

Unconsciously she ran her hands down her flat stomach to her hips and thighs, brushing the beads of water from her. She must change and drag herself out of this depressing mood that had captured her. She knew she had been unbearable. Rothus said he understood, but he would only be patient for so long. She missed him. It had been two days since they had made love. She dropped the drying cloth and tied the wrap around her hips then slipped into the sleeveless top. Today would be different. It must be. She turned back to Rothus who floated on his back watching her.

"Rothus, I'm going back to the barkin. I've lost something and I need to search for it in my room."

"What is it?" he asked, stroking towards her.

"Guess. I seem to have lost it two days ago. I have been absolutely miserable without it. It was in the bedroom the last time I saw it, and only you can help me find it again." She smiled when his puzzled expression dissolved into a grin. "I'll meet you there," she said, "unless of course you would rather swim for a while longer." With that, she made her way up the embankment pleased with herself.

Half way up the incline she spotted it, the sun reflecting brightly off the smooth surface. Puzzled, she stopped and leaned forward to peer at the object. Already her heart beat more quickly as she realized what it must be, for there was nothing on Zendar that shone as such in the sun. Crouching low, Dreanna brought her face down until she was close to the strange shape. She withdrew, excitement building as she looked to Rothus who had almost reached the water's edge.

"Rothus, come quickly," and she turned back to stare at the object.

"What's wrong? What is is, Dreanna?" There was worry in his voice as he stepped from the water, scooping up his sword.

Unable to wait, she reached out, strangely afraid. As her fingers closed around it, she waited, expecting something to happen. Half-buried in the black earth, the object was warm from the sun's rays, almost hot to the touch. She gently pulled it free.

Old. Older than anyone, anything she knew. Older than anything she could imagine. The strange material from which it was fashioned told of that. She wiped the dry film of mud from the lower half. Only the length of a hand span, it weighed almost nothing. Narrower at one end, smooth flowing lines broadened it to twice this width at the other. As thick as her thumbnail, it had a series of three different sized holes running down the center of the thinner end.

Her hand closed on it, and a deep sense of awe, of history and heritage swept over her. Tears filled her eyes. Dreanna raised her head, taking a deep breath that shuddered weakly as she exhaled. To hold something that had belonged to her ancient ancestors was humbling.

"Dreanna, what is it? What's wrong?" At her side, a still naked Rothus, sword in hand, glanced nervously about them.

"Look," was all she could say as she held out the object.

He looked down at it, confused by her emotion.

She wiped her eyes with her forearm and stared into his eyes, a wistful smile touching her lips. "It's of the Ancients," she said. "Look at it. There can be no other explanation."

As he studied the object, Rothus reached out as he too realized the nature of the object. His fingers stroked its surface. He looked up at her. "Where did you find it?" now full of surprise and awe at the find.

"Here," Dreanna said pointing. It was..." She stopped with a sudden start. "The old man! The Friend of the Ancients." She looked around to ensure she was right. "Yes, this is where he fell." She looked down on it again. "It's his."

The sun gently steamed the narrow path through the forest of reed trees along which Dreanna, Rothus and the two guards hurried. In the humid air, the bodies of the four dripped and shone in the sun with sweat. Only a few days since the rains had ended and once again each tree showed the beginnings of fresh leaves on the stiff, horizontal branches that reached out around the trunks of the reed trees like the spokes of a wheel. Although all of the ravines were still full, much of the water in the newly created small streams and rivers was gone. The rain water that had soaked into the earth was slowly evaporating, filling the air with moisture.

The excitement of Dreanna's discovery had helped to chase away her doldrums. She played up to Rothus, teasing him one moment, talking excitedly about her find the next, bubbling over with new-found energy. Her excitement was enough to hurry them on their journey to Bonstag. All had been awed by the ancient piece, but also by the responsibility of finding the owner. Dreanna only hoped that the traveler was still in the village and had not continued on his journey. There were questions to be asked. She wanted to hear *this* story, of how he came upon it. Only in the rarest of cases were artifacts of their ancestors held by individuals. All were kept safe and displayed by the Ancient Keepers in the temple at Orrdamoor. If the traveler could not be found, then they would have to think again.

The day had been disappointing, much of her excitement exhausted. The old man had not been found despite searching through the afternoon. As the day waned, Rothus had encouraged her to begin the journey home lest they be caught in the dark. Nearing home had helped to raise her spirits and now, much to the guards' displeasure, she ran, daring Rothus to catch her. When he refused the bait, she turned her back on him, and marched ahead.

Two men stepped out silently in front of her. Startled, she jerked to a halt, their rough, travel-worn appearance alerting her to danger. Dreanna wheeled at the noise behind her; sudden guttural sounds of pain. A cold trickle of fear ran through her. Both guards lay lifeless. Eyes wide, Rothus lay pinned to the ground, a sword at his neck. Two other men stood between her and Rothus, weapons red with blood. Dreanna's sword was out of its scabbard before the two could approach closer. They stopped, grins spreading over their faces.

"Come now, girl, don't make it worse for yourself," said one, his swagger confident as he moved closer. Dreanna flicked the blade towards him, drawing him up short. She glanced behind her to the others who laughed aloud at their companion. The first one eyed Dreanna's sword point and spoke again.

"Listen, girl. We can wrestle the sword from you, but there is an easier way. Grecus, we don't need the lad. Cut his throat."

"No!" Dreanna shouted as one of the men jerked Rothus' head from the path, a dagger in hand. Distracted, her sword was wrenched from her by one of those behind her. She snatched her dagger free and slashed the arm that gripped her. The man howled in pain but she was grasped by another. Dreanna fought, kicking wildly. Finally the dagger was twisted from her grasp and her hands were bound behind her. Four men stood over her as she lay panting on the ground.

"I'll bet you would give a wild ride, wouldn't you, girl?" one of them jeered at her, wiping his mouth with the back of his hand, his eyes traveling over her body, caressing its curves.

"The slit cut me," said the one who pressed a cloth to his arm.

"Shut up," the leader of the six hissed. "Get her up and let's be off this path before someone else comes along. Quickly now. Gag the two of them. No noise. Drag the other two from the path."

Pulled to her feet, Dreanna was held firmly on each side and led into the forest. She could hear the others behind her and turned to catch a glimpse of Rothus. One of the captors jerked her around.

"Don't you worry girl," he smiled. "We'll take good care of him." His laughter was joined by his companion, the two of them pulling her along faster.

The fear started to grow. They hadn't tried to rob her. They couldn't possibly know about the ancient piece she had found. They hadn't even searched her. They hadn't hurt her. They wanted her alive and unharmed and were taking her somewhere...just like the Suru had tried to do.

Lanos felt little concern for the two young ones until it turned late. Allowing for the time to travel there and back, whether they found the Friend of the Ancients or not, they should have returned by late evening. He had insisted on it. This morning with Doros and Colonar he had traveled to the village, a quiet, worrisome trip. They checked with Rakosur first but the innkeeper shook his head.

"She was here, Lanos," said Rakosur, his face lined with worry. "She showed me what she had found. I cautioned her to keep it to herself.

She asked about the Friend of the Ancients that visited you, but I have not seen him. She insisted on looking for him, so I suggested a number of taverns that she might check. With the guards they left to do so. When they didn't return, I assumed, successful or not, that they had returned home."

Checking the taverns that Rakosur had suggested revealed that the four had been there. A further search of the inn where Rothus stayed revealed nothing. Returning to Rakosur's, the worry and guilt Lanos felt surfaced as anger.

"We don't even know where to begin looking. Something must have happened to them on the streets or on the way back home."

"It was the Suru!" blurted out Doros, his eyes blazing with a mixture of fear and impatience.

"Quiet, Doros. Keep your voice down," the old man cautioned. "We don't know that, although it seems the likeliest possibility." His voice was low, expressionless, but the pain as he spoke etched the lines deeper still into his face.

Doros lurched to his feet, rocking the table. A few heads turned their way at the disturbance. "We have to do something. We can't just sit here."

"Sit down, Doros. We will do something, but we must think first."

"Think? There's nothing to think about!"

"Then what would you have us do? Search the whole countryside in the hopes of bumping into her?"

The anger and sarcasm stung Doros and he slumped to the table, his face red with frustration and embarrassment. Lanos put his hand on his grandson's arm.

"I'm sorry. I just need time to think." Doros and the others remained silent after the outbreak, the noise of the small crowd of patrons filling the void. "Andar must know," Lanos said quietly. "Rakosur, if you would make arrangements for Colonar, Doros and I will return home, pack a few things, and set out." Doros stared intently at his grandfather as the old man continued. "I don't see any other course of action. There are only three paths that cut into the one from our home to the village. We could risk following one of them in the hopes of finding whoever might have taken Dreanna, but they have a lengthy start. My legs aren't what they used to be, and if we did catch them, then what? What could an old man and a single young warrior do against who knows how many? No, we will seek out Andar. We know the path he took and where he is going." His confidence grew as he spoke. "The Suru wanted to take Dreanna alive. I don't believe that they will harm her. In that lies our advantage. That gives us the time we need."

Lanos finished, and looked to Doros who stood waiting.

Part Two

Suru Stronghold

Chapter One

The cloak snapped restlessly behind Bonara as the gray-bearded merchant hurried along in swinging strides. It was dusk, and the sky waxed purple as he moved confidently along the misting path that led to the smith's dwelling. Soft, muffled clanking from the pieces in the pouch fastened to his side fueled his excitement. In just a matter of days he would use the pieces to gain entrance at last. If he had calculated correctly, he would be in time. *They* would not yet have awakened, and the opportunity for knowledge and power would be unfathomable. His pace quickened. He knew each step drew him closer to his destiny.

Everything had gone well, if not according to plan. Although the Suru had not been successful in removing the daughter, nevertheless the smith had left, abandoned his home in search of her attackers. Then a stroke of good fortune. His spies told of the daughter and her male companion being abducted or killed by common thieves or trailmen. Bonara laughed in pleasure, for then the elderly man and the young one had gone in search of the smith. Bonara shook his head again at how fate had aided him. He would have just as soon had Suru kill them all and be done with it, but his compromise with Grenfeld had worked out after all. Why Grenfeld cared if they lived or died, he neither knew, nor cared. That the homestead was abandoned was all that mattered.

Ahead, the trees were thinning, and as soon as he rounded the gentle bend in the path the barkin came into view. Bonara didn't hesitate, for his men had arrived earlier to ensure his safety. He ignored the barkin, hurried past it and the other out buildings and scrambled up the boulder strewn embankment, stopping breathless at the top to overlook the pond.

Spellbound, he gazed at the deep, clear water. There it was. Undisturbed for thousands of years; and he was about to uncover it. "Radic." The man was at his side. "Begin at once. Day and night until it is done."

Bonara sat before the hearth in the smith's great hall, contemplating the fire. He had stood in the darkening night with feverish eyes and watched his men as they began to move earth and boulder to create a channel to divert the water. It would take days. Now, after the evening meal, he tried to control his mounting excitement. *Patience. Soon it will be revealed. The final gate will be breached, the secrets mine.*

Reclining by the fire, Bonara held the pouch loosely in his hands. He rolled it back and forth, feeling the pieces sliding and rubbing gently against each other. Loosening the cord, he tipped the bag, letting the contents fall lightly into his lap. Thin and flat, they appeared identical at first glance. The length and width was the same, but the circular openings within each were of a different number and location. He let his fingers glide lightly over them, turning each with a gentle nudge.

Bonara felt the blood drain from his face as he stared at the pieces in his lap. *Five.* He counted them again, over and over, his hand returning to the pouch, his mind refusing to accept it. *Six. There must be six!* His head spun. He needed them all. *Without even one, it is all for nothing.* His hands darted to the pouch yet again, and he found it; the opening in the seam along the side of the bag. It wasn't large, but big enough for one of the pieces to fall through.

Where? A terrible dread assaulted him. *It could have happened anywhere.* He tried to think of the last time he had handled the pieces. *During the rain, when I was holed up in that tiny inn on the outskirts of Bonstag.* But since then he had traveled the forest many times.

Think. Think. He closed his eyes and slowed his breathing to gain control. *Relax, open your mind. Let the source bring the thoughts to you.*

The girl. He remembered one of his spies had said that the daughter had been to the village, inquiring about a gray-bearded old man who had visited them. He knew that he had them all before he had visited the site in the guise of a teller. He had slipped and fallen. *That must be it. She found it, and assuming it was mine, had tried to return it. Why else would she be trying to find me? She must have it!* Bonara's excitement was quickly dashed. *She's gone, taken by someone. They would have taken it after killing her. It's suddenly gone wrong.* He sat, gathering control and calming himself. *But I must try. I must find the sixth key.*

"Take our best men. Go to the village and question the people she talked to. You will find someone who has knowledge of her disappearance. You *will* find the trail and follow it and bring back the piece. Tanir, do not return without it."

"Yes, Lord Bonara."

Chapter Two

Andar's sandaled feet pounded the trail that led steadily westwards along the highlands. In the humid air, his legs churned tiredly, sweat running in tiny rivulets down his torso and legs to disappear into the soil. His pace the first days had been relentless. Although he had wound his way through the Belnor Mountains without incident, their ravines had exhausted him with the many vertical climbs. Doggedly, he had maintained a punishing pace, hour after hour, stopping only to eat a small portion of reedbread and dried sleerak, then pressing forward again. The solitude of each new dawn, created a terrible ache of loneliness that burdened him further. He was goaded onward by the fear that the Suru might attack again before he could find them. Possessed by the thought, harried by fear and guilt, he ran and ran. Until today.

Today his body could not fulfil the demands of his will. All morning numbness had crept up his legs to his torso. He shook his head and closed his eyes, hoping to clear his blurred vision. Staggering sideways, a loose rock twisted his ankle and he plunged over the edge of the narrow trail, unaware of the swirl of branches and rocks that battered him.

Consciousness returned quickly, fear changing to panic. Lying on his back, he raised his head and viewed his prostrate body, sweat beading his forehead. His arms and legs refused to move. Andar stared at his right hand, willing his fingers to tighten. Nothing. His lean form twitched with effort as he tried again and at last he saw them spasm and curl. Fear slowly waned as he watched his feet stretch and relax, then his knee bend slightly. A feeble laugh accompanied the flood of relief. He lay still, listening for an animal's stirring, anticipated an insect's sting. After a time he moved: rolled his weight sideways, wrestled to all fours, pushed up to his knees, then his feet. His movements, so heavy and awkward, scared him.

Although he had not fallen far from the path's edge, he struggled on stiff legs to regain the thin meandering line that cut through the reed trees. Staggering like a drunkard, Andar found a wider spot on the trail and cursed when he tumbled to the ground. His swollen tongue poked at dry lips and his hands shook as he fumbled with his drinking gourd. He raised it to his lips and drank greedily, forcing himself to lower it and turn to his food pouch. He ate more than usual, realizing the foolishness of his rationing. He would sleep more at night and alternate his jogging with walking. In a weakened state, he would be easy prey for the first malbar or trailman that came along. The meal finished, with weary disgust Andar eased himself around the trunk of the tree out of sight of anyone traveling the path. Almost immediately the minions of sleep pulled him down into their netherworld of darkness.

Tugging on his shoulder dragged him back from his deep slumber. When he shook off the veil of sleep, the source of the disturbance stilled his breathing. Clenched in the jaws of the warlum was Andar's food pouch, the strap, still over his shoulder, pulled taut. Anchored in a thigh-sized hole, the pinkish white flesh of the creature rippled in waves as it pulled its head back. Andar stared into the slitted green eyes less than an arm's length away. Although more scavenger than predator, when aroused, the warlum with its sharp broad teeth was more than formidable.

The powerful tugs dragged Andar slowly across the ground. He knew that as soon as he moved, the warlum would react on instinct to the sound. Andar squeezed the hilt of his sword, trying to gauge his strength, when another stronger pull decided for him. He whirled his blade up, pivoting it around his wrist, slashed at the strap and rolled away, putting the bole of a tree between him and the creature. The warlum reared upwards, its rage-inflamed crimson neck arched above him. Andar froze as it swayed back and forth into view around the reed trunk. Without the noise of escape, the nearly blind creature bobbed aimlessly then began to shrink into its lair still clutching the pouch in its jaw.

Andar sagged in relief as the last of the creature disappeared. He stumbled to the trail, staggering away from the creature to ensure he was safely distant. He leaned against a reed tree and slid to the ground, his movements awkward and stiff. The rest had restored little of his strength. He thought that he was probably half way to Kempa, his route having taken him in a westerly direction, past many small villages similar to his own. Already the forests were beginning to thin, occasionally giving way to reed grasses. Though the terrain would level making traveling easier, he knew his condition would slow him. He would be lucky if six more days would see him there. He would walk the rest of the day, make camp early and if lucky bring down some small game with his bow. Drying it over the fire and cooking some reedbread would give him a quick source of food for the following day. He struggled upright and set off again, stiff muscles complaining painfully.

Night arrived, and the tiny translucent bubbles on the leaves of lichen began to release the green moisture into the air cooling the plant. The mist danced in quiet graceful swirls about the fire, until venturing too close, it disappeared into the coals. Andar sat exhausted, poking the coals, alternately covering and uncovering the tiny cooking pan that contained his meal. Inside was the layer of soft reed found between the spongy bark and the core. The fibres, cut and mixed thoroughly with water, then allowed to sit, resulted in a thick even paste. Baked in the lidded pan above the coals, the resultant bread would be bland to the taste but ease his hunger and keep his strength. While eating, he smoked the strips of meat that had been lying in readiness on a crude grill fashioned from the remains of the tree. He had been lucky to see a spotted narlot, careless at a stream. The arrow had not killed the small, elusive creature, but pinned it to the earth long enough for Andar to dispatch it. Not particularly tasty eating, it would nevertheless help to sustain his strength.

Curled in his cloak in front of the flames, Andar stared morosely into the coals. He realized that the world he had left behind so many years ago hadn't changed. He had simply forgotten what it was like. The incident with the warlum had shaken his confidence. He could not begin to fathom what else lay ahead. He knew he must steel himself for other events to come, as he knew they must. Slowly a new resolve strengthened his purpose. He would do whatever it took to stop them. Nothing else mattered. He would find a way. The flames swam dizzily before him. He would do whatever it took to stop them. Whatever it took...

In its death dance, the green mist of two more solitary nights cavorted before Andar's fires. Having finished the small narlot, he had stopped early both evenings to hunt game and roast it on a spit. Now traveling through reed grasslands, he was careful to heed Rakosur's warning and stay on the trail during the day to avoid clingers. He had seen them for the first time the day before when he came across a long legged bradez lying on the edge of the path, covered in the squirming, fist-sized creatures. The black earth dwellers had swarmed the grass grazer, latching on to it with claw-like jaws, weighing it down with sheer numbers. It was dead from blood loss, the sucking continuing still.

Andar took his water gourd and followed the sound to a nearby stream. Although he was eating plentifully of the tender shoots of reed grass, and had shot several small fury narlots, he had hoped for a bradez that would supply him with enough meat for the rest of the journey. The daily hunting took too much time. Much of his strength had returned, although he was leaner than before. At the stream, the face that stared back was sombre. He peered with sunken eyes at his haggard appearance. The tanned skin, stretched tightly over his cheek bones made him look more like Doros, only much, much older, age having descended suddenly these last days onto the wooden, unsmiling mask. He swiped angrily at the water's surface, rippling the water and marring the image. The distorted stranger's face in the water seemed to silently laugh at him as he rose to leave.

The third day after encountering the warlum he made better time. Occasional whips of head high reed grass that leaned inwards over the path caressed his shoulder. As he walked, Andar ate some of his hoarded rations from the previous night, only too aware of approaching dusk.

Ahead through the gathering mist, the sound of voices floated towards him. Wary, he tensed and slowed, apprehension and mistrust his first thoughts. From around a bend, the faint glow of a fire coloured the mist. He reached out with his sense, not prying so as to alarm them, but sampling the mood of those ahead. He strained, focusing his hearing as well, but couldn't sense any menace, and only heard the sound of a crackling fire and quiet laughter. Companionship. On the trail alone, he hadn't realized how much he had missed it. How he had missed his family. Rounding the bend, the glow of the fire mellowed the reed grasses around the clearing, forming a roofless shelter, cozy and warm. He approached the band of travelers, still unseen, estimating their number at eight or ten, more men than women. The variety of travelworn tunics and cloaks identified them as trailmen, nomads who travelled from village to village, a restless people with few possessions who rarely settled anywhere for long. Relaxed, engaged in conversation, none sensed his aura. Finally he was noticed by a thin, bearded fellow who sat back from the others, watching the fireside proceedings. The man spoke softly and conversation ceased, all turning in Andar's direction, hands moving instinctively to swords.

"I am alone, and seek nothing more than the warmth of your fire, and the companionship of others, friendly and trusting as myself."

"R' fires yours. Hav'in r' food, hav'in r' ale, sharr'in r' fire," replied a figure rising from near the fire, his mutilated speech that of the trailman. His tunic was thread bare, as was a light evening cloak. A green, fine-line tattoo scrolled from one cheek over the bridge of his nose to the other. He motioned Andar forward, moving aside to present some room within the circle. Conversation returned to the group, eyes glancing his way as he settled himself.

"Well'comed friend. Bordor, mine name. Tanto, drag some ale for r' traver. And drag sum foods for'is belly."

One of the women, wild looking, red tattoo lines running down her cheeks and neck, handed him a gourd of reed ale and disappeared from the fire's edge.

"So ware yuu trek friend."

His self-appointed host, whom Andar deemed leader of the group, was heavy-set and had the same dishevelled look about him that all possessed, but his darkly tanned face was friendly and open, the warmth of the fire mirrored in his eyes and speech.

"Kempa. I'm traveling to Kempa," Andar replied accepting some meat from Tanto.

"Archorus bless, but we trek the same, trek the same. Haps we trek as one." It was more statement than question, the rest of the group pausing in their conversations to hear his reply.

"Many thanks for your kind offer, but I travel light and travel the day long. Perhaps on another day, on another journey, our paths can travel as one." Andar added the final traditional statement of refusal carefully so as not to offend. None seemed to be taken.

" Be'it. Deed, yuu treks easeelite. No tak'en time ta'eet. Small left on yurr bones."

"His looking good ta'mee," said one of the women around the fire, causing a clamor of laughter.

" Best hold ta'er tight, Freelar, for she's sniffin' new meats," and again a chorus of jeers and laughter answered.

Andar glanced towards the girl who leered at him, the puffy glow of too much ale upon her. The grime of more than a few days travel marred her attractive face. Intricate tattoos snaked down the side of her face and neck to meet in the hollow between her breasts. Freelar, the thin bearded one who had first noticed Andar, frowned at her but said nothing. Aware of his displeasure, she leaned towards Freelar, mouthing several kisses in his direction while grabbing a breast and squeezing it, moaning. She broke into laughter again, shifting her glance once more to see if Andar was watching. Andar concentrated on his food as the last of the laughter died away.

"Mind tem ones. Much fights tween'em," said Bordor as his eyes fell on Andar's sword. "Yuu treks easeelite, but much fancy. Yurr longpiece a fine fancy. Uthers much fancy too," he said, a touch of envy in his voice.

Andar glanced down at his sword, unconsciously touching the grip. He recalled the many hours that had gone into making it. He said as much, explaining his occupation. When Bordor waited expectantly Andar knew he had no choice. To not offer the trailman a look would offend. He passed the sword to him. Bordor inspected the hilt and pommel then eased the blade a little from its sheath to view the edge. His eyes widened.

"Purple blade," he said. "Heard of tem in legend. Eyes never seen. Not think real. Not til now."

"It takes much time and many firings to create," said Andar. I wasn't sure they were real either until it happened."

Bordor ran his thumb along the exposed edge. "Keeps edge sharp." He pushed the blade back into the sheath and handed it to Andar. "Much fancy friend," he said, eyes lingering on the sword.

As the conversation lulled, in ones and twos they moved off, seeking wraps for the night. Soon, Andar did the same, lying apart from the others, glad for their company but desiring his privacy. He had been grateful for the evening but looked forward to the dawn and moving forward. It wasn't long before the bonds of sleep wrapped around him.

He slept fitfully, tossing and turning, a myriad of jumbled images moving in and out of his dreams. The warlum towered menacingly over him but, as it drew nearer, its face was that of the Suru he had killed in the pool, eyes staring coldly, mouth twisted in a laughing grin as the image faded away. The girl from the fire replaced it, squeezing her breast at him, her appearance sad and bloated as she mimicked the actions of a seductress. She smiled and the face changed into Katrena's, soft and oval, long brown hair falling down to frame hazel eyes. Her tiny jaw opened to speak, but as it did so she was suddenly beside the lumbering cart, calling him. He turned at the sound of his name. His name. The last thing she said before the half dozen smooth, greenish-brown reed logs rolled from the cart. Even as he shouted, had taken his first futile step, he saw in slow motion the first of the logs strike her. Her eyes were locked onto his and he read the surprise, saw it turn to pain, and then fear. One after another they fell, each slamming into her, piling one on top of the other, until she was all but buried, only her head and shoulder visible. It was over in an instant, his useless strides taking an eternity to bring him to her side. She said nothing, but her eyes never left his as the light faded from them. He screamed, launching himself at the weight, unable to move it, kneeling back at her face, stroking it, attacking the logs again. In his dream, the logs became one large smooth towering mass, pressing in on him, suffocating him, frightening him. He couldn't get past it. It flamed the fear in him and then, his sleep disturbed, he rolled to a new position and sought the elusive rest that sleep would not bring.

Chapter Three

They came for him in the night, two of them, Freelar and another. Silhouettes against the night sky, weapons drawn, they moved in stealthily, a sword's length apart. Through the fog of an uneasy sleep, Andar watched them, trying to determine if it was real or if he was dreaming. It was the quiet whisper of 'ready?' that alerted him to an imminent attack. Already they were too close for him to rise to his feet. He tightened his grip on the dagger he slept with.

When they attacked he tossed his pack in Freelar's face and rolled under the descending sword of the other. As the blade cut his back, Andar thrust the dagger, aiming for the man's belly and felt warm blood splash over his hand. Still on his knees, he pulled the dagger free and slashed to his left. The blade missed its mark, but kept Freelar back giving him time to gain his feet. Yelling for help, Freelar lunged at Andar.

Other figures rose, shouts filling the air. There was no choice but flight. Andar dodged Freelar's thrust and ran towards the path. A women rose from where she was sleeping and slashed at his leg. He swatted her arm aside as another shadow loomed before him. Andar ran at it, swinging his arm, bowling the man over. Then he was past the group and the path, a pale lifeline in the green mist, was before him. He ran, the sounds of pursuit close behind him.

He set a pace that was punishing but one he knew he could maintain. When the sounds behind faded, he slowed but kept moving to ensure his safety. A thin coat of perspiration covered him when he finally stopped but his breathing was light. The wound on his back stung from sweat and his hand shook as he sank to the ground, nerves getting the better of him now that the immediate danger had passed. He knew they wouldn't follow him at night, but he still listened for the tread of their footsteps.

He cursed his naivety. Toughened physically for the journey, he was no longer prepared for a world beyond the peaceful existence of his home. First the warlum. Now the trailmen. Andar examined the wound as best he could. It wasn't deep and the bleeding had slowed. After apply some salve, he tried to use his sense, as Maudasa had instructed, to encourage the healing. Sitting in the middle of the path, looking down the trail, he directed the energy of his source inward, visualizing the wound closing from within. After a time he rose unsure of his success, feeling foolish for time wasted. With a last look down the trail and a resigned breath for the work ahead, he left the path in search of the things he needed.

Winding through the grass under the light of the two moons, he worried that he might encounter clingers, even though he knew they retired to their burrows in the evening. He slipped between the thick stalks, sidestepped the small black holes and soon found a small reed tree growing in the tall grass not far from the trail. He cut it down with his dagger and back at the trail stripped the bark and outer layer from some of the small branches, then used the dry reed crystal core to fashion a small, smokeless fire. After removing the bark from the thin trunk, Andar shaved strips of the outer layer of wood from it then cut these into long, finer strips that he pushed into his mouth, one at a time. He chewed on each gently as he cut the next. When he had six softened strands he knotted them together then braided them into a bow string. After he shaped the bow from the trunk, he strung it with the braided cord and proceeded to fashion arrows from the thin branches drying over the fire.

He cut a handful of them, then as a grim afterthought, cut more again. If he had to kill the women, he would. He was vaguely aware that he should be alarmed at the thought, but he wasn't. The world had changed little since he had retreated to his smith shop so long ago. He worked methodically, devoid of any emotion. He had learned. He would do whatever was necessary. Andar whittled the heavier ends of the shafts needle sharp, testing each one with his thumb, stopping several times to restring the bow as it gradually stretched the cord. When finished, he nocked an arrow. It sped from the bow, its flight quick but inaccurate without vanes to steady it. He would have to be close to his targets. He hardened the points over the coals, set the bow and arrows by the fireside then settled to wait for dawn.

In the early morning, Andar sat where the path ran arrow straight. Behind him, it curved sharply. If he had to run he could quickly disappear from sight, safe from arrows. Shortly after dawn he heard distant voices and soon they came into view. His presence brought a shout of amazement. Two in the lead drew their swords and charged, the curses loud and coarse. Others behind yelled angry cries of encouragement. Andar gripped his knees, ignoring the bow that lay in front of him. Without being properly cured, he knew its limitations. They had to be closer. He couldn't afford to miss with the first arrow. The distance narrowed dangerously. Finally, his heart pounding, he stood.

Although green, the bow was thick. He pulled fiercely with his shoulder and back muscles until the tip of the arrow almost touched his hand. When he released, the arrow drove into the centre of the closest man's chest. His mouth flew open in a great noiseless shout as he rose up on his toes. The second man halted in doubt. As he turned the arrow caught him in the side. It tore through his stomach exiting in front on the left. Horrified, he stared at the shaft, one hand curiously touching the bloody tip as he staggered back. Andar scooped up the remaining arrows, ready for flight. The rest of the trailmen had stopped.

"Put my possessions in a pile where you are. Walk back along the path and keep in sight." Andar spoke loudly, hoping to mask his fear, for there was still many of them.

"Not live long, friend," shouted Bordor. With that, the remaining three men and one of the women surged towards him. Andar wheeled and ran around the bend and down the trail. He held the steady ground eating pace, the sounds of pursuit soon diminishing. It was an hour before the trailmen caught up to him again. The bodies of a few clingers that had surfaced and crawled towards him lay at Andar's feet where he had methodically stepped on them. Hidden within the reed grasses only a few feet from the trail he could almost reach out and touch the trailmen as they warily passed by. Freelar was in the lead with one of the women, his eyes wide, darting everywhere. The remaining three women followed, heavily burdened with equipment, so that the others could be free and unencumbered. Bordor and Tanto formed a rear guard. Andar let them pass, then stepped to the path, drew the bow and released. Tanto screamed when the arrow passed through his thigh, his bow falling from his hands as he staggered forward. The others whirled about.

"If he moves, if anyone moves, I will kill him," said Andar as he leveled another arrow at Bordor.

Tanto sank to the ground, moaning and clutching his leg, while the others stood watching. The two at the front of the procession hesitated.

"Put the bow down or I will kill him." Andar's voice was flat and emotionless.

"Freelar," Bordor shouted. "Down. Put down!" Slowly Freelar, at the front of the group, dropped the bow, glaring at Andar over the distance. Unable to maintain the draw on the bow any longer, Andar eased the pressure, but didn't lower it.

"Put all of my things in a pile where you are. Lie down on the side of the path and let me pass. Bordor will walk in front of me. If anyone attempts to interfere, he dies. Do it now."

Andar's arm was beginning to ache and he let the bow relax further. Slowly, they did as instructed. When ready, Andar drew the bow again, moving in closer to Bordor.

They moved past the three women. Andar felt their eyes burn into his back, wondering if one or all were rising to jump him from behind. He risked a quick glance but they were still on the ground. Andar approached the remaining two.

"For this, yuu soon dead," said Freelar.

"Don't talk." Andar said, taking the arrow from Bordor and pointing it at Freelar. Then they were past the last two. Andar released his draw on the arrow, grabbed Bordor by the hair, and pulled him back towards the others. He wheeled and drew the bow again as they started to rise.

"Slowly," he said, covering them with the bow. "Walk back the way you came until you're out of sight."

"We both trek same trail, same way," said Bordor. "We meet. When-"

Andar pulled back harder on the bow, pointing it at Bordor's chest. "Move."

Bordor turned sullenly away. The rest followed him. Andar lowered the shaking bow, his arms exhausted. Watching the retreating forms, he set it down, gathered his equipment then backed down the path. When out of sight he turned and started to jog once more towards Kempa.

As the sun grew warm on his back, he berated himself. He had let his guard down and they had taken advantage of him for the fool that he was. He would not let that happen again. He would not take any chances. He would trust no one.

Chapter Four

Dreanna's hands began to ache and throb as the ropes cut into her wrists turning her hands cold. She twisted and pulled at the bonds, trying to loosen the cords and work some circulation back into them. All the while, they walked westward through the dense reed forest along a winding trail that would skirt her homestead. Dreanna knew the path. She had travelled it once or twice with her father when delivering some goods to customers. Since her capture, none of the men had spoken. Beneath the worn apparel was the unmistakable mark of discipline. One forged ahead to act as a lookout while the others walked in single file in front and behind her. When she attempted to see Rothus, she was roughly turned about. Rothus protested, and she heard an answering blow. After that she made no further efforts.

Stopping for a midday meal, her hands were untied so that she could eat. A long cord was attached to her ankle and tied to the wrist of one of her captors. Rothus, his hands also untied, ate some distance from her. He looked unharmed and smiled encouragingly at her, although he said nothing. Soon she was pulled to her feet again, her hands rebound. Dreanna protested to her dark faced guard that the bonds were too tight, but he only laughed.

"There's no need to hurt her." She turned at the sound of Rothus' voice. One of the others made to strike him, but stopped at a shouted command from another who appeared to be the leader.

"Her young lover friend is right. There is no reason to damage the goods. Grenfeld would be more than displeased. Loosen the ropes, Martar, and be quick. We are wasting time." Rothus glared at Martar as he did so, but said nothing. Within moments they were again marching westward.

That evening, when they stopped for the night, sore and exhausted, Dreanna sank to the ground and began to drift off to sleep. She was awakened by a kick, her hands untied, and some reedbread and game thrown onto her lap. The food was tasteless, but she forced herself to eat as she scanned her captors. Fear was immediate when she realized that Rothus was nowhere in sight. Dreanna reached out with her sense, searching for a trace of his aura. Nothing. She struggled to her feet, attracting the attention of her guard.

"Rothus! Rothus!" She turned to the guard. "What have you done with him?" Her breath came in short gasps, her heart pounding.

Martar came menacingly close, speaking in a loud whisper. "Shut up, you fool. Your Rothus is all right. He just went for an evening walk. Now keep quiet and eat."

"No! Where is he?" The concern for his safety chased her fear away. "What have you done with him?"

"Keep quiet, I said." He was at her side now, one hand grasping her throat. "Now sit down and eat your food or-" Without warning, he was shoved violently to the ground. He uttered an angry oath and reached for his dagger.

"Enough!" Rothus stood over her guard, his eyes angrily focused on Martar.

Dreanna looked up. "Rothus! You're alive!" She threw her arms around him, burying her face in his chest. Looking to the side, she saw her guard rise to his feet, the dagger in his hand.

"The masquerade is over." Rothus motioned towards Martar. "Leave us now."

Martar paused for a moment then with a bowing nod of his head stepped back and stalked away. Dreanna, still in Rothus' embrace, looked from the retreating figure to Rothus in confusion.

"Rothus, you know this man? He obeys you?" Her confusion faded as the first traces of comprehension surfaced. She eased from his grasp, studying his empty face, trying to read there what her heart did not want to accept.

"Dreanna, things have happened. Things beyond my control. I did not-"

Her blow struck him across the face.

"You… you are with them? You are one of them?"

"Dreanna, when-"

She pushed him further away. "You didn't have the courage to face my father as the other two did. And I made love to you!" She launched herself at him, striking and clawing his face.

He grabbed her arms, drawing her close as he controlled her. "You must believe, understand, that things have changed." Before he could continue Dreanna spat in his face.

"My father will kill you. I will kill you."

Rothus released his grip on her with one hand and wiped his face. His voice was devoid of all emotion. "That may very well be, but I don't think so. Martar!"

The guard returned quickly, a smug look on his face. "Bind her," said Rothus, "but not so tightly that you do her harm. Grenfeld will be displeased if she has been mistreated, and I am sure you don't want to feel the wrath of his anger."

Martar ambled towards Dreanna with an easy smile as his eyes caressed her body once again. "Come along now, darling. Martar won't hurt you." He led her to the opposite side of the camp where he bound her hands, threw a cloak over her shoulders and attached the cord to her ankle once more. Stretching out the cord, he looped it around his wrist then sat under a nearby tree, grinning at her.

The fear and helplessness grew as Dreanna watched Rothus in conversation with the others. His manner was casual and relaxed as he traded stories around the fire. More than once they responded to his comments with a round of laughter, their eyes darting to her, hunger and envy on their faces. Each time, her spirits fell. The fear built, crippling her, reducing her to the child that she had been a short time before. With shaking hands she pulled the cloak tighter over her face and cried.

When her tears finally stopped, she sat in the dark. Never had she been so frightened, felt so alone. She moved, adjusting herself to the ground as she sought to escape the discomfort in her side. She sat up with a start. *The ancient piece.* She still had it with her. It dug into her side. She fought to suppress her aura, the sudden excitement that they might sense. Dreanna looked around at her captors, but all were busy in talk or idle activity. She moved her hand slowly until it closed on the pouch. Easing the top open, she withdrew it, her actions hidden by the cloak. *I must bury it.* She wouldn't let it fall into the hands of such as these.

At the base of the tree Dreanna rolled over putting her back to the fire. Where she lay, one of the roots grew towards her, disappearing under the black soil. Carefully so as not to make any noise, she scraped away the soil beside the root. Soon it was necessary to use the very artifact itself, and she said a silent prayer asking forgiveness. When large enough, Dreanna placed it in the hole along and under the root then pulled the soil in over it. She smoothed the surface, obliterating all traces of her task.

The act helped to bolster her spirit. It was small consolation, but they would never get it. She would not give up, that much she had learned from her father. She would fight them.

Chapter Five

The next day Andar travelled swiftly, determined to lengthen the distance from the trailmen. By evening the reed grass had disappeared, replaced once more by a new-growth forest of reed trees. He camped for the night on the trail between two of the many small ravines he had been passing. The events of the previous two days had left him exhausted as never before. Numbed by the tension and physical strain, he ate staring vacantly at the ground, his thoughts turning to Dreanna, feeling uneasy for her safety, despite the presence of Rothus and the guards he had enlisted. The memory or her tearful apology for having done something to start this madness brought a lump to his throat again, as it had that night. He pushed it aside, turning his thoughts to the journey ahead and the man Gartonnar said he must find. Finally he fell asleep, a piece of half eaten meat in one hand, his sword in the other.

Late the next morning he crested a tree covered hillock that overlooked the town of Kempa. He felt not the slightest sense of elation as he surveyed the city. Although he had visited other cities and towns many years before, Andar had never seen one so large. It sprawled along a flat plain, the river on the west side churning south as the last of the rains drained from the low lying mountains in the north. The trail flattened out, widening as he passed the simple barkins of farms, each field of reed grass dotted with countless workers hurrying to harvest the new crop while it was still young and tender. The trail turned into a rutted road and soon he was at a gate house, where guards questioned him briefly.

Andar entered and followed the dirt road, already baked bone dry by the sun, the raised walks that lined the roadway once again unnecessary until the next deluge. The smell of too many people crowded into too little space permeated the air. Unlike Bonstag, the air was already much drier here. Almost all the people were dressed in light, flowing robes that covered much of their bodies from the sun. Andar realized that clad only in his wrap and weapon harness, he was drawing too much attention and soon stopped to slip on a tunic that he pulled from his bag. Many narrower steets intersected the main road as his steps took him past shops and houses. He pressed further towards the center. As in all towns and cities, here the reed logs of the buildings were darker, their structure simple in nature, testifying to their age. A second storey had been added to many of them, wealthier merchants and officials gaining status in the oldest, most desirable part of the city. The buildings crowded together and blocked out the view, making him uneasy. He had never been used to the confined spaces of villages and cities, but knew today it was more than that. He was aware that his journey had taken a toll on him. He wasn't himself, and knew he must search for a tavern where he could eat and rest.

He settled on The City's Gate, a tavern that boasted clean rooms. Inside it was comfortable, the food good and plentiful. He ate the roasted gorny and baked cornut hungrily, attracting the attention of the barmaid who marvelled at his appetite, wondering aloud if it applied to all things. Andar ignored her and kept his head down until finished. Upstairs, behind the barred door, when he finally lowered himself onto the bed, he found sleep immediately.

He slept the night through and half the next day. After a large meal and a too-expensive bath in the tavern's cleansing room, Andar felt better than he had for days. At the tavern, he began his inquiries for the man he sought then continued his search at other shops and taverns along the street. After a midday meal, he wound through more back streets and alleys as he searched for the shop of Joshura, the man that Gartonnar had told him about.

Two days later, he found the tired establishment crowded together with others in similar disrepair. He stopped for the briefest moment in front of the door, unsure of what he would say, finally realizing that he would say or do whatever it took to get the information he needed. Andar shouldered the rounded door open and, once inside, dropped the bar to lock it. A musty odour hung in the air. He moved quietly through the gloom of the shop towards a counter along the back wall, some reed crystals tinkling as he brushed by them, the clear, high pitched tone out of place. The room was a clutter of objects arranged on benches and tables. Countless bolts of material were piled high, while pots, bowls and other articles balanced precariously, threatening to tumble from shelves. Ropes, weapons, and tools of every description hung from the low ceiling. As he reached the counter, a woman appeared from a back room. She was tall, dressed in a worn, patched robe that hung from bony shoulders. Her face, although not old, was gaunt with sad eyes that darted from his face to the counter as she lowered her head.

"I would do business with Joshura," said Andar.

"What is you want? I can serve," she said, her head still lowered.

"I don't wish to speak to you. It is Joshura I want." Andar could sense the aura of another in a back room. A male. Anger flared, his voice turning into a snarl. "Fetch him for me and be quick."

The two dull curtains of hair veiling her face parted and the sad eyes reappeared when she raised her head. "As you want." Like her eyes, her voice was hollow.

"Tell him if he is not out here quickly, I will drag him out."

She nodded her head imperceptibly and disappeared through the back doorway.

Andar saw that his hands were shaking and placed them on the counter, hanging his head as he took a deep breath. He realized he was angry. And frightened. Frightened that the man wouldn't know anything. That he wouldn't talk to him. That this one chance for information might end here. His heart began to race. He knew he mustn't lose control. Andar heard muttering from the back room, a voice raised in annoyance, then a muffled slap. Soon a balding, overweight man stepped through the doorway and appraised Andar. Although his shoulders and chest were broad, his youth was spent. His gray beard was unkempt, but he smiled warmly as he approached.

"What good fortune," he said. "I have returned this moment from important errands. Now pleased to serve. I am Joshura. Well come to my humble shop. How can I help?"

"I have heard that you apply designs to the body," said Andar.

"Yes." He rubbed his hands together in a great show of pleasure. "In all of Kempa no craftsman better skilled than Joshura. Nothing too hard for me. Even the most-"

"Then there is probably little that you have not seen," Andar said quietly, cutting him short as he drew a small piece of parchment from his pouch and began unfolding it on the counter. He shielded the parchment from the man's gaze.

"Yes. That true," Joshura replied, his curiosity sparked by the parchment and Andar's action. He broke into a crafty smile. "You have a questionable design to put upon another? Without his or her word? Takes much planning and be very difficult. More expense." He smiled again, his voice trailing off.

"No," replied Andar as he watched Joshura's face. "This design is already on a person. On several." As he spoke, Andar opened the final fold revealing a sketch of the tatoo he had found on the arm of both Suru. He saw, for the briefest moment, the look of recognition in Joshura's eyes.

"Very simple design, not worth my talents," said Joshura. "I not suggest it. We have fine samples I can show. I get some."

Andar's hand grabbed Joshura's wrist firmly as the merchant turned away. "I am not interested in finding a design for myself, as I think you know," he said. "I am very interested in finding the persons who have this design."

Joshura looked down at the hand gripping his wrist and slowly pulled his arm free. "I know nothing of this design. That is all." He turned again, moving to the back doorway.

Grabbing the counter, Andar swung over it, driving both feet into Joshura's broad back. Propelled headlong through the doorway, Joshura crashed into a table and chairs. The woman, who stood by a shelf, screamed as she whirled around. Sword in hand, Andar stepped through the doorway and pulled her to him by one of her thin arms. Joshura struggled to his feet, knocking chairs aside with his bulk. Fear and rage played across his face.

"Sit down," Andar said. Joshura started to speak but Andar took a threatening step forward, his sword raised. Sitting, Joshura glared at him. Andar pulled the woman close again and spoke to her, his voice cold and hard. "If you would live, you will sit down beside him. I don't wish to hurt you."

She nodded, her hands trembling as she shuffled towards Joshura and sat passively beside the shop keeper, the fear in her eyes now replaced with a blank stare. Below her right eye, the red puffiness of a bruise was beginning to show.

Andar glanced at Joshura then the woman. "What is your name?

"Dajata."

"Dajata, this does not concern you, but you must remain here until I find the information I seek. I won't harm you as long as you don't interfere."

She nodded slowly then turned her head to look at Joshura.

Andar stepped closer to the shopkeeper. "I don't have time to waste. The information is of great importance to me. Great importance. Understand that." He held the merchant's gaze for a long moment. "The mark I showed you is that of the Suru." Joshura's eyes widen slightly. The shopkeeper glanced towards the door, as if the mere mention of the name would cause them to appear.

"You have heard of them and I am sure you have seen this mark. I need to know where to find these people."

Joshura stared at Andar in disbelief, then let out a low, mocking laugh. "You are mad. No one knows where they live. Visit them?" He laughed again, louder and harsher. "Fool, you trail travel too long. Easier ways to get killed."

Andar's face remained impassive. "It's *very* important to me. I believe you etched these designs for them. I think that you have means of contacting them. Tell me how to do that."

"You wrong. I never-"

Andar's sword snapped forward, stroking the man's thigh. The motion was so quick that it took Joshura a moment to realize what had happened. Blood seeped from the cut as he grimaced in pain, grabbing the wound, holding it together.

"You droeur, I never -"

The blade whirled again in a short quick arc, the tip slashing across his right arm. Joshura gasped at the new pain, moving his hand to stop the flow of blood from his arm. Blood covered him, smeared on his arm and leg from his attempts to staunch the bleeding. He looked imploringly at Andar.

"You have but two hands. You will bleed to death very quickly if this continues," Andar said.

"They kill me if I send you." Joshura stared at Andar for a long moment, understanding seeping into his thoughts. "You... you don't want hire them. You want..." He paused, his breath coming in ragged pants. "Revenge? Revenge for what done to you?" Despite his fear and pain he laughed again. "You are fool."

"If you do not help me, I will kill you," Andar said quietly.

"Do so. Better death here than meet death at hands of Suru."

As he spoke, Andar saw the truth of it, but in the merchant's eyes he also saw the desire to live. His blade cut again, frustration driving it deeper into the other thigh.

"Stop!" the woman yelled. "Stop! I tell you." She had jumped up from the chair, her hands covering her eyes. She lowered them to her mouth and looked at Andar. "I show way. No more." She dropped her hands, her face reflecting fear and loathing.

"How is it," he asked cautiously, "that you would know where to lead?"

She motioned towards the struggling shopkeeper. "He is father. I go with him there. Help him do markings. I know way." Ignoring Andar's sword, she moved to fetch a cloth for her father.

"This is some trick to save his life," Andar said lowering his weapon.

"No, fools speak truth," Joshura whispered, his voice weak from blood loss and pain. He looked at the woman. "You never smart. Now we are both dead."

She paid no attention to him, but spoke to Andar as she wiped the tears from her face. "The markings are part of ceremony. Must be done at Suru fortress. Father goes one time a year when they tell him. I show you how to go. I will draw map."

"Yes, you will show me, but to make sure there are no mistakes, when the map is drawn, you will come with me. That way your father won't send warning to them. I'll kill you if there is any treachery." Andar turned his gaze to Joshura as he finished.

The shopkeeper smiled weakly at Andar. "Risk my daughter's life?" He looked at her, his head rolling back as she reached to bandage his arm. "See what you have done, girl." Silent laugher shook his chest.

As she wrapped the cloth around Joshura's thigh, Dajata looked fearfully from Andar to her father, her frail body seeming to shrink further with new fear.

"You will stay here," Andar said to Joshura. "We will close the shop. Don't go outside so as to arouse suspicion from your wounds. If anyone asks, you were attacked and robbed. Your daughter has gone away on business. Is that understood?"

The man nodded weakly as Andar turned to Dajata.

"Do you know The City's Gate tavern?"

She nodded.

"I must return there to gather my belongings. You will come with me. My dagger will be close at hand." He turned to Joshura. "Remember, your daughter's safety depends upon you." Andar took the woman's arm, but she held back, looking at her father. Andar dragged her to the front door. "I will be following you, never far away. Don't do anything stupid."

She looked at him with sad, hollow eyes. "Or you kill me? You are same, no different."

Andar stared back at her then pushed Dajata outside, letting the bar fall to lock the door as he closed it behind him.

The back door of Joshura's shop opened quietly. Sitting in the chair, the shopkeeper heard and smiled bitterly. He looked up to see death moving silently towards him.

"I expected you," he whispered to the sombre figure before him. The drawn face stared at him in silence. "We know each other," Joshura wheezed. "She right. We are same."

His eyes went wide as the blade of the dagger slipped between his ribs and found his heart. Andar's hand remained firmly pressed over the merchant's mouth, until his chest slumped. He wiped the blade clean on Joshura's tunic and left by the back door.

Chapter Six

Doros chafed at the pace Lanos kept day after day, but held his tongue. There was little that could be done. His grandfather's elderly face was haggard, showing the effects of the last six days. More than once he ended the day with dragging steps, sometimes staggering with weariness. Doros had argued with his grandfather to let him go on ahead, to try and overtake his father, but the old man just smiled and insisted that they stay together. Doros glanced to his left at him and wondered if his grandfather could continue.

The morning of their departure, Doros had felt a rush of exhilaration. For the first time he could leave the confines of his home and explore the world. It was a quest, a great adventure unfolding. What did it matter that the princess he must help to rescue was his sister? The next moment, embarrassed at his foolishness, his concern for his sister would sober him. But always, there underneath, was his unbridled enthusiasm for the journey.

Their pace had been slow but steady, the midday meal the only break before continuing on to dusk. Tonight, like other nights, Lanos talked little, wrapping his cloak around him after the evening meal, falling into a deep sleep. As the mist formed, Doros sat quietly by the fire, feeding it, guarding the camp. He pulled his cloak tight against the dampness of the mist, the tiny bubble-coated leaves of lichen releasing the green moisture around him. He leaned against the trunk of an ancient reedtree, staring into the darkening forest, listening to the night sounds build. Bark bugs and their deep pulsing tone filled the silent void creating a backdrop for the screech and squeal of narlot and sukins. The firelight played across his face as he viewed the small bundle that was Lanos lying by the fire. A splinter of guilt pricked at him for the impatience he had shown his grandfather. He rubbed the ginger stubble of beard on his chin looking once again into the night. He knew his grandfather was doing his best, but he was an old man. This journey was beyond him. Doros' mouth set with determination. If his grandfather faltered, he would carry him. He pulled his cloak tighter and heaped some wood on the fire.

Doros awoke with a start to the sounds of someone moving about. Although he slept lighter now after days on the trail, he saw with annoyance that again Lanos had managed to awake before him and begin preparing breakfast. Doros struggled upright, his cloak moist from the night. With awkward, shuttling steps, his grandfather approached and offered him some hot ree, smiling warmly.

"I imagine we are half way to Kempa now, perhaps a bit further," Lanos said testing his legs, stretching them lightly then turning towards the early morning sun and its warmth.

"Do you think Father is there yet?" Doros asked, yawning, wiping the sleep from his eyes. He blew on the steam drifting from the top of the tankard.

Lanos turned to Doros. "I would think so," he said and continued his stretching.

"Will he still be there when we get to Kempa?"

"I don't know. It depends on how successful he is finding information about the mark. Even if he is still there, we have to find him."

"How will we do that?" asked Doros, sipping the reed tea. It was a problem he hadn't considered.

"Now that is a good question. Maybe you can give it some thought and come up with an answer. I could use a little help with that."

Doros studied his grandfather who once again stood facing the sun, stretching and kneading his legs. He looked down into the bottom of his tankard of ree, then back at Lanos. It felt good to be needed. Yes, he would give it some thought.

Later that morning, with Doros in the lead, they came upon four dead bodies splayed across the path. One young woman was sprawled upon her back some distance from the others. She had evidently been the last overcome by the malbar, and at the end had broken and tried to run. The other three, father, mother and a younger child, lay in a small group surrounded by the bodies of many malbar.

The two approached in silence, eyes darting everywhere in search of other winged creatures, though it was evident from the bodies that the carnage was a day, maybe two days old. They stepped over the thick, rounded carcasses of the malbar, their open, yellow eyes seeming to watch them pass. The stench of death was thick in the air as they stopped before the three bodies.

It was the first time Doros had viewed malbar deaths at close quarters. The eyes of the dead stared sightlessly up into the morning sun, the skin on their faces stretched tight from swelling, already split in places. Tongues, swollen, black and misshapen, protruded from their mouths. Doros stood, a sick feeling building in his gut, unable to remove his eyes from one of the malbar. It lay close to the woman's feet. Embedded in its head was her sword, stuck there, just as his had been many days before. His eyes shuttled back to the woman and saw the dagger clutched in her swollen, purple hand. He turned away and was sick, retching until dry heaves ended his vomiting. Lanos stood beside him, his hand on his back.

"We must go now, Doros."

"Grandfather, we can't just leave them here," Doros said as he wiped his mouth, his eyes wide and filled with sadness. "We have to bury them." His voice was strained. He knew he was on the verge of tears and fought for control.

"Yes, we could. They should be given a proper burial, but others will have to see to it. We have something we must do that will help others that are still alive. We don't have the time. Let us go."

Doros allowed Lanos to pull him away from the woman and soon they were moving along the trail once more.

That night, their simple meal finished, rather than retire immediately, Lanos lingered by the fire. Doros brooded silently poking the flames with a stick. Neither spoke as the night darkened, the two moons casting conflicting shadows over the small clearing beside the trail.

"That could have happened to me," Doros said, staring into the flames, his voice barely audible. "I got my sword stuck in the malbar's head. I hated Father when he told me about it, but he was right, wasn't he?"

"Yes he was." Lanos pulled the cloak closer about him as he stretched his legs out in front.

"I might have been killed if you and Father hadn't been there. I want to listen to him, but, but... he's always so angry, yelling at me."

"He was frightened. He's your father, and so is always worried that something might happen to you. That maybe he hasn't done or said something that would ensure your safety."

Doros stared off into the night, his eyes distant and unseeing as he wrestled with his grandfather's words.

"He has lost your mother," said Lanos. "Someone is trying to take your sister from him. He's not himself. Hasn't been for some time now. He's only trying to protect you."

Doros sat in silence, deep in thought. The droning of bark beetles, thousands strong, filled the void. He looked at Lanos, his face solemn. "Thank you, Grandfather. Now you must get some sleep so we can make good time tomorrow."

The old man smiled at the tone of his grandson as he rose painfully to his feet. He flexed his knees then pulled the hood of his cloak up. "I think you're right, my young warrior. Good night, Doros."

Chapter Seven

For Dreanna the days were long and uneventful. Her captors followed the trail that led west through low lying mountains, camping on the outskirts of the towns and villages they encountered. Whenever they would pass others on the trail, she would be surrounded by her guards, a knife held to her side. On the rare occasion when they were overtaken by those going in the same direction, her captors would slow their pace, ensuring those who passed would forge ahead. She had never been so far from home, and as the distance grew, so did her fear. Escape was impossible, her hands always bound, a guard always near. She had tried to speak to Rothus, but he would have none of it. He kept distant from her, one or another of the men guarding and caring for her needs. It was as if he were a different person from the one she had come to know.

Tonight she lay outside another town, deep in depression. Help was so near, yet beyond her reach. Rothus and Serdor had left the group and ventured into the village for supplies. The others sat talking and drinking around the fire, their mood buoyed more each day as they journeyed closer to home. The reed ale flowed freely, the banter rising as the night progressed. Dreanna suddenly stiffened as their conversation carried clearly through the misted night.

"How would Grenfeld know? Are you going to tell him?" The speaker, a big boned man with narrow eyes, wiped the trickle of ale from his chin and eyed Dreanna hungrily. "When was the last time any of you had anything so young? I ache just thinking about it." He took another swallow of ale and challenged the others. "Why should we pass up such a treat? I tell you, no one will be the wiser with the other two gone."

One of the men shook his head. "Go ahead, Dredar, get yourself killed. What's to stop the girl from telling Rothus when he gets back? No, it's just the ale talking. Me, I'll wait until I get home, and so will you. Now drink up and put the girl out of your mind, otherwise you surely won't be able to sleep tonight."

Dredar said nothing, but sullenly drank more ale, his eyes on the form shrouded in the mist outside the circle of firelight. The men drank and talked further and, when Rothus and Serdor returned from the village with some supplies, Dreanna's tension eased as the camp settled for the night.

A rough hand clamped over Dreanna's mouth, a dagger point at the soft skin under her chin. When her eyes found the face close to hers, she recognized the coarse features of Dredar.

"If you make a single sound, I will push the tip of this dagger into your skull. Is that clear?"

Fear blotted out all thought so that she did not answer. He moved his face closer to hers until she could smell his breath when he repeated the question. She nodded ever so slightly, feeling the press of the dagger with her movement. Slowly he moved his left hand from her mouth, down to her breasts. His eyes held hers as he fondled her. The odour of ale and sweat struck her as she looked away out into the dark. Dreanna ground her teeth, fighting the pain as he squeezed a breast. Her eyes snapped back to him, but he warned her again with the dagger's tip. His hand travelled down her stomach.

A shadow passed over them and Dredar's face slowly moved away from hers as his dagger shifted from her throat to his. She lay panting, watching him rise, terror bright in his eyes. With a curse, Rothus flung him by his hair backwards away from her.

"Are you all right?" Rothus asked without taking his eyes from Dredar, his own dagger clenched in his hand.

"Yes," Dreanna whispered.

"Dredar, you would dare, in my presence, disobey my father's orders? Disobey mine?"

"I meant no harm, Rothus. She has bewitched me! I could not help myself."

"Then you are a danger to us all. Stand up."

He stood slowly, new pleading on his lips. With a jerk, he brought the dagger up, lunging for Rothus who slid back. As Dredar's arm swept by, Rothus plunged his dagger into his chest. Behind him now, Rothus encircled the man's neck, holding him upright as he pulled the dagger in further. Finally, with a push, he cast Dredar from him.

Rothus stared at the other men who had awakened and gathered around them. "Let no one else disobey my father's orders. Bury this fool." Without looking at Dreanna he stalked away.

Dreanna was numb. The attack on her had been frightening, and now this new revelation. To discover that Rothus had procured her for his father filled her with dread. She curled up beneath the cloak, a frightened child once more. What had she done to deserve this? How could anyone who had seemed so wonderful turn out to be so evil? Worse still, how could she have not known?

Days of journey took them through reed grasses the likes of which Dreanna had never seen before. Towering, plump stalks, stretched for as far as the eye could see. As thick as her wrist, the stalks were more yellow than green, their aged skin smooth and tough, no longer fuzzy with tiny hairs. They soared three and four times her height, the tops flowering red with the days bloom.

To her young mind the distance they had travelled seemed impossible to retrace. Ever onward they pushed leaving the grasses for new reed forests that reminded her of home. They travelled past other towns and villages, the names of which she sometimes caught, but had never heard before. Finally, from the crest of a winding ridge, she saw a city, larger than Bonstag by many times. They skirted it, and soon came to a river where a large log raft floated against a dock. A rope stretched over the raft and across to the other side of the river. After payment, the ferryman and his helper silently pulled them across, taking turns walking the length of the raft as they held onto the thick rope. While they were across, Dreanna was held tightly, the dagger tip pressed against her back to ensure silence. A dark reed forest enveloped them once more as they travelled onwards, further from her home.

The sun beat down on Dreanna as they crossed a narrow ridge, the ravines falling away steeply on each side to the ragged bottom below. The path was stony, huge slabs of rock exposed, the soil all but washed away by the rains. Even the usually sturdy reed trees had not encroached upon this section of the trail. The heat from the sun reflecting off the rocky surface baked them as they walked single file, eyes cast downwards against the blaze.

All heads rose as the running footsteps of a figure sounded on the path ahead. The front scout dashed towards them, his manner alerting the others who quickly freed swords and bows. Almost immediately the approach of the rear guard was heard. The scout reached them first, drawing up short, excitement loud on his face. He was young, breathing in panting breaths as the account tumbled from his lips.

"A group of men, ahead of us and approaching this way. Heavily armed. I didn't watch further because of our position. Felt we would need all the time we could get." He finished, his face flushed, awaiting approval for his actions.

"You did well, Gonsun," said Rothus. "And behind us, Cabbor? Much the same I would think."

"Aye, Rothus," said the rear guard. "They are coming on quickly."

"Whoever they are, they chose their site well. Cabbor, take half the men down trail, two lerds distance to make your stand. Serdor, the other half the same distance up trail." He turned to the young warrior.

"Gonsun, fetch the woman. You will stay here with me and help protect her. Quickly now, there is not much time."

Gonsun raced away to grab Dreanna as Rothus unslung his bow and set the quiver of arrows at his feet. Back with her, Gonsun faced down the trail, imitating the action of Rothus. Dreanna stood watching the preparations for battle.

"Dreanna, sit down between the two of us. A large body of men is about to attack us. I do not know who they are or what they want, but nothing good can come of it."

"Father! He has come to rescue me. It must be so!" and she stepped forward to pass Rothus. He grabbed her arm and pushed her to the ground.

"I think not. Perhaps a band of trailmen. You do not want them to rescue you."

Her eyes blazed as she settled on the ground. "He will kill you," she said, but he was not listening. Men had appeared at both ends of the trail, double their number. Rothus eyed them and their position critically. Although the slopes on each side of the trail would prevent them from being attacked from all sides, the absence of reed trees left them exposed and vulnerable. Rothus nocked an arrow and waited.

"Gonsun, don't loose an arrow unless you are sure of a target. Don't rush your release."

The attackers advanced slowly, confident at having trapped their quarry. When in range of their bows, Rothus' men released. The arrows arced in silent flight, two of the enemy going down, the rest launching their arrows in retaliation. One of Rothus' men fell. Two of his men held packs and equipment aloft, shielding the archers as both groups of attackers edged nearer. Another of Rothus' men fell to arrows. Casting their bows aside, the attackers on the upper part of the trail rushed them. Some fell from arrows before they closed, then swords clashed.

Rothus bent the heavy bow back smoothly, pushing forward with his left arm, as he drew the arrow. With a soft whispering hiss it sped away. The arrow struck one of the attackers knocking him from his feet. Wild shouts of attack came from down the trail. Rothus saw that now they too had cast aside their bows and rushed his men. His bow rose and a warrior fell, an arrow through his throat. Then the ranks closed and hand to hand combat began. Rothus chose his targets carefully, releasing the arrows without hesitation, his targets often only a hand's width from his own men.

"Rothus!" The voice was that of Gonsun, panic creeping into it. Rothus saw that two attackers had broken past his men and were racing towards them.

"Take the man closest to us," said Rothus, his voice calm and steady. They were closing rapidly as his bow string twanged and the arrow sped away, slipping past the first man, knocking the trailing warrior down with its impact. Gonsun released a second later. The arrow whistled up the trail, off target, careening wildly to the left. The warrior doubled his efforts to reach them. Gonsun cursed as he bobbled an arrow, glancing up and then down again to his bow. A shout came from down the trail and Rothus saw that all his men had fallen and six warriors were racing towards them, swords drawn. He plucked an arrow from his quiver and turned to face back up the trail, to the lone attacker closing on them. The man leapt forward, drawing his sword back for a strike. Rothus released and turned his back as he focused on those down the trail. The arrow struck the attacker and passed through him. He fell on the stone trail a body's length from them.

"Take your time, Gonsun," said Rothus. "We cannot afford to miss, not now." He released an arrow down the trail felling another attacker. "Dreanna, take the dagger from my belt. If more than two of them get past me, be prepared to use it...on yourself. I...you do not want to be captured by them. Hurry, take it."

She looked up at the broad shoulders that pulled the bow once more. He released an arrow, catching a man in the thigh. Dreanna stared at the men charging towards them, the battle lust in their faces, bodies splattered with blood. The meaning of his command paralyzed her. Her trance was broken by Rothus' shout.

"Dreanna! Take the dagger now!"

She jumped up and pulled the dagger from its sheath as Rothus stepped away from her and towards the attackers. Dreanna planted her feet, and held the small blade at ready, the way her father had taught her.

Together, Rothus and Gonsun pulled down two more men. The remaining attackers, stalked towards them. Respectful of the accuracy of his bow, they shielded themselves with the dead bodies of two of their men. A shout came from down the trail. Her heart sinking, Dreanna turned. Her spirits buoyed as she saw that there the enemy had been defeated. The last of Rothus' men ran tiredly towards them. Dreanna slumped in relief as their attackers checked their advance, turned and ran.

Rothus clapped Gonsun on the shoulder as the other man lowered his bow. He took a deep breath of relief before he looked towards Dreanna. Their eyes met for a moment and held, the look of elation fading from her face.

"I missed, Rothus," said Gonsun, his face turned away. "I panicked and missed."

Rothus turned to him. "You did fine, Gonsun. "As his men approached, he walked to Dreanna and extended his hand for the dagger.

Dreanna looked again into his eyes, searching for something, but found nothing. This was no longer her friend, her lover. He had given her no reason for his treacherous actions. The blade of the dagger was a blur in the sunlight. Rothus' hand whipped up stopping it just short of his chest. Dreanna winced in pain as he twisted her wrist. The dagger dropped at their feet.

"Cabbor, tie her hands."

As Cabbor pulled her away, Rothus stooped, retrieved his dagger, and walked down the trail to check the condition of his men.

Chapter Eight

With the woman, Andar crossed the river to the west of Kempa. Threats of death had kept her tongue still. They had stopped for a late midday meal after walking for several hours and now ate in silence, neither of them having spoken since leaving the city.

Cutting another piece from the brown, prickly fruit, Andar studied her. Swathed in her robe, she sat apart from him, her head hanging down exposing a long white neck, black hair once again veiling her face. She would be easy to control, her aura had told him as much. The intangible life force around her was almost nonexistent, only the smallest energy emanating from her. It was the pace at which they travelled that was the problem. He had known that taking her would slow him down, but they travelled at less than half the speed he was accustomed to, and by the end of the first hour, he had been ready to strike her, assuming it to be a ploy to delay him. Finally, after watching her move, he understood how feeble she was.

"What do you have on under that robe?" he asked abruptly.

Her head rose slowly, the hair falling back. Beads of perspiration covered her face from the heat. Her sombre eyes studied him. "Nothing," came the quiet reply.

Andar returned her gaze, shook his head then rummaged in his pouch to find an extra wrap. He threw it to her. "You're slowing us down too much. I'll carry all of the supplies. You're too weak. That robe also slows us down. Take it off and bundle the supplies in it. Wear my wrap instead. Cut a piece of it to cover your breasts. Hurry, we're wasting time."

She looked from him to the wrap and back again. Andar wiped the blade of his dagger and threw it to her. It stuck with a thud in the ground beside her foot. She had kept her eyes on him during the throw, not flinching when it struck. Finally Andar broke their silent battle and looked down the path, biting into a last piece of reed bread.

Dajata felt the weave of the wrap then opened it to gauge its size. She looked furtively moment to moment to see if Andar was watching her. Using the knife, she cut and tore a long strip from the material. She rose, turned her back to Andar, and undoing the tie of the robe, let it slip down her body to the ground. Andar resisted looking in her direction, but found himself doing so nonetheless. He gaped at the pitiful sight before him.

On her gaunt frame, the bones of her vertebrae and ribs stood out in clear relief, covered by pale emaciated flesh that had never seen the sun. The waist was pitifully small, her back flowing down past sunken buttocks to meet skeletal thighs. Covering her were a myriad of bruises, as fresh and blue-black as yesterday, as old and yellowed as days before.

Andar tore his eyes away after only a moment, but the image refused to leave. He had shaken and threatened, been ready to kill this wretched creature that stood naked before him. The shame burned his face as he lunged to his feet, stepping down the path away from her. Anger returned for the fat, bald man she had called father. He must have been responsible for the beatings. Andar encouraged the thought, hiding his own disgrace, glad now that he had killed him. He shook his head, trying to rid himself of all thought and turned back to the camp.

She stood in the same spot, a pale skin-covered skeleton. The supplies were bundled in her robe, the dagger held loosely in her hand. The maroon wrap clung to her hip bones, extending half way down to her knees. The strip of material she had cut ran around the back of her neck to crisscross over tiny breasts and was then tied behind her. Andar looked at the bundled equipment at her feet. She had tied it neatly, using the full sleeves to form a strap which he could sling over his shoulder. He took the dagger from her, grunted his satisfaction then collected those supplies he had been carrying. He hoisted the bundle and motioned for her to take the lead.

"We must travel as fast as possible," he said. "You'll set a pace you can maintain. Don't exhaust yourself. I don't want to carry you as well as the supplies."

She nodded silently and without speaking set off down the trail.

That night they made camp in a small clearing beside the path. It was typical of many sites along the trail, used by trailmen and travellers alike. A supply of wood was piled by the ashes as trail etiquette required, a large reed log in front of the fire pit for seating. They had travelled west, but Dajata indicated that the next day they would take a southern path. After eating, Andar stripped some of the outer bark from a tree and chose a piece of cooled coal from the fire. He handed both to her.

"Draw a map of the route we will take," he said sitting.

Dajata held the bark and coal loosely in her hands, making no effort to begin.

"Do it," Andar ordered, annoyance coating his words.

She looked at him nervously. "I can not."

Andar's anger flashed. "Do it. At the shop you said you'd draw a map to the Suru's stronghold. Do it."

"I can not. I said to make you stop...stop what you do."

Andar stared at her without speaking, his anger and frustration building.

"You don't know the way to the Suru stronghold?" His voice trembled with the thought.

"I know way but can not draw it."

"Draw the map now," he said his voice deadly quiet.

"I can not. They are deep in forest, away from everything. I know signs, marks to follow when I see. Here, I can not remember."

Andar rose and drew his sword. "Draw the map now."

Dajata held his gaze without expression then lowered her eyes to the bark and began to sketch. Andar slid his sword back into the sheath and sat watching her, wondering what he would have done if she had refused. Could he kill her as he had her father? What purpose would it serve? There *had* been a reason for killing Joshura. He would have sent word of warning to the Suru. He watched her struggle with the map, her brow knit in concentration, her mouth twitching with the effort. As the time passed he saw her frustration and agitation grow until, with a curse, she hurled the bark from her.

"I can not," she said. "I try! I can not." With a shuddering breath she covered her face with her hands and lowered her head, the veil of hair descending once again.

Andar studied her, then rose and retrieved the bark, examining it when he sat.

"Kill me now." Her voice carried faintly above the crackle of the fire.

Andar saw she had risen to her feet.

"You will when done with me. Do now. Kill me."

As she spoke she stepped toward him, one hand clawing for his eyes as the other reached for his dagger. Andar's hand encircled her wrist, preventing her from drawing it. She struggled, new found strength in her slender form. He pulled her hand from the dagger and slapped her. The blow knocked her to the ground where she lay still. Andar raged above her.

"Malshead, what's wrong with you? I need you. My daughter's life is in danger and you are my only hope of finding those who would take her from me! Why would you expect me to kill you? I won't kill you. Why would I kill you?"

Dajata struggled to sit up, raked her hair from her face, then pushed and dragged herself to the other side of the fire, where she sat in silence. Andar hurled the map into the night then sat staring into the fire. Neither spoke as the fire burned down to coals, the mist swirling about them, at last disappearing as it was sucked inwards by the heat of the embers.

"You have daughter?" she asked.

Andar stared at her over the fire. It was the first time she had spoken to him other than her rage moments before. She studied him in return, her gaze steady.

"Yes, I have a daughter." The lines in his face soften.

"You never said this. Do this to save her?"

"Yes."

"And a wife?"

His face hardened again. "No, she's dead." The reply was quick and sharp, leaving a hostile silence between them. Images of Katrena's burial returned: the taste of dust on his lips from pushing the dry soil into the grave, the cries of his children as they did their part, the heartfelt words of the mourners who cared for his wife. Andar closed his eyes as he recalled the evening and the drinking and the deaths.

He had found a small tavern, needing to be alone in his sorrow, needing to retreat from the world that had taken her. He drank until the depth of his darkness was complete. It only took the words of the two beside him who demeaned his drunken state. They were course and uncaring of his grief and his anger grew as he warned them off. He didn't recall much. Perhaps they found him an easy target. Perhaps they were drunk as well, for they never heeded his warning.

Moments passed until she spoke again. "Why do Suru want daughter? Who does this?"

He looked at her and realized he was talking with her really for the first time. "I don't know. I have to reach the Suru, to find answers, to stop them, to kill them. Whatever I must do." He turned away, picked up some wood and added it to the coals, hiding his fear and anger from her.

Dajata fell silent, her turn to stare into the flames. The silence stretched into the night.

"Why did he beat you?" Andar was surprised at how hungry he was to talk to someone.

Without looking up, she shrugged. "I not please. He always angry. No reason." Her voice was without emotion.

"Why didn't you leave? Run away."

"I try. When younger. Brought me back. Things worse."

Andar rose and approached her, a length of cord in his hand. Dajata shrank back from him, but he pulled her hands together, binding them, testing the knots carefully. She said nothing, but watched him with guarded eyes. He checked the binding for a second time.

"I have to make sure you're here in the morning," he said. Andar pointed to a spot by the fire. "Lay down here." With the rest of the cord, he tied her feet then threw her tattered robe over her. Andar lay down on the opposite side of the fire facing her. He pulled his cloak around him against the evening mist. "Sleep now. We have to make better time tomorrow."

Dajata lie back and tugged her robe about her. She examined his face, the drawn cheeks, dark circles under his eyes. His skin was deeply tanned from the sun, the coarse black hair streaked with gray. She studied him, puzzled, until finally, "You not wish to take me?"

Andar opened his eyes. "No. No I don't wish to *take* you. Go to sleep."

He closed his eyes, but she continued to watch him. Long into the evening Dajata lay awake, confused by this man who did not want to take her.

They travelled south for several days along paths seldom used, encountering no one. Whenever the path divided, they took the left fork. It steered them west, but always veered again to the south.

The reed forests they traversed had the mark of age upon them, the trees soaring to heights which Andar had never thought possible. The mottled brown-grey trunks were an arms' spread in diameter, the bark no longer soft and leathery, but thick and tough. Many of the valleys were wider and not as deep, the crests between them flatter. The differences made the land unfamiliar, alienating Andar and making him uneasy.

They left a narrow, overgrown trail they had been following through a forest and made their way down the steep incline of a smaller ravine. They angled down the slope and although there was no obvious trail, Dajata paused only momentarily near a jumbled pile of boulders then continued. At the bottom, they walked downstream for a short distance then began the climb up the other side. Andar followed as she found the seemingly invisible clues and wound her way up the slope.

Her attitude toward him had changed little since her outcry and attack several days earlier. He expected nothing less. He glanced up and caught the roll of her skinny buttocks as she climbed, the shortness of her wrap almost exposing her. Andar looked away. He looked up again, this time watching her small feet pick their way over and around the rocks and boulders.

Dajata came to a level grade halfway up the incline, stopped momentarily, and turned to look back the way they had come. He followed close behind her, head down, his eyes watching her feet. At her hesitation, his head rose, eyes flicking past her wrap as they sought her face. For a moment his cold green eyes met hers. With a wave of his arm he motioned her forward again and she continued her climb without saying a word.

He had spoken little but treated her well. He still carried all the supplies and never seemed to tire. As for herself, she felt better. Walking the first days had exhausted her so much that she had collapsed when they stopped for the night. Before he would allow her to sleep, he forced her to eat, and when she had eaten, he forced her to eat more. On those first mornings, she was so painfully stiff that she felt she could not rise, but with abrupt encouragement from him, she had managed. However, now she was no longer sore, and had acquired a good appetite. For the first time in her life her skin was turning brown. She liked that it helped to cover the bruises.

She was only too aware of him below as she picked her route up the incline. She restricted her stride to keep the wrap from rising up her thighs, holding the front of it tightly, pulling it down all the while trying not to attract his attention. She was puzzled by this prudish action, but knew somehow it had to do with the distain in his voice when he made it clear that he didn't want to take her. But she did not trust him, for she knew what men were like. There had been many men. Men that her father had brought home. Some had been kind and understanding, but they too had used her. The others had been animals, less than human.

This one was not like that, but he was driven. He was as one addicted to the cher root, living for it, nerves exposed, teetering between anger and joy, a puppet of its seductive power. Such was this man. She had watched his face when he was not aware. She saw the worry and sadness, the anger and frustration. It lurked just under the surface, held in check. The time would come, soon she felt, when control would be lost, and the terrible, pent-up flood would burst. When it happened, she did not want to be within reach of that rage, for there was a frightening hardness about him when he sat before the fire, evening after evening, saying nothing, only honing or polishing his weapons.

The sound in the distance began as an ominous, deep-throated rumble that brought Andar to a nervous halt. He called to Dajata to stop. She turned to him and saw the unease in his stance as he listened to the roar.

"It is great waterfall. At foot we cross river and marsh on both sides," she said.

"How will we do this?" he asked uneasily.

"Suru leave reed boats hidden. We find one of them."

Andar grunted his approval and motioned her forward. The rumble grew until the thunder of the water filled his head. Even the power of its roar did not prepare him for the spectacle as they emerged from the forest to stand at the base of the falls. The massive wall of water thundered down, its clamor shaking the reed trees on either side. Great clouds of mist curled upward from the frenzied melee at its base where the water leapt and churned before continuing downstream to the wide flood plain. Bound on both sides by marsh, the plain was hundreds of yards wide and extended downriver as far as the eye could see. Running through the center, the Great Kalimar River flowed eastwards.

"We look here along shore," Dajata said, breaking the spell the falls had cast over Andar.

He pulled his eyes from the rushing water and motioned Dajata forward. In a short time they found the hollowed out reed log lying among the foliage. The walls of the craft were thin, both ends shaped into long tapered points that would cut the water cleanly. It was light and together they pulled it to the water's edge and began paddling awkwardly across the marsh, the cool mist from the falls coating them and their tiny boat. Unaccustomed to water craft, their progress was slow as they meandered through purple water reeds. These jutted out of the foamy water, their coloured berries tapping the sides of the boat, slowing their progress even more. At the edge of the marsh their boat entered the flowing river, was caught broadside by the current, and carried rapidly downstream. Andar looked over his shoulder at the falls quickly receding behind them.

"Paddle harder," he said and dug his paddle deeper, straining from the weight of the water. The boat rocked dangerously as his weight shifted, water spilling over the side.

"Turn front of boat towards falls," she yelled to him. "Point up river!" Andar paddled furiously, finally turning the nose so that it cut through the current, slowing their downward course.

"Now paddle up river and across," she said over her shoulder.

Andar understood, leaned forward, and pulled at the water. The craft began to turn away from the side he paddled and soon the current grabbed the nose. Broadside once more, they were washed downstream.

"Change side to side. Paddle both sides," Dajata yelled.

Andar fought the current and turned the nose into it again. Although they paddled nonstop, they were still pushed downstream until at last they drove the boat from the current into the calm of the marsh on the other side. Andar dropped his paddle in the boat and leaned back, his muscles exhausted, arms limp by his side. He fought to capture his breath.

"Why didn't you tell me to point the boat into the current before we entered the river?" he asked. "Why didn't you say something?"

Exhausted, Dajata pushed herself upright and turned to him. "I thought you know. Why you not know boats?" she said and turned around again.

Andar stared at her back. He had never paddled a boat across a river before and been completely unprepared for it. *My search for Dreanna's attackers might have ended here. If the woman had drowned, who would have guided me?* Shaken by the thought, he picked up the paddle and began once more. Dajata joined him and finally they made it through the marsh and pulled the boat onto the shore where he hid it among the undergrowth. Shouldering the supplies, he stood looking at her.

"We go back up stream near base of falls," Dajata said in answer to his unspoken question. Without further word she started back along the edge of the marsh. At the base of the falls she led them up the side of the gorge to the top, then turned west, and for the rest of the day followed the crest between two ravines.

That evening Dajata told him that it would take four or five more days to reach the entrance to the stronghold of the Suru. Sitting exhausted before the fire, Andar stared into the flames, his earlier realization at the river haunting his thoughts. He didn't know what he would do when he reached the Suru. He only knew that he must find them. He looked across the fire to the woman. She sat slumped against a boulder. Her face, like her limbs, was beginning to tan, imparting a healthier appearance, but tonight it was drawn and tired.

"You have been to this Suru camp before," he said.

"Yes, you know that."

"Tell me about them."

Dajata leaned forward, wincing as tired muscles complained. She pulled her knees up and circled them with her arms as she looked across the fire at him. "I do not know about them. Only they kill people and my father puts markings on them."

Andar stared at her, the first stirrings of anger beginning to surface. He held it in check. "You've been to their camp. You've seen them. Tell me what you know." Despite his efforts, traces of a threat tainted his voice.

She returned his stare, too tired to be frightened. "Before we arrive, they blind our eyes. Take us to a room where father makes markings. The ones we mark have hood on their heads. When done they lead us out."

Andar waited, but when she said nothing else, he turned his gaze to the fire. Without any knowledge of them, he didn't know what he would do. Like earlier that day, a sense of helplessness overwhelmed him. When sleep finally came, it was troubled and full of the same frightening dreams.

Andar awoke with a start, sensing something was wrong, something out of place. He relaxed the grip on his dagger when he saw that it was Dajata's aura that was the source of his awakening. It was stronger and pulsed with some subtle difference that he could not define. He saw that she had nursed the coals back to flames and was making ree. It was late, for already the morning mist had evaporated. Andar sat up with a start when he saw that her wrists weren't tied.

She looked at him. "Last night you not tie them."

"You didn't try to escape," he said as he watched her pour the ree.

"You would catch me." She shrugged her shoulders and turned away.

They had travelled without incident for the greater part of the morning and now walked beside a meandering stream at the bottom of a narrow valley. Andar felt uneasy, his sense tingling with a variety of impressions, aware that the boulders and jutting slabs of rock would shield others from him. He loosened his sword in its sheath and warned Dajata to slow down. She looked at him as if he were foolish, yet slowed her pace. Andar scanned the slopes looking for anyone that might be triggering his sense, but could see nothing. Finally they rounded a twist in the ravine and Dajata drew up short with an exclamation of surprise. A small band of men crouched upon the ground eating a midday meal. They were on their feet quickly, each with a sword in hand. Their apprehension disappeared quickly as they saw the two of them.

"Well'comed friends," said the closest of the four, a short fellow with curly hair. He slipped his sword back into its sheath and wiped the grease from his mouth with the back of his hand. His faded gray eyes, cross hatched with wrinkles, studied them as they approached. He smiled with easy charm. "Rare to see kin trek tis trail. Come. Hav'in arr food, hav'in arr ale, sharr'in arr fire."

Dajata didn't move, waiting for a signal from Andar who eased up beside her.

"Thank you, friend," Andar said, eyeing the men. They were trailmen of the same cut as those he had encountered earlier, but he felt he had little choice lest he provoke them by refusing their hospitality. "We shall share a meal and friendship with you and then take our leave." He nudged Dajata forward, but after a few steps she came to an abrupt halt. A hand went to her face as she turned away. Andar's stomach tightened.

The Stone Sleeper was spread-eagled on his back, all four thick limbs stretched tight and staked to the ground. He raised his head, black eyes squinting against the sun as he watched them. His mouth hung open, his jaw moving as if about to speak. A pink tongue wiped his bruised and swollen lips as the shaggy head eased back, eyes closing.

Andar's heart began to race. Bark beetles and leaf reed mites crawled in and out of the cuts, gouges, and tears in his massive frame. On his chest, strips of thick tissue had been cut and peeled back, insects crawling upon the bared sinews. Earlier wounds had dried in crusty rivers that flowed over the dark grey flesh, but others more recent still oozed blood. Several sharpened reeds had been driven through his flesh and into the ground.

The brutality was like nothing Andar had seen. He felt the turmoil build within him as his heart hammered against his ribs. An enormous, shaking pressure raced to his arms so that he struggled to keep them from trembling as he handed his dagger to Dajata and stripped himself of the supplies he carried. The curly haired trailman and a second one, tall, thin, and hard faced, ambled towards the Stone Sleeper, motioning Andar and Dajata closer.

"Tat's right. Give yurr pip a chance," said the shorter trailman, looking at Dajata. "Ever se'you a sleeper 'fore? Drox, but he's a tough ol shakir. Hard to git morenaa grunt outta him. When we cuts off his jollies, he'll squeal. What say swee girl? Ever sees a set like that?" He laughed and stepped closer to the Sleeper as he studied Dajata. "Yuu wanna whack 'hem?" With that he kicked one of the creature's legs, the stake driven through it pulling at the flesh.

Andar and Dajata continued to approach and were at the feet of the Sleeper. The remaining men followed behind them, anticipating a show. Dajata's eyes were wide in horror, her hand in front of her mouth as she tried not to vomit. Andar drew his sword.

"Yurr pip squeamish is she?" said the tall one, his lip curling in disapproval as he rested his foot on the head of the Sleeper. He looked to Andar. "Go then frien. Strok'em with yurr longpiece."

Andar turned to Dajata, his voice a barely controlled whisper. "Cut him loose." Then with a scream Andar slashed the tall trailman across the neck. Dajata saw his head fall away, the face frozen in disbelief. The headless body remained upright for a moment then tumbled to the ground as Andar leapt past the crumpled form and attacked the other man. Dajata stood rooted to the spot, disbelief preventing her from turning away.

The shorter man's eyes were wide with terror as Andar hammered blow after blow upon the man's sword. Savage energy from weeks of pent up emotion drove Andar to cut and slash and cut at the man again. Gone were any lessons of timing or skill or finesse as rage drove him forward. With a surge of speed he sent the trailman's sword rebounding outwards then opened the man's throat open with a lightning back cut. From behind Andar, curses filled the air as the two remaining trailmen rushed him, swords drawn. Andar charged them, rage still ruling his actions. The two men split up, then attacked from both sides, but Andar was everywhere, leaping first at one to slash and parry, then assaulting the other. He felt no fear, no fatigue, only unbridled hatred and a lust to kill.

The two trailmen tired quickly. One broke away and ran towards Dajata, who stood frozen watching the battle. Too late she brought the dagger up. The dagger dropped from her grasp as he twisted her wrist. His arm encircled her neck.

"Stop! I'll cut the slit's troat."

Andar and the remaining trailman lowered their swords hesitantly.

"Put yurr-"

Before the threat could be shouted, Andar's sword arced slashing the neck of the man in front of him. The head, still partially attached, fell to the side as the body collapsed. Andar whirled and stalked towards the remaining man who held Dajata. Shocked, the trailman hesitated.

"Kill her and the pain you've inflicted on this creature will be nothing compared to what I'll do to you." Andar approached, his eyes holding those of the trailman. "Let her go and I'll let you live."

Her captor grabbed Dajata roughly by the hair and pressed the sword's edge tightly to her neck. A thin trickle of blood ran down from under it. "Stop or 'er head jumps!" he screamed, the fear raw in his voice.

"Let her go. If you don't, I'll free the Stone Sleeper and let him have you."

The trailman's eyes flicked in horror to the creature who watched him.

"Let her go and live," repeated Andar as he lowered his sword.

The man lowered his blade slightly. "Yurr word you let me go."

"Let her go now," Andar said his voice hollow.

"Yurr word! Swear by Dukor!" the trailman screamed, panic shining in his eyes.

"My word," said Andar.

"Swear by Dukor!"

"I swear."

The trailman threw Dajata forward to the ground, whirled and bolted down the ravine. With a snarl, Andar leapt past Dajata and raced after him. The man looked over his shoulder at Andar bearing down on him, and screamed. He never turned to defend himself. Andar caught the man's trailing leg, severing the foot and halting his flight. He paused, his sword held overhead as he stared into the eyes of the trailman. Even as the sword descended, the truth of his action. He *wanted* to kill him. He stood over the body, breathing deeply, the killing lust slowly receding.

In shock, Dajata watched Andar turn and walk towards her. His face was lifeless. She cringed when he reached down to help her up, but she clung to him for a moment, steadying her nerves. Dajata stepped back and put her hand to the trickle of blood that ran down her neck to her chest.

"He was going to kill me," she said to herself as she smeared the blood on her chest. She looked at him, her eyes wide in awe at his rampage. "You stopped him. Stopped them all."

"I still need you," he said, his eyes expressionless as he turned away.

Andar approached the Sleeper. "I'll free you and help treat your wounds. After that it's up to you whether you live or die." He raised his sword to cut one of the cords, but paused. "I don't hate the way they do." The blade slashed one of the bonds.

"You hate, friend. Maybe not the Sleepers." The creature's voice was deep and rich.

Andar stared at the craggy face but said nothing. One by one, he cut the cords, the Sleeper's head turning to watch. Andar drove the point of his sword into the soil and bent to pull out one of the stakes driven through the flesh of the creature's leg. The Sleeper remained silent, no trace of pain on his face as it was withdrawn. One by one Andar pulled them free sending fresh rivers of blood running down the gray skin into the soil.

Andar took the pouch that held the powdered crystals from his harness. Created those many years ago to fight the poisonous bites of the malbars, it helped prevent infections and promoted the healing of wounds. He mixed the powder with water and after he applied the paste over the many cuts, punctures and tears, he bound the Stone Sleeper's wounds. When done, with much effort they propped up his heavy body with equipment from the dead men then lit a fire close by, a supply of wood at hand. Andar doubted the creature's chances at survival. His great reserve of strength was gone, weakened from the amount of blood that had been lost. He tried to probe the Sleeper's aura, to gauge his chances, but either the creature didn't possess one, or it was so weak that he couldn't sense it. Andar hunted and brought down some small game, but by the time they were finished their ministering, the two moons were casting gentle shadows on the ground as the mist creapt down the sides of the ravine to their fire.

Andar had grudgingly accepted that they would not be proceeding and now, as always, stared into the flames of the campfire, wrapped deep in thought, a wall between him and the other two. Dajata had avoided him as much as possible and drew back when he bound her arms. The creature's eyes blinked in surprise at this, but he said nothing. The fire dwindled, dimming in the dark, the mist caressing their forms as it crept over them, drawn inwards to the fire's embers where it dissolved into lazy coils of shimmering heat.

"My name is Rigersor." He spoke for the first time since being freed. "I will survive. I owe you my life. I would know the name of the man who has saved it, and why."

Andar looked at the lined, battered face, shadows chiselling valleys across its grey surface. It could have been a statue carved in stone.

"Andar, from the village of Bonstag. I saved your life… because of them," and he motioned in the direction that he had dragged the corpses. His thoughts were distant as he stared out into the night. "It is others such as them that I seek."

"And why must you do this?" Rigersor asked, the deep voice gently prodding Andar from his trance.

Andar's face weakened as a vision of Dreanna formed before him. She was teasing him at Rakosur's tavern. For long seconds he couldn't speak then his face turned hard. "That's my concern, Sleeper. In the morning we leave. We've wasted enough time."

The morning filtered down the sides of the valley. The sun, shuttered by the reed trees, patterned long shadows across the valley bottom. In the cool morning breeze, they ate their morning meal without talk. The Stone Sleeper showed remarkable signs of improvement and was able to sit unaided. They left him what remained of the food and with a nodding farewell Andar motioned Dajata to lead the way.

"Good fortune, Andar. Perhaps our paths will cross again," the Sleeper called after them, but if Andar heard, he made no reply.

Chapter Nine

Bonara's mood was foul, his patience growing shorter each day. Although he tried to control it, little by little his fear grew, threatening to suffocate him. The walls of the room at the inn on the outskirts of Kempa were a prison. Unable to do anything but wait, his nervous energy ate away at him, undermining his confidence.

His men had found traces of the girl's kidnappers. An old man and his wife, travelling quietly in their age, had heard noises ahead of them on the path. Fear had hidden them in the trees, but they had heard much of what had happened and told others in the village. Finally, Bonara's men had found the couple and determined that the kidnappers had headed west towards Kempa. Bonara feared that by now the girl and her companions were likely dead, the key in the hands of those responsible. But he had to try. He sent his men racing westward in the desperate hope of finding them. As of yet, he had received no word. He followed them west, hoping to meet them returning with his precious piece, but a long march now found him at Kempa, waiting. He assumed his soldiers had ventured farther west. Successful or not, they were to meet him here at the inn.

Time crawled as each day's passing assaulted his very reason for existence. Without the sixth key, all was lost. He would never be able to gain entrance. It had only been the strangest of flukes and thousands of years of erosion by the rains that had allowed him access to that first sanctuary so many years ago. That would never happen again. A quiet knock at the door disturbed his thought.

"Yes?" he said, carefully controlling the hope he always felt arise when someone knocked. Too many times it had meant nothing.

"My Lord Bonara, the men have returned," said his man servant. "One waits below in the common room."

Bonara bolted from his chair towards the door. He swung it wide, hardly able to control his voice. "Have they been successful? Do they have it?"

"I do not know, my Lord." The man's eyes found the floor and he shifted from foot to foot. Bonara exhaled and his shoulders slumped forward.

"Send him up," he said, not wishing to see the man, but knowing he must.

The soldier appeared, close to exhaustion. His face was haggard from lack of sleep. A blood-stained bandage wrapped his arm. Nervously he stood before Bonara.

"What news, Resnic? Why is it that Tossmor does not appear before me?" Bonara's voice was cold and flat.

"My Lord, Tossmor is dead. All are dead except for us four."

Bonara's eyes widened in disbelief.

"We found her, my Lord."

Bonara staggered a step forward in surprise. "You found her? Alive?"

"Yes, but we were unable to return with her," said Resnic, shifting uncomfortably.

Bonara stood deathly still, anger slowly replacing his confusion. His eyes seared Resnic. "And you let her get away?" He raised his hand to strike him.

"My Lord! Nearly all of us died trying to wrest her from them. I have never seen men fight so fiercely. One of them, a bowman, killed nearly half of our men."

Bonara stared, his eyes focusing tighter on the soldier. "Describe this man to me."

"He was tall, but thin. Dark hair worn long. The bow he used was larger than any I've seen." Resnic paused, the fear and respect in his eyes, echoed in his voice. "He never missed, my Lord."

Bonara was silent, the light of wonder and hope beginning to infuse his eyes. "Could it be? But it must be so! Why else would they not have killed her? Grenfeld's son. It must be him. Grenfeld must have sent his own men under his son's command to steal the girl when the Suru failed." He looked up at Resnic, grabbing and shaking the man's shoulders. "Rothus will be taking her back to Grenfeld. All is not lost! With any luck, she may still have the key. It will delay matters, but the key can still be returned. Well done, Resnic."

"My Lord?"

"Never mind. Retire for the night. You are now in command. We leave tomorrow for Dashindar and Grenfeld. Make the arrangements. Go."

As the door closed, Bonara began to shake uncontrollably. His nerves these last few days had been tested to the limit. The relief he felt almost undid him. He staggered towards a chair and collapsed in it.

"The fool. He almost ruined everything. He still may have. If so, I'll kill him myself."

Doros and Lanos stood at dusk on the rise overlooking Kempa. In the distance, lights flickered throughout the sea of buildings that seemed to stretch forever in all directions. Both weary travelers viewed it with a mixture of emotions. Even as they rejoiced at their arrival, the very magnitude of the city below unnerved them.

"Grandfather, you could fit five, ten villages the size of ours within this one," said Doros.

"Yes. Finding your father or the man he seeks will be a challenge."

They made their way slowly down the incline towards what appeared to be an inn on the outskirts of the city. The journey of the last few days had taken its toll upon Lanos. His legs had not been able to endure the constant pace and he limped badly. He had refused to stop, except for the noon meal, but their pace had gradually slowed along the trail. Others had passed them frustrating Doros further, but he had said nothing, the condition of his grandfather all too evident.

Much to their relief, the structure below did prove to be a small but sturdy inn. The thick door swung inward to a gentle push, heavy warm air from a fire in a hearth reaching out to embrace them. Many torches bounced flickering light off the low ceiling lighting up colorful wall hangings. A few robed patrons occupied the tables, sipping ale or eating a late meal. After paying for a room at the small bar in the corner, Doros helped Lanos negotiate the stairs that led to the sleeping quarters. The old man grimaced as he struggled with each step, leaning heavily upon his grandson.

"My legs are hardly what they used to be, but they'll be fine in the morning. All I need is a good night's rest… a good night's rest," and he trailed off, out of energy and breath.

The room was small and simple. The lamp's glow cast soothing shadows from roof timbers that angled steeply up over two narrow beds. Lanos hobbled across the planked floor to one of them and sat, fumbling with the cord on his cloak. Doros lifted it from him as he fell sideways, then spread the cloak over his grandfather and stood looking at him. Exhaustion claimed Lanos for the night as Doros closed the door and ventured downstairs to the tavern.

The warmth from the hearth and the solid walls reassured Doros as he sat at a table near the fire. The stew was thick and tasty, the reed ale a strange red color but welcomed. All but two of the patrons had retired for the night. Unlike Lanos, sleep was a stranger to him as he contemplated how the last few days had crippled his grandfather.

Grandfather had always just been, Grandfather; kind and understanding, full of bits of knowledge, able to show him many things. Doros had never noticed his age. But now his grandfather's face, so tired and wrinkled, scared and upset him. To think that just walking had exhausted him so was beyond Doros' understanding. He realized, with guilty pride, that he was more than a match for his Grandfather. He was much stronger, could last longer. But it made him feel sad, for it was as if Grandfather was dying.

Doros took a sip of ale. The taste of the murky red liquid was different, distinct with the local brewmaster's touch, but so welcomed after days on the trail. He drank deeply. It was sweeter than it should be, he thought. Not like that which Rakosur served. He shook himself. He must stop thinking such useless thoughts. He must think of what they were to do next. Of what *he* must do next, for he was sure that Grandfather could not continue on their journey. How would they find his father *if* he was still here? If he had left how would they know where he had gone? He remembered that his father was searching for someone here in Kempa. He couldn't remember the name he was sure Grandfather would. Yes, he thought, Grandfather will remember.

Doros watched three men descend the stairs from the inn above. The gray bearded one in the lead, slighter of build and height, spoke to the trailing member who had the gait and demeanour of a soldier. The man bowed, wound his way through the tables and left by the door at the far end. The bearded one spoke briefly to his remaining taller, heavier companion, then sat at a table near Doros.

A foggy image swirled in Doros' mind. The newcomer seemed familiar, something about the beard and the shape of his face. Doros raised another spoonful of stew as he watched the man's companion return with two tankards of ale. The man's face was worn with years, and the many battle scars gave him a brutal appearance that had Doros staring despite himself. As he sat, the man slid the ale across the table and eyed Doros who quickly looked away. Both men sipped their drink making idle conversation to which Doro listened as he ate. It seemed they were waiting for someone to arrive. The voice of the shorter, bearded one did seem familiar. It was different in manner, soft yet confident. Doros was sure he had heard it before. He made an effort to listen more attentively.

"The man should be here at any time, my Lord," said the heavyset fellow. "I think that we are perhaps early."

"Yes, yes," the other replied impatiently. "Kaymar, we must make this fellow realize the importance of contacting them, of preventing them from attempting to trace and capture her. Nothing must happen to her until I reach her."

The voice, so distinct yet elusive, tantalized Doros, as did the subject.

Kaymar's gaze shifted to the tavern door as it swung open. "Here he is now, my Lord."

Both watched the approach of the new figure who accompanied the soldier. Doros risked another look at the short, bearded one beside him.

This time, the grey beard and thin countenance leapt at him as he remembered the visit from the old storyteller. Yes, it was him. He turned away as the soldier and his companion, a tall lean man swathed in dark clothing, reached their table. Doros felt the eyes of the newcomer study him.

"Let us sit over here," he said. "I do not like the heat as much as you." They moved over to a table near the back of the tavern, behind Doros.

"Now we can speak," said the newcomer, after he had settled opposite Bonara.

Doros heard the words faintly as he finished his meal. He strained to catch their conversation, aware that they did not want anyone to hear.

"To the point," began Bonara, his gaze intense on the man in black. "The girl has something I need. I must have it. But Grenfeld sent his son to take the woman when your men were unsuccessful."

"They are not my men, Bonara. I simply have means of contacting them, of making arrangements."

"Yes, fine. Then you must contact them, immediately. Rothus has the girl and continues on to Dashindar."

Doros felt the hairs on the back of his neck rise when he heard the name. The heat from the fire seemed to enfold him as blood rushed to his face. It was all he could do not to turn his head and stare at them.

"I must leave immediately to join them there," said Bonara. "Now that I know where she will be, now that her father has left his home, I have no further need of the services of … your acquaintances. Not that they have been very effective. It would seem their reputation is exaggerated."

"Don't talk like that. This man who has protected the girl, her father. He must be truly exceptional, or very lucky. He's the reason for the complications."

"Perhaps you're right, but he's unimportant now. Word must get to… them, to cancel the arrangement. When can this be done?" asked Bonara.

"Word will go out tomorrow. A group of new apprentices is to be led to the stronghold. It will take six days before they arrive."

"I'll have one of my men bring a letter to you tomorrow to present to them," said Bonara. "When and where shall he meet you?"

"He can find me at the Red Spear Inn. Have him bring it there at first light."

They rose and the dark one took his leave. Doros, almost beside himself with what he had overheard, wished he could shrink into nothingness for fear that somehow the storyteller might recognize him. When those remaining raised their tankards and drank, he summoned his courage and keeping his face averted wound his way through the tavern and up the stairs. He had much to tell Lanos.

Chapter Ten

Dawn's hazy rays filtered through the morning sky, barely lighting the alleyway where Doros had taken up his vigil crouched behind several hooped barrels. This morning in the tavern, Lanos had watched Bonara pass a note to his tall, battle scarred accomplice. As the man left the tavern, Lanos had hobbled behind him outside and nodded to Doros who had taken up careful pursuit. Now he sat across from the rundown building that the dark clad visitor from last night had entered.

The plan had not been hastily conceived, for Lanos was beside himself with anger and frustration. When he heard of Rothus and Grenfeld, his face went white and he cursed them both and all their ancestors until he was out of breath. Doros stood wide-eyed at the tirade. He had never seen his grandfather so distraught.

"After all these years that Droxeur comes back to upset our lives once more!" Lanos pushed himself from the bed and paced the room, limping painfully.

"Who is he, Grandfather? Who is this Grenfeld?"

Lanos stopped pacing and stared at Doros. "He's a nasty son of a narlot who knew your mother and father many years ago and finally left Bonstag when he couldn't get what he wanted. And now he's back with this erront that is his son." Lanos limped to the bed, sat and cursed his legs, for they were no better despite the few hours rest. Then he cursed Doros.

"And now you want to follow someone to others, and then follow *them* to the stronghold of the Suru? Have you lost your senses?"

"But Grandfather, even though you remembered Joshura's name, there is no guarantee that we can find him. If I can follow them to the Suru, that might be the fastest way to find Father."

"Yes," said Lanos, "but that's assuming that your father has found Joshura and the directions to the Suru." He spat on the floor and rubbed his swollen knees harder. "What if something should happen to you? By all our ancestors, we've already lost your mother. Your sister is missing and your father…is…we don't know where. If something…"

"We have no choice, Grandfather. We must do all we can to find Father and tell him about Dreanna. And Rothus."

At last it was agreed upon and in the morning, after following the black clad man down a backstreet, Doros had entered a narrow alley to hide behind the barrels. Vermin scurried about him after food scraps cast off from the back doors of taverns and houses, the dank odour of refuse and animal waste held in the air by the last traces of mist. An old man, a piece of gnawed cher root clutched in his hand, lay sprawled on his back at the far end of the alley.

Doros peered cautiously through the crack between two of the barrels when he heard the sound of footsteps. The figure of a boy about his own age walked hesitantly down the alley, searching, finally drawn towards the building that the man had entered. At the door he hesitated, then rapped upon its scarred surface. It opened to reveal a shadowed figure that held out a hand. Placing something in the upturned palm, the boy was admitted.

Doros slouched behind the barrels, his confidence slipping away. The plan had seemed sound and he had accepted it with a mixture of pride and excitement. Here, waiting alone in the damp alley, he felt his courage fading. Grandfather was not nearby to give him advice. Another young figure appeared and the procedure was repeated. Doros bit his lip in worry. What if when they left to meet the Suru they did not come out the same way? More footsteps disturbed his thoughts, and this time two boys travelled the backstreet, each approaching from an opposite direction. The first to arrive at the building paused, eyed the other one suspiciously, then approached and knocked on the door. It opened and after receiving the offering, the figure admitted the boy. Finally the second boy approached and was admitted. The door closed silently behind them.

Doros was sweating even though the morning was still cool and damp. He leaned back against one of the barrels, wiped his upper lip, his heart pounding as a new plan began to form. The boys didn't know each other. No one would know him. He wouldn't try following them and risk being detected. He would *join* them.

Already six had arrived. How many more before they left? Clutching onto one of the rough barrels Doros pulled himself up wondering from which direction the next one would come? He had to get whatever it was that gained them admittance. As he stepped from the alley a figure rounded the corner down the street. Doros held his breath and clenched his hands to hide the trembling as he walked towards the approaching figure. They drew closer then passed each other. Doros walked further then chanced a look back again. The boy had already found the building and was preparing to knock. Doros leapt into an opening between two buildings, his heart racing as he cursed himself. He had been too late. He could only hope that another would come his way.

Two more boys arrived, both from the other direction. How many more? Had they said in their conversation last night? He wracked his brains trying to remember. With each one it lessened his chances of being able to join them. Footsteps to his right startled him. Sweating, he inched back from the edge of the building, pulling his dagger from the sheath. Doros held his breath, afraid that his hoarse breathing would give him away. As the boy passed, Doros stepped out behind him, raised his weapon and swung for his head. The glancing blow from the pommel of the dagger jarred Doros all the way to his shoulder. He caught the boy as he collapsed and dragged him out of the street and between the two buildings. Doros leaned against the wall and sank to his haunches as he tried to control his trembling.

"Stop it. Stop being a child," he muttered to himself. "Hurry or it will all be for nothing."

He knelt over the prostrate form, horrified to find blood oozing from the boy's head where the pommel had struck, but relieved to find his victim still breathing. Doros searched, looking for whatever it was that each had presented the guardian of the door. The round token was not striking, but different than anything he had seen. There was nothing else on him that could serve as admission.

Doros bound the boy with strips cut from his tunic, dragged him further down the alleyway into the shadows, then started for the building afraid his resolve might desert him. At the door he struck the marred surface. It swung open without warning and the silent figure stood, hand outstretched. Doros held his breath as he handed the token to him. The shadowy figure stepped aside, motioned him to enter, and the door closed silently behind him.

They were naked. It was the second day of travel and all of their weapons, clothing, and supplies were wrapped in cloaks which they carried beneath one arm as they ran. Led by one Suru, for so Doros surmised him to be, a second trailed, occasionally encouraging them with a blow from the flat of his sword. Doros had never felt so tired in his life. Sweat ran down his face and neck to cover his chest. His legs were so painful from the first day that he felt like they would give out at any minute. More than once he had felt the slap of the blade on his back and feared he would never again see his grandfather.

They stopped, giving them a few precious moments to gain their breath and take a mouthful of water. Bent over from the waist, his lungs heaved like bellows as he laboured to suck in more air. Then again they were on their seemingly endless run through the forest.

When the first gruelling day had ended they had collapsed at the campsite. After a brief meal, they were instructed to sleep around two fires that they built. In the morning the ordeal had begun again. When the evening finally brought a halt to the second day's travel and he lay in a heap on the ground, Doros wondered how he would be able to continue. His bold plan to steal into the very midst of the enemy now seemed a foolhardy way to die and he turned his face from the others as the tears suddenly began. They were given their meagre meal of reed bread and when finished one of their escorts, a lean hard man with close cropped blond hair, rose and stood before them.

"Before it has begun, many wish to make the journey, but once started they wish to be safe at home once more. The journey for you has started and will be a long one, full of many hardships, but many rewards as well." He pointed to one of the two fires. "After tonight there is no turning back. In the morning those who chose to sleep around this fire will continue." He pointed to the second fire. "Those who choose this one… will make the return trip to Kempa." He let the silence linger as his eyes searched their faces, only the crackling of the fires disturbing the night. His smile was grim, his voice soft. "Think well what you would do with the rest of your life."

The silence was overpowering as each of the young men fought to keep their eyes averted from one another. Already the group was divided between the two fires and Doros could not help but wonder what results the morning would bring. For him there was no choice. He curled up where he lay using his forearm as a pillow and tried not to be afraid.

When morning came, four of their number had chosen to leave. After breakfast they were allowed their clothes and weapons and one of the Suru led them away. As soon as they had departed, the equipment of the remaining boys was returned and their blond leader instructed them to dress.

"Welcome, brothers. You have passed the first test. Your choice has been bold, befitting of those who would become Suru. From here it is a four day walk to your new home, to new beginnings."

The Suru rolled and tied his cloak, slung it over his shoulder, then led the way south. Surprised at the change of events, the boys looked at each other in confusion and relief then followed their master.

Some distance from them the Suru wiped the blade of his sword and slid it back into the sheath. He took a last look toward the bodies of the four boys that lie at the bottom of the ravine and set out to catch up with the others.

Chapter Eleven

After the attack on the trail that evening, in the hollow of an overhanging ledge of blue-grey rock, Dreanna watched over the small fire. Its glow barely illuminating her huddled figure. They had found the small cave-like opening half way up one side of the ravine. Rothus and another sat apart from her, talking quietly. The four others had been posted, hidden to stand guard against the possibility of pursuit from the men who had attacked them. The faint, delicate aroma of baking reed bread hung in the twisting mist. She tended the baking with care. It distracted her from the killing and horror of the afternoon. She had never seen men kill each other. Never seen such violence. The world and everyone in it seemed to have gone mad.

It had not been her father come to rescue her. She realized how foolish that hope had been, yet she had clung to it until the very end, desperately searching the faces for her father. The men attacking had appeared rough and unkempt, but what frightened her was their uniform desire to get to the three of them. Could these men also be after her? She had been beside herself as the two had broken through, their bloodied swords coming closer. She had watched as Rothus calmly stood his ground and cut them down.

Using the corner of her cloak, Dreanna removed the lid of the pan to check the progress of the bread. The last of the moisture from the dough evaporated, adding the scent once more to the tumbling mist. She replaced the lid and sat staring out into the night. So many dead.

She could still hear their dying moans, still see the bloodied corpses scattered along the trail.

She had been angered and confused as she watched Rothus cradle the head of one of his injured men, talking quietly to him, reassuring him, making promises. The man's arm had almost been severed. There was only one thing that could be done, and when Rothus was finished, he had sat with his head bowed. Everything she had seen of him today reminded her of the Rothus she thought she knew. His empathy and sorrow for his men, his courage and prowess with the bow in the heat of battle: these did not match the cold calculating traitor that had professed to love her then stolen her away from her home. Perhaps if she could talk to him, reason with him, there would be an answer. But she had tried that and was met with cold rebuke.

They journeyed for three more days and after crossing another river began winding their way through a young reed forest. The limber branches of the young trees hung in long arcs weighted down with new seed pods that clung to the underside of the leaves. The spear shaped, rubbery leaves formed a canopy of shade beneath which the travelers found a cooling respite. Despite the temporary relief from the sun, all were showing the effects of the journey. Rothus had given organizational command to Portend and stayed aloof from all, speaking only when necessary. More than ever he avoided Dreanna, letting one of his men feed and watch over her during the day.

In the dark, between the reed trees, the Suru glided silently. Nothing betrayed his presence, the green garb blending with the mist floating above the ground. He circled the encampment, studying the position of the men, their weapons and the girl. All were asleep except for the guard who stared sightlessly at the figure of the girl across the fire. He closed in behind the guard then waited for the fire burn down. As the light dimmed he crawled closer, hugging the ground, the mist a covering shroud. The guard shifted and the Suru froze. As the mist swirled and cleared, the sentry's back materialized out of the mist. The Suru slipped his grooved dagger from the scabbard. His feet eased silently under him and he began to rise. Then he froze, for the girl stirred.

Dreanna's green eyes opened sleepily, unfocused and confused. She rubbed her nose, eyes hardening when she saw Rothus across the fire watching her. The mist coiled and cleared momentarily and her eyes widened in surprise. Her face softened, then her lips parted and she spoke to him, her first words in days.

"Rothus, my love, come to my side." She saw his face tighten and he lowered his head. "Rothus, darling, do not save your expertise for a rainy day at home when my father is there. Do what you do best, here and now. Come to me quickly. Come to my side before someone should awake. Quickly my love."

Finally alert to her warning of danger, Rothus rose and stepped toward her, seeking his sword hilt. As the mist shifted Dreanna saw the silent figure materialize again, then spring from the green undulating floor, a dagger in his hand. The widening of her eyes as she looked over Rothus' shoulder warned him of the direction of the attack. He spun attempting to draw his sword, but was too late. Dreanna's scream raked the night when the Suru slammed into Rothus, sending them both toppling to the ground near the fire's edge. Rothus grabbed the hand that held the dagger and the two rolled and bucked on the ground as shouts from Rothus' men rose. The Suru somersaulted off of him, but Rothus held onto the wrist and bought a moment's delay. He released and rolled away as his men surrounded the Suru.

"Don't kill him!" Rothus yelled drawing his sword.

The Suru, dagger in one hand, sword in the other, was constant motion, spinning, and weaving. He pressed the six men outwards, keeping the circle from closing on him, testing the defences of each. With a flick of his wrist, the dagger flew into the chest of one of the men as he lunged smoothly catching another in the thigh. The men rushed him, but his sword was a blur as he twisted and turned, dancing out of reach of their blades. One of the men caught the Suru's arm with a slash, but fell to the assassin's sword. Rothus opened a wound in his thigh, and the blade of a third found his stomach. Still, he evaded their rush, inflicting wounds on two more of Rothus' men. Panting, the men stepped back to regroup, eyeing the bloodied form of the Suru who staggered on his injured leg, a hand held to his side to staunch the flow of blood.

The assassin studied the men and his lip curled contemptuously. He launched himself towards the two in front of him. His sword caught the shoulder of one of them as the blades of three others impaled him. Without a sound he fell to the ground. Rothus stood over him and delivered a kick to the inert form. He looked up at his men who stood staring at the Suru.

"He gave us no choice, Rothus," one of them said.

"I know." He looked at Dreanna for a long moment then turned back to the man who had spoken. "Drag him out of the camp and let us tend to our wounds. We have a long night ahead of us."

Chapter Twelve

Andar followed Dajata south, his unease growing as they journeyed closer to the Suru stronghold. The changes in the reed forest added to his unrest. When he saw the first tree he was sure it must be deformed, affected by a sickness. But soon another and another appeared. They were like nothing he had seen before. Dajata sensed his uneasiness.

"Have been so since first I came," she said, "Every year more."

She shrugged her shoulders in acceptance and began walking again as he ran his hand across the trunk of one he passed. Unlike the reed trees, with their smooth trunks and straight branches, the rough trunks of these sent thick, crooked limbs skyward, their branches multiplying in dizzying numbers as they divided. He reached up and pulled a leaf free, rubbing it between his fingers. It wasn't thick and rubbery like the spear shaped leaves of the reed trees. These reddish leaves were parchment thin, almost fragile, without any continuity to their shape. He released it and watched it flutter to the ground. Soon the reed trees disappeared altogether and they walked through a landscape of fluttering crimson that he could have never imagined. It stretched off into the distance, a canopy of red that blocked out the sun. Beneath them a strange foliage began to appear as they ventured deeper into the red forest. Waist high sticky fronds clung to their bodies as if intent on capturing them. It stuck to their legs and arms, grasped the bundled supplies and tangled around Andar's sword sheath. It layered them, tearing loose from the stocks, until the weight slowed them down. Finally

Dajata headed down into another stoney ravine bottom, leaving the unworldly forest behind. They stopped to pull the green remnants from them, washing the sticky film from their bodies before setting off along the valley floor. The experience had unnerved Andar, but as they travelled along the valley bottom the familiarity of the shaded slopes eased his nerves. They struggled up a steeper slope back into a familiar reed forest once more. Here on the crest where the flood waters never reached, giant trunks soared high above them. Then down again they ventured into the next valley, slipping and sliding as they crushed the tender new reed shoots that softened the ravine's walls until the next rain would wash the sides clean.

Dajata leapt from the rock to another, landed surefooted and gathered herself for the next jump. Her newfound physical strength and endurance exhilarated her and she had begun to play a game with it, testing and pushing herself until the man behind her was forgotten. She made a satisfying leap, landed with tanned legs spring-tight, arms poised in perfect balance, and realized that she felt wonderful. She felt strong and alive and happy. And free. The thought unbalanced her and she scrambled quickly to prevent a fall.

"Be careful," came the warning shout from behind her. "I don't want to carry you as well."

Self-conscious now, she recovered quickly and chastised herself for playing games, thinking foolish thoughts. Her joy slid away, replaced by the familiar sadness. It was only the illusion of freedom, presented by the outdoors and her new physical state. She was as much a captive as ever.

That evening Andar squatted by the fire studying Dajata who sat with her chin upon her arms, eyes downcast. Although she seldom spoke to him, he sensed her silence tonight was different and realized uncomfortably that she had become the other person in his life. The one he ate with and slept beside. He had felt her eyes upon him and in return he had watched her. He had come to know something of her and he knew something had happened. *Perhaps she is ill, but she looks well.* Although still thin, her face was filling in, changing her appearance. The tanned skin glowed in the fire's light, her high cheek bones cupping moody brown eyes. Since they had left the Sleeper, he had sensed a difference in her aura. She had seemed somehow more alive. But tonight she was as she had been the day they first met. Tonight her eyes were weary or sad in their empty stare.

"What troubles you, Dajata?"

She raised her head slowly, one hand drawing her hair aside as she looked at him.

"What troubles me?" Her voice was cool and controlled. "When will you kill me, master. If you do not, what do I do? Go back to my father and beatings?" She was on her knees now, her voice edged with bitterness. "Shall I beg? You leave me, I not survive. I not survive to find village or town without master. You can not save me from Suru. They kill me for leading you." Anger bared her teeth as she scooped up a pebble. "*That* troubles me *master*." She rose to her feet and hurled the stone at him, waiting, challenging him.

Andar stared at her, guilt silencing him. He *had* turned her life into a nightmare, just as someone had done to him. He had betrayed who he was. Who he thought he was. He stood silently before her, knowing his words were inadequate.

"It's not what I would have chosen to do, taking you from your home and…" The image of his blade slipping into Joshura flashed before him. "…and bringing you here. But I had no choice. I don't mean you harm, nor will I let harm come to you, but I would do the same again if it would help save my daughter." He looked into the night when his voice faltered, then continued. "When you have taken me to the Suru, I'll release you at the nearest town if that is your wish. I swear this before our ancestors."

The night noises retreated, the fire flickering gently. Dajata lowered herself to the log and sat. She stared at him then slowly shook her head. "How you understand?" she said, then slipped from the log and turned away from him and the fire.

Dajata sat looking out into the forest as the night pressed in around her. Finally she reached down and pulled together a small pile of soil to represent Zendar, laid a reed tree leaf near it, and placed one of her sandals to create the third corner of the triangle. She knelt in front of it and began to hum the melody of the Telling Song. The gentle notes floated in the air as she rocked back and forth, the evening mist curling up over her knees. She shut out the world, and felt only the gentle sway of her body, heard only the song of her people, and the anger receded. She continued then sat, more accepting, more at peace. She believed him when he spoke of releasing her. He would fight like a madman to protect her. But he didn't know the taste of freedom he had given her. He would never understand.

Chapter Thirteen

By noon of the following day Dajata said they were within a half day's march of the Suru stronghold. Andar had decided that he would approach them openly. They would not know who he was. In that lay his sole chance for an audience. He removed the bundles of equipment and supplies, keeping only his weapons, then turned to Dajata.

"I hope to return within the day. Wait here for me. Don't show yourself or light a fire. When I return we will take a path in whatever direction I must follow. We'll search out a village. You can stay there and wait for my return with my daughter. Then I'll escort you back to your... back to Kempa."

Dajata's eyes smouldered. "When you don't return, *master*, what shall I do?"

He detached the dagger and its sheath from his harness and threw it at her feet. Andar stared into the fuming brown eyes. "I will return." Without further word he set off.

He ran to release the tension. Soon he would face them and get some answers. He pushed harder, seeking the confrontation, wishing it over. Then reason surfaced. Guards would be posted to warn of unwanted visitors. He mustn't appear as a threat. He wiped his brow and settled into a walk.

Although he could not see them, it didn't take long before he could sense the presence of others. Then two of them were there, silent deadly statues of dark green materializing out of the forest ahead of him. Although his heart pounded, his mouth dry, it came as a relief to have found them. He looked behind him not surprised to find two more motionless figures watching him a few feet away.

"I would speak…" but he went silent as one of them motioned him to follow. Andar breathed in, his chest fluttering nervously, and followed as the others fell in line behind him.

Silently they wound their way deeper into the forest. The Suru twisted and turned, their feet skirting soft soil, moss and lichen. No telltale markings were left to show they had passed this way. Andar tried to follow their example, the concentration a welcomed distraction. The forest became dense, young reed trees interspersed among massive, old world ones. The heavy lower limbs of the giants were intertwined with each other, and Andar realized that what he had thought at first to be new trees, were in reality branches that had grown downwards, taking root in the earth. The ancient giants had created a wall of near impenetrable reed wood. Passage seemed impossible yet the Suru slipped between the barricades with ease.

Other Suru surrounded them. Cold and impassive eyes appraised his physical stature, viewed his weapons and studied his face, taking his measure. Posted guards became more frequent and soon Andar walked a gauntlet of prying eyes intent upon stripping him bare and exposing the fear that he hid inside. Finally the Suru compound materialized, one building at a time, growing into a rambling complex beneath the shadows of the elderly reed trees. Few of the ancient giants had been felled, the squat structures constructed among the massive trees. The building timbers were weathered, stained dark with time, ground cover growing upon the walls, blending the structures with the forest around them.

Following a narrow path, Andar discerned pockets of bare earth on either side where the ground cover had been removed. Here green clad figures sat in observance or practised the art of warfare. Regardless of the nature of the activity, all were carried out in complete silence. Surrounded by walls of vegetation, the violence within each pocket was eerily tranquil. The lines of a large building became visible. As they neared the structure it loomed out of the forest, the steep roof covered thickly with lichen, the high walls barely visible beneath clinging vines. It was a dark brooding monolith; the gaping doors a hungry mouth waiting to devour him. Andar mounted the broad stone steps, hesitating at the door as he watched the lead Suru enter and disappear into the darkness beyond. He felt those behind him press close. With a dry swallow, he pushed his fear and uncertainty down and stepped inside.

Worn floor planks in a wide entranceway narrowed to a long unlit hall. Nothing adorned the woven mats covering the walls that led to two doors at the end. Torches illuminated a carved symbol centered on each door. The symbol, the same as the ones on the dead Suru, held his gaze. Torch light played shadows across their carved surfaces making it seem as if they pulsed with a heartbeat. They halted in front of the doors, the guards becoming statues, eyes fixed upon him, waiting. His heart raced with the fear of the unknown, drops of sweat falling to hit the floor with a tiny patter. Without warning the ponderous doors swung inward, the groan of hinges twisting his stomach.

The silence was complete as Andar stepped inside. The peaked roof soared above him, tiered rows of empty benches filling the side walls. There were others present on the dirt courtyard, but his eyes were drawn to the bearded figure seated on a dais. The elderly Suru Master's shoulders were still broad, the back straight. His presence seemed to draw him across the room. Andar slowed his breathing, pulling in and reinforcing his aura against the piercing wedge of the Master as he attempted to breach it. At the dais, his escorts halted, bowed then stepped away leaving Andar alone. A dozen other Suru, seated on both sides, inspected him, the tentacles of their probing efforts pushing at his aura. Andar held them at bay, pulling his aura inwards.

"You will remove your weapons and place them on the floor behind you," said the Master, his voice quiet but commanding.

Andar held the man's gaze. "I come-"

"I will not repeat it. Remove them or die now."

Andar looked at his guards then removed his bow, arrows and sword, and placed them behind him.

"Step forward. My eyes grow dim with the years and I wish to view closely a common reedsmith who has dared broach our stronghold."

Andar walked towards the dais, the soles of his feet slippery in his sandals from nervous sweat.

"That is close enough. If you are capable of dispatching two of our brothers, I have no doubt that even without your weapons you are a threat. I may be old but I am not careless."

Andar halted. "Someone has-"

"If he speaks again cut out his tongue." The Suru Master rose from his chair and stepped down. At a distance he circled Andar. "Strange. You are tall, but thin. Not young. You have been a reedsmith for many years, not a fighting man, despite your earlier training. Yet still you managed to kill our brothers." He stepped back to the dais and sat. "There is something to be learned here." He stared at Andar, pushing again with his sense. "Could it be that you are simply blessed with stronger attributes than most? I can't pierce your aura to get a sense of who you are, of what makes you unique." His pale blue eyes studied Andar for moments longer. "Now you may speak."

"I come to the Suru seeking those who threaten my daughter."

The Suru Master stared at Andar but said nothing. Finally, he leaned back in his chair. "We have allowed you to enter our stronghold, the first to do so, uninvited, for as long as any can recall. This because of the respect we hold for your apparent skills. Above everything we value the fighting skills that we have dedicated our lives to achieve. Those skills and our commitment to fulfill a contract are the pillars we live by. Are you so naive that you believe we will give you such information, abandon our contract because you request it? Suru honour demands that it be carried out." He rubbed his close cropped beard then looked to a guard who stood near a doorway. "Bring the boy in." The Master returned his attention to Andar.

"No, we cannot do what you ask. I'm afraid you have forfeited your life for nothing."

The door opened and Andar's face blanched as Doros was pushed towards him. A myriad of bruises, partially hidden by dirt, covered his face and torso. Blood had congealed in his nostrils.

"Father!" He rushed to Andar who wrapped his arms around his son. He held Doros at arm's length and inspected him.

"Are you all right?"

Doros' voice quivered, on the verge of breaking. "I'm fine now that you're here."

"What are you doing here? How did you get here?"

"It would seem that you are not the only one who is resourceful," interrupted the Master. "Somehow he managed to infiltrate a group of candidates and when he arrived avoided discovery for a number of days. Master Shottan detected the subtly hidden rhythms of his aura that did not...shall we say, fit the pattern of our usual recruits. He has been very stubborn and uncooperative with the questions we have asked.

Andar's faced reddened as his eyes narrowed on the Master.

"They have Dreanna, Father! She's gone."

"You have my daughter here?" Andar said, loosening his grip on Doros' shoulders.

The four Suru near him tensed.

"No, Father. It was Rothus." Doros' words pulled Andar back to him.

"What? That can't be. He killed one of them himself."

"The Friend of the Ancients who visited our home," said Doros. "I overheard him talking in Kempa. He hired the Suru, but when they failed, some other man sent Rothus to get Dreanna without the Friend of the Ancients knowing, and now she's gone, but she has something of his and he needs to get it back, so he's going to...to Dashindar where he thinks Rothus will take her." The words tumbled out in a stream and Andar struggled to understand what had happened.

"What did he want of Dreanna? What could she possibly have that he would-"

"His name is Bonara," said the Suru Master. "Since none of you will be leaving, I will share the information with you. It was he who sought us out to remove your daughter and bring her here. He did not wish her harmed, but merely wanted to lure you from your home. Why, I do not know. It was of no concern to us. What your daughter possesses, I do not know."

"Who is this other one who sends a coward disguised as a lover to steal my daughter?"

"We know nothing of that man or of the abduction of your daughter by this man Rothus."

"Grenfar, Grenfold. Grenfeld!" said Doros. "That was the name of the man."

"Grenfeld." Andar whispered the name. He saw Grenfeld's face contorted with hate. He could hear the threats that he hurled at him and Katrena. *Could it be? After all these years?* "You're sure that is the name you heard?"

"Yes, I'm sure."

"And Dashindar is where he is taking her?"

"That's what the gray bearded one said."

"I doubt that will happen," said the Master. "When news of the failure of our second brother reached us, another was sent to honour our contract. Your exceptional talents, whatever they may be, helped you to survive and saved your daughter from abduction by our brothers. But your daughter should arrive here tomorrow. If she does not, it would mean one of our brothers has failed again, but I do not think this Rothus will have the... shall we call it luck, that you did?"

Andar's head swam with the information. Despite everything he had done, his leaving had triggered a chain of events that had only worsened the situation.

"You have grown silent." The Suru Master addressed Andar, his voice tolerant, almost fatherly. "It has proven interesting, although perhaps not for you. We have your son. What do we do with him? Your daughter will soon arrive and then we must deal with her."

Andar's eyes blazed as the Master continued speaking.

"But that is not all." The old warrior motioned with his hand and when the guard opened the door, two figures entered. One wore the green of the Suru, the other a short wrap and a band that crisscrossed her breasts. Dajata, wrists bound behind her, was led in, eyes wide in terror.

"She has good reason to fear. It was her who led you to our stronghold and she knows the penalty for treason. Very few have been entrusted with the secret of its location."

"She had no choice. I forced her to lead me here," said Andar looking at Dajat's face, white with fear.

"Yes, we found her father's body."

Dajata's eyes rose hesitantly to the Suru Master. "His body?"

"Yes, he is dead, a knife through the heart. When we attempted to contact him, one of our own found him. It saved us the trouble of dealing with him."

"But he was alive when we left," she said, her eyes seeking Andar. She saw the truth in his face as he looked away. "You killed him? You killed him after we left?" Her voice was strained and incredulous as she shuffled towards him. "Why? No, don't answer. I know. You are killer. You not going set me free at near village. I was right. I dead from the start." She spat at him.

Andar stood motionless, the spittle running down his face.

"And then we have this problem," said the Master. Once again he motioned and a group entered. One, taller than the rest, his hands bound, walked in the middle of the warriors who surrounded him with spears. Dried blood matted the flaking gray skin of his head. His black eyes sparkled as the torch light caught them. The Stone Sleeper was halted before the dais and he gave what Andar could only assume was a smile.

"When we went to take the woman he appeared, protecting her. That seemed a rather strange event. What magic do you weave that encourages a boy to find his way unknown into our stronghold? That causes a woman to reveal the location of our encampment, even though she knows the penalty is death? That causes a mutant creature to defend a travelling companion of yours? What power do you have, common reedsmith of Zendar?"

Andar stood silently for long moments, staring at him, shocked with the new developments. Finally he spoke, his words heartfelt, but tainted by fear.

"I have no special power, no magic. Someone threatened my daughter. She..." His voice cracked and he clamped his jaw tight as his eyes shifted to the floor. Then Andar looked to Doros who stood beside him. "She and my son are my life, my strength. Nothing," and now his voice was strong, tempered by fear for them as he looked to those on each side then returned his gaze to the Suru Master, "nothing, will stop me from finding and bringing her home."

"Brave and noble words," said the Master, "but hollow. We train our brothers to accept reality. The reality of the life they have chosen. The reality of the situation they find themselves in, *and* to act accordingly. You would have been wise to do the same, reedsmith."

"My name is Andar, from the village of Bonstag, and while I still breathe, I-"

"We do not care what your name is." We will test you tomorrow, possibly learn something from you, but in the end you are a common reedsmith who will die in this great hall after witnessing the death of your companions.

The blood drained from Andar's face. He stepped back, then again, spinning about and crouching to scoop up his sword. The dirt floor behind him was empty.

The Master laughed. "You are pathetic, and yet that makes your survival all the more puzzling. We will use you and the others so that our brothers learn of your strengths and your weaknesses. You and they will become part of our training, for you see, we know that fighting skills alone are not enough." His eyes shifted to Doros. "Bring the boy forward."

Andar moved towards his son but the swords of his guards were four walls confining him. Helpless, he watched Doros dragged before the Master who rose to his feet.

"For someone so young, you show great promise. It is unfortunate that you did not realize what we had to offer. Tomorrow you will provide a learning experience for some of our newer recruits. Several will be given the opportunity for their first kill. You should be honoured."

Doros looked to Andar, searching for help. "Father?"

The swords kept Andar at bay. "Let him go! He has done nothing."

"Silence. Take the boy away and bring the woman forward."

White-faced, Dajata stood before him as he addressed her.

"Death is your reward for leading this man here. We have some brothers who have an aversion for killing women, a definite weakness. Tomorrow we shall put one of them to the test and see if he can slit your throat. Remove her."

His eyes turned to the Sleeper who stood ringed by Suru, each spear point held against his flesh. "And you, mutant, offer a rare experience for us. I have heard of your kind, sometimes born to normal parents, killed at birth. Then why are you here?"

Rigersor stared blankly at the Suru Master and shuffled his weight absently from foot to foot.

The old warrior laughed at the vacant stare. "Rumors tell of Sleepers being capable of speech, of reason. It would appear this sad fool can do neither. Nevertheless, he should provide an interesting challenge for some of our more advanced brothers. He will make for fine sport."

"That is the difference between us." Rigersor spoke, his deep voice filling the chamber. He smiled at the look of surprise on the face of the Suru Master. "I kill out of necessity. I believe it makes me the better human."

The Master recovered quickly. "Aren't we the clever beast. We shall see how smug you are tomorrow in the great hall." He dismissed Rigersor with a wave of his hand and turned to Andar.

"You, reedsmith, shall be last. You will watch them die as a consequence for your actions. I am sure that it will also make your last efforts more worthy. You would be wise to honour our ancestors tonight, for tomorrow you journey to join them."

Chapter Fourteen

Dreanna awoke with a frightened start, a hand firmly over her mouth, another on her arm. She tried to scream, but the pressure increased ensuring her silence. A figure leaned in close to whisper in her ear.

"Dreanna, don't struggle. If you wish your freedom, you must do exactly as I say. Do you understand?"

Her eyes stared wildly at him, but some of the tension seeped from her body.

"I'm going to remove my hand. Don't speak, we'll talk later. Follow me. Do you understand?" Rothus slowly relaxed his grip. When she remained quiet, he checked for signs of movement from the others. There were none. Rising, he pulled Dreanna to her feet, away from the fire and into the night.

Neither spoke as they wound their way through the forest, the minutes ticking by without alarm from any of the others. The layer of mist, broken by their strides, swirled upwards in tendrils then settled to the ground again behind them. Dreanna heard something scurry from the trail ahead of them, the brittle undergrowth rustling in the dark. Rothus stopped when they approached a darkened heap directly ahead of them. He lifted a small pack, passed it to her then shouldered a larger one.

"Now it begins," he said. "They will follow us at first light. We must put as much distance between us and them as possible. Are you ready?" She nodded her head, made as if to speak, but he cut her off. "Good, let's go." Without further word he turned and struck off deeper into the forest.

The night was endless. They marched through the dark with reckless speed, trees, shrubs and animals materializing out of the dark and the mist. Without a trail, the rubbery pointed leaves of the reed trees poked and buffeted them. A spiked narlot, disturbed at his feeding, hissed at them, his orange eyes following them as they passed. They neither stopped nor ate, but varied the pace rather than resting. When the first thin rays of morning broke through, Rothus called a halt.

Dreanna collapsed without removing her pack. She lie still, the exhaustion creeping over her until it was a weight pinning her to the ground. There was no way she could continue. Her legs were heavy with fatigue, and even now she could feel sleep reaching out for her, drawing her in. She closed her eyes and exhaled, once, twice, welcoming the pattern. In, out, in, out. Someone grabbed her arm and pulled her back from slumber's abyss.

"Dreanna, there's no time for sleep. You must eat quickly then we start again. It won't take them long to catch up. Eat."

Dazed, she took the reed bread as Rothus finished speaking. Her lips felt thick and wooden. "And then what do we do?"

"I don't know," he answered wearily.

"Why, Rothus, why?" The question was without malice or anger.

His lips tightened as he turned away. "Eat, for soon we move on." He refused to speak to her further. After the short respite Rothus set a pace Dreanna could manage, but as the morning sun rose, she stopped mid stride on the trail.

"Stop!" she said watching Rothus' figure gradually pull ahead.

He halted and turned, his face tired and drawn. "What? What is it?"

"We're travelling north, not east. My home doesn't lie to the north. You know that."

There was impatience in his voice. "Even though we try, we can't outrun them. Our only chance is to lose them. They will be expecting us to go east, back towards your home. That's why we head north."

Dreanna wrestled with his logic, searching his face for some trace of the truth. "Why should I believe you after everything you have done?"

He looked at her without saying anything before lowering his eyes. "Do as you will," he said and wheeled about.

Dreanna watched him stride away until the forest drew him in. She turned and looked back the way they had come and then ahead once more, just catching sight of Rothus as he disappeared among the trees. With a deep breath she followed him.

She struggled with his answer. Was it another trick to lull her into trusting him? Perhaps this whole escape was a ploy to force her to travel more quickly, and the men would simply follow behind them. But she had heard Dashindar was to the west and they were travelling north. She watched him stride ahead, ignoring her. It would be easy to fall behind and elude him. Perhaps he wouldn't follow her. A chill ran through her even as she wiped the sweat from her face. Could she even survive alone? She knew the answer and pushed herself to catch up.

Time crawled by, the monotony and effort of their march through thick undergrowth draining. They passed through an area of waist high plants. The sunburst of short, sharp leaves cut their arms and shredded their tunics when they brushed against them, slowing their progress as they tried to avoid the plants. Hanging chokvines, entwined in the lower branches of the reed trees groped for them, sensing them with hairlike feelers. As they cut their way through the foliage, a clear path lay behind them for their pursuers. By evening they left the vines behind and wound their way through a forest of young reed trees. Rothus stopped and looked down at the black soil, their footprints clearly visible.

"A blind man could follow us. We must find a route where our tracks will be concealed. It won't be easy, for there is none better than Portend." Rothus looked at Dreanna. Though her jaw was set, her face reflected exhaustion and pain. He lifted the pack from her.

"Do we rest here?" she asked, without looking up, her voice a whisper.

"Not yet. I'll carry your pack, but we must keep going."

"No! I can do it." With tired arms she reached for the bundle, but he moved it away, fending her off as she struggled to take it. Dreanna struck him, her tired arms flailing. "I hate you!" Energy spent, her shoulders sagged. "I hate you," she mumbled, almost incoherent from exhaustion.

"Yes, hate me for what I am, for what I did, but don't blame me when my father's men catch us. They were right. You are the weak little child that I found and used."

Her head snapped up. She raised her arm to strike him, but he grabbed it and glared back at her. She pulled free.

"Saving me won't make up for what you've done. It won't right matters. If my father doesn't find us and kill you, I will." She whirled and started off once more leaving him to follow.

He continued harassing and pushing her. They hadn't stopped moving for two days and nights, with little food and no more than a few minutes rest. Rothus found a bare, rocky slope leading down into a ravine and they traversed it carefully, avoiding the sparse vegetation and soil. They travelled the bottom of the dry valley, made their way up the other side and down again into another. The bottom of this one was covered with rock making travel easy as they moved north.

That night, on the verge of collapse, they crawled into a small cave. They crowded together, uncomfortably close, the cool dampness of the cave chilling them. Rothus shoved some reed bread into Dreanna's hands. Both ate silently, without a fire, too numb for speech. When finished, he moved his hand to the hilt of his sword and fell asleep beside Dreanna.

Dreanna felt the warmth of her sleeping wraps and pulled them up tightly around her neck, snuggling deeper into her bed. She didn't feel like rising, content to languish in the warmth and let grandfather start the breakfast this morning. But now she couldn't get comfortable. Doros had done something; put something hard in her bed that poked her in the side. She opened her eyes squinting into the morning sun that warmed her. Framed by the mouth of a cave, the sun lit up the valley floor below and cast the opposite side in morning shadows. She moaned at the pain of stiff muscles and the reality of her surroundings as she struggled to sit up. The ordeal of the last two days bore down on her, but her moans caught in her throat as she fell forward pressing her face to the rocks.

Voices cut the morning air, loud and clear, as if they were right outside the entrance. She raised her head slowly. They were there, directly opposite the cave entrance on the opposite side of the ravine. She ducked down again and after a few minutes the voices became fainter. Dreanna crawled to the lip of the entrance and eased her head outside. They were past the cave now, Portend slightly ahead of the rest, moving deliberately down the valley. She turned back to Rothus, shaking him awake, her hand over his mouth.

"They've found us," her whisper harsh as she pointed in their direction.

Rothus shook free of sleep and crawled to the entrance. He watched them for a moment. "Quickly, gather your pack. We must leave now. If they were able to follow us here, soon they won't find a trace of our passing ahead and will double back."

At the cave entrance they eased forward. Looking left, Rothus saw they were some distance past them now and on the ravine bottom. He glanced to the right and cursed quietly. The floor ran straight and true for as far as he could see.

"We go now, before they turn about. Up the side is our only hope," he said. "Try to move from tree to tree, rock to rock to stay out of sight. Ready?"

Dreanna nodded in reply.

"Let's go," he said and surged out of the cave entrance.

They scrambled up the ravine side, looking over their shoulders. Half way up the side they saw Portend stop. After some discussion and hand pointing, he began to travel back up the valley floor towards them. Dreanna and Rothus looked at each other and climbed faster, expecting the shout of discovery any minute.

It came when they had almost reached the crest. Looking down, Dreanna saw them bound forward, shouts of victory on their lips. She redoubled her efforts to gain the top, close on the heels of Rothus. They broke the crest and to their surprise found a wide, well trodden path.

"Drop your pack, Dreanna." She did so without question. "Run. We've got to put some distance between us and them. Find somewhere to make a stand." He pushed her forward and she sprinted ahead.

The night's sleep had helped revive her and without the weight of the pack her feet flew over the path. Encumbered by the supplies and his weapons Rothus was hard pressed to keep up with her. They ran, concentrating on the path beneath their feet and the bend ahead. There were shouts behind them. Risking a backwards glance, Dreanna saw that the men had gained the crest and begun pursuit. She was tiring, her pace easing up as she sucked in air. The gap between them and their pursuers was slowly closing, but the bend in the trail was getting nearer. Rothus pulled up beside her.

"I'm going ahead. Try to round the bend and prepare a defence."

Dreanna nodded her head, too tired to reply. She watched Rothus pull ahead, concentrating on him to shut out the pain that stabbed at her side. As he drew away, her fear at being left alone grew. She glanced back. The men had gained greatly on her. She could see their faces contorted with strain. Hear their heavy breathing and the bounce of weapons against pounding thighs. Dreanna ran faster, driving her feet against the ground. Her foot caught and she pitched forward. She fought for her balance, taking short choppy steps, but her momentum was broken and it took valuable seconds for her tired legs to start again. Behind her they raised a shout at the sight of her staggering. She had to look and saw their mouths drawn back as they gulped air, sweat streaking their faces. She turned around and Rothus was gone. He had reached the bend.

Tears ran down her face. She no longer thought nor felt anything. The world ceased to exist except for the hazy image of the path ahead of her. Even the shouts of those behind her became muffled and distant. She was at the bend. Turned the corner.

Hideous and huge, the Stomuant towered over her. Half-formed hands, rough and flaked, clutched her, dangling her helplessly. The creature's breath from a blackened mouth caused her to gag as the lumped and crusted face swung close to inspect his catch. Then Dreanna's scream died on her lips as the blow from the Stomuant jarred her head, spinning her into oblivion.

Chapter Fifteen

Andar sat on the thin sleeping mat, his back against a wall. His hands and feet were bound. The stench of vomit emanated from a bucket in the corner. Overwhelmed by the events he sat defeated, arms loose by his sides, his eyes unfocused. He closed them and the battered face of Doros appeared, calling to him for help. *And I can do nothing. Tomorrow they will kill my son, and I can do nothing.* Andar wiped at the tear that ran down his cheek, then crawled to the bucket and vomited again.

He knew it was his fault; that they would kill his son. That he would never know what happened to his daughter. A shudder racked his body and he buried his face in his hands. *I should have stayed in Bonstag and protected her. I should have never left.* But he had. The Suru Master had been right, for there was always a consequence.

Andar raised his head and looked toward the door as he sensed someone's presence. He identified the aura, but little else, for the Suru Master's defense was too strong to be penetrated. The door swung open and he entered the room, wrinkling his nose at the pungent odour of vomit and sweat.

"From this display it is hard to believe you are the same man who killed two of ours," he said, disdain in his voice as he stepped closer to Andar.

Andar looked up with empty eyes. "I fought with the first one in the water with... my daughter there to help. The second attacked me in the rains, and Rothus killed him with his bow." He closed his eyes wearily. "I'm no warrior."

"Yet somehow you found your way here, no small feat. And you were able to win the loyalty of that excuse for a human." The Master walked the small room as he gathered his thoughts. "There are things about you reedsmith that impress, although from your state at this moment, no one would agree. Tomorrow we will watch and learn of them. Beyond that you are of little use to us, for I believe you to be beyond change. Your son could be another matter. These traits you possess, whatever they are, I believe are also present in him. There is the same strength and conviction that we saw in you earlier, before your present, pitiful condition. I believe he has the potential to become one of us. We only need to shape and mould him."

Andar looked at the Master, his eyes no longer empty as anger gave him strength. "Become one of you? He has seen what you are, what you do. He will never listen to your lies and posturing. I have raised him to know better."

The old Suru stopped in front of Andar. "Then you have a choice. Tomorrow you die, but I offer you the chance to save your son. Tell him to say that he has seen our skills and the brotherhood that binds us together. Tell him to plead with us for a second chance. That he wants to live. We will spare his life. Let him think that he will be fooling us. Eventually he will see the wisdom of our way of life and change. But make no mistake, reedsmith, if you do this, he will become one of us."

Andar struggled to his feet and stood facing the Suru Master. "You would have me help you destroy my son?" He hopped awkwardly towards the Master who stepped back. Hidden doors sprang open and two Suru stepped into the room, spears levelled at Andar. The Suru Master motioned for the two guards to step back and he approached Andar once more.

"I would have you save your son's life. Don't be a fool. Don't let your emotions rule, for that can be deadly. It can cost you your life, or more to the point, that of your son. If you wish to save him, send word to me and I will have him brought to you." He held Andar's glare then turned and strode from the room. The two Suru backed up slowly and disappeared, closing the doors behind them.

Andar sank to the floor and buried his head in his arms.

The Reedsmith of Zendar

Four guards closed tightly around Andar and escorted him. Silence seized the great hall as he stepped inside. The yellow flickering glow of torches lit the cavernous room where the Suru sat, tier upon tier, peering down from on high to the narrow, earthen court below. A sea of undulating green, their sheer numbers shook his courage. Exhausted from the previous night, he tightened the wall of his aura, blocking out the threats and noise and bloodlust he sensed, and found a place of calm. He clung to it, shoring up the walls further by envisioning Katrena's face and feeling her presence.

Andar struggled to slow his breathing, and stay centered, for the Suru Master had been right. Today he must not let his emotions rule his actions. His life and those of his children depended upon it. Last night he had made his decision and now clung to it knowing it was the only one he could live or die with. The Suru Master looked down from the dais and spoke.

"Your decision is a foolish one, reedsmith. Perhaps you were incapable of even making one, but the result is the same. Your fate and that of your companions is of your choosing." The Master looked to a Suru who stood nearby. "Bring in the others."

Andar turned and watched as Doros, Dajata and Rigersor were brought in separately and led to stand beside Andar in front of the dais. Beside him Doros smiled a quick weak smile at his father. Andar sensed his state of near collapse and sent a quick stroke of encouragement through his son's weak aura. Doros reacted, pulling himself upright and flashing a smile in return to Andar.

"Very touching, reed smith, but a wasted effort, for your son is about to die for the benefit of the Suru. Take the boy center court-"

"No," shouted Andar, stepping towards the dais. The swords of the four Suru near him leapt from their sheaths. Ignoring them, Andar shouted at the Suru Master as he put his desperate plan into effect.

"I challenge the Suru to defend their way of life. I offer a challenge that you must accept."

All eyes in the great room focused on him.

"The very foundation for your existence is your training and skill in the arts of stealth and death. I challenge any one of your brothers to do battle with me. If I win, you set me and my companions free. If the third brother you have sent after my daughter is successful, she is released to me. If he is not, you will not send another after her."

The Master sat listening, spellbound by the bold challenge. At last he smiled grimly at Andar. "I knew you must be a resourceful, clever man. Already we learn more about you and why you have survived. But you have not thought this through. We have no reason to accept your challenge. We have nothing to gain from it." He turned back to those that guarded Doros. "Take the boy to center court."

"But you do!" Andar's voice was loud, feigning confidence as he spoke directly to the mass of warriors. "You have much to lose. You have already lost respect among yourselves. I found my way here to your sacred stronghold. My son has penetrated your defenses leaving you unaware that he had done so. This woman did not fear you enough to refuse to lead me here. And now your Master refuses to pit your best against a lowly reedsmith. By doing so, he condemns and makes a mockery out of everything that you have trained for and believe in. Does he have such little faith in the brotherhood that he will not risk the reputation of the mighty Suru against one outsider?" Andar turned and looked once more at the Master as did all of the assemblage, tier upon tier.

The elderly warrior stood silently upon the dais, fighting to keep his anger under control. He smiled coldly. "There is a power about you, reedsmith. Call it magic, call it will." He raised his face and looked over the throng of warriors who awaited his words. He returned his gaze to Andar. "So be it. The Suru accept."

The tumultuous roar that filled the stronghold shook Andar to his core.

Chapter Sixteen

Shouts of approval rang down from above as Doros clutched his father's arm, panic in his voice.

"Father, you can't do this. Since I've been here, I have seen them do things that I would not have thought possible. They'll kill you!"

Andar looked into Doros' eyes, bright with terror and forced a smile as he fought to hide his own fear. He placed his hands on his son's shoulders, struggling to ignore the chanting which grew louder by the moment.

"This way we have a chance, if only a small one."

The Suru Master raised his arm, calling for silence. The crowded hall settled quickly, all eyes upon the old warrior.

"So it shall be, reedsmith," he said, lingering traces of anger filling the quiet void. He raised his voice. "Verdazan!"

Andar watched a figure in the front row bound lightly over the knee wall and approach the Master. His movements were fluid, muscles bunching and rolling smoothly beneath the green garb. The raw boned assassin was a hand shorter than Andar, but heavier. Still chafed by the way he had been tricked into accepting the challenge, the Suru Master glared at Andar, then spoke to the Suru who turned to face Andar.

"To honour your courage and skill, you may choose the weapon," Verdzan said.

The courtesy did little to hide the menace in his voice. The warrior's pale blue eyes studied Andar as he waited for an answer.

"Swords," Andar said quietly.

The faintest trace of a smile touched the Suru's lips. Andar saw the reaction, the seeds of doubt sown.

"Bring his sword," commanded the Master.

While Andar waited, he whispered to Doros, knowing his words were pointless, but unable to stay silent. "If things do not turn out…well, act immediately. Make for the doors behind me."

Before Doros could reply, Andar accepted his sword and turned to face the Suru who stood relaxed, the tip of his sword resting on the earthen floor as he watched Andar. The warrior's calm, powerful presence weakened Andar's resolve more as he approached the man. A murmur went up when he drew the sword and the assemblage saw the purple blade.

"And so we learn further of you, reedsmith," said the Suru Master.

Andar cast the sheath aside and loosened his nervous grip on his sword. It was the one weapon that he had mastered above all. Gartonnar had called him a natural, for when he fought, it would become an extension of him. He knew it must be so today if he was to survive. The assassin's blade came up and they circled each other.

He sidestepped to the left, forcing the Suru to respond, trying to judge the man's movements. If he could last but a few moments with the Suru in the heat of battle when everything moved too quickly for thought, his instincts would take over and he would have a chance. The assassin edged closer, the long thin blade drifting in lazy circles and sweeps in front of Andar. Then the Suru leapt forward and their blades met in a flurry of strokes and parries that were invisible to the eye. Six, eight, a dozen ringing contacts and Andar ceased to think . Everyone disappeared as the rhythm of sword and body became one.

Andar breathed easily, attacking and defending deftly with quick parries. He turned his adversary's blade aside at the last moment, twisted his body, and the point of the Suru's blade impaled empty space. He beat the man's sword aside, lunged smoothly, expected the counter and rolled with the block. He whirled his sword's tip in a tight circle over the man's blade, slashed at the warrior's throat, then leapt free of the new assault and began his attack again.

Crouched on the ground, Doros watched, his heart racing as his father battled like never before. Rigersor solemnly watched the human, who had saved his life, fight again for his freedom. And from the side, Dajata watched the man who had saved her life, who had killed her father, who had made her feel free and new while still a captive.

Andar's tanned skin glistened in the torch light as his feet shuffled and danced across the packed earth. Darker, sweat-stained blotches marked the green garment of the Suru as he tirelessly attacked and counter attacked. Andar swung his blade quicker. Annoyance replaced the easy rhythm of his exertion. The Suru's blade slipped past his guard and only a last minute twist of his torso prevented the slash from being lethal. A murmur rose from those in the tiers as the Suru pressed the attack. Andar blocked two more slashes then stepped back pressing his hand to the wound which bled profusely. Sensing victory, the Suru renewed his assault.

Andar retreated, absorbing the blows. The blood ran down his thigh, his footing becoming treacherous. The Suru backed away, letting the wound do its work. Andar rushed him. There could be no letting up now. He leapt and lunged and whirled his blade and leapt again. He deflected a lunge, stepped close and smashed his fist against the warrior's jaw. The Suru caught Andar in the arm then backpedaled, but Andar drove forward, stepping on the Suru's leading foot. The Suru staggered and Andar threw all his weight into a blow that struck his sword guard. The weapon spun from the Suru's hand. Andar's blade whirled overhead, stopping at the top of its arc, his eyes locked on the Suru. The warrior's pale blue eyes were without emotion as he waited for death. In the silence, time seemed to stand still as Andar tensed his sword arm for the final blow.

"No Father!"

The cry stalled the pounding blood lust then another voice screamed at him.

"Kill him! Kill him!"

The spark flamed into a roar and his blade streaked downwards, but someone slammed into him knocking him sideways. Andar's arm shook, his sensibilities lost. He looked to his sword, the tip embedded in the earth, then to his son who struggled to his feet beside him. The Suru stared at both of them as Doros took his father's arm and guided him to the ground where he sat in a daze.

"You have won your freedom, reedsmith, and that of the others."

The hall and those watching came back into focus. As he searched for the Suru Master, his eyes passed Dajata who gave a twisted smile of triumph.

The Master turned to the defeated warrior who stood with his head bowed. "Verdezan, you have no place here. Leave us now."

The warrior raised his head and locked eyes with him then his stare moved from Andar to Doros. He stooped, retrieved his sword and offered it to Andar who pushed it wearily away. Verdazan's face whitened as he turned to Doros. He bowed to him then walked towards the doors.

"I believe you to be a man of honour," said the Master. "Your word, that our stronghold, its secrets and location are not revealed to anyone. You must ensure this, not only for yourself, but for the others as well."

Andar's head swam as Doros helped him to his feet. He shook it to chase away the dizziness before looking to the Stone Sleeper who nodded. Dajata held his eyes but didn't acknowledge his unspoken question. Andar looked back at the Suru Master. "You have my word. For all of us."

"So it shall be," said the Master. "We received word last night. Your daughter will not arrive here." You leave within the hour."

Andar stared at him. "I have given you my word, *our word*, never-"

"And you have mine. "I do not know what has happened to your daughter." He rose from his chair. "Leave now, reedsmith. "You have earned our respect with your courage and skill. We wish you long life. Today no Suru shall cause you harm. However, this is the brotherhood of the Suru, bound by tradition. It would be unwise to return, ever again." He descended the dais and walked towards the exit. The tiers of warriors began filing out, their voices subdued, and soon the four were left alone in the quiet of the great hall.

Chapter Seventeen

As they left the last of the Suru buildings behind, Doros was unable to take his eyes from the broad gray back of the Stone Sleeper who trod the path in front of him. Dense with bulky muscle and covered by thick skin, the Sleeper created a wall blocking Doros' view, making him feel small. Coarse hair, matted and unkempt, hung stiffly over the non-existent neck. Doros tried to pace himself with the massive thighs, but found it impossible to match the strides of the Sleeper.

Andar walked behind Dajata, his hand held to his bandaged side struggling to keep up to the others. Although the healing power of the reed salve would do its work, the blood loss had left him weak. Rest was what he needed to end the tugging on the edges of the cut so that it might heal. Through the pain he reconsidered the course of action he had planned for them. He felt the Sleeper would agree to his request. Doros would fight the decision but see the importance of returning to Lanos. Dajata would be the problem. Looking up he saw that Rigersor and Doros had paused, waiting for the others. Andar reached them and eased to the ground, indicating that the others should do the same.

"Rigersor, I have need of your service," Andar said, eyeing the heavy features of the Stone Sleeper.

The black eyes studied him and he nodded in acknowledgement before he spoke. "You have saved my life twice. I will do whatever your wish, or die trying." His deep voice made it sound like a simple statement, without the dramatic overtones it might have held.

Andar nodded sensing that with him few words were needed or would be offered. He turned to his son. "Doros, what you've done makes me very proud. Perhaps I should have let you accompany me but it was fortunate that you stayed with Grandfather and that you were able to bring me knowledge of Dreanna's capture. Again, you must carry a message, this time back to your grandfather." Andar held up his hand as Doros began to object. "I know that you would rather stay here but someone must tell Lanos what transpires. He must know that you have found me, that I am well, and that we know where Dreanna is being taken." Doros stared sullenly at his father. "But there is more, Doros. Someone must return home, must watch and try to discover what is happening. Why are our lands so important? Perhaps the town council will need to be informed. It will be dangerous spying on those who have overtaken our home, but I now know that you're equal to the task."

"What you say is true." Embarrassed, he looked at the ground then back to Andar. "I don't know if I can find my way back to Kempa. It all happened so quickly."

"Rigersor will guide you."

Doros was on his feet, pleading. "You're wounded. You're going to face the people who kidnapped Dreanna. He..." and Dorus motioned self-consciously towards the Sleeper, "must go with you. Let the woman guide me back to Kempa."

"No," Andar said quietly. "You must reach Kempa safely, and knowing what she knows now, I would not trust her with your company." He saw the disdain and loathing on Dajata's face, but she remained silent. "Also, two warriors are safer than one. Dajata will stay with me until-"

"No! No! You promise release at nearest village." She scrambled to her feet and charged towards him, her brown eyes fuming. "You killer. I never should believe you. I was right. Killer. Assassin!" She spun around and stalked to a tree where she stood with folded arms, her stare hateful. Andar watched her then turned back to the others.

"She will stay with me as we move north towards the path the Suru spoke of. If we follow it to the west we should come to a village in three or four days. There I'll release her and continue on to Dashindar."

"Liar." Her lips were twisted in a contemptuous smile. "You are liar.

Even they not believe you," she said.

Rigersor looked from Dajata to Andar and spoke. "I will do as you wish, but you will be left to face your enemies alone."

"Yes," said Doros, his voice earnest. "You need someone, someone to help you."

"Gartonnar told me before he took of the Flowers of Dallipon that there is always a choice. This is the one I've chosen. I know where Dreanna is headed. I know who did this." Andar struggled to his feet, wincing from his wound. "Come now, we must start. There are still several hours of travelling time and the rains are getting closer every day. You must get to Kempa before they begin."

Rigersor rose and stood silently. Dajata stood resolutely by the tree, glaring at Andar as Doros approached his father. There was a frightened weakness in his face as his eyes searched Andar's.

"Is it true? Did you kill her Father?"

Andar averted his eyes, but finally looked at his son's pleading face. In it he saw the answer his son waited for, the answer he could not give.

"Yes," he said his voice barely audible.

"Why, Father? Why?"

"I had no choice, Doros." His words were wooden and again he heard Gartonnar say, "There is always a choice." Andar saw that his son

Doros continued to search his face, trying to accept the meaningless answer. "And today if I hadn't stopped you?"

"Things have happened, things that have changed me. I should have stopped myself, but I couldn't. I'm the same, but different. What I feel at times, I..." He stared into Doros' frightened eyes. "Don't worry Doros, soon this madness will pass."

Doros swallowed and blinked away tears then put his hand on his father's shoulder. He managed a smile. "I know you, Father. I know who you are." The two stood for a long moment then Andar hugged Doros feeling the strength in the young arms.

"Now my young warrior, you must go. I'm sure that grandfather and you will know what to do."

"Good-bye, Father," Doros mumbled and quickly turned away to follow Rigersor.

Andar watched the two disappear from sight then shuffled to Dajata.

"You can't travel to Kempa," he said. "Not now. With your help my wound will heal sooner. I need you to carry the supplies and assist me. I said that I would set you free at the nearest village after we found the Suru. This I will do. Nothing has changed."

"Something changed. You killed my Father. That is the change." She stalked to him, her face red with anger. "You do anything to get what you want. Kill me if it helps you. I hate you!" She leapt towards him and struck his face and chest with her fists. Andar staggered backwards, but she pressed the attack. He blocked her blows, each becoming weaker until her head fell forward against his chest, large sobs wracking her body. Ignoring the pain in his side, Andar put his hands on her shoulders. She shook free, and shoved his hands away. Tears stained her face, but she no longer cried.

"Do what you want," she said drawing herself upright, thrusting her face close to his. "But not pretend concern for me."

Andar's eyes lingered on her, but she held her stance, shoulders back, her eyes challenging him. He picked up his pack slowly and put it in her arms.

"Until I'm able, you'll carry the pack. We travel north. Lead the way."

As he fell in behind her, Andar checked the wound in his side. It had started bleeding again.

Part Three

Beyond the Northern Mountains

Chapter One

In the hours they had travelled since leaving the others, the pain in Andar's side had numbed his senses. The cloth he held to the wound was soaked with blood. He stumbled once more over a tree root, new pain radiating out from his side. Ahead of him, and getting further away all the time, Dajata was little more than a blur of colour in a landscape of green. As her shape began to waver and become unfocused in the dying light, he called to her.

"We spend the night here. Prepare a fire and a meal while I rest."

Dajata retraced her steps and dropped the pack at his feet. "Yes, Master," she said, her voice without emotion. She left the path in search of wood for a fire.

Andar eased to the ground and struggling with one hand pulled a gourd and his extra wrap from the pack. He poured some water over the blood soaked cloth that he still held pressed to his side. After the congealed blood loosened he eased the cloth from the wound. He cleaned it with more water and inspected it. It still bled, but the reed salve had prevented any infection and the outside edges of the wound were starting to heal. If he rested for a few days, it would heal much quicker, but all he could think about was getting to Dashindar. Andar held the spare wrap to the wound, closed his eyes and leaned back against the tree trunk.

Noises filtered through the heavy stupor that blanketed him. Andar's head lolled and he stared at a blurred, red-yellow haze that floated before him in the dark. The fire came slowly into focus as he realized that he had fallen asleep. He couldn't see Dajata anywhere and jerked upright, pulling at his wound and grunting in pain. Movement to his right verified her presence and he leaned back, eyes closed. He heard the pad of her footsteps. She stood in front of him, holding some reed bread and the dried, stringy meat of netic in a bowl.

"My Master awakes. Would it please him to eat now?" The anger of earlier was gone. She stared sullenly over his head.

"I'll eat now," he said. "Don't call me master."

She lowered her gaze until her eyes met his. "You beat me if I not stop, Master?" She knelt and placed the food beside him on the ground. "You like beat me now, Master, before eat?" Her voice rose sharply as she lunged sideways and grabbed a thin reed stalk. "Here, do now. Beat me now!" She pushed the reed into his hands and threw herself across his legs. "Do it. Beat me!"

Andar tried to push her from his lap, but she clung fiercely to his harness. The pain from his wound flared.

"Hit me. I should be beaten."

"Stop it. Get away from me." He shoved her roughly, but she pulled and threw herself against him once more, her shoulder driving into his side. Andar cried out in pain and angrily raised the reed overhead as he looked at her. She was beyond reason, the madness in her eyes frightening as she pushed her face near his. He raised the reed higher.

"You teach me be good. I have been poor daughter. Beat me!"

The words struck him, breaking the spell. He lowered the reed and cast it aside. The madness left her and there was nothing left but the sad realization of what had happened. She lowered her head onto his lap, sobs shaking her shoulders as she curled up and held onto his legs. Andar reached out and put his hand on her shoulder. She didn't flinch or draw away and soon her tears ran down his leg. He stroked her hair and stared at the night sky. After a time, Dajata rose and left him. The next morning she was no longer sullen and didn't address him as master, but she spoke only out of necessity and avoided looking at him.

The Reedsmith of Zendar

Mid-morning of the third day since their release from the Suru they travelled a winding trail that steadily lead them to the North. Andar was still unsettled. He had treated her no differently than had Joshura, justifing his behavior because he needed her. Needed her still, if only for a short time, until he healed. Perhaps to ease his own conscience, he asked her to walk with him rather than lead the way.

"What will you do when we reach the village?" he asked.

She shrugged her shoulders, eyes focused on the trail. "Joshura is dead, I am free. He was terrible man, but was my father. I knew nothing else." Her voice was tired and sad. "I knew it wasn't right, but you not know what he like. I could not escape. No one else. Nothing to do but accept. Maybe I stay in this village. Maybe someone needs a travelling companion. I not know what happens, no more than you."

He thought about what she said. Finally he offered, "When I return this way with my daughter, I'll stop at the village. If you're there I'll guide you east."

"You forget who guides," she said. Is not a guide I need." She paused for a moment, then spoke, choosing her words carefully. "I think you not return. You think as father should, but your actions... not always good. You are danger to others and to you. I not think you return."

"You haven't had a partner and children. I lost my wife and I am in danger of losing my daughter. I won't let that happen. Her life is worth the risks I take, any methods I use," he said, erasing the doubts he felt earlier. "

"You right." Her voice was melancholy. "I not have a family like you. I not remember my mother. No brothers or sisters. Only father." She was silent for a spell as they walked. "There good...is good in you, but the journey changes you. If you save daughter...your daughter, I hope she finds you same. Same father she knew."

As they walked Andar thought about what Dajata said. He remembered his conversation with Doros. 'I am the same, but I am different. Things have happened, things that have changed me.' In the short time that this woman had known him, she too had seen differences in him.

The afternoon meal was short with little conversation. On the path again, Dajata looked remorsefully at Andar's side. When he had inspected it during their stop, she saw that it had broken open again near the front where her shoulder had struck him. It bled more today and he had slowed their pace.

As she glanced up, Dajata saw a malbar as it wheeled about and dove between two reed trees ahead of them. A second and a third soared skywards from where the first had disappeared. They righted themselves and plunged again towards the earth as other rose.

Andar grimaced in pain as he pulled his sword and cautiously advanced. When they cleared the trees, both saw an elderly man fighting vainly against the many malbar that swooped at their prey. Two of the winged creatures lay dead at his feet, victims of the double bladed staff that he wielded. He swung awkwardly at another that sped towards him, missing the creature who raked him with its talons before winging skywards. The old man swung again and again, his arms slowing as he tired. The malbar tightened their circle, sensing victory. Then one of them slammed into the man's back, the fangs finding their mark.

Andar surged forward, clutching his side, his limping run carrying him out into the open. He yelled as he ran, distracting the creatures who as one wheeled about and sped towards him. He ran doggedly towards the old man, ignoring the approaching malbar. His sword clove in two the malbar that still clung to the back of its victim. The old man rolled onto his side and Andar's eyes momentarily met his as he straddled his body.

"Stay down," Andar said, and then the rest of the malbar were upon him.

From the trees Dajata watched in horror and awe. He had leapt to the old man's aid without a warning shout to her. He was suddenly gone, racing to protect a stranger. She saw him straddle the fellow and turn to face the overwhelming odds. Then she realized the truth of her words was being borne out. One moment he was cruel and malicious, using others to suit his purpose, and the next moment he was throwing his life away for an old man whom she was sure he could not know. She watched spellbound the one sided battle. The fool was going to get himself killed.

Andar slashed and turned, slashed and turned in an effort to keep them at bay. Their attack was constant but predictable as they swooped again and again at his head and shoulders.

"Behind you," and he turned at the last moment to the old man's shout. His blade streaked across his body, severing the head of the malbar. It tumbled from the body, the carcass slamming into Andar, momentarily jarring him. He felt the bite of teeth on his shoulder and swung his sword over and down, raking the creature off. Above and to his right he saw another dangerously close and whirled his sword up once more to cut it down. Pain shot up his leg as the creature he had knocked from his shoulder fastened its jaws in his calf. His blade sliced into the grotesque face, lifting the top of its head off. Andar struck again at the jaws still embedded in his leg. The remains of the head and body fell away leaving teeth protruding from his flesh.

The malbar soared upwards to begin their diving attack once more as Andar clasped his side. Blood flowed freely from the reopened wound. He saw that the old man had gone still as the poison raced through his system. And then the remaining four dove at him. He drew his breath and grasped the hilt of his sword with both hands. The two on the right were close together, one beside the other. He surged upwards and struck across them in an attempt to disable the two with one cut. Both staggered from the blow and Andar threw himself to the ground to dodge the remaining two behind him. One missed and soared skywards, but the other slammed into him, fastening itself to his back with its claws. Andar struggled to his knees and grabbed his sword with both hands again as, wings flapping, the malbar sank its teeth into him. Andar bowed his head and heaved the sword up and over his shoulder. It struck home and the creature shuddered and went still, but his sword fell from his hands. Andar struggled to rise beneath the weight of the dead malbar, its claws still embedded in his back.

Two disabled creatures were crawling towards him, while above, the last malbar began its swooping dive. Andar pulled a foot under him, but the ground swirled around him and he collapsed as the poison took effect. His eyes began to close, but for a brief moment, he saw a pair of long brown legs planted before him.

Dajata held the twin bladed staff in trembling hands, her breath coming in nervous swells. There was no time to fend off the two crawling creatures for the airborne malbar was almost upon her. With the butt of the staff on the ground, she lined up the blade as the creature hurtled closer. It struck the point and she saw the curved blade pierce the broad chest. The force knocked her backwards loosening her grip, but she held on as the malbar jerked and spasmed. It pulled and clawed its way down the staff towards her. Horrified she threw the staff from her.

Scuffling noise at her feet drew her eyes. One of the wounded creatures reached for her foot with skinny, hooked claws. Dajata stumbled back, staggering and tripping over another carcass. The two creatures kept coming, oozing trails of blood behind them. Andar's sword was in her hands and she was slashing and chopping at the writhing forms. Finally all was still. Splattered in the greenish black blood, she was violently ill.

Chapter Two

Dajata staggered to her feet, her eyes wild as she gaped at the carnage. She choked back a cry when she saw that the malbar was still fastened to Andar's back, the creature's split head oozing blood. Her body trembled from the battle, but she pushed the hair out of her face and with his sword still clutched in her hand, knelt beside him. Although he still breathed, the puffiness had started in his face and hands. She bit her lip in fear, for she knew it might already be too late. Dajata dropped the sword and pulled his dagger from its sheath. Carefully she slipped the blade under one of the claws and pried at a talon. The hooked tip tore through his skin creating a small pool of blood that sat on his back. Andar groaned quietly as she did another, then another, until finally it was done, and she pushed the creature off of him with the blade of the dagger. Dajata pulled the broken teeth from his leg then inspected his face once more.

The swelling was getting worse. She knew he needed the salve, and quickly if there was to be any hope of survival. Dajata grabbed the pouch from his side then cursed as she glanced towards the trees where they had left their supplies. *The water gourds.* She sprang to her feet and ran hard, her new muscles propelling her across the dried grass. At the pack, she tore it open, snatched up a gourd and raced back, leaping over the carcasses when she reached Andar. Her eyes flicked towards the old man who groaned softly. He lay crumpled on his side, the stiff grass pushed against his wrinkled face. *He will have to wait. He has only been bitten once.* She knelt, then cursed, leapt up again and ran back to the supplies for a drinking cup in which to mix the paste. *More time wasted!* She found one, ran back and threw herself to the ground beside him. She tipped some of the powder into the cup, added water then mixed it with her fingers until she had a dull, yellowish liquid. Dajata placed it on the ground and struggled as she rolled Andar onto his back. She grabbed his neck and harness, pulling him into a sitting position. His head fell forward as she fought to hold him with one arm while she reached across him for the cup. It lay on its side, the liquid seeping through the crumpled grass into the dry soil.

"No!" Dajata lunged towards the cup, letting him fall back. She snatched it up, shook more powder into the cup and mixed it with water. She placed the cup carefully and wrestled Andar upright once more. His eyes were open but unfocused, his jaw already stiffening so that she had to pry it open with her fingers. Too quickly she attempted to pour the liquid into his mouth. Much of it ran down his neck and chest.

"No, no! Drink!" She tilted his head back and slowly poured the mixture in, a little at a time, rubbing his throat, waiting for his mouth to empty.

Her shouting stirred the old man who slowly turned his head in her direction. Dajata looked at him. Through glassy eyes he watched her. His hand motioned feebly and awkwardly and he pursed his lips, trying to speak. His eyes implored her for the cup. She had forced most of the liquid down Andar. *Is it enough?* She looked at Andar, then back to the old man. His eyes begged her. Dajata added powder to the cup, mixed some more and waddled on her knees to the old man's side. She propped him up, put the cup to his mouth, and he drained it with her help. Wet eyes glistened in gratitude and Dajata forced a smile as she patted his boney shoulder.

She scuttled back to Andar and for the first time saw the wash of blood from the wound in his side. She put her hand over it and he moaned again. *Now you are going to bleed to death?* She inspected the bites. They were already red and inflamed. Dajata checked the remaining salve powder. There wasn't much left. The blood continued to seep slowly past her hand. She looked around for something to use to stop the bleeding, but there was nothing. With her free hand, she pulled the strip of material from her breasts. Kneeling on the edge of the cloth and holding it with her teeth, she cut off a piece, folded and pressed it to the wound, then bound it to his waist with the remainder of the wrap. She emptied the last of the powder from the pouch, mixed it to a paste, and pressed it into the rest of the wounds. Returning to the old man she did the same.

Dajata wiped her brow and glanced skywards at the swollen sun. She looked to the shade of the trees, then at the bodies littering the ground. Soon the stench of the malbar would become unbearable. She dragged two of the carcasses out of the way to clear a path to their supplies. The sweat rolled down her face and chest as she grabbed Andar's wrists and pulled against his dead weight. He barely moved. She heaved again, leaning back and driving with her legs. This time, he slid across the dry grass. She dragged him until she couldn't continue, dropped his arms and sat exhausted at his head.

"Do not make easy for me. Do not help." She pulled some grass and threw it at him. "Your fault, stupid Master." Dajata stared at his swollen face then bit her lip as she looked away. *Stupid Master.* She climbed to her feet, grabbed his wrists, leaned back and pulled. After three sessions she reached the shade of the trees. She let his arms drop, fell on the grass beside him and lay panting, her body shining with sweat despite the shade. Dajata found the other water gourd in the pack and drank greedily. She looked at Andar and then back to the open field. *Now the old man.*

Dajata was surprised to find his eyes open and alert. Some of the glaze had disappeared, but although his lips moved attempting speech, he couldn't manage it. His arms and legs moved weakly as he lay. The old man's gaunt frame changed her mind. She eased him into a sitting position then wrapped her arms around his chest and with surprisingly little difficulty dragged him to his feet. She pulled his closest arm over her shoulder and wrapped one of her own around his waist. Although wobbly, his knees were locked and he was able to stand with her help.

"All right," she said, pleased. "Now we walk to the trees." Dajata took a pace forward. His legs didn't move. "Come on, try," she said, attempting to pull him forward with the arm about his waist. His toes dragged in the dirt and he began to fall forward. She struggled to regain their balance. "Come on," she demanded, glaring at him. His weathered face struggled to keep its composure. Dajata closed her eyes. "It is all right. Not your fault," she said. She started to lower him to the ground, but stopped. *You are not heavy.* She released his arm, ducked low in front of him, and let him fall across her shoulders. She staggered, but fought with shaky thighs to stand upright, balancing him carefully before she started walking.

The grass swished under her feet, carrying the old man sending a shiver of satisfaction and energy racing through her. Dajata reached the trees and lowered him to the ground. She sat panting for a moment, then settled the old man and checked the sky once more. She looked at Andar. "I must get wood to light fire. Will be a long night."

Dajata sat by the fire. She fed it constantly, worried that the carcasses of the malbar might attract other animals. Andar's condition had worsened. The swelling continued and he was feverish as night approached. Sweat beaded his swollen face and his limbs had begun to stiffen. She fretted over him, bathed his face with the little water they had, but felt helpless against the poison coursing through his body. She doubted that he would last the night. Carefully she dabbed water on his swollen tongue which had begun to protrude from his mouth. *Stupid Master. Why had he risked his life and his journey to save his daughter for this old man?*

"You must live, stupid Master," she said crossing her arms. "You promised to take me to village." She piled more wood on the fire and pulled Andar's sword closer to her before she looked back at him. "You not want to be liar again. She curled up beside him as the mist swirled about them. "*Stupid Master.*"

Chapter Three

Dajata awoke, the cool dampness of the morning lingering in the shadows under the reed trees. She rose from Andar's side. Somehow he was still alive, though his whole body was swollen, the fever worse. Dajata looked away from him and closed her eyes.

"If you wish to see him live, you must administer more of the salve."

The quiet voice startled her and she whirled around. The old man sat opposite the remains of the fire. Although his white hair was a swirled yetcher's nest, his face haggard, he looked at her through clear eyes. During the night she had forgotten about him. She stared now, open mouthed.

"You must get more of the salve into him if he is to survive," he said.

"You are better."

"I have been bitten many times before. My body can deal with the poison better than most. I'm still weak, but I'll live, thanks to you." He shifted his gaze to where Andar lay. "And thanks to him." His eyes moved back to Dajata. "Quickly, mix some more salve and I will help you. We must try to save this man of yours."

"He is not...we..." She stammered but stopped abruptly as she realized the truth. "There is no more salve."

The old man stared at her then tried to stand. "Here, on my harness. There is plenty in my pouch. Come on girl, help me get up. There'll be plenty of time for introductions later."

Already tired from the long night and the ordeal the day before, Dajata breathed heavily as she pulled the makeshift platform that held Andar and their meagre supplies. Her legs were on fire and it felt as if the skin on her palms was about to rip off. Sweat stung her eyes and ran down her body as she glanced up at the old man. Still weak from the poison and unable to help pull the crude sled, he walked slowly, leading the way.

It had taken both of them to gradually trickle more of the salve mixture into Andar and by the time they were done the old man was exhausted. He lay back and smiled at Dajata as she stared at Andar.

"Trust me, your man is strong. That he survived the night is a good sign."

"He not...is not my man," she said, bristling at the reference for a second time. "We travel together, that all. Whether lives or dies means little."

The old man raised an eyebrow but said nothing.

"If your...travelling companion is to survive, we must get him to my home. It is not far. My Besha will take good care of him."

His name was Didav and he had shown her how to lash together two thin reed trees to make the platform that she pulled. Although Didav walked slowly, he was gradually pulling away from her. She staggered to her left, the long grass beside the narrow path swatting her in the face. The dry grass rustled quietly at being disturbed, a clinger falling at her feet as she fought to control the handles of the sled. At last, her legs gave out and she slumped to the ground on her knees.

"Wait," she whispered. He didn't hear her. "Wait!" and with relief she saw him turn and shuffle back to her. He slid down the bole of a reed tree and leaned his head back. Dajata saw that he too was in a state of exhaustion. His breath came in quick, rasping pants. He smiled at her ruefully.

"I like to think it is the poison rather than my age that causes so much difficulty, but my wife would disagree." Worn teeth flashed a smile. "We'll rest here a while."

The distance to Dadiv's home, although not far, seemed impossibly long, only accomplished with many stops. When his homestead came into view, Dajata gave a cry of relief and thanked their ancestors. The small weathered building was set in a clearing surrounded by well kept gardens. In one of them his wife Besha worked between rows of charott, loosening the soil with a flataxe. She turned her round face at the sound of the dragging sled. Upon seeing Dadiv, she dropped her gardening tool and hurried towards them. Her eyes went wide at his condition. He fell into her arms when she reached him, the last of his strength gone.

"Divi! Divi! I was so worried. Our ancestors have brought you back to me."

Didav's wife brought two rees to the table. They sat together, safe in each other's arms. It was an old homestead, handed down to them from Besha's father when he passed. The floor boards were still soft and pale, recently replaced by the two of them. It had taken much time, and now Besha rubbed them with a sandaled foot as she sat with her husband.

"She sits long with him for someone who doesn't care if he lives or dies," she said, sipping at her steaming tankard. There was a gleam in her brown eyes that wasn't hidden by the heavy eyelids. She slipped an arm through his. "I was so worried about you, Divi. When you didn't come home yesterday, I thought that I had lost you." Her voice cracked and Dadiv put an arm around her shoulders and squeezed her tightly.

"I'm fine, Besha. A day or two and I'll be good as new."

"A day or two," she said, looking up at him with watery eyes. "You expect me to wait a day or two?" She snuggled into him and held him around the waist. "You *are* getting old."

"We've done everything we can. Will he survive, Divi?"

"I don't know. He's very strong, but was bitten many times, so many times." His voice trailed away as he recalled the incident. "He came to my aid against terrible odds, Besha. I think I was already bitten. Another would have thought it too late, but he came." He turned and looked into Besha's wrinkled eyes. "I would have never seen you again."

She hugged him quickly. "It's all right, you're here now. We're together again." She drew away and wiped her eyes with the back of a plump hand. "We must do everything we can to save this fellow. We owe him much."

The three nursed Andar, sitting with him through the days and nights. They poured the salve into him in small amounts, yet day after day the fever refused to slacken, his breathing threatening to stop at any moment.

The fourth day after the attack Dajata sat bathing his face, chest and arms. The swelling had receded, but the fever continued. Although lean before, she could see him wasting away. She wiped his face, studying the sunken eyes and hollow cheeks then brushed back the damp hair, warm from the heat of his brow. She dropped the cloth into the bowl and walked to the window. In the gardens the crops of ander, charott and cornut grew in neatly cultivated rows. Beyond the ander under a tree, Didav sat on a bench drinking as he watched Besha work the garden. Besha joined him and the two sat, hands entwined, their hips touching as they talked. The scene anchored Dajata to the window, and soon tears ran down her face.

"Dreanna." The word was only a whisper. Dajata wiped her eyes and hurried to him.

"Dreanna." It was still a whisper but held a desperate urgency. Andar's head rolled back and forth as he repeated it over and over. Dajata leaned above him, calling his name as she wiped his forehead. His hand, weak and shiny with sweat, closed on her arm. His eyes, still veiled in fever, studied her in confusion.

"Dreanna?" The hope in the whisper caused a lump in Dajata's throat and she fought to hold back fresh tears.

"No, it is Dajata."

She saw his confusion melt away, then disappointment replaced by fear. His grip tightened on her arm, eyes intense as he stared at her.

"Help me." He tried to raise his head. "Help me." His voice weakened and trailed off as he sank back onto the bed and lost consciousness.

Dajata removed his damp hand from her wrist and laid it beside him. She wiped her eyes then took the cloth from the bowl and wrung it out. Tenderly she dabbed at his face.

"I will help you, stupid Andar."

Chapter Four

When Andar awoke, everything ached. He wondered why he couldn't hear Lanos moving about, then noticed the ceiling wasn't his own. It was too low, the reed log joists too small and close together. Walls made of thin, polished reed trees shone from the light through a large window. The events of the last days came back in a rush, flooding him with thoughts and images: the old man, the malbar, falling. *Where am I?* His eyes found the plump figure of a gray-haired woman who sat beside him sewing. A brown robe, pulled snug around her ample waist, fell in loose folds to the floor.

"Wuhh..." Andar tried to speak, his throat dry and tight. He closed his eyes, his throat burning with the effort.

The old woman lowered her sewing and wiped his brow with a damp cloth. "This is a good sign. You do not seem so hot any more. Maybe the fever is finally breaking and you will wake up for us. That would be a good thing, don't you think?" She slipped the needle through the coarse fabric and continued with her sewing.

"Where am I?" Andar forced the three words from him, wincing at the pain.

Besha dropped the sewing, her eyes wide as she looked at Andar. "Divi! Dajata! Come, come! He's back."

Andar heard the trample of feet as others appeared at his bedside: the old man from the grassy field. Dajata. He listened to their chatter as they smiled and hugged each other. He watched the old man grab the gray haired woman and dance, twirling her about. Dajata smiled, pleasure lighting her face as she spoke with the others. She looked strange, different, and then he realized why. He had never seen her smile before. The celebration quieted as all three paused and looked at him. Besha stepped forward and raising Andar's head, held a cup to his lips.

"Slowly. You mustn't overdo it." She removed the cup and stepped back, smiling at him.

"Welcome back, Andar," said the old man. His face shone with pleasure.

Andar studied him, giving thought to the old man's words. "How long?" he asked.

"Ten days."

It struck him like a blow. "I must leave." He attempted to rise, but even before they reached to restrain him, he knew something was wrong. He could barely move his head. Summoning all his strength, he raised it and saw his wasted body. His head fell back. "Ten days," he whispered. He closed his eyes and turned his face away from them.

"Didav, Besha, if you would leave him for now, I think he needs some time alone."

"Yes, of course. Come along, Divi. Let's leave the two alone. I'll make you some ree."

"By the landsite, we'll not be having ree today. I'll pour us some ale."

"Yes, yes, Divi, you're right. Now come along and we'll celebrate."

As they left the room, Dajata sat on the bench beside Andar. The silence was awkward. Uncertain of what to say, she rose and moved to the window,.

"What are you doing here?"

Dajata turned to him and smiled nervously.

"Why have you not made good your escape?" His voice was bitter.

The hurt lasted only a moment until the cold indifference that she had learned to live with replaced the pain. She walked stiffly towards him.

"I still needed you."

Andar stared at her. The words, his own, echoed from the past as she walked from the room.

The first days for Andar passed slowly. He was confined to his bed by Besha who fussed over him, bringing him soups and stews, cooking for him constantly. Dajata made few appearances, only coming when asked to do so by Besha, to deliver some food or collect an eating bowl. As Andar gained strength, Didav spent time with him, talking, questioning, and learning of Andar's quest. After many days, against Besha's wishes, Andar climbed out of bed, stiff and sore. He began with solitary walks that lengthened until finally he turned to his weapons . Slowly his strength returned and with it his impatience to leave. Didav cautioned otherwise.

"Only now has your side healed. To leave now would be foolhardy."

"It's been too long since the malbar. The closest village to the north. How many days journey?"

"Three, no four I would say, in your condition."

"I'll leave tomorrow." Andar held up his hand silencing Didav. "No, friend, I must leave. I can't rest while Dreanna is still in danger."

"I understand. I'll send Besha and Dajata to town after the midday meal to fetch whatever supplies you need."

"To town? You said the nearest village is three or four day's journey."

"The nearest village to the north. Is that not what you asked? Our village is a short journey to the west."

"Does Dajata know this?" asked Andar.

"Of course. She and Besha have been there several times during your illness."

The sun's rays slanted low over the field as Andar approached Dajata. She worked in a garden behind the house, turning the soil, banking it against the thick stalks of the cornut. The tasselled, red tops swayed back and forth above her head in the gentle breeze. He stopped to watch her, recalling her smile on the first day he had awakened. She hummed to herself as she worked, something Andar had never heard her do. She wore the new wrap that Besha had fashioned for her. Although the material was coarse it was bright and multi-coloured, unlike the drab piece Andar had cut from her robe. She had fastened a matching top in the same manner as she had on the first day. The similarities in her appearance ended there.

The wrap did little to hide the long legs that were now shapely and tanned a golden brown. Toned arms flowed from her shoulders. The criss-crossed top now cupped rounded breasts that swayed slightly from her efforts in the garden. The shiny black hair hung about her shoulders, dusting them as her head swung back and forth. It wasn't the same woman he had met in the shop in Kempa. Didav had told him how she had killed the last of the malbar, peeled the dead one from his back, made camp and then brought them safely to Didav's home. This was not the frail creature he had first met. She caught her breath in surprise when she looked.

"You startled me."

"I'm sorry. I was looking for you and became distracted."

She studied him openly, her head erect, shoulders back. He felt embarrassed, caught like a voyeur staring at a woman in a private moment. Yet he couldn't take his eyes from the mantle of black hair that framed her face.

"What is it that distracted you? Is someone here?"

"No, Dajata, there is no one else."

"You are leaving," she said, her voice guarded.

"Yes, tomorrow." He paused as he struggled to find words. "I know I can't make amends for what I have done to you."

"You have said so before. I know why...why you did it."

"Your speech. It has changed somehow. It's different."

She blushed and looked at the ground, kicking the earth with a sandaled foot. "I been...have been practising. Beshi have been helping me. I want to talk better. I want to sound like them." She looked up at him. "And you."

He looked at her, but her face was devoid of any emotion. "Didav told me what you did at the battle with the malbar."

Dajata shrugged her shoulders.

"Why? Why did you do it when you hate me?" He could read nothing in her face as she stood watching him. She pulled a green, oblong fruit from one of the cornut stalks sending its top swaying violently back and forth. She picked at the layered husk as she stood in the twilight.

"Why did you save Didav?" she finally asked.

"It was the right thing to do. The only thing to do."

Dajata shrugged her shoulders again, but said nothing.

"Why did you not leave when I was safely here?"

Her lip curled in annoyance and she answered quickly. "You *are* stupid master." Angrily she swung her head away. Her hair whipped about as she squinted into the setting sun. Dajata turned back to him, her eyes mere slits. "No where to go. There was nowhere to go. The village is small. Nothing there for me." She picked at the cornut, pulling the brittle petals back as she looked towards the small cabin.

Her sudden anger silenced Andar. Finally he asked, "Then what will you do? Will you stay with Dadiv and Besha?"

The suggestion seemed to drain the anger from her. "They are kind and gentle people. They wanted me to stay. But they are old. Have...they have each other. I do not belong here."

"Will you return to Kempa?"

"I have no brothers or sisters. I sure... I am sure the shop is gone. Someone would take it. If I returned I not think they would give it to me. No, they kill me... will kill me one night in an alley." She shrugged her shoulders indifferently again, her manner as casual as if she were planning an outing to buy food at the village market.

"Then what will you do?"

Dajata shook the dirt from her sandal, her head finally coming up. She met him squarely with her eyes. "I would travel with you to the north."

Andar's face betrayed his surprise. He saw her mood alter again and before he could speak she answered brusquely.

"There is no place here for me. To north in a larger village or town, maybe I will find something, someone." Her voice trailed off as she looked at the last of the sun. When he said nothing, her head snapped back to him, eyes sharp. "You do not wish I...wish that I travel with you? You not take me to the village?"

"Yes, of course I will. To the north. I'll see you to the village there. I owe you no less."

Dajata stood silently before him. When she said nothing further he nodded his head awkwardly. "Good night."

Dajata remained, her hands idly holding the cornut as she watched him return to the cabin. She raised the fruit and bit into it but spat it out, wiping her lips. She cast it aside. She had known it wasn't ripe, wasn't ready. She picked up the flataxe. *He owes me no less.* Dajata jerked the flataxe up and drove it into the ground. "I do hate you, stupid man."

On the morning of their leaving Andar and Dajata stood at a table packing their last provisions. Didav appeared with an object wrapped in cloth. He carried it with care, as if it were fragile. They ceased their preparations and turned to the old man who stood ramrod straight before them, his eyes alive.

"To you I present this gift. It is one of thanks, but is given with more than gratitude. My father bequeathed it to me as did his father to him. So it has been passed down through the generations from the days of the beginning." The reverence in his voice was unmistakable. "I have no son or daughter. It was not meant to be. I've waited long for the right person..." He paused and smiled, "persons to arrive on which to bestow the honour and responsibility of this gift. You, Andar, and you, Dajata, are those people."

Dadiv placed it on the table and slowly unwraped the object. Each worn layer was ritualistically lifted aside until the last covering was lowered and Andar and Dajata stared in wonder at the ages old artifact. Dadiv slipped his hands under the cloth and held the object out to Andar and Dajata. His voice trembled as he spoke.

"I entrust this to both of you that you may protect it and keep it safe. Let that which was our forefathers' be a constant reminder of our humble beginnings on Zendar, for only knowledge of our past can ensure our future." His voice quivered as he spoke but he smiled, as if passing the burden of care on to another had set him free. "The honour and responsibility are now yours," he said as he handed it to Andar.

As long as Andar's hand, its golden surface reflected the sun. Thin at one end, the other thickened with contours that held small indentations. Dajata leaned closer, her eyes tearing up as she studied the smooth shape. She looked at Didav. "It is so old, but looks as if one of our ancestor's hands could have held it yesterday. May I touch it?"

"Certainly, but be ready to feel a tingle when you do. And don't touch this or this," he said pointing to two areas. "I believe it is a tool or a weapon. It can be very powerful when the user wishes it so."

Dajata reached out hesitantly. A light tremor passed through her and she pulled her hand away.

"A strange feeling, isn't it? It's a physical bonding between the device and the user that occurs when touched with the bare hand. I have held it so often that the sensation often goes unnoticed with me. It didn't hurt did it?"

"No," she said as she rubbed her hand. She looked at Andar. "You try. Touch it."

Andar reached out with his free hand. The tingling sensation travelled up his arm from his hand to eventually settle upon his whole body. Within seconds, although still present, it dissipated becoming almost unnoticeable. When he removed his hand the tingling faded away as if dissolving within him. He smiled self-consciously at Didav.

"To possess something of our first ancestors is an honour I can't repay."

Didav cut him off with a raise of his hand. "It must be passed on. I'm old. You two are the chosen. It is a sacred honour to accept and care for it. A lifelong responsibility. It's not something to be repaid." He looked at Dajata. "Do you accept this task?"

She swallowed nervously as she looked at him, then stood, taller and her voice was clear. "I do."

Didav swung his glance to Andar. "Andar, do you accept this task?"

Andar looked down at the ancient object, then to Didav. He turned to Dajata, who stood with her head held high. "I do," he said as his eyes met her's.

Didav placed one of Andar's hands upon the object and then Dajata's atop his. "Then it is done.".

Andar and Dajata stared uncertainly at each other then removed their hands from the object.

"I have never shown another the Ancient Ones' tool. As the keepers, you must know how it works. Watch."

Didav took hold of the object at one end, his hand slipping onto the contours. He closed his eyes to concentrate on the tingling bond for the last time. After a few seconds he opened them and smiled. "I will miss it," he said. "Each time I hold it, it is like experiencing The Telling Day, only with this, my renewal with our ancestors has been as often as I wished. Yes, I will miss it. Now watch."

Dadiv moved his finger onto one of the forbidden spots and then held his other hand in front of the object. A pale yellow band of light shone from the end onto his outstretched palm. It lasted only a moment and then stopped.

"Hold out your hand, Andar." Didav pointed the end of the object and the light shone onto Andar's palm.

"It's warm. Soothing," said Andar.

"Yes, now watch." Didav pointed the object at the leaf of a nearby reed tree. A thin, brighter beam of light burst forth, A section of the leaf disappeared, the rest of it dropping to the ground. Andar and Dajata glanced from the object to Didav. His pale green eyes smiled at their unbelieving looks.

"Yes," he said. "I do not understand such majik or how it works, but it can be very powerful. It won't work for Besha, or she is not able to make it work. Believe me she has tried." He laughed a quiet chuckle. "Yes, how she has tried." He looked down at the object. "It took much time for me to be able to burn little holes in a leaf, but I am sure it was meant for much more than that." He looked up at the two of them. "Now, let me teach you what I know."

Chapter Five

In Dashindar within Grenfeld's estate walls Bonara paced restlessly back and forth trying to contain his anger. *Stay in control. Grenfeld's son will have returned with the girl. She will have the key and all will not be lost.* He glanced towards the door that Grenfeld would use to make his entrance. Bonara knew Grenfeld had kept him waiting to reaffirm his mastery here in Dashindar. *Fool. Dashindar is all you will ever amount to. A brutish warrior who can think no further than revenge.* He sat, breathing deeply, trying to decide if their alliance had been worth the frustration.

Years ago, he had heard of Grenfeld. Bonara had needed men in the early discovery days and for a price Grenfeld had supplied them. Bonara's recent efforts to displace the smith had proven unsuccessful, and he had approached Grenfeld once more, again careful not to reveal the existence of the cavern beneath the smith's house. When Grenfeld heard the name of the village, a transformation occurred.

"Bonstag." He had repeated it over and over again, as if in a trance. "I knew a man from this village." His voice was cold, eyes dark with an unspoken memory. It was as if he had been transported to another place and time. And then Grenfeld had spoken the reedsmith's name and their alliance had begun in earnest.

Bonara played upon Grenfeld's obsession with the smith's wife then broke the news of her death. He nurtured the hatred that had lain dormant for so many years, and hatched the plot to abduct the man's daughter.

"So much better than killing him. Steal away his only daughter as the smith stole Katrena from you."

Grenfeld would arrange for the Suru to abduct and bring the daughter to him. A message would be sent to the smith, drawing him away – to Grenfeld and his revenge. Bonara didn't care what he did with the smith or his daughter. It had taken time to convince Grenfeld that using the Suru would be better than marching to Bonstag with a small army. To do so would draw unwanted attention.

Bonara rose and paced back and forth. He slumped in the chair again, tapping restlessly on the arm. *As soon as I regain the key, I'll sever the relationship with him.* Movement at the door brought his head about.

"Lord Bonara. What an unexpected pleasure." Grenfeld's solid frame crossed the floor. He smiled pleasantly as he watched Bonara rise to face his host.

"Grenfeld," he answered curtly, annoyed at himself for showing his impatience.

"It's Lord Grenfeld now. I have you to thank for that. I rather liked the sound of it when you first introduced yourself as such. What do you think, Lord Bonara?"

"Very proper, Lord Grenfeld." *The man is irritating beyond belief.*

"What brings you to my humble estate? News that the Suru have been successful and my prize is on the way?" Grenfeld wandered to the table and poured them some reed wine.

Bonara accepted the wine. *Play the game, but show him who is in control.* "There were some complications."

Grenfeld studied him silently.

"Nothing that could not be handled."

"What happened?"

"It seems some trailmen made off with the girl."

"What? Some common trailmen took our prize?"

"I had thought of contacting you immediately," said Bonara, carefully watching Grenfeld. "Perhaps you could have sent your son with a group of men to pursue these...trailmen, but I felt I could deal with it myself." He watched his host's face redden and felt satisfaction. "No, I didn't wish to bother you, so I sent a group of my own men to track them down."

Grenfeld's face darkened. "You acted without my knowledge? What did these trailmen look like?"

"They appeared to be trailmen, but were well trained. The leader was tall, young with long dark hair."

"What happened?" asked Grenfeld, eyes fixed upon Bonara.

"I instructed my men to find, kill them, and bring the girl to you."

"You sent your men after my son to kill him? And you show your face here?" Grenfeld advanced dangerously close to Bonara, his hand upon the dagger.

Bonara fought the urge to step back, suddenly aware that he might have misjudged Grenfeld and pushed him too far. He fought to compose himself and steady his voice before he spoke.

"Your son? What do you mean?"

"Don't play games, Bonara. What happened?"

"Rest easy, Grenfeld. Your son is safe. I did not know who had taken the girl when I sent my men in pursuit. It was *not* part of our agreement that you would act on *your* own without informing *me*." Bonara's confidence returned and he held Grenfeld's stare. "I had no way of knowing. My men caught up with your son, and they did battle. Neither your son nor the girl was injured. They made good their escape with others. Some of my men returned with this news and from the description they gave, I determined that it must have been your son. I assume by now he is back with the girl."

Grenfeld's face had registered relief, then confusion as he listened to Bonara. "Back? No, he is not back."

"Come, Grenfeld, let's not play this game any longer. Summon him so that we may conclude our business."

"Game? I play no game." Grenfeld's face was livid with anger. "I sent my son for the girl, but I have heard nothing from him. And now you tell me you have sent men after him and he does not return. Who is playing games?"

Despite himself, Bonara stepped back, suddenly aware of the danger.

"He should have arrived. Many days ago." Bonara could feel the sweat break out on his forehead. "Something has gone amiss."

"What has gone amiss is that your men have killed my son and kept the girl for themselves." Grenfeld stepped closer and grasped Bonara's tunic as he pulled the dagger.

"Think, Grenfeld! Stop and think! I don't want the girl. Only four of my men out of twenty returned home. They swear your son, the girl, and others escaped. If something has happened to them, it has been after they had the encounter." Bonara held his breath, his eyes wide.

Some sense of sanity filtered into Grenfeld as his breathing slowed and the tension left his hunched shoulders. He released Bonara, lost in thought. "The young fool. If he has let something happen to the girl, I'll kill him myself." He stared at Bonara. "We'll talk later." He turned on his heel and strode from the room.

Bonar felt his legs go weak. He walked to the chair and fell into it. His hand shook as he wiped the sweat from his face. Once again the missing key had eluded him. Bonara stared at the floor, the news leaving him devastated. Without it his life's work had been wasted.

Dreanna fought to hold the noose away from her neck as she struggled to keep pace with the other captives who walked silently in line. More than once she had slowed causing the coarse rope to chaff her neck. Now the slightest tug on her raw skin made her jump in pain. She stumbled, but before she fell the Stomuant who walked beside her caught her arm and pulled her up.

"Look where walk human," he said his voice deep, barely coherent.

Dreanna watched his towering bulk lumber ahead, knotted muscles sliding under the crusted gray hide. Almost twice her height, countless coloured stones adorned his harness, glittering whenever the sunlight stabbed through the trees. Others encircled his thick neck, wrists and ankles. Like all of the creatures, a wrap of gaudy material hung from his waist.

In the first days of the march, other captives had joined the line of misery. In twos and threes, young men and women for the most part, were roped into line until Dreanna guessed that there must be close to thirty prisoners. Many were from small northern villages. Some had the mark of trailmen on them. All wore the dazed look of misery and fear of the unknown. In the last two days no further captives had joined them and the Stomuants had increased the pace northwards.

Dreanna looked ahead at Rothus. Despite how she felt toward him it helped to know that she wasn't alone. She watched his foot carefully navigate a tree root that stretched across the path. He would exaggerate his movements to alert her to possible footfalls. But now, in their fifth day of captivity, exhausted from the punishing pace, she faltered again, and the rope tugged on her neck. As it did it also pulled on Rothus' neck.

"Dreanna," he whispered, "you must try harder. You must keep up."

"I can't," she answered wearily.

"You must. You're strong. You can do it. I'll try to keep the rope slack so it doesn't pull. Now walk faster."

She glared at his back, but quickened her step.

"Good, I knew you could do it."

The days were long, never-ending ones of hardship. Falling brought the wrath of the nearest Stomuant who would drag the offender to his feet. However, despite their impatience, the Stomuants never struck them. The pace was punishing, taking them to the edge of exhaustion. Then each night around the fires they were fed generous portions. Together with the night's rest, it sustained them for the next day's march.

Day after day as they travelled northwards the temperature dropped. The sun still shone brightly, but now there was a cool freshness to the air that Dreanna had never experienced. It was as though the air had been cleansed, making it easier to breathe. The reed forests gradually thinned out and the lichen disappeared, taking with it the green mist. No longer did the drone of bark bugs fill the evening nights.

This morning they had awakened to a layer of white mist that floated above the ground. It drew the heat from their bodies, attacking fingers and toes, leaving them tingling with pain. Dreanna shivered beside Rothus and the other captives as they huddled around the coals of the fires and warmed themselves in the morning sun while they ate. The march began again and now they traveled a desolate terrain of earth and rock. The cracked surface was dotted with waist high plants, their solitary circular leaf of brown open to the sky. Dampened by the mornings white mist, as the day progressed, the edges shrivelled in the sun.

At midday they stopped for food. From a crude hovel made of rocks, the Stomuants pulled out animal hides. They slipped their heads through a hole that had been cut in the center of each blue fur. That evening it was only the thickness of her crude robe that allowed her to sleep. The next day, like the other captives, she walked with it wrapped about her. The Stomuants appeared to be impervious to the growing cold.

When Dreanna saw the distant mountains she fought to control her panic, for tales told of the Stomuants living beyond them. Now the harsh reality of her fate was clear. She would never see her home again. Her tiny village would exist only in her imagination and dreams.

The mountains became larger and higher each day until she felt sure they would fall upon her. Yet still they grew, huge vertical thrusts of black rock that formed a barrier in both directions as far as the eye could see. Their craggy peaks loomed above them, white caps glistening in the sun, rivers of white running down their sides. As they neared them, Dreanna couldn't understand how they could continue. They would never be able to pierce the impenetrable black barrier of rock or survive the unfathomable cold that seemed to issue from these giants. That night, as she lay curled up by the fire, Dreanna couldn't stop shivering from the cold. She heard a rustling beside her and raised her head to see Rothus move carefully closer.

"Dreanna, turn and face the other way. I'll lay in close behind you to keep you warm." The light from the fire flickered weakly over his tired features. Dreanna started to protest, but he cut her off. "We must stay alive, both of us. We must help each other. Now turn around."

Too cold to argue, Dreanna struggled with weak arms to turn her back to him. Rothus slid up behind her, pressed his body against her and pulled his hide on top of hers, covering them both. He slid his arm over her side, pulling her tightly into him. When the tremors from the cold ceased, Dreanna couldn't think of anything except the warmth as the world around her faded away. Someone held her and she was safe.

"Thank you, Rothus," she murmured as she drifted asleep in his arms.

Chapter Six

It had been two days of slow but steady travel since they had left Dadiv and Besha. The parting had been difficult. Besha hadn't cried but she had held Dajata who sobbed in the old woman's arms. Dadiv had been solemn, saying little to either one of them, wishing them long life, calling upon the ancestors to aid Andar in his quest to reunite his family. Then the two elders had stood together, arms wrapped around each other and watched Andar and Dajata until they disappeared into the forest heading north.

That evening, Andar sat and watched the mist materialize as dusk turned to night. Beneath the moons' silent travels, it grew into wisps that gathered into small roiling pockets that swelled and churned until the carpet of green covered the forest floor. It twirled and danced out of harm's way as Dajata's feet cut a path through it towards Andar. In the distance the piercing scream of a werkemp temporarily silenced the chanting rhythm of the skeletal gripons that hung tenuously in the trees about them. Andar looked up when Dajata stopped in front of him. She handed him a cup of reed tea and turned away.

"Dajata, sit with me."

Her eyes flicked his way as she sat next to him by the fire. She sipped her tea, waiting silently. They had hardly spoken during the two days on the trail. She had been melancholy, neither avoiding nor encouraging conversation. Although Andar was growing stronger each day, he still tired easily and hadn't encouraged talk.

"The Ancient Ones' tool that Didav entrusted to us causes me worry," said Andar as he pulled his rolled sleeping wrap up onto his lap and began undoing the ties.

"Why is that?"

"It's one thing for Didav to have it in his possession safely at home." Carefully he unrolled the wrap and lifted the object from the blanket where he had hidden it. "We're traveling. Anything could happen to it."

Dajata looked at the object, still wrapped in the worn cloth that Didav and his ancestors had used for countless years. She leaned back, thinking about what he said. "I agree with you. But what choice do we have?"

"When we get to the village, you should keep it with you there."

Her eyes widened. She sipped her ree studying him silently. "You trust me with it?"

"It belongs to you as much as me. It's your responsibility as much as mine. We both know that I might never return. Then it would be lost."

"Do not talk of such things," she said. "You will return."

Andar poked the fire coals before he looked at her. She stared into the fire, her face impassive, nothing betraying her thoughts.

"Why do you now believe that I'll return?"

"Because I want you to." She stared at him, and her face flushed, silence hanging in the air. "This ancient piece... the responsibility must be for you as for me. You must return. I not...do not want it alone."

"Yes. Yes, you're right," but like his eyes, his thoughts were distant. Finally, he looked at her. "Fate seems determined to keep our paths as one."

"Yes." Her voice was soft and quiet. She stood. "Good night."

He watched her retire to her robe on the other side of the fire.

"Good night, Dajata. Sleep well."

It was the morning of their fourth day of travelling, the village expected around each bend in the trail. The forest they travelled had thinned out, but the reed trees were ancient, the girth of their trunks so large that they could only be encircled by the spread arms of ten men. Andar stepped from the trail and placed a hand upon the deeply creased bark as he gazed upwards. He pulled his feet free of the vine crawlers and struggled back to path through the waist high fronds clustered around the base of the giants. From the powdery trail that wound its way between the trees, Dajata had watched him approach the tree.

"Never have I seen such as these." His voice reflected the awe he felt. "It is hard to imagine their age," he said, suddenly embarrassed by the way she studied him. He stepped past her. "We should go."

He had increased their pace the day before, testing himself, disappointed that he wasn't stronger, but worry for Dreanna pushed him again today. He believed that by now she would have arrived at Dashindar. The thought of Rothus quickened his heartbeat and lengthened his stride. It helped little knowing where she was. Whatever Grenfeld was about, he was certain it did not bode well.

Andar caught his breath in surprise when the first drops of rain hit the path creating tiny puffs of dust before him. He cursed and looked skywards. Without a set of reed shards hanging nearby there had been no warning. Now it was too late.

The plummeting drops increased. He glanced at Dajata who had also stopped and was staring upwards. She slipped her pack from her shoulder and opened it. Andar did the same and quickly found his face protector. He slung his supplies onto his back again then unrolled his cloak, slipping it over his shoulders and the pack. Tying the face protector to his harness, he pulled the hood of the cloak over his head, hoping they would find the village before the rains became too strong.

"It's not here. My face protector. It is missing."

"Missing? Check again. It must be there."

"It is not here." He heard the growing panic in her voice.

"Put your cloak on. With luck the village is just ahead. Hurry."

They set off, but as they raced down the trail the din increased, drops spattering loudly on the leaves and fronds. Although not yet large enough to damage the foliage, the barrage was growing quickly. The rain thudded against their hoods, soaking through, wetting their hair and running in small trickles down their backs. The cloaks offered some protection, but they grew heavy, slowing them, making their movements awkward and tiresome.

The rains developed quickly. Already the drops had doubled in size as well as intensity. The constant drumming on his head and shoulders became draining, and the hood, plastered to his head, no longer offered any protection. The rain soaked through, a sheet of water washing over his face, blurring his vision and making breathing difficult. He reached for his face protector and slipped it on.

"Andar!"

He barely heard the muffled cry but realized immediately why Dajata must be calling. He spun around and found her bent over, holding her hood out from her head as the water cascaded from her nose and mouth. Gasping for air, she shouted his name again.

"I'm here," he yelled, bending over her to shield her head with his body.

"I cannot see. I cannot breathe. Put your protector on and go. Take the artifact."

Andar knew they had to find shelter quickly. The force of the rains had doubled again, beating down on them, the drops now striking with the force of blows. He had never seen anything like it. Even though he could breathe, the constant pounding would soon have him unconscious. Dajata had less time.

Andar released his cloak, peeling the sodden mass from him. Exposed to the rain, the watery pellets pummelled his back and head, goading him to move faster. Already Dajata was doubled over, on the verge of collapsing. He heaved his cloak over her, jamming his knee under her chest to prevent her from falling. Slipping his pack off, he backed underneath Dajata and surged upwards, balancing her on his back. He held her arms with one hand then grasped his pack. Burdened by her weight and the punishing rain, he staggered forward down the watery trail.

Even though he could breathe with his protector in place and was sheltered from the punishing rain by Dajata's body, he knew he couldn't travel far. Her weight, and that of the pack and the two sodden cloaks, forced his feet deep into the mire, threatening to bear him to the ground. His own pack was a dragging anchor as he pulled it through the muck. He veered from the path into the forest of aged trees, desperate to find shelter if they were to survive. Each sucking footstep in the thick mixture of soil, water, and debris, challenged his balance and sapped his strength. The air was filled with the tearing of leaves as the drops punched holes, shredding them. The rain veiled the world in a shroud of silver so that seeing further than his hand was impossible.

Andar bumped into a tree trunk. He tottered, fighting the dead weight that threatened to unbalance him and send him crashing to the ground. He dropped his pack and hooked a foot through its strap. With his hand in front of him he staggered forward, contacting and fending off the trunk of another giant. His legs burned and his breath became ragged. A few more steps and he knew it would be over. There had been nothing from Dajata since they had begun, but he could feel her stubbornly holding onto him.

His leg stuck calf deep in the dancing froth. He fell sideways, one hand contacting another invisible trunk, its bulk obscured by the deluge. As he slid around the bole of the tree, his hand disappeared. He staggered forward, half falling into an opening. Grasping the lip of the entrance, he reached inside. His shoulder caught, but the opening widened as it went deeper into the trunk of the tree.

Andar sagged forward to his knees and fought to unload Dajata and the rain-soaked cloaks that clung to him. She fell, tangled in the watery folds. The rain beat at him, hammering his exposed skin and holding him to the ground by it ferocity. Somehow he struggled to his feet, reached for and found Dajata. He dragged her towards the fissure in the trunk and jammed her into the entrance. She became stuck in the opening. He pulled her free and tore his cloak from her as she pulled at her own. Her pack dropped to the ground and when he shoved her again, she disappeared into the trunk. Andar's head rang with the blows from the pounding rain. He grabbed the lip of the entrance and squeezed himself inside, banging into Dajata who cried out as her head struck the inside of the trunk.

"Andar." Her voice was a painful, searching cry, barely audible as the rain beat the ground outside.

"It's all right. I'm here."

She squirmed, twisting around to face him, bumping into him and forcing him beyond the entrance. The rain tore at his back. He jerked forward, colliding with her and forcing her against the trunk once more. Pressed against her, he felt Dajata's arms reach for him and she buried her face against his chest, sobbing quietly. Andar removed his face protector and held her head, stroking the side of her face. She clutched him tighter. Outside, the deluge continued, holding them captive in the hollow. Neither moved nor spoke as they stood pressed together supporting each other. Finally Dajata raised her face.

"I couldn't breathe. I thought-"

"Shh, we're safe now," he said. He brushed the hair from her face and touched her forehead with his lips. They lingered and Dajata raised her face to him, touching his lips hesitantly with hers. She pressed against his lips lightly then pulled his mouth down harder as he responded. The kiss was long and passionate. Andar slipped her top from her shoulders and felt the press of her breasts against his chest. His hand moved down to her buttock. The roar of the torrent outside disappeared.

Both of them fought with the other's rain soaked wrap, tugging it upwards, hindered by the confined space. They clutched each other, desire heightened by the constraints of the space and their rain-soaked bodies. Dajata pulled herself up, wrapping her legs around him. She cried out as the rain pelted her feet, but Andar pushed her back against the trunk, burying his face in her shoulder as they thrust against each other. He held her, stayed with her, finding the strength somewhere to keep her pressed against the inside of the tree as she clasped him tightly. Finally, his lips against her ear, he said the words he thought he would never be able to say again. She squeezed him tighter, and soon he felt her tears on his shoulder.

They stood together, Dajata's head on his chest, arms wrapped around each other. Neither said anything. The rain outside thundered down making conversation nearly impossible. Andar leaned down towards her upturned ear.

"I was in a dark place. You saved me."

She hugged him fiercely, pulling herself up to kiss him, tenderly at first, then long and hungrily. His passion matched hers and soon they both stood breathless. Dajata's eyes were wet.

"You not... have not changed. There always been much good in you." She looked at his chest and kissed the scar from the Suru's sword. "I watched you stare into the fire. I see your pain. Hear it when you talk of your daughter. The pain made you hard and cruel, but sometimes I... would see who you were. The real Andar would show himself. That is the master I love."

The roar of the rains tore about their shelter like a beast in search of prey. Only the thickness of the trunk muffled the sound. They stood entwined, everything somehow less threatening now that they were together.

"We can't stay here," said Andar. "My legs are cramping. We have to find someplace else. A larger shelter where we can rest. Where I can carve you a new face protector."

"But it is impossible to go out without a protector. How could I?" asked Dajata as she peered around him to look outside. "This is a great rain. Greater than I have seen. You cannot carry me. Even with a face protector, we cannot walk in it."

He looked out the fissure, the world beyond the crack in turmoil. "You're right. I don't know what we can do."

Dajata shifted uncomfortably, trying to work some blood in her legs, bumping her elbow on the trunk. "This tree is so big. Why the hollow have to be small?"

"We were lucky to find it at all."

Dajata caught her breath. "What about the Ancient Ones' tool? Could we use it somehow?"

"I don't know if we can even make it work."

"You did when you were with Dadiv. Not much, but some."

Andar looked down at her, then bent awkwardly and kissed her nose. "We have to try."

He peered outside and saw his pack and sleeping wrap tangled in Dajata"s cloak. He hooked the sodden mass with the guard of his sword then dragged it to the entrance. By bracing himself against the sides of their narrow shelter, he climbed above Dajata who crouched below him. She unrolled the soggy blanket then shoved it outside, clutching the wrapped bequest to her. Andar lowered himself.

"You saw Dadiv make part of the leaf and other things disappear," said Dajata.

Andar watched her unwrap the artifact. "If only we could make the rains disappear."

"I could not make it work, but you were able to create some heat with it. Try." She held it up to him on the wrap.

Andar felt the tingling the moment he touched it. His hand slipped onto the contours and he pushed the spot on the side with his finger as Dadiv had instructed. He pointed at the trunk wall and encouraged the tingling energy that had settled over his body, but nothing happened.

"Nothing," he said. "It worked before, but not now."

"Try again. You tried many times before the light happened."

He shut out the sounds of the rains, focused his sense and drew his aura inwards to his core where it vibrated with the artifact's energy. Then he directed it down his arm. A pale light shone, lighting up a small circle on the trunk. Andar lost his focus and it disappeared. Dajata reached out and touched where the circle had been.

"Andar, it is warm. Try again."

He concentrated on the tingling, helping it grow, encouraging the vibrations to intertwine with his aura. This time he felt a force begin to pulse within him. Suddenly the light brightened, lighting up the interior like midday. Startled, Andar relaxed and it disappeared.

"Look!" said Dajata. Where the light had been, a shallow hollow had appeared. She reached out to the depression. The smooth concave surface felt warm to the touch. "How can this happen? There is only warmth.. Nothing is burned, yet is gone."

Encouraged, Andar focused on the energy that now pulsed more easily within him. This time when the light burst forth he held his concentration, moving his hand left and right while maintaining the beam.

He rested between efforts, but when done he had widened the space within the trunk so that they could stand without touching each other.

"What they must have been able to do," he said. "You try."

Despite her best efforts, she was unable to create the light.

"I cannot do it. I feel the tingle, but it does not grow like you said."

"Perhaps it is only the men who could control it, make it work," Andar said, aware of her disappointment.

"Then you do it. I cannot stand much longer."

Gradually Andar enlarged the interior of the reed tree, carving the walls furthest away from the fissure. He worked slowly, the concentration exhausting. When large enough, they sat together and fell asleep in each other's arms. Night was falling when they awoke, the sound outside incessant as the rain continued. He pulled their packs inside and they ate some reed bread from their supplies. As his control over the artifact improved, he carved their living grotto more quickly, working round the trunk, creating enough space for them to lie down for the night. It was Dajata's idea to use the heat of the artifact to gradually dry out their cloaks.

Andar pinned Dajata's cloak to the wall with the dagger and created the pale yellow beam, but when the process proved too slow, he became impatient. Suddenly there was a flash of brighter light and he looked at the hole in her cloak. He turned to find Dajata, hands on her hips, staring at him.

"That was my best cloak. You must buy me a new one," she said. "Tonight we will have to share yours. Do not ruin it too."

When he had dried them, Andar spread his cloak, lay down and held his arms open to her. Although the floor was smooth, it was hard, but wrapped together in the cloaks they were safe. Exhausted, not even the rain could keep them awake.

They sat inside the trunk in front of a small fire. Andar had created a hole above it to allow the smoke to escape. He had enlarged their wooden cave, experimenting with the artifact until he was comfortable controlling it. He had to rest often, for the effort and concentration tired him quickly, however now he could narrow the beam to make thin cuts or expand the circle of light to smooth large areas.

"We can't wait for the rains to stop," he said, poking the fire. I have to get you to the village so that I can continue on to Dashindar."

"So that *we* can continue to Dashindar," said Dajata. She sat silently defiant, arms crossed prepared to ignore his arguments.

Andar closed his eyes and took a deep breath. He would not risk her life on the journey, but before he could begin, she spoke.

"You too have changed my life. I not...will not go back. I will not let you leave me."

"It would only be-"

"You will not leave me. I know you would have me safe in village, but I must help in this. *We* must find Dreanna."

Andar pulled her close, elated at her determined response. There seemed little to gain in arguing with her now. He would deal with it later.

It took several days for them to make the preparations that would enable them to continue. Andar enlarged their lair, as Dajata called it, so that they would have room to work. Using the Ancients' tool, he cut strips of reed wood from the wall of the trunk and fashioned a simple shelter that was strong enough to withstand the rain, but light enough to drag along the path while under it. He fashioned a hand held shield so that he could venture outside for brief forays in order to find a younger reed tree that Dajata could use to prepare some reed bread to replenish their supplies. When he carved a new face protector for Dajata she smiled, teasing him at the decorative touches he added to it, laughing at his feeble explanation. She threw herself upon him, playful wrestling ending up as lovemaking once more.

When all was in readiness, Andar assembled the sloped shelter outside and the two ducked under it. They grasped the bar and lifted the front of it so that they could stand. The rain beat on it, the drumming louder than ever as the drops exploded off the bark covering.

Dajata looked at the tree that had sheltered them. "It was a good tree. It was a good first home."

"It was a good home," said Andar. He bent over and kissed her then the two of them leaned forward dragging their shelter in search of the path.

Chapter Seven

The cold seemed to thicken Dreanna's muscles so that her movements were slow and awkward. Her face burned from the chill air. It felt like a fire ant had crawled inside her nose and was biting her. In her furry wrap, roped in line behind Rothus, she shuffled forward with the others. They were approaching the base of one of the mountains, winding their way between immense boulders that had fallen from lofty peaks. Jagged, larger than any barkin, the rocks lay strewn like pebbles at the foot of the huge mountains.

The path through the barren ground was almost non-existent. A cold white film now coated the rocks making footing slippery and treacherous. Eventually the path led into a wide natural rift that sank into the side of the mountain. Sheer gray walls, speckled with glittering specks of green, rose on either side as they followed the narrowing crevice that lead downwards. The fissure closed overhead, the sky disappeared, the light fading as they ventured deeper into the passage.

Dreanna found herself blindly following the others, her rope now a lifeline in the dark. Cold sweat beaded her face as her eyes strained to see anything. Ahead a torch flared and cast a feeble glow down the passageway towards her. Another and another were lit and placed in cracks along the wall as the Stomuants led the way forward. She saw that the passage had changed. The floor was smoother and more level, the ceiling rounded, the walls ran straight and true. They were no longer walking in a winding crevice. It was a tunnel. It led into the mountain, but she couldn't comprehend how anyone could live here, in the dark and cold.

They ventured further and further into the mountain. Without daylight or being able to judge distance, time became immeasurable, the monotony of the march through the shadowy shaft dulling her senses. With nothing to see or hear, a pall settled over her until she felt like a sightless allaca, spindly legs swinging forward as it crawled aimlessly in the dark. Neither food nor water was dispensed. She could tell from her empty stomach and weakening energy that they must have travelled far.

In the distance a brighter light appeared. She saw that the tunnel opened into a large cavern carved into the rock. The low, domed ceiling arched above them as if supporting the weight of the mountains. Torches festooned the rough stone walls, specks of blue minerals shining in the light. Along one side, recesses had been cut into the wall, each containing a sleeping wrap. Crude stone tables and benches occupied one end of the room. Opposite the entrance tunnel, Dreanna saw the dark opening of the tunnel as it continued through the mountain. All the captives were herded to a corner away from the tables. Dreanna sank to the cold floor beside Rothus who curled the rope between them.

"Rothus, how can this place be?" she asked, her voice tired but still filled with awe. "How can they have dug such a tunnel?"

"I don't know. Maybe they didn't do it. Maybe they found it and use it," he said looking about them.

The Stomuants sat in casual conversation at the tables. Their deep, guttural voices were occasionally punctuated by barking laughter.

"But if they didn't dig the tunnel, who could have?" Dreanna asked.

"I don't know." He looked at the opening on the opposite side of the chamber. "And it continues. I think it will take us under the mountain to the other side."

Dreanna gaped at him in disbelief. "That is impossible. No one could do that."

"I have been to the first city of Norrdamoor. I have heard the Friends of the Ancients sing of them," said Rothus. "Sing of the Stomuants. The words are taken from the book of Ancestral History. It's written that they come from the wastes on the other side of the mountains. I never understood how such a thing could be, but look around. There is nothing here but a few supplies. The tunnel continues." He surveyed the wet walls. "I think they will feed us and let us sleep and then we will continue walking the tunnel tomorrow. This is just a resting place."

Dreanna went silent, the finality of her capture reinforced by Rothus' suggestion. Some reed bread and meat was dropped into her lap along with an empty drinking cup. They ate silently, weary and disheartened by this new development. Rothus turned to her, his voice hesitant.

"Dreanna, you must believe me. I never meant you any harm."

She tightened inside, the blood draining from her face. "No, Rothus, not now. Do not-"

"I must. We don't know what will happen, what fate might bring us tomorrow. I must explain. You must listen. Please!"

"If you must," she answered turning her face away, staring at the cavern wall.

"It's true that my father sent me to get you, but when I met you, when I... when I learned what you were like, I couldn't do it. My father's men acted without my orders, and when they did, I couldn't stop them. You don't know my father. I had to wait until the right time to set you free and return you home." He stopped, his eyes bleak and tormented as he waited.

Dreanna looked at him for the first time since he had begun. She watched him lower his eyes, unable to hold her gaze. "Why do you explain yourself to me now?" she asked, a flicker of hope within her. He looked back at her, but didn't say anything, and Dreanna faltered when the answer she sought wasn't forthcoming. Her lip curled in distain. "Is it the desire for forgiveness that makes you present this story?"

Rothus looked away from her, his mouth set in grim acceptance. His voice was hollow. "Yes, forgiveness."

Dreanna released the breath she had unconsciously held, raising her head as she spoke. "Much but not all has been beyond your control. Your story is a sad one. I pity you, the way you have been led, the way you have been used. I feel sorry for you, but I don't know if I can forgive you. You ask much."

The colour drained from his face. "It's enough that you try. I won't end my efforts to return you to your home. This I swear by the Mother Ship."

Dreanna looked around them, taking in the wretched captives, the Stomuants who sat at the tables eating, the gloomy chamber, and returned her gaze to Rothus. "I fear they are brave but empty words." She turned and lay on her side, pulling the wrap about her.

After some morning food, the march through the tunnel continued. Dreanna was now convinced that Rothus had been right in predicting that the tunnel would take them to the other side of the mountains. The temperature had gradually risen, and when they stopped at another carved chamber for food and sleep, their wraps were collected. The air now seemed somehow less dense, breathing easier. After another day's marching, it was with a feeling of relief that she saw light at the end of the tunnel. When she finally stepped out into daylight once more she had to shield her eyes. There was warmth to the air without the heavy closeness that she was familiar with. She looked behind her and saw that indeed the mountains loomed above her. They had just passed underneath them in little more than three days.

They travelled down the side of the mountain through rock and boulder strewn slopes. The pace was unhurried, the rope seeming merely a formality, the prisoners all but ignored. On flat terrain again, it wasn't long before they came to several buildings. Most were large simple structures constructed of heavy stones, set roughly in place. The walls were high, the doors large and the roofs steeply sloped. As they approached, a number of Stomuants emerged from one of the smaller buildings and stood awaiting their arrival. The foremost, who seemed to be the leader, spoke.

"Greetings, Merki." Compared to the others, he was shorter and more lined and weathered than the others. Large folds of lumped skin hung down from the aged and rutted face. Small black eyes, almost hidden, burned brightly.

"Greetings, Garda! replied Merki, the leader of their captors. "The mother stone makes you look well."

"Good words, greatest gatherer. You collect many this time." Garda turned to look at the captives.

"Yes, was a good hunt. Much to gain from this pack. Enough talk. I need sorrays for my men."

"Course. You rest first or bring them out right way?" asked Garda.

"Now. This pack humans worth much. I want to collect for them."

"Will do," said Garda. He led his men towards one of the taller buildings.

Dreanna drew a breath in surprise, her hand going to her mouth when the mounts were led out of the building. Now she understood the soaring roof lines, the huge size of the doors. The reddish-orange sorrays lumbered towards them, stout legs moving smoothly over the sandy surface. Their tremendous bulk swayed from side to side, many harness straps on each swinging in time with the beast's movements. Thick necks held their broad, earless heads erect. Slit against the sun, heavily lidded eyes studied the newcomers with passing interest. Supplies were lashed in place and the Stomuants clambered upwards to sit on the broad backs of the beasts. With few words, the procession headed north, leaving the mountains behind.

Dreanna walked in the shadow of one of the immense beasts. Large worn nails encircled heavy foot pads that landed silently on the sandy soil. Above, their heads swung left and right in gentle swoops, snouts testing the air. The Stomuants, clad in their jewelled harnesses and bright wraps, sat tall on the backs of the beasts, swaying from side to side in the sunlight. Despite herself, the vision of them in gaudy attire, perched upon gigantic beasts moving silently in a long procession through the featureless wasteland, created a bizarre, impressive sight that she could not help but watch with awe.

Trees appeared. Unlike the smooth trunks of reed trees that soared skywards, the thick tortured and twisted trunks of these were scarred with countless gnarled knots where branches had made futile attempts to grow. Others that had survived were likewise stricken, twisted and deformed as they reached towards the sun. Dreanna could almost feel the pain in their tortured trunks and limbs. Her depression continued, the unknown terrifying and numbing. Like the other captives who walked silently with her, heads bowed against the sun and their fate, she no longer observed or cared where they were going.

For a long, hot day, they walked the featureless wasteland. Her feet started to bleed although she had ceased to feel them. When night fell and their captors let them stop, she collapsed onto the gray sand, and fell into a restless sleep. She was awakened with a sharp tug, and the captives continued their march as the sun rose over the mountains .

On the second day the temperature climbed but the air lacked the earlier humidity. After the midday meal, buildings appeared on the horizon, blurred in the shimmering waves of heat that rose from the earth. Dreanna saw that unlike the earlier crude structures, those ahead were squat affairs that hugged the ground with a uniformity that suggested order. The walls were plumb; the surface of the pale green stones chiselled smooth and fit with precision. All were only one storey high each was surrounded by large section of land.

As they moved into the village Stomuants appeared in doorways and on the street to watch their arrival, some shouting greetings, others staring silently at the captives. Interest waned quickly and soon Dreanna and the others were herded into a large building. The rope was removed from their necks and the Stomuants left without comment, locking the massive wooden door behind them. In the corner of the barren room on the dirt floor was a pile of sleeping wraps. Scant sunlight seeped through the narrow windows set high on the walls.

The vacant faces were downcast as they realized their journey had ended without any hope of escape. One at a time, they sank to the floor. A woman, older than Dreanna, but still young, started to quietly weep. Soon another sobbed, burying her face in her hands. Silence descended upon the room when shuffling footsteps outside stopped at the door. The sound drew everyone's eyes. Some of the captives huddled together, others moved away from the door. It opened to reveal four female humans, their gaunt faces tinged with a grey pallor. They carried trays heavily laden with food and water which they placed on the floor. No one moved as the door closed. The woman who had been crying moved, adjusting her position and all eyes flicked towards her, but she turned away from the food and started crying again, long shuddering sobs that disturbed the silence. Dreanna watched the others. Watched their eyes drawn to the food in the middle of the room. Finally a man rose unsteadily to his feet. He walked slowly to one of the trays, took a piece of meat then shuffled back to his place. Soon a second, then a third approached and took a piece.

Dreanna looked up at Rothus who extended the food towards her.

"Refusing the food will change nothing. It will only cause us hunger and weakness. Here, eat."

Dreanna looked about at the others who sat silently eating, then back to Rothus who motioned with the food to her. She took the pale meat and cup of water, eating slowly, tasting nothing. When finished, she took a sleeping wrap from him and curled up on the floor. She said nothing when he lay down close to her, her contempt for him fading as depression set in. Little seemed to matter now. She heard someone crying, someone else getting sick to their stomach. Pulling the wrap tighter, she stared into space and for the first time in days spoke to Rothus.

"What will they do to us?"

"I don't know. I don't think they'll harm us. They have fed us, kept us warm. They need us for something."

"I'm frightened, Rothus. What could they possibly want? I want to go home. I want things to be as they used to be." Her voice trembled and for the first time since their ordeal started, the tears began.

Rothus dragged himself closer. "Don't cry, Dreanna. I'm with you. I'll protect you. I won't let anything happen to you."

She rolled against him, reaching out for him. "I'm so scared."

"You're not alone. I'll never leave you." He wrapped his arms around her and drew her in close. "I'll hold you. Know that you're safe tonight, and that I...and that I'll never leave you."

Dreanna buried her face in his chest, and sobbed until sleep finally took her.

The next day and for several after their arrival they were treated well. Food was plentiful and they were allowed to venture outside into the large courtyard of their building. The surrounding walls were high, the entrance barred by a sturdy gate. Two Stomuants stood guard. With the other captives, Dreanna and Rothus walked to release tension. Talk of their future and what it held in store for them soon became exhausted. On the final day of their confinement several large vats were brought to the courtyard and the men prisoners taken from the yard. Soon they returned carrying water in buckets. Back and forth they travelled until the vats were filled. One of the Stomuants pulled a female close to one of the vats. He made a great pretense of sniffing her.

"Human stink. Take off clothes. Clean now." He turned to all the others who stood watching. "All humans, clean now." When no one moved, the Stomuant looked about at the prisoners. "I come back. All must be clean or all will pay."

As the Stomuants left, Dreanna looked at Rothus. He took her arm and led her to one of the vats at the far end of the courtyard.

"Use the water while it is still clean. I'll do the same."

Dreanna looked about her and saw that others had begun to undress beside the vats. There was little modesty left.

When finished bathing, they stood expectantly in the courtyard. The gates opened once more and the Stomuants entered. One of them inspected them as a number of humans were led into the courtyard. Tired and beaten, many of them could barely walk. A gray pallor tainted the skin of some.

"The exchange session," said Rothus as he stared at the fragile bodies. Most were thin and marked by bruises.

What does it mean?" asked Dreanna, unable to take her eyes from the new arrivals. "If they were captured like us, why were they treated so terribly?"

"I overheard two of the Stomuants talking. These people have been here for some time. They've been returned by those who bought them."

Rothus paused, wishing that he had never started, aware that many around him were listening. "Stomuants have little patience for us or our mistakes. Anger comes quickly to them." He nodded to the last of the group entering the building. "If we can't perform our jobs any more, then we are returned here to be exchanged. We are rested until better then sent out again.

"Humans!"

Dreanna jumped at the shout. All turned their eyes to the Stomuant who stood at the entrance of the courtyard. He pointed to the outside.

"Walk. Time for payment."

Bent over from the waist, Dreanna straightened slowly, arched her back and felt the strain in her muscles slowly dissipate. She rolled her shoulders and neck attempting to loosen the stiffness.

"Work."

She quickly bent over, working the soil in her row with the crude blade, pulling weeds free with her other hand. She shot a malevolent look at the woman who had shouted the warning. As the days passed it became increasingly difficult to feel sorry for her. Difficult to remember that the field boss had once been like her. Human.

Dreanna slashed at the ground, hacking the earth apart. She fought to control the dread that threatened to overwhelm her. *One day I'll be the same. Even now the rocks are changing me.* She shuddered believing that she could feel something different about herself. She glanced to the woman working in the next row beside her. She was tall, a raw boned woman with shorn hair who was maybe twice her age. It was rumoured that Swenden had lived in Kempa and had been a captive for a hundred days or more. It wouldn't be long before she would be taken from the field. Last night, Swenden had almost been numb from talking about her approaching fate. Dreanna had learned much last night.

"That is the horror," Swenden had said. "You wake each morning after a nightmare. Examine yourself for any changes. During the day you question all of your thoughts and actions." She had been talking to

Dreanna, her bald head hanging down, as she stared at the dirt floor where her hands constantly smoothed the dry soil in sweeping movements. She raised a hand and examined it.

"My hands look bigger." Her brow furrowed and her eyes met Dreanna's. "They are bigger. Stronger."

Dreanna had said nothing as Swenden continued, but listening to the woman's rambling, the fear grew inside her as she learned what her fate would be.

"Everyone say your mind start to change first. You start think different as your will and emotions bend to the stone. The will of the stone. Then you not look for the physical changes because you no longer care."

Dreanna shook her head, trying to chase away thoughts of last night's conversation and concentrate on the weeding, but the seeds of fear were not to be so easily dismissed. *Will I even know when I stop worrying about the changes? Will someone tell me of them? Will I listen? Rothus will tell me, or will he already not care because he has changed? Will he be repulsed by me if he lasts longer?*

Dreanna felt as if her head would split at any moment as the worry and fear tore at her. *Is that a sign that I'm already changing?* She bit her lower lip attempting to stop it from trembling, and tasted blood. *I've never done that before. What am I doing?* She freed a hand from the weeds and slipped it inside her wrap, grasping the piece of material she had hidden there. It was small, but she squeezed it tightly and ran a finger over its rough surface, again and again. As he was about to be taken away, Rothus had given her the small piece of cloth, torn from his wrap.

"Remember me whenever you hold this," he had said as he pressed it into her hand. "Remember me. I love you. You must know that, and know that I will come back for you."

And then he was gone, taken from her. She closed her eyes, squeezing the cloth with all her strength, thinking of him and his final words. Thinking of him helped to break her chain of frantic thoughts. Knowing he loved her allowed her to accept, that despite everything that had happened, she loved him too.

A shout from the field boss and soon they were shuffling towards the stone structure where they spent all of their time when not working. Dreanna walked behind a male human who was little different than the field boss. His skin was thick and gray, his hair a coarse tangled mass falling over the boney face. A lifeless stare from humourless eyes completed the picture of what she was to become. That and worse, for she was a woman and now knew from Swenden's rambling last night, what would eventually be in store for her. Dreanna shuddered and extended her hand back to the girl behind her who had been captured at the same time as she had been. She momentarily felt the other girl's hand in hers.

Their Stomuant's home was on the outskirts of Kirgongant, the village where they had arrived. Many from her group had been bought here in the village and were nearby at the homes of other Stomuants. Her thoughts returned to Rothus and the final look he had sent to her as he had been led away.

"Stop!" The voice was loud and commanding. Everyone ceased moving. "Turn. Face me." As one they turned to him, heads and eyes downcast. The silence lengthened as they stood staring at the sun baked ground, the heat on their shoulders. Dreanna lifted her head ever so slightly peering upwards towards the Stomuant. The black eyes of her owner were focused directly at her. Quickly she dropped her eyes, staring once more at the ground.

"Continue. All but this one." Like the others, Dreanna looked up. His thick calloused finger pointed at her.

Chapter Eight

Andar paced back and forth along the covered porch of the tavern watching the steady torrent of rain. It fell relentlessly, the coursing runoff in the wide eaves drowned out by the thundering deluge on the roof. In the street the water performed a feverish dance as each large rain drop hammered the watery mix of leaves and dirt. A carpet of boiling froth, it swept under the buildings and walks, chopped and churned into pockets of swirling debris by the pilings. He leaned on the railing staring into the silver barrier that held them virtual prisoners.

A would-be patron, wrapped in an evening cloak, trod along one of the many covered walkways that linked all of the structures in the village. The bearded man looked up as he approached Andar, nodding a silent hello. He glanced at the teeming downpour, shrugged his shoulders and smiled at Andar who nodded in return. Conversation outside of the tavern's double roof was impossible. The fellow slipped past and entered. Closing his eyes, Andar took a deep calming breath. If the villagers in Skagdar could accept and adapt to the fury and violence of the rains, he could too. He had already discovered that here travel in the rains was not an option.

Although they had only dragged the sloped shelter for half a day, the task had proved exhausting. Once again, Andar had knelt in the muck hanging wearily over the handle of their structure. Beside him, Dajata also rested on the bar, eyes closed, gasping for breath. The shelter had grown heavier with each step. The mire beneath them sucked at their feet and opened up below the dragging poles until either he or Dajata would collapse from fatigue. Then they rested, sitting in the muck, eating from their pitiful supply of food. But the Ancients had blessed them and finally through the curtain of rain the gray shadow of a single building became visible. They yelled at each other, mouth to ear.

"Our ancestors have answered our prayers. It must be the village," shouted Dajata through panting breaths.

"I think you're right, but village or not, we'll seek shelter here." Andar straightened from the railing at the touch of someone behind him and Dajata slipped under his arm, wrapping hers about his waist. He looked down at the upturned face that smiled and motioned him towards the doorway. Andar looked out at the rain once more and let her lead him inside.

They lay naked in bed in the small room above the tavern. The muffled noise on the sloped ceiling served as a constant reminder that once again they would spend another day in the village. Dajata slid on top of Andar, resting her elbows on his chest. When he tried to speak, she kissed him on the mouth, silencing him.

"No, you waste your time. We start this journey together when the rains stop. I not take a chance of losing you. We do this together."

"We *will* start this journey together. I *will* not take a chance. You often forget to use will."

She punched him. "You *will* listen to me. We *will* go together."

Andar studied her solemn face then wrapped his arms around her. "I love you," he whispered.

Dajata smiled and wriggled on top of him, pressing her hips against his. "You have proved that many times."

"Let me prove it again," he said and pulled her closer still.

When the rains ended, they travelled quickly, the forced confinement in Skagdar allowing Andar to heal and rebuild his strength. After crossing the Kalimar River once more, several days of travel through reed forests finally brought them without incident to the outskirts of Dashindar. Located in a clearing, it was surrounded by farms, the various crops making the cleared land a tiled mosaic of colours. As they approached the town, farmers in the fields paused to study them. They leaned on their duggips, the wide brims of their woven hats drooping low over their eyes as they watched them pass by. The narrow road snaked around and past them and their small homes, leading to an opening between two towers. The city wasn't walled, but towers stood at regular intervals around the town's perimeter. They weren't challenged, but Andar felt the eyes of the closest guards when they entered.

Inside, the uniformity of the buildings and the grid of the streets identified it as a newer town. Each building sat upon pilings, the double, steeply sloped roof ending in a covered porch. The streets were frequently interrupted by the covered walkways that linked them. They moved among the townspeople who bustled with new found energy now that the rains had ended. While merchants sold their wares on the streets, children ran and played underfoot, the outdoors a renewed attraction. On a main road, they found a tavern and were soon drinking ale as they waited for their meal. The tavern was almost empty, tables and benches neatly in place, the noise from playful banter missing. A small fire flickered in the hearth.

"How do we find the man who has your daughter?" asked Dajata, wiping the froth from her mouth.

"We'll ask everyone until we find someone who knows him. If he had money to hire them to take Dreanna, then he must be of some importance. He'll be known."

"Then what do we do?"

"I don't know. Walking into the Suru encampment didn't work very well." He shook his head at the memory. "This time we are dealing with one man in a house. If we find out where he lives we'll go there and look around."

"What does this man…What is his name?"

"Grenfeld. His name is Grenfeld." Andar's face hardened.

"What does he want with your daughter? Why is he doing this?"

"I don't know. He was my wife's mentor before I met Katrena. She was no longer interested in him, but he wouldn't leave her alone. He blamed me for stealing Katrena away from him. That wasn't how it was, but that's what he believed."

A gangly serving boy with a head of untidy black hair brought a tray of meat, reed bread and cornut to the table.

"An acquaintance of mine is said to live here. I wonder if you might know of him," said Andar.

The youth wiped his hands on the soiled cloth at his belt and hoisted a sandaled foot onto the low bench. "I have probably served most of the folk in Dashindar, so if your friend makes his home here, I'll know him." He smiled importantly and leaned forward resting his arms on his raised knee. "What's his name?"

"Grenfeld," replied Andar.

The lad's smile disappeared. "At the end of the street. The two storied building." He turned abruptly and left. Dajata's and Andar's eyes met over the tray of food.

"This man is not well liked," said Dajata.

"I didn't like him then. I have less reason to like him now," said Andar. "It was only because Katrena interfered that I didn't kill him then. By the landsite I wish I had." He looked away to the window, the anger in his face replaced by fear when he looked back to Dajata. "If he has hurt Dreanna-"

"Dreanna is good," Dajata said. "He would not have done all this just to hurt her."

Andar stared at her. "Then what does he want?"

The sound of scabbard and harness creaking turned their heads as men filed into the room spreading along the sides and back of the tavern. The last man to enter was short in stature and powerfully built with thick shoulders. He stood at the doorway surveying the two of them. Grenfeld walked towards them, each deliberate footstep accompanied by a satisfied smile. Andar rose to his feet, his hand moving to the hilt of his sword. Grenfeld stopped two sword lengths away, the smile disappearing.

"I believe you are looking for me, Andar from the village of Bonstag."

Andar paced the confines of the small room where they had been imprisoned. The walls were thick, the door heavy and locked, the windows barred. He strode past Dajata who sat on the floor and kicked the door, cursing.

"Stop. It was not your fault. How could you know?" said Dajata.

"I should have known. I did the same thing at the Suru encampment! I should have known he would have spies or guards. He took Dreanna. Of course he knew I would come." He stood with legs splayed, hands clenched at his head. "And you! I never should have let you come with me."

Dajata stood, pulled his fists from his head and stared into his eyes. "Listen to me. You saved me from a terrible life. Your love for your daughter taught me how to love someone. Do you think I let you send me away? Leave me? You taught me better. It is not what you did to your daughter. It is not what I do to you."

Andar held her hands, closing his eyes as he regained control. When he opened them he moved her hands around his waist and wrapped his own about her shoulders. They stood together in silence.

Behind one of the walls of their prison, Grenfeld straightened up from the small peep hole, a smile on his face. He reached out caressing the hole with his finger. Tomorrow he would begin with the woman. He would make it last a long time. Yes, tomorrow his revenge would begin.

Bonara watched as Grenfeld consumed his morning meal. His host, sitting at the table dressed in colourful finery, was pleasant and outgoing.

"Really, Bonara, you should try the roasted volver." Grenfeld raised a delicately carved cup and sipped the hot ree, then wiped his lips on a cloth. "My cook Tarus is the best in the town. He insists that the volver be caught alive and fed grain for days. Says it plumps them up and makes them tender." He sipped the tea again and laughed. "Perhaps I should try that with the next girl from the village. Do you think it would work?"

"What a clever idea. You really must let me know," said Bonara, raising his cup to hide his distaste for the man.

"Cheer up, friend," said Grenfeld. I'm sure my son will arrive any day now with the girl." He nodded to the manservant who approached to remove his plate. "Bresar." The man froze mid step, his eyes searching Grenfeld's face. "I understand Bresar that Tarus has put you in charge of supplying and preparing the volver."

The man shuffled nervously on his feet. "Yes, my Lord. It is a great honour."

"It is a great responsibility. You know how much I enjoy my volver."

"Yes, my Lord."

"Good. Then I'm sure I won't be disappointed. That it will be just as plump and sweet as always. Am I right, Bresar?"

"Yes, my Lord."

"Good, now you may take my plate away." Grenfeld turned to Bonara once more.

"Yes, you must have faith, Bonara. My son and I differ on many things, but I have taught him well. If, as you say, something has happened, he will find a way to return with the girl."

A tenuous knock on the door interrupted them. It opened and one of the servants eased inside, trailing apologies even as he broke the news. "My Lord, the men return. Even now they are coming up the street to the gate."

Grenfeld looked to Bonara who had sprung to his feet upon hearing the news.

"Do you hear that, Bonara? The day is complete. My son returns with the daughter of the man I have already captured. Now I have three prizes."

"Yes, yes," said Bonara, his head dizzy with the sudden excitement of the girl being found, of the return of the key. He couldn't sit again and paced about the table.

Grenfeld looked at him in amusement. "Patience my friend. Could it be that you were...by the Mother Ship, it's the girl isn't it? You're taken with her! So be it. I have the man and his new love. I no longer have any need of the daughter. Take her with my blessings. I-"

The door flew open and a number of men entered. Three of Grenfeld's servants assisted four battered, dishevelled figures that staggered towards the table.

"The girl! Where is the girl!" Bonara screamed the moment he saw that Dreanna wasn't among them.

Grenfeld took in the few men. "Shut up, Bonara. Portend, where is the girl? Where is Rothus? Where are the rest of the men? What has happened? Speak man and be quick."

"My Lord, we are all that is left. With your son, we found the girl and made off with her, but we were attacked by a band of men." Grenfeld glanced at Bonara. "We fought long and hard, my Lord, and even in the face of heavy odds we managed to escape; Rothus, the girl and others of us. Later we were attacked by a Suru, but we managed to kill him and save the girl. But then, my Lord, I swear before Kaptan Dukor, we were set upon by a band of Stomuants. More men died, my Lord." He paused uneasily.

"Go on, man. What happened next?"

"Your son and the girl were captured by them. We fought to free them, but there were too many of them. We fought until there were but four of us left, and then, knowing that we must get word to you, we fought our way to freedom and have carried this news to you that we might return with a large force and rescue them."

"Gone! The girl is gone? You let her be taken?" Bonara leapt at Portend and struck him across the face knocking him to the floor. He straddled him, but Grenfeld sprang forward and pulled Bonara off.

"Bonara, control yourself. She was just a woman. There are others in town."

"Just a woman? This isn't about a woman! This isn't about your stupid revenge. She held the key to power and knowledge. She alone could enable me to finish my quest. And now she is gone, and with it the secrets and power of the past."

"Get hold of yourself," said Grenfeld. "What are you talking about?"

"It's over," Bonara whispered, his eyes glazed as he pulled away from Grenfeld. "It's over," and he left the room.

Grenfeld knocked upon the door. It had only been a short time since the return of his men, but Grenfeld had little patience, especially when he felt he had been a pawn in another man's game. He had watched Bonara leave after hearing the news from his men. Although he had not understood the words, it confirmed his suspicions. He had always wondered why Bonara had been compelled to stay and await the return of Rothus. There was always something else. Now he would find out what it was.

The voice that bade him enter was low, barely audible. He found Bonara slouched in a chair staring vacantly out the window. The face had aged. Bonara swung his head towards Grenfeld, empty eyes watching his entrance. A smirk marred his lips as he addressed Grenfeld.

"Alas. You are too late my friend. It's over. A life's work, over and done."

"Trouble sits heavy upon you, Lord Bonara."

Bonara smirked again. "It's not Lord Bonara anymore. Simply Bonara, town merchant, for that is what I am. What I will always be."

"What is it that you hoped to be…before this loss overtook you?"

Bonara rolled his head to the window again, staring silently for a time. When he turned back, Grenfeld saw a trace of excitement in his eyes. "What would I have been? I will tell you. I would have been the most powerful man on Zendar. The knowledge and skills of another race, much more advanced than The Ancients, would have been mine."

Grenfeld kept his eyes upon Bonara. He thought they could be the musings of a man crazed by the cher root, but Bonara had never seemed as such, and even now, in these strange mutterings, he did not seem so. "Bonara, there is but one race, the race of man, unless you wish to think of the Stomuants as a different race, but they certainly are not more advanced than us."

"Yes, we may be the only race, the only *living* race on Zendar." Bonara laughed, a quiet empty sound that echoed in the room. "No, I am talking about a race that lived thousands of years before we even arrived on Zendar in the Mother ship. The Dremords; a race that travelled the planets, in control of a vast empire, Zendar being but one of their conquests." Caught in the excitement of his tale, Bonara levered himself to his feet and approached Grenfeld. "Even before the Dremords arrived, this planet was inhabited by others." His thoughts travelled back to the first time he had viewed the remains of them deep in the catacombs. "Yes, others were here before them; a race more similar to us in appearance. But they were conquered. For the Dremords, Zendar was a colony ripe for harvesting."

"But something happened. I haven't been able to find the reason why, but Zendar's air began to change. Something happened in the heavens, something that even the Dremords with their vast powers were unable to stop. The air was becoming poisonous for them to breathe. Not all could escape on the few planet travelling machines still here. To survive, adaptation to the new environment was needed. They created giant underground caverns where they retreated to sleep away time until their thinking machines could make changes to their bodies." Bonara's energy seemed to evaporate. He struggled back to his seat.

Grenfeld pulled his chair opposite him, eased into it, studying the man's face and voice for some sign of lunacy.

"This is a fascinating tale you weave, but what proof do you have? It would seem the ravings of a madman."

"Believe or disbelieve as you will, for it matters not. I could lead you to any of five caverns that I have unearthed in my quest to find one remaining Dremord alive." He saw Grenfeld's eyes widen with interest. "Yes, I have found their caverns, their sanctuaries. With my own eyes I have looked down upon their giant remains and wept with the frustration of doing so. Time and time again their machines failed to make the changes necessary for survival. The caverns, now tombs, hold only the remains of the Dremords. It took years of searching to find each new cavern, but always I was too late. Perhaps many, many years too late, I don't know. I have entered five of the chambers. There was still hope that in this last one there might remain some that are still alive, who have not been awakened yet by their machines, only to die."

Bonara lapsed into silence, his gaze moving away from Grenfeld to the window. Grenfeld found himself caught up in the tale, wondering what they might look like, what powers they might possess that he could use.

"Go on Bonara," he urged. "What prevents you from entering this last cavern?"

Bonara drifted back to the present, staring blankly at Grenfeld. His hands fumbled with the small pouch at his belt. He eased open the drawstring and let the contents slide out onto the table; five thin gray pieces, each with varying sized holes. Grenfeld eyed them with sudden new interest. Here was tangible proof of something out of the ordinary, for he saw at a glance that they were foreign in nature.

"Five of them. There are five. Only with all six can I gain entrance to the final cavern. There were six, but one was dropped and then found again. Found by the daughter of the man you hold prisoner."

Grenfeld pressed his thumbs together resting his chin upon the pommel of his prisoner's sword as he awaited his arrival. The purple hue of the blade shone gently in the sunlight from the window. The first of many prizes, he thought to himself as he admired the blade that until now he knew only as a legend. Bonara sat to his left, quiet and subdued despite the plan the two had agreed upon. Grenfeld was more pensive than usual, wondering if he was making a mistake. The course of action they had decided upon was hard for him to accept.

They had talked all afternoon, gradually drawing the information from Bonara until finally Grenfeld was convinced of the authenticity of the merchant's claims. Bonara had brought forth other strange and mysterious looking articles, none of which were of this world. Yes, he believed the story was real, and so would be the immense power that other devices might contain.

The door opened and the captives were brought before them, hands bound securely behind their backs..

"Where is my daughter? What have you done with her?"

Grenfeld looked upon the man who stood angry and defiant, demanding his daughter. He saw the weathered toughness of the lean body, the grim determination in the face. He had seen him fight many, many years ago. He doubted that few men were as skilled. If anyone could get the girl back from the Stomuants, he could. It was his daughter; no one would fight harder.

"Where is she Grenfeld?" Andar yelled stepping forward despite the two who held him. They grappled with him, kicking his legs, bringing him to his knees.

"What, no pleasantries after all these years?" said Grenfeld rising and stepping forward. "Nothing would give me greater pleasure than to tell you that I have her and have been making love to her for days."

Andar surged upwards, his face twisted in hate. A blow from behind stunned him and he slumped to the floor.

"Stop it!" yelled Dajata, struggling against her guards.

Grenfeld looked at her then back at Andar. "Yes, that is what I would like to tell you, but I don't have your daughter. I never have. My son was not successful. The two have disappeared."

"Liar," said Andar, struggling to sit up.

"He speaks the truth."

Andar turned his gaze to the speaker, noticing him for the first time. He took in the gray beard and thin face. "You. What part did you play in this? Where is my daughter?"

Grenfeld stepped between Andar and Bonara.

"Your daughter and my son have been captured by the Stomuants, and you are going to get them back."

Chapter Nine

Rothus felt the blackness rise and swirl around him, unaware of his imminent contact with the earth. When he crumbled to the ground, he was already unconscious.

"By The Mother Stone, this one stupid," said the bald Stomuant who stood over the inert body. "This one big stupid. Can't touch without him attack." He walked around Rothus, stopping to nudge him in the ribs with his foot and roll him over. "Look him. Back from exchange, already useless from beatings." The Stomuant shook his head in disgust as he turned to his companion. "I say I kill him. Too much waste time." He looked down at the figure sprawled on the ground and nudged him with thick blunt toes. "Stupid one cost Gurgios much money." He shrugged to his companion. "Gurgios waste time."

Dreanna won her battle with the weight of the meat, turning it on the spit then hurrying to the table to prepare some reed cakes. Although tired, she worked quickly, often hustling back to the spit to turn the huge cut of meat. She moulded the dough into large, round portions then carried them to the oven beside the fire. Pushing the coals aside, she placed the dough inside then rolled the stone slab over the opening. She wiped her brow with the back of her arm and leaned tiredly against the warm cover. She could rest for a moment, although not for long.

Korados would soon be home, as would his mate, Laposa. The food must be ready.

Being chosen as the house servant by Korados had terrified her. When he had taken her inside, she had hardly been able to function, but he had shown patience. She had heard that he was considerate, that his slaves were not abused. Stern, without the cruelty that was characteristic of many of the Stomuants, some said. Others argued that he was simply practical and did not want to pay the exchange fee.

She had learned that he was a powerful Stomuant who made decisions for their people. Both warriors of high rank, often in council, Korados and Laposa were seldom at home during the day. When the food was prepared, her only other job was to care for Jakerda, their young child, who after being nursed by his human mother, had been taken from her. At three years, his skin was a pale gray, much lighter than that of either Korados or Laposa, his black hair no coarser than Dreanna's. Although Jakerda only came to Dreanna's waist, he weighed as much as her and was already stronger.

In the evening, before Dreanna was allowed to retire with the others, it was expected that she sit and play and talk with the young one. Korados and Laposa would watch the two. Dreanna had been the most terrified of this time, fearing they watched, ready to punish her if she did anything wrong. But nothing of the kind had occurred and she realized that Korados and Laposa *were* different than other Stomuants. At meetings in his home, he was demanding and gruff. More than once she had seen him attack another who showed disrespect or who did not fulfill their obligations. But it was at night, when they were alone, that she saw his daily countenance seemed a facade. In his dealings with Laposa and his son, and even herself, there seemed little of the quick, volatile Stomuant that was in evidence during the day.

That evening as she entertained Jakerda, he noticed the swatch of material that Rothus had given her protruding from her wrap. He snatched it, examining it. Dreanna lunged for the cloth with a startled cry and caught it, but the youngster held it tightly in his grip. As he pulled, the material tore, her only connection to Rothus torn in two. Weeks of fear and loneliness released a flood of tears as she held it to her chest, sobbing uncontrollably.

Laposa began to rise but Korados put a hand on her shoulder. The two watched as Jakerda approached Dreanna, his face a mixture of confusion and concern. He pushed the remaining material he held into Dreanna's hands. Still sobbing, she stared at the two pieces, closed her eyes and held them to her face. Jakerda reached out again and laid his hand upon the side of Dreanna's head.

"No cry, Dreanna."

Korados and Laposa looked at each other.

"Laposa put Jakerda to sleep." Korados looked at his son. "Nothing wrong." When the two left, he sat and watched Dreanna until she regained control of herself.

"Can I go now?" Dreanna asked, her voice thick with tears.

"No," said Korados. When he saw the stricken look on her face, he added, "Jakerda not need be sorry. You not need be sorry. Accident. Good accident. Much encouraging."

Dreanna looked at him through watery eyes, unable to make sense of what he had said. In the silence that followed, she composed herself further. When Laposa returned she sat beside Korados and took his hand in hers.

"Why this important?" He pointed to the cloth clutched in Dreanna's hand. "Why so much sad when taken from you?"

Dreanna looked down at the cloth, crumpled and wet from her tears, then up at them, and no longer cared. She didn't care if she said things she shouldn't. She didn't care if her anger, fear, and hatred came out. She spoke of the Stomuants' cruelty and her terror and fear of changing, of never seeing her home again. Dreanna told of her family and spoke of Rothus, and the words poured from her, and she saw him and felt him near. She told of their capture and of her love for him. And when she had finished, Dreanna felt stronger for having stood up for herself and her kind. Now it didn't matter what they did to her.

Korados remained silent for several moments then spoke, his speech slow and halting as he tried to express himself.

"We start as one, now two different people. Yes, we people. Not creatures or Stomuants... like you call us. Strong warriors. Owe life to The Stone. We hunt, capture you... to show we better, to show we right to stay by The Stone. Strong from it. You stay small and weak."

Korados stood and walked to a window staring out into the night then returned to Laposa. She raised her hand and Korados held it, staring at her before he turned to Dreanna again.

"We hunt you for more. We stay with The Stone. It is power, life for us. But there is... result. We need you. We cannot have young. We bring you here to survive. You give us young. Until change take place. Then you like us. Can not have young. So we gather more."

"You weak, but we not live without you. We hunt you. You fear, hate us." He looked at Dreanna. "Good for all that you fear The Stone. If not, no one survives."

Dreanna sat fascinated. She realized that she might be the first to understand the tenuous position of the Stomuants. She now knew what was in store for her and was numbed by the knowledge. She would mate with another human captive and even as the stone started to change them, they would have children. Children who would not be like them. And the more they changed, the more their children would be... different. They would be taken away from her to be raised by others. This was to be her life.

Days later, when Dreanna left Korados' house and returned to her quarters, she found Rothus lying in a corner of the compound, barely alive. She ran to him, pulling his face from the dirt floor and cradling him in her arms. She cried over him. Cried because she had found him and they were together again. She cried because Korados had found him, and she knew why.

Chapter Ten

The soaring peaks and jagged cliffs of the mountains cast Andar and the other men in shadows as they trudged single file through the bleak wasteland towards the dark cathedrals of stone; sentinels that guarded the home of the Stomuants. White mist came in waves making the clear visibility nonexistent from one moment to another. Sparse patches of blackened reed grass grew scarcely knee high among the scattered debris of rocks. Among it, thick bodied trees, gnarled and deformed, fought the dry cold, struggling to survive. Andar had never seen the likes of these tortured giants, the surface of their trunks and branches deformed with countless crusted knots, their limbs twisted and stunted from lack of rain.

He led the way at a steady pace, shoulders hunched high, his cloak pulled tight against the cold wind. None of them had experienced cold like this. It was the fourth day and the temperature had dropped, but he bore the cold without complaint, as did the men.

His weapons, trail bag and cloak had been returned to him and he had been supplied with all the food and equipment that he requested. He knew little of the mountains or what to expect, but gathered together some rope, extra wraps and foot coverings. He had chosen nine of Grenfeld's tough seasoned warriors, ones he felt he could depend upon. They were close in age to him with a life's experience that would temper their lust for adventure with a desire to return safely to their families. So far they had not let him down. None had complained and now held a grudging respect for him as they had learned of his own tough unyielding character.

The impossibility of his task had long since been submerged by his determination. It must be done. Somehow, he would find a way to cross the mountains, find his daughter, free her from the Stomuants and return to the woman who had shouted her love for him as she had been dragged away.

For half a day, they wound their way silently through the huge boulders at the base of the mountains, choosing a ravine that sloped gently upwards. By the day's end, although their progress up the side had been limited, the further decline in temperature was all too evident. As they huddled together eating some reed cake, Andar felt a strange stinging tightness in his fingers as he moved them. He had little doubt that as they journeyed higher, it would only get colder. Now he knew how ill-prepared they were for the journey, but who if anyone had ever climbed the Northern Mountains? He cursed himself for not bringing the Ancient One's tool, but who could have know the cold. With it he could have created heat to warm them. But he had wanted to keep it safe and so had hidden it in Dajata's sleeping wrap. Looking at the haggard faces of the men, he knew a decision had to be made. When night came, once again without a supply of reed wood, they huddled together, sleeping fitfully.

It had been difficult, but finally, with much debate, when the pale light of morning hazed into existence, only five continued up the steepening incline. Wrapped and bound with double layers of sleeping wraps under their cloaks, they increased their pace, striving to keep warm and decrease the nights they would have to spend on the mountain. The others, without their sleeping wraps and with a minimum of supplies, raced down the slope homewards. Everything they could spare to keep the advancing five warm and fed had been relinquished in the hopes that it would keep them alive.

As Andar climbed, the winds disappeared, but the temperature continued to drop. Their breath changed into white mist as they exhaled, and a cold white substance appeared in patches beneath their feet. Soon it became a thick coating on the ground into which they sank, wetting the wraps they had bound onto their legs and feet. The incline became steeper, almost vertical in some places. Often they had to backtrack and seek an easier route upwards. Fingers were numb and bled as they scrambled over boulder and rock.

With one hand tracing the wall to his left, Andar walked carefully along a ledge, avoiding the sheer vertical drop to his right. His eyes watered from the cold and despite having wrapped his face, he felt as if he were wearing a tight mask. He turned to the four men behind him.

"We'll eat and rest on the ledge ahead."

They nodded agreement and together shuffled forward along it. The rock face yielded to the left, the ledge widening quickly as it disappeared around the corner. When Andar stepped around the rock face, the Stomuant towered above him, his face a frozen scowl as he stared downwards. Staggering back, Andar crashed into the man behind him. Both fell heavily to the ground, almost tumbling over the edge of the precipice. Andar fought for his sword within the tangled cloak, his eyes drawn to the Stomuant who surveyed them silently. Andar stared at the creature, waiting for the attack. Finally he found his sword hilt, but realized there was no danger. His head fell back and he closed his eyes, his racing heart slowing as the tension drained from him. He heard the frightened men panting and cursing behind him as they too understood.

Andar struggled to his feet. The wind had suddenly stilled and the ominous silence was complete. He was still too shaken to venture forward and studied the frozen giant from where he stood. A huge slab of rock from a landslide had fallen on the Stomuant's leg, crushing it and pinning him to the ledge. Andar took a step forward, still unsettled by the size and frightening appearance of the creature, even in death.

"May the ancestors forgive me," said Taburt behind him. His voice was quiet and filled with fear and awe. "How could we have known? No reward is enough."

"It's dead. It can't harm you, said Andar."

"This one can't. It's the ones that are alive that I fear." The other men nodded and mumbled agreement.

Andar turned back to the Stomuant. Snow covered his shoulders and lay along the arm that held a spear out in front of him. On his leg there were terrible cuts and gashes from his attempt to cut himself free. Behind him the ledge disappeared, buried by the avalanche of stone that had ended the creature's life. Andar turned back to the solemn faces of the men. Their eyes refused to meet his as they stared at the dead giant.

"We can't continue this way," he said. "Warka, lead us back the way we came," he said to the man at the far end. With nervous glances at the Stomuant, the others followed Warka.

They backtracked and soon stopped for something to eat. All were quiet, heads downcast as they chewed the small portion of reed bread. At last Taburt, the oldest of the men spoke.

"Every man here knows I am no coward." The other men nodded their heads in agreement. "I was glad to be chosen to rescue your daughter. It is a just cause." He looked at Andar. "I have children of my own. I have only... to see such creatures..." Embarrassed, he looked away. "Forgive me, but I realize the folly of this venture. I wish to see my family again. Neither the wrath of Grenfeld nor his money can make me continue. I pray the Ancients guide you in your quest, but I will start homeward now." The men were silent, until the one beside him nodded.

"I too will return with Taburt," he said.

Andar studied them then looked to the other two.

"I will continue with you," said Warka.

Andar's gaze shifted to Pagar, a whiskered, thick bodied man.

"As shall I," he said quietly.

"Then let us start, each on his own journey," said Andar as he rose. They clambered to their feet.

"May our ancestors watch over you," said Taburt.

"And you," replied Andar.

The two started down the mountain and were soon lost to sight. Andar shouldered his pack and turned to the remaining men. "There is not much time left before dark, and even brave, foolhardy men know better than to travel a mountain slope at night."

The new route that promised to lead them over the mountains was a twisted, tormented affair that cut back and forth along the face of a steep cliff. After eating at midday, Andar noticed a change in the air just before large flakes of white began to fall. He held out a curious hand to one, catching it on an upturned palm. It was cold and melted almost immediately. As they increased, the flakes landed on their heads, shoulders and arms. Soon the sky was filled with white as it fell faster and faster, the flakes growing larger, covering the ground. Hand sized flakes of white cold clung to arms and legs. It weighted down their heads and shoulders making breathing difficult. Visibility was impossible. Andar shook his shoulders trying to free the growing mass that clung to his body. With a sinking heart, he realized that the rains, white rains, had come to the mountains.

The heat from their bodies seeped through and melted the traces of white that were not shaken free. Soon they were soaked, the sticky flakes now clinging more tenaciously. In desperation Andar grabbed at the men in the whiteness, his voice muffled by the thick air.

"We must find some shelter. Grab my cloak. Hold on to the one in front of you."

Turning, he hugged the cliff to his right. He felt the grasping tug on his cloak and blinded by the wall of white, ventured forward along the ledge, seeking the shelter of a cave, an overhanging ledge or a crevice into which they might crawl. They shuffled through the growing layer of white rain, each step harder than the last as it rose around their ankles then deepened to their calves. It clung to them, weighed them down and sucked the heat from their bodies.

It began as a distant rumbling sound that seemed to come from above. It grew until the air seemed to vibrate. Confused, they stopped, waiting.

The tumbling mass struck them, tearing the hand behind him from his cloak as the other two were swept away. The force ripped his cloak from him as the wave of white raced by. Sheltered by a thrusting slab of rock above him, he fought the spray that threatened to drag him over the edge. He dove in the direction of the cliff wall. His head crashed into it and he staggered back into the fringe of the racing wall of white. It tore at his face, blinding him then hit his chest toppling him over onto his back. With a mouth full of cold, he twisted and turned his back to the wave, crawling towards the cliff wall. Reaching it he struggled to his feet, clutching the wall. He spit to empty his mouth. Clawed at his eyes to clear them. The madness of the rushing wall tore past him overhead as he pressed against the rock wall.

A cascade of white showered down onto the ledge from the wave as it hurtled over him. The pile of white grew on the ledge, sliding back towards the rock face where he stood. It spread to his feet then rose to his knees. Andar kicked and stomped, breaking free and scrambling on top as the rising mound threatened to bury him. It rushed at him faster. He slipped and fell, sliding backwards into the rock wall behind him. In a moment he was pinned there as it flowed around his waist and chest, the pressure tight and unyielding. As fast as he shoved it aside, it slid down onto him until only his head remained free.

Andar noticed the silence before he became aware that the slide of white had ceased. He was shivering uncontrollably now and needed to rest, but flake after silent flake swirled in to settle on him. He realized that where the wall of white had failed to bury him, the falling flakes would succeed. He freed a hand, then the other, and pushed and scooped away the snow to free his shoulders. He worked feverishly despite his exhaustion, the fear of death driving him. He hunched his shoulders and levered himself with his arms, rocking his body back and forth, packing the snow to force some space around him. Finally he clambered free and lay on top of the white mass. In seconds the large flakes stuck to him, draining his energy. Somewhere, he found the strength, fought to his knees and beat them from him. He couldn't feel his hands and feet. His fingers barely moved and he realized they didn't hurt any more.

Andar crawled up the pile before him then slid down to the right. Blinded by the flakes, he stumbled forward. The shivering had stopped and he no longer felt cold, but when he fell he could barely get up. Sleep beckoned him. It would be fine to rest for a short while. He wasn't cold anymore. He would be fine. He raised his arm to wipe away the flakes that covered his face, but his arm hurt him. He saw that the wraps covering it were frozen. He raised his other arm to pull at the material, but his hand wouldn't move. He cursed, but the words were slurred.

He knew he was dying. He shook his head violently, throwing the white from it, trying to clear his mind, but his thoughts wouldn't crystallize. He staggered a step, a second, then toppled over the edge of the cliff into the swirling white void below.

The door to Dajata's prison opened to reveal a figure framed in the doorway. Grenfeld smiled, a glint of white teeth in the dark. He executed a subtle bow, but did not enter the room.

"Forgive me for not visiting you earlier. My affairs have kept me preoccupied. So much to do when you have so many interests." He smiled again and leaned against the door frame. "May I come in?"

Dajata drew herself upright and raised her chin, but inside she trembled. She had known men such as him. She felt her heart race as he stepped into the room and swung the door closed. She had been used by others, sent at the whim of her father. But that had been a lifetime ago, when she had been little more than a hollow shell. Before she had met Andar.

He loomed out of the darkness into the light of the torch, crowding her back towards the small bed. In the cool of the room she felt his warm breath on her cheek. It smelled of reed ale. She felt it on her neck, on the hollow between her breasts as he bent lower. She stared at the top of his head, angry that he saw her tremble. His head snapped up and he smiled; the same cruel smile that others had. It was their smile, those who had used her. But she had survived and met Andar. Grown stronger and changed. She wouldn't let this man or any other cower her. Not anymore. Her trembling ceased and Dajata smiled back at him.

Grenfeld saw the defiant smile. He moved behind her. Despite her resolve, Dajata gasped when his arm came over her shoulder, the dagger stopping short of entering her chest. Its point pressed against the soft flesh of her breast.

"If you move, I will kill you," he said. She felt his tongue lick her ear, then the bite on her earlobe. She stared ahead, eyes wide, the prick from the dagger's point demanding her attention. She sensed him fumbling at his wrap. Confusion as the warmth ran down her legs. Then the smell of his urine soiled the room. With a harsh laugh he removed the dagger and shoved her from him.

"You will learn. I have much time and patience to teach you."

Dajata stood with her head bowed. She steeled herself, drawing strength from Andar, from the way he loved her, and she him. She turned, raised her arms in defeat to Grenfeld, stepping to him. She laid her head upon his chest and wrapped her arms around his waist. Grenfeld rubbed her buttocks, working her wrap upwards. Dajata moved her feet, spreading her thighs for him.

The spray of her urine ran down Grenfeld's thighs. He cursed her and tried to push her away, but she clung to him, emptying herself. With a violent shove he threw her across the room, his face contorted with rage as he drew his dagger. He took a murderous step towards her then slowly lowered his arm, his breath coming in long shudders. He stood in the darkness, watching her.

Grenfeld's eyes bore into her as his hand moved down to his damp thighs. He brought it up to his face, smelling her scent. He said nothing as he moved towards the door. With a hollow thud the door closed and she was left alone.

Chapter Eleven

Rigersor had scowled at the sky as the flakes began. Huddled on the mountainside east of the five men that remained, he tore off a piece of dried meat, pulled the cloth from his face and stuffed the frozen strip in his mouth. He held it there until it started to thaw then chewed absently as he watched the others. He wanted to approach them and tell them that their route was pointless, but knew that would be folly. The men would be terrified of him, Andar no doubt enraged. His only choice was to let them explore this mountain face and determine it was impassable.

The journey back to Kempa with Doros had been quick and uneventful. They had reached the town, and soon Doros had returned with Lanos to the Sleeper's meagre campsite where Rigersor sat among a thick copse of trees tending a fire.

Doros nodded silently to him then turned to Lanos. "Grandfather, this is the...the one I talked about."

"Sleeper is what you call us. You can call me that. There is no shame in what I am."

The old man had paled at his first sight of Rigersor when the Sleeper rose to his feet, but Lanos steeled his nerves and with wary steps approached him.

"Doros has told me of the part you played in this quest, and for that you have my thanks and that of our ancestors."

"It is nothing compared to what your son did for me. I would do more to help him find his daughter."

"There is more that you can do." Lanos glanced at Doros who nodded.

"Grandfather agrees with me. Father is..." His emotions got the better of him and he looked off into the distance before returning his gaze to Rigersor. "I never knew what Father could do. He is the best swordsman on all of Zendar, of that I am sure." His voice had risen with pride and he stood straighter. "But he is only one man, and we don't know what he has yet to face. If you really wish to help him, to repay him, then leave us. We know the way back to Bonstag. There is no danger to us. We'll watch as Father has said. The danger lies in Dashindar where he is headed."

Rigersor studied the young face then looked to the old man. "You agree with this young warrior?"

"It's what we both wish," said Lanos.

"I have given my word to your son to protect you both."

"Easy to fulfill your word with a safe journey," said Lanos, the challenge in his voice.

Rigersor smiled. "I see where your son learned how to manipulate others." He took a deep breath and looked skyward, squinting into the sun. "It is still early. If I leave now I will make good distance."

Rigersor had travelled the mountains before and knew he had to immediately seek shelter on the narrow trail, even though he was on the outskirts of the white death. He hurled himself towards the rock wall. The run-off tore at him, but crouched low under an outthrust of rock, his frame solidly anchored, there was little danger. He knew it wasn't the case for those ahead of him.

Before the last of the white slid past him, Rigersor started up the mountainside again. He forged ahead, encountering the pile of churned white rain on the trail before him. The immense pack he carried hindered his movements and weighted him down. He waded into the barrier, hugging the wall, fighting the crumbling slide towards the precipice. At times it was white powder into which he sank waist deep, the next minute, boulders of white rock, hard and unyielding. The wind had ceased but the steadily falling flakes all but blinded him, visibility little more than an arm's length. Only the sound of his deep breathing seeped through the silent air. That he was too late he didn't doubt. Unlike him, the men had been directly in the path of the rushing wall of white. He would fight his way to the other side and look for his body. He would do that much for the man who had saved his life.

A moan carried faintly to his ears. It startled him, so sure was he that all must be dead. Then Rigersor renewed his efforts, charging the mound on the trail in front of him. He forgot the yawning chasm to his right, slashing at the barrier with his hands. He staggered, losing his balance, and almost fell over the edge.

The figure appeared white and ghostlike an arm's length from him. In an instant it vanished. Rigersor didn't hesitate. He focused on the spot where he had last seen the apparition, and hurled himself forward, head first over the edge of the trail to the depths below.

Rigersor's heavy body punctured the white surface and he descended into its soft embrace. It was light and air entrenched near the surface, cushioning his fall. As his body sank, he spread his arms and legs to slow his sinking. He was twice his height below the surface before his descent stopped. He immediately pushed outwards against the white, creating a breathing space. He listened for any sound, but there was nothing. He called out Andar's name, the confines muffling and choking the sound of his voice. He shouted again then listened to the empty silence . He knew that to search would be futile. Andar could be within reach of him even now and he would never know.

Again he heard an almost inaudible groan that died. Rigersor yelled, but there was nothing. He thought he might have imagined it and yelled once more, and then again. In the white silence, he stood perfectly still, eyes closed, listening. At last, he was rewarded by another feeble cry. Now he had a direction and tunnelled his way carefully in pursuit of the ghost whisper, calling out and listening.

He had not landed far from Andar, but had plunged deeper than him. With a gentle cascade of white, the ceiling above him gave way and Andar fell upon him. The Sleeper clutched the cold body and lowered it gently. He examined him quickly and his heavy brow furrowed.

Andar's body was very cold and stiff. Even the torso was bereft of any warmth. Only the slightest heat seeped from the scalp. But he would try.

Rigersor shucked the pack from his shoulders then used his staff to poke an air hole above him. Next he used his weight to create more space, driving outwards with his back and shoulders. Already much of the heat in the white rain, generated from the tumbling and swirling down the mountainside, had vanished. It was hardening quickly as it cooled but Rigersor fought doggedly to create a small cave for them. Soon, breathing heavily, he sank to his knees and tore open the huge pack. He pulled many sleeping wraps free, dug further and unearthed a container made of reed wood, then a larger gourd. After spreading two of the cloaks, he pulled Andar onto them. With a curved dagger from his belt, he cut the frozen cloak and sleeping wraps from him until the bluish white body lay exposed. It was worse than he had thought, and for a moment the futility of his efforts struck him. But the man was a survivor, so he began.

Methodically, he smeared paste from the larger of the two containers onto Andar's body. From head to toe he applied it, rolling the stiffened body onto its stomach and coating the back, buttocks and legs. Setting the paste aside, he opened the second container and began sifting the yellowish green powder over Andar's body. He began at the skull and sprinkled the stone crystals, watching them land and stick to the paste. The reaction started immediately. He agonized over how thickly to layer the potent crystals, for he had never used them on a human with delicate skin. He rolled Andar's body over and carefully continued, letting the crystals drift down in the gloom of the cave. Finished, he pulled the two wraps tightly around Andar then added three more. The heat from the crystals had to be contained in order to warm the body.

Rigersor found a drinking mug in his pack and put some of the paste and crystallized stone into it. The cup became warm as the two substances reacted. Carving some of the hardened white rain from the wall, Rigersor filled the cup and watched it melt. He added more and soon had a half cup of yellowish-green, warm water. He pried Andar's mouth open and poured a little of the liquid within. Much of it ran down the wraps but he saw that some trickled down his throat. Patiently he coaxed the liquid down a little at a time. When almost gone, he added a pinch more of the powdered stone and forced the rest into Andar's mouth. Then he sat back. There was nothing more to do but wait.

Andar began to moan, the sound bringing a smile of satisfaction from Rigersor. The moaning increased as blood travelled once more to Andar's extremities. Rigersor knew the pain would increase as his body responded to the warmth. He knew the pain would be intense, for much of the human's body had been stiff, set in its own fluids. Another few minutes and he would spread the reed wood salve. It would soothe the burns from the stone powder and help the tissues and muscles survive their reawakening.

Although still unconscious, Andar rolled his head from side to side, his groans loud and continuous as the pain increased. His eyes flew wide, a single cry of pain echoing in the cave. It died away as his eyes, filled with agony, focused on Rigersor. Red-faced and dappled with sweat, he stared in recognition at the Sleeper. Rigersor relinquished a grim smile.

"We meet again, Andar. I know the pain is great, but it will get worse before it gets better. You are a man familiar with pain, so I know you will bear it with quiet dignity as befits your race." A smile passed over the large mouth again. Andar said nothing but rolled his eyes up towards the ceiling of their cave as the wave of pain grew. His mouth closed and his face tightened. Drops of sweat ran down his blotched cheeks.

"I must remove the wraps and apply the salve now that the blood has started to return. If I wait any longer the flesh may die and so will you. It will hurt, but it must be done." Without waiting, Rigersor began to un-wrap his body. He moved slowly, being as gentle as possible. At times he would wait patiently until Andar's pain-filled breath slowed before starting again. When he finally peeled the last wrap from him, his eyes leapt to Andar's face. Rigersor clenched his jaw as he viewed the raw, red skin. He had used too much of the Stone powder. Applying the salve would be all the more painful. Scraping some from the container with the edge of his dagger, he turned to Andar once more.

"I cannot help but feel that you have done something to anger those ancestors who might have influence over your fate."

Andar's eyes returned to the broad face of the Sleeper. With effort, he controlled his panting breath. Through a clenched jaw his words escaped. "Spread the salve." His eyes closed as he clenched his fists. Rigersor looked down compassionately at the slight frame and began.

Rigersor chipped with his sword at the shiny white walls of their cave, opening a doorway to a new tunnel that they would excavate upwards. The heat from their bodies had gradually melted the surface of the walls turning them rock hard. They had moved from cave to cave, tunnelling upwards as the white rain built up above them, darkening the one they were in.

"It will not be long now. I think the white rain will end any day and we will be able to continue," said Rigersor.

"I pray to our ancestors that you're right. The delay has been too long," said Andar as he jabbed angrily at the wall. His face still bore blotches of red, but his strength was returning as the reed salve did its work. Rigersor fed him constantly from the large food store he had carried. When questioned why he brought so much, Rigersor had pointed out that Andar had begun his journey with ten men.

Rigersor pushed his sword into the snow floor. "Enough. Let us rest and eat."

It had taken days for Andar to accept that Rigersor had done the right thing in leaving Doros on the outskirts of Kempa. The Sleeper had travelled back towards Dashindar, caught in the rains as had Andar and Dajata, but unlike them, to make up for lost time, he had journeyed part of each day, his tremendous strength allowing him to do so. He had reached Dashindar and set up a camp in the forest by the trail, waiting for Andar and Dajata to arrive or leave the city. When Andar had finally emerged from the city with the soldiers, he knew that all was not well and had followed them. When it became apparent that they were headed north towards the mountains, Rigersor had gathered and fashioned supplies along the way.

Andar chewed on the tough, dried meat and studied his companion, who ate in silence. They had talked much, sharing stories, learning much about each other.

"You have never said where you come from," said Andar, opening the conversation.

"Where else but from the North? A small village called Downet. Not so far north, not so close to the Stone, as to turn people, but close enough that... I think you can see. My parents were normal, at least on the outside, but the stone must have affected one or both of them." He picked up the gourd that held melted white rain and drank. "They hid me, protected me from the outside world. They loved me. When I was discovered, they were killed as punishment for the love they showed. I escaped."

"Are you not filled with hate for us? For what they did?"

The Sleeper was quiet for a long spell, his thoughts deep and veiled by silence. When he finally spoke, it was with a softness that Andar had not heard before.

"My mother. She taught me that it is only their fear that makes them hate so. She taught me that if I hate, as they do, then I am like them. Then they killed her and for a long time, I hated as they did. I killed as they did." He stared at Andar, coming back from the distant memories that haunted him. "But I have met some humans, such as yourself, who have proven my mother right." Silence hung in the air until Andar spoke.

"You know a route across the mountains? You've crossed them before?"

"When I was searching...for somewhere to belong." He shrugged indifferently. "It was a long time ago. Since then I have accepted what I am, and what I cannot be." He smiled at Andar. "The route is further to the west."

Two days later, the white rain stopped and they tunnelled to the surface. The sky was clear, bright sun warm on their faces. It made the freshly fallen white rain blinding. They donned the eye protectors that Rigersor had fashioned and set out. Travelling was slow through the powdered surface, but Rigersor steered them to near vertical rock walls where the whiterain had not clung. On these they climbed. The air remained still and the sun warmed them as they scaled the mountain, clinging precariously to tiny cracks and crevices, sometimes trudging up inclines littered with the debris of rock slides. More than once, using the rope, Rigersor pulled Andar past nonexistent hand holds. He had enormous reserves of strength, and at times Andar struggled to keep pace with the Sleeper. Much of his own strength had returned and his determination grew with each cliff and peak they conquered. Gradually breathing became difficult as the air grew thin. The sun's rays were no match for the temperature as it continued to drop with their climb and by the end of the first day, as the evening air tightened its cold grip upon them, they huddled in a hollowed out bank of white.

Late in the afternoon of the third day of climbing, they reached the summit. Standing side by side in the bitter cold air, they gazed at the forbidding mountain scape below. Shadowed from the sun, the mountains thrust jagged, white pinnacles through clouds of mist that blanketed them half way down. Ponderous sheets of white rock filled the valleys and crevices that ran in twisted paths down the mountain. If anything, the northern side was even more rugged and unwelcoming than the one they had just climbed.

"*This* is your easier way down the mountain?" Andar asked.

"No, not here. Now we must travel east. Come, it is not far."

Andar saw it in the distance, a thin line that zigzagged in steep graceful curves down the mountainside. He couldn't fathom what it might mean or who would have built it. Guessing his thoughts, Rigersor answered the unspoken question.

"It was built by the Stomuants. When I do not know. It is hollow and was used by them to send stone, their stone, down the mountain from the mine. The route it follows, although longer, is the easiest and fastest."

When they finally reached the tube, Andar saw that it was about the diameter of his shoulders, the halves of hollowed out reed trees fastened together to form a chute. Wherever the tube went over the steepest inclines, crude steps and scaffolding had been fashioned to build and support it. Following the path of the tube would be easier. He rested his hand on it, the smooth hard surface as good as the day it was built.

"Rigersor, how long will it take us if we follow this route?"

"Four days, maybe less if we push hard."

Andar studied the surface of the tube and the flowing route it took as it descended the mountain. He ran his hand back and forth over the tube.

"We're going to use this," he said, suddenly excited. "Rigersor, do you see how smooth and slippery it is? Yes! We're going to ride it straight down the mountain!"

Chapter Twelve

Andar stood holding the makeshift sled steady on the top of the tube as he watched Rigersor slip over a jagged rocks and climb down the slope near the pipe. The Sleeper stopped not far from him.

"This is far enough. You are going to fall off as soon as you start," he said.

"Just make sure you stop me from shooting by."

"It is hard to walk down a mountain with a broken leg. Even a Sleeper knows this."

A sleeping wrap had been wet, and as it froze, moulded over the sides of the pipe to form a curved platform upon which Andar would lay. He held the front edges of the frozen wrap and swung one leg up and over it. Cautiously he lifted his other from the ground. There was a moment of jittery balancing, and then he crashed heavily to the ground on the other side of the pipe. He rubbed his arm as he looked ruefully at the sled that now hung upside down. Slowly it started to slide down the pipe, but Andar reached up and stopped it. He had travelled less than the span of his hand.

"Well done," said Rigersor.

Ignoring the Sleeper, Andar climbed to his feet, pulled the sled back on top of the pipe, and mounted it again. This time he travelled the length of his body before toppling off sideways. He wasn't quick enough, and the empty sled picked up speed as it travelled down the pipe. Rigersor stopped it, pulled it roughly from the tube, and climbed back up to Andar. He threw it down beside him.

"Are you ready to get started?"

"What I need is some way to get more leverage to be able to balance myself." Andar stared at the wrap. "And I need something to rest my feet on so I can keep them up. Maybe turn the bottom edge up near the back and let it freeze there."

Rigersor shook his head and turned to his pack. Pulling out some reed bread, he sat down and ate.

With his sword sheath frozen into place across the front of the wrap, Andar had something that would help his balance. After several more practice runs and falls, he was able to travel the distance to Rigersor, who viewed the contraption with distaste. Although still sceptical, he helped fashion another larger one and grudgingly practiced with his craft.

"I'll go first," said Andar. "If we squeeze the pipe with our thighs we should be able to control the speed, and the pipe levels out in places so we should slow down there as well."

Rigersor only grunted. Andar tied his pack on his back and lay on top of the sled, one foot resting lightly on the ground. He gazed nervously down the curving length of the reed pipe that disappeared into the mist far below, then looked at Rigersor.

"With our ancestors' blessing, I'll see you at the bottom." He took a final breath, lifted his foot and, with the scraping sound of frozen wrap against pipe, he was gone.

The added weight of his pack increased the speed rapidly. The front edge, bent upwards, thudded as it slid over the rough joints that connected the reeds. In a moment, he was past where Rigersor had stood and stopped him. Alarmed at his speed, he gripped the sword sheath tighter, pressed his thighs against the pipe and creased his eyes as the sled tore through the frigid air. The speed somehow made balancing easier, but already he was racing down the mountain out of control.

His speed continued to build. Andar knew that if he made a mistake, or if the pipeline were broken, he would be smashed against the rocks in an instant. On he sped, his face numb from the wind. He concentrated on the gentle bends in the pipe, shifting the pressure slightly from one hand to the other. At times his speed decreased as the decline lessened, but without fail it accelerated before he could stop. With sudden dread, he realized that if he couldn't stop himself, neither could Rigersor. He was heavier and his speed would be greater. If he overtook him, they would both careen off the pipe to certain death.

Time slipped by as he sped on, his body stiff from the tension and cold. He shot into the white mist half way down the mountain and everything disappeared. Andar leaned to one side as he felt the beginning of a curve, overdid it, and corrected at the last moment. He streaked out of the mist into a clear patch, then the shroud of white closed around him and he was racing blind again. All the time, he strained to hear the ominous approach of Rigersor behind him.

He wasn't sure, but the mist started to feel warmer. Beads of moisture on his face ran down his chin and neck to seep under his wrap. He shot out of the mist, leaving it swirling behind him. He felt more confident in his control of the sled, felt the exhilaration of the speed. Ahead he could see the pipe straightening out as the decline lessened. He could feel the wrap beneath him begin to soften as it warmed from the milder temperature and the friction. It created drag and helped slow the sled further as he pressed against the sides. For the first time, he felt he might yet succeed.

As he gazed ahead, his eyes widened. It was the end of the run where the rocks fell out and were collected. He clamped his thighs tightly against the pipe, striving to stop his craft. His speed lessened, but he was still going too fast. He stared at the approaching end and the rubble strewn upon the ground at the end of the pipe. He squeezed harder, and his efforts slowed him still more as the softened material dragged on the pipe.

He wasn't going to stop in time. He slid his elbows downwards and pressed against the pipe with them as well. At the last length of pipe he felt the bump from the final joint pass under him. Andar wrapped his arms and legs around the pipe and squeezed with all his strength. He slowed more, more, then slammed into the supporting brace under the pipe. It broke the grip of his arms and he slid further, started to fall over the end. His feet, caught on the support and with a painful lurch brought him to a stop.

Hanging over the end of the pipe, Andar stared down at the rocks below. He inched his way up and backwards, pushing on the pipe until he lay once more on top. Beneath him the wrap was a soggy mass that hung limply over the pipe, but he didn't notice the cool wetness that soaked him. Andar closed his eyes, resting his head upon the pipe, oblivious to everything .

The sound was barely audible at first, but continued to grow. It wasn't until he could feel the vibrations that he realized what it was. Rigersor's voice cut through the air.

"Move, Andar, move!"

Andar peered over his shoulder and saw Rigersor bearing down on him at an enormous speed. He only had a moment. There was no choice. He pushed himself upright and looked for a place to land. The pipe was shaking now with Rigersor's weight, as Andar felt the wrap slide beneath him and he fell over the side. At the last moment he remembered the supporting structure and swung an arm wildly towards the closest beam. He caught it with the crook of his elbow and hung on.

The pipe trembled above him and Rigersor's arms, wrapped around the pipe, struck the beam onto which Andar clung. The Sleeper's legs struck it and Andar saw Rigersor's body slip off the end of the pipe as his heavier weight carried him over the edge. The huge frame, stretched out from the end of the pipe stopped, then began a pendulous swing back. Relieved, Andar saw that Rigersor had grabbed the end of the pipe and held on. But now the Sleeper was swinging on a collision course for him. Andar relaxed his grip on the beam and slid downwards just before Rigersor smashed into the post. Andar tightened his grip and stopped his sliding descent. He looked up to view Rigersor's scowling face.

"I told you it would work," said Andar who slid down the post before the Sleeper could reply.

The sun was warm on Andar's back as he sat eating some stale reed bread at midday. If he closed his eyes, it brought back memories of home and the lazy heat of prophetic days that ran one into another with their similarity. Days that he had grown dissatisfied with. Days that he blamed on his slow, sedentary life. If only it was the same again, he thought, the ache coming back as he pushed aside images of his scattered family.

They had travelled for three more days, passing the exit of the tunnel used by the Stomuants, unaware of its presence. Having ventured beyond the mountains once before in his search for a place to belong, Rigersor approached the outpost carefully, giving it wide birth. Andar followed nervously, awed at the sight of the towering, reddish-orange sorrays. From a distance the animals made the three Stomuants who tended them appear small. The beasts stood passively outside the buildings, dipping their snouts into the stone troughs, then raising their heads high to let the feed slide down long necks. As Andar and Rigersor watched, the creatures turned their heads in their direction and sniffed the air. The two froze when the Stomuants turned and surveyed the terrain in their direction. Finally, the Sleeper motioned for Andar to follow and they crept past them along the trail away from the mountains, ever vigilant for others who might approach.

As they travelled the dry gray soil, trees appeared unlike any Andar had ever seen. Thick bodied trunks stood stark and twisted in the sandy wasteland. The heat continued to build, welcomed after the cold of the mountains. When they saw the buildings in the distance the following day, they approached cautiously, staying hidden among the trees and rock formations. From behind a stand of small reed trees they studied the village. It wasn't walled, the neat stone buildings spread out without any apparent order. In many of the gardens humans worked under the supervision of others who, in appearance, resembled the Sleeper. Fruitlessly, Andar scanned the faces, looking for Dreanna with no success. He turned to Rigersor.

"There are other...Sleepers here who seem to be accepted. Those who are in charge of the captives."

Rigersor looked out over the field at the figures in the distance but said nothing.

"When you came here before, were you not tempted to stay? To try and fit in with the others?" Andar asked.

"No," he replied. "I am not one of them. I was born of human parents, raised by them. I do not belong here. They," he said pointing to the others, "have no choice." He was silent, deep in thought before he spoke again. "Those that you see, that you thought were Sleepers like me, are not." He waited for Andar to understand so that he would not have to tell him, not have to speak it. When he saw the confused look, the Sleeper spoke the reality softly, as if the gentle tone would lessen the pain. "Like your daughter, they are captives who have been here longer. Captives who have changed. Who are changing still, as are all the others." He saw Andar's surprise turn to horror.

"Dreanna? No. No, it can't happen to her." Andar's hand shook as it went to his mouth and he turned back to stare at the captives in the field. He wiped at his eyes. "How long? How long before it starts?"

"I don't know. I have not lived here. It is working on us now as we sit here. We have been here days and we have not changed. I believe it takes much time."

"Then we must find Dreanna, and quickly."

"How?"

"I don't know. We'll start with this...village, one home at a time if we must. Start with the biggest home, the wealthiest. Dreanna is proud and strong. Those with the most wealth and power would want her. And if he does not have her, we'll search the next and the next until we do."

Andar lay tired and filthy behind a low rise outside a compound in which captives were held. The sandy soil stuck to his skin as he peered through some cut branches at the humans who appeared tired and abused. He was confused, for there were no gardens to be tended and the prisoners were left to sit or wander listlessly within the compound. The place he surveyed was unlike others that he had crawled close to in the last five days. He had been here before dawn, keeping his eyes on the yard, but despite waiting, he had seen no sign of his daughter.

Rigersor remained among the closest boulders, awaiting developments and protecting them from behind.

With a final glance, he saw two Stomuants approach the compound. He watched them enter the doorway, but they re-appeared almost immediately dragging a dishevelled male between them. Long black hair hung down over his face and his feet dragged on the ground as they pulled him along. The prisoner struggled and threw his head back as he fought against his captors, trying to free his arms. Without hesitation one of the Stomuants struck him. The prisoner slumped and they continued once more. But the moment was enough to rivet Andar's attention, for the man he recognized was Rothus. Andar fought the urge to leap to his feet and pursue them. He remained prone until they were out of sight, then crawled furiously back to Rigersor.

"Did you see them? Did you see which way they took him?" he gasped, ducking behind a boulder, popping up to peer in the direction the Stomuants had been heading.

"Quiet," said Rigersor. "What is wrong? That was a man, not a woman."

Andar continued to duck and bob until finally he spotted them between two buildings in the distance. He grabbed Rigersor by the harness and pulled him.

"Quickly, we must not lose them. It wasn't my daughter, but the man who took her. I'll not lose him, not for anything."

They followed cautiously, skirting houses, bands of Stomuants, groups of other human workers. At times they lost sight of the three and, close to panic, Andar had to be restrained by the Sleeper. Finally they were led to another property, complete with a large home, compound and gardens. They dragged Rothus into an outer building and left. Andar and Rigersor lay studying the compound and surrounding buildings. The fields, although carefully tended, were empty with not a Stomuant or human in sight.

"There must be others. There are gardens," said Andar.

"They must be somewhere else."

"I think I should crawl in and speak to him. Get him while I have the chance." Andar's voice was strained.

Rigersor studied him. "He probably does not know where your daughter is. Talking to him will only risk getting captured or killed."

"I must see him. I must!"

"Wait, someone is coming," Rigersor said drawing Andar's eyes back to the compound and the building.

A young girl was leaving the main house and approaching the quarters. Andar's stomach turned and his jaw clenched as he lowered his head onto his arm. It was hard to breathe. *I've found her. She's alive.* He raised his head, the tear tracks silent communication to Rigersor.

"It pleases me that we have found your daughter," he said quietly.

Andar turned his head slowly to his friend and companion. Unable to speak, he forced a feeble smile before turning to stare once again at the compound.

Andar crawled towards the compound and its building keeping the humans' quarters between him and the main house. He didn't see the huge Stomuant leave the house and head towards the quarters. Rigersor did, and drawing his dagger began to follow Andar, winding his way towards the buildings, trying to catch up.

When Andar reached the window and peered inside, his thoughts exploded in a swirl of emotions. Dreanna held Rothus in her arms, stroking his hair. Rothus tried to speak, but she held a trembling finger to his lips, hushing him as she rocked him gently. Andar fought the confusion and white hot anger as he watched Dreanna cradle the one who had abducted her. Then a Stomuant stooped low and stepped through the doorway. For only a second Andar watched the lumped gray body straighten and tower over his daughter, then grabbing the window ledge, he leapt through the opening, pulling his sword free when his feet hit the floor. All three pairs of eyes focused on him.

"Father?"

Dreanna's disbelieving cry rang out as Korados' hand found and rested on the hilt of his sword. Andar pointed his blade at the huge figure, watching the Stomuant expectantly. Dreanna pulled free of Rothus and in tears staggered towards him. She cried openly now, tears running down her face.

"Father? You've found me?" Her hands reached for him as he enfolded her with his arm. She buried her face against his chest, her voice wracked by sobs. "I'm sorry, Father. I'm sorry. I stopped believing that you would ever come. I should have known." For uncounted moments the three stood still, the silence in the room complete.

"Father! Behind you!"

Andar swept Dreanna aside as he pivoted, his sword ready to strike the new threat. Rigersor, dagger clenched in his teeth, paused in the window and turned to look behind him. Finding nothing, he grimaced as he realized she viewed him as a threat. Andar spun again to eye the Stomuant who remained standing at ease, his weapon undrawn. Then Korados spoke.

"Only a father finds tunnel through mountains. Finds daughter. Not taken captive."

"I know nothing of your tunnel, but I do know that I'm leaving with my daughter. Now draw your sword."

"You travelled mountains?" The voice registered surprise. "I am impressed."

"Enough talk. Draw your sword and let us be done."

Dreanna pulled away from Andar and ran towards Korados. Taken by surprise, Andar was a step behind her.

"Korados, don't do this," she said.

Andar caught up to her. "Dreanna, get back."

"No!" She shook herself loose from his grasp. "He will listen to me. He must listen." She turned back to Korados. "It can't be this way. Things must change. Somehow we must learn to share the world. To live together without killing each other. It must start somewhere. Let it start here."

Korados smiled, but his eyes were sad. "You right. You speak what I wish could be. But we dare not leave The Stone. Is our history, our life. You loath it. But we need you. Peace? Together?" He smiled sadly. "Needs too different. Only dream. Not real." He looked up from Dreanna to Andar. "Take daughter and this other. Go. I not alarm others." He looked

THE REEDSMITH OF ZENDAR

back to Dreanna. "My gift for...taught...what you taught son. My son. For what he taught me." He smiled at her. "One dreamer to other." He turned to leave, but Rigersor called out.

"If we knew of the tunnel, it would save us time and hardship, perhaps the life of the girl. Tell us of its location."

Korados eyed the Sleeper. "I go with you to entrance. Have time talk. Learn of others." He turned to Andar. "You wish this?"

Dreanna looked to her father. His eyes sought an answer in hers. Without hesitation she nodded.

"You can trust him, Father." She looked up at Korados. "I know him. You can trust him."

Korados smiled down at the diminutive figure. "Meet in woods, behind this building. Dusk. I bring mounts." He waited for a nod from Andar and then without further comment, he was gone.

Andar's eyes left the back of the Stomuant, travelled past his daughter to the figure still slouched on the ground. Dreanna saw the darkness settle on his face.

"I don't know what will be worse, to kill you now or leave you here to become one of them. For what you have done to my family..." and he raised his sword as he took a step toward him.

Dreanna stepped in front of her father.

"Father, you must listen to me. So many things have happened. We have all changed. I see it in you. You're different. So am I, so is Rothus. You don't know, couldn't know what has happened to me or him. What has happened between us. But know this, Father, he loves me, and I him."

Andar stared at her, attempting to make sense of it. He looked at Rothus who climbed unsteadily to his feet.

"You have the right to kill me. I've done dishonourable things, driven by another's purpose and mind. This I admit, but it's as Dreanna says. I love your daughter and have tried to make amends."

"It's true," Dreanna said as she stood beside Rothus. Her voice thickened. "I won't leave without him."

Andar struggled with her words. He didn't want lose her again.

"As you say, I have changed too and been unable to think clearly until recently." He looked at Rothus. "The measure of a man is proved by his actions. Words can be uttered easily. For now, it's enough that Dreanna loves you." Turning, he walked towards Rigersor and the window. "Come, we must go before it's too late."

The tough, hairless hide of the sorray beneath Andar creased and smoothed with the bobbing motion of its neck as it shuffled across the sand in a ground eating gait. Despite the midday sun, the temperature had begun to cool as they neared the mountains. Korados said they should reach the tunnel's entrance by dusk that night.

There was little talk among them despite Korados' notion that they might do so. When they stopped for brief respites to water the mounts and eat, pleasantries were exchanged, but little else. At first Andar and Dreanna rode together, the former clasping his daughter tightly, however, after the first break, Dreanna kissed her him lightly on the cheek and told him she would ride with Rothus for a time. He saw her smile, the shine in her eyes, and watched her walk to him. When they embraced he knew that it was as it must be. His fear for her, the mistrust of him, still chased each other, but he knew right now it was beyond his control. It would take time.

All stood silently before the tunnel opening until finally Korados broke the silence.

"No…collecting parties out, no danger from others." He turned to Dreanna. "Safe journey. My son will miss you." He stepped back and motioned them entrance with his arm, but Dreanna approached and put her hand upon his rough forearm. She stared intently at him, at a loss for words.

"Thank you," she whispered, unable to say anything else. She grasped Rothus' hand and together the two stepped into the tunnel.

"I owe you much, Korados," Andar said. "For caring for my daughter, for your help tonight. I won't forget." He stepped into the tunnel and Rigersor followed.

Inside Andar used striking stones to light the torches they found, and armed with them, they began the walk through the mountain, Dreanna and Rothus leading the way.

Their pace was slow, favouring Rothus' condition. They rested often in the tunnel and in the caverns where food had been stored. On the third day of their trek, the pale glow of evening light filtered in towards them and soon the tunnel opened up to the sky. The air was crisp, the night clear, thousands of stars winking above them as they stood at the mouth of the tunnel overlooking the treeless, boulder-strewn terrain. Dreanna left Rothus and stood beside her father. She wrapped her arms around him as she looked out onto the scene below.

"Father, I can't believe it's over, that we're here. I know we're far from home, but for the first time in a long time, I feel happy. We're free. Free to go home to be with Doros and Colonar and Grandfather." When Dreanna gazed up at him, she saw that he didn't share her joy. "Father, what's the matter? I know we still have far to go, but aren't you happy that it's over?"

Andar looked down at her and forced a smile. "There is much that I haven't told you. Much has also happened to me. Some that still needs to be settled." He looked off into the distance. "There is someone who awaits our return."

Part Four

Release from the Hunger

Chapter One

Far beneath the surface, silence was a shroud that filled the stone-hewn rooms, now, as it had for thousands of years. Beneath the dust that covered the sealed capsules, the creatures imprisoned within waited for release.

Thoughts floated on the edge of their subconscious.
Images flickered; memory fragments of a life frozen in time.
Images, brutal and powerful materializing, one after another.
They rose, leaking out, oozing anger; danger, survival, existence.
Hunger. Now the subconscious knew nothing else.
Nothing else except the hunger, the terrible hunger.

Dajata sat in the dusty courtyard on a bench beneath a reed tree watching Grenfeld's display. Like every day, she had been summoned to walk the grounds of his estate with him. Again today, they had stopped to observe his men in the yard. Grenfeld approached two soldiers who were training together and held out a hand for one of the men's swords.

"Sandor, you're a fine swordsman," he said to the young man. He turned to the other soldier. "To throw your opponent off guard, fake a lunge. Begin to step forward with your foot and draw back your sword to convince him of your intent. Then," he paused dramatically, "move immediately into an overhead slash. But it must be quick. Don't advertise it with movement of your arm. Use your wrist to speed the blow and catch them off guard. Like so." Grenfeld took a stance, raised his foot as if to step forward, and the blade whirled about, invisible to the eye. "Aim for an arm or wrist. The blow is quick, but does not have the power of your arm. Try." He handed the sword back to Sandor who took his stance. "Slowly at first until you get the feel of it."

Sandor executed the movement smoothly. Grenfeld clapped him on the back.

"Well done. Practise that. It just might save your life one day."

As always, Grenfeld had faced her, watching her watch them as he performed. The forced camaraderie of the moment had been heavy and awkward, like an ill fitting cloak about his shoulders. He took her by the arm extolling the virtues of the soldier, conversation light upon his lips.

It had been like that ever since Andar had left. The day following their first encounter in her jail, guards had escorted her to a room on the second floor of the main house. Although small, it was clean and bright, furnished with a fine bed, table and chairs. Woven curtains adorned the window, and a rug of braided watertithe warmed the floor. All necessities that befit a guest, but the bars on the shuttered windows that opened onto the courtyard spoke clearly of the nature of the room. She had been placed there and the door locked once more. Although she had known who it would be, when the knock came, she had questioned who it was. Grenfeld answered.

"May I come in, Dajata?"

"The jailor asks of his prisoner if he may enter? What game do we play now?"

She heard the bolt being drawn and the door swung wide to reveal Grenfeld dressed in a finely crafted robe of green. His hair had been cut shorter and he wore a warm smile as he stepped within, closing the door.

"I trust that this room will serve you better while we await the return of the search party," he said, motioning with his arm about the surroundings. His voice was soft and smooth as he smiled. Freshly groomed and clad in the fine robe, his presence was impressive. The ease with which he had changed his image surprised and unsettled her. She stumbled in her composure, but as she watched him approach, she saw that the eyes were the same. They were cold and calculating, frightening in a new way. Dajata steeled herself for whatever he might attempt.

"A room with bars is still a dungeon no matter how nicely furnished," she said.

"Bars are also to keep others out. There are many who envy what I have, what I have accomplished."

Dajata snickered at his answer. "What do you want?"

"I wish to ask your forgiveness for what occurred yesterday. I cannot believe my actions. Finding out that my son had been taken by...by Stomuants, I was not myself." He stepped closer and she saw the pain on his face. "He is my only son. Surely you can understand how upset I was."

"And today you are not?" she questioned contemptuously.

"Today as well, and tomorrow and the next until he returns safely with the help of...with the help of your travelling companion." Grenfeld walked to the table and rested his hands on the back of one of the chairs. "But the shock has been dulled. I am closer to being myself again. The things I did, the things I said, were the acts of a tormented man, out of his head with grief and worry. Asking forgiveness is perhaps too much. At least accept this room as a token of my remorse."

So it had begun. At first she ate alone in her room. Then she was invited to use the eating area of the house. It wasn't long before Grenfeld joined her for the occasional meal. She was allowed to walk with a guard in the yard, then Grenfeld would accompany them, and then only he would walk with her. Soon Dajata realized that he was courting her.

Standing silently at the edge of a low plateau, the weary travellers looked down upon Dashindar, all lost in thought. One towered head and shoulders above the others, his bulk casting a long shadow as he stood behind them. The girl, youthful and pretty, leaned against the younger of the two other men, her face marred by tired eyes that often closed. The man at her side, held her about the shoulders, his eyes filled with uncertainty as he looked towards the city below. He waited for a sign from the last figure who stood apart from the others. He was worn and weather beaten, scars tracing patterns upon the brown skin of his lean body. But the green eyes were intense as they focused on a two story building barely visible in the distance.

"We'll make camp here," he said at last. Tomorrow we go down into the city."

"You don't know my father. Let me go with you," Rothus insisted, agitated by Andar's plan. He looked to Dreanna for support.

"No, you must stay here. If you come with me, there would be nothing to stop him from killing me or Dajata. I'll tell him I'll return you when he frees Dajata."

"It's all right, Rothus, Father knows what must be done," said Dreanna. "He'll see that I'm safe." She reached out and pulled his arm around her. "You must trust him."

"I trust him," Rothus said, as he removed her arm and locked eyes with Andar. "But you don't know my father like I do." He stalked away from the fire and sat by himself. Dreanna started to follow, but Andar held her back.

"Leave him. He's worried for you and needs time to deal with that."

She cast another glance at Rothus then sat down, pulling her feet up under her, staring at her father. "Tell me more about her, Father. Tell me about Dajata. She must be very special."

Andar looked at his daughter and smiled. The lines of worry that had gathered on his journey eased. "Yes, she is special. Special like you, like your mother." He was silent, thinking of Katrena, realizing that he had not done so for a long time. He felt guilty for the briefest moment, but realized there was no need. "She is caring and sensitive and strong despite everything that has happened to her."

"Is she pretty like Mother?"

Andar smiled at his daughter and her enthusiasm for this woman she had never met. "Yes, she is pretty. Not like your Mother, but in a different way." His eyes left Dreanna as he envisioned her features. "But enough of this. You will meet her and be the judge. Now get to sleep. We have much to do tomorrow."

Dreanna stood up and threw her arms around his neck. She squeezed him tightly, pressing her face against his. "I'm happy for you, Father." She kissed him quickly then went to Rothus.

Bonara slumped in the chair looking listlessly out the window of his room. Periodically he closed his eyes, his head falling back onto the chair. He slept intermittently, only to awake with a start and stare once more down at the small patch of yard that had become his world.

He too was prisoner here at Dashindar. Not of Grenfeld's device, but of fate and the cruel injustice it had dealt him. At first he had fought back the waves of depression that threatened to crush him. Gradually, day after day, when they did not return, he had become more dejected. He saw his dream and life's work slipping through his fingers, just as the key had done. Soon, he didn't leave Grenfeld's house. Then he confined himself to his room, taking his meals there, staring out the window. Waiting. Waiting for what he knew would never come.

He dozed again. Noise intruded upon his restless sleep, the sound of running steps in the courtyard. Blurry-eyed he looked down to see that Grenfeld, the woman, and his men had stopped and were staring at something. Bonara leaned forward. All were looking toward the gate where the figure of a man and woman were framed in the opening.

Bonara held back the spark of hope that flared. *Is it him? Yes! And the girl is with him. Does she still have the key?* It was too much to hope for, but he was on his feet, racing for the door.

Below, Dajata walked then ran towards Andar. She hurled herself into his arms, clinging to him until her arms ached and her breath was scarce from the pressure of his embrace. She felt his lips upon her face as he kissed her, and finally she was able to whisper, "I knew you would come back to me. I knew you would."

Grenfeld stood deathly still. The blood drained from his face as his eyes rested upon Andar's daughter. His world was spinning as he stared at her. Before him stood the image of Katrena.

Bonara raced across the dry courtyard, past Andar to Dreanna. Before she could move, he grabbed her by the shoulders.

"The key! Where is the key? Do you still have it?" His eyes were wild as he screamed, spittle spraying from his mouth.

Dreanna struggled to escape his grasp. "Let go of me. Let go!"

Andar grabbed Bonara and threw him to the ground. Several of the guards drew their swords, moving towards him as Bonara screamed and sputtered unintelligible curses. The gates slammed shut with a thud, and Andar drew his sword, eyeing the approaching guards.

"Enough!" Grenfeld's shout cut through Bonara's babbling and the confusion, bringing the advancing guards to a halt. He pulled his eyes from the image of his former love. "Sheath your swords. Sheath yours as well, Andar. Bonara, get to your feet and control yourself."

Andar lowered his sword until the tip rested on the ground, but didn't return it to his scabbard.

"So you have returned." Grenfeld's voice was measured and cold. "I am truly surprised, for in truth, I never expected to see you again." His gaze settled on Dreanna. "But you always did manage to twist my life around."

"The key. Where's the key? Do you still have it?" Bonara crossed to join Grenfeld.

Andar looked at him then back at Grenfeld. "What is this fool talking about? What does he want?"

Grenfeld relinquished his attention from Dreanna, eyes shifting to Andar. "You know nothing about it, do you? But your daughter does, don't you, Dreanna?"

Dreanna looked at the two in confusion. "I don't know what they are talking about, Father. I don't have a...a key, whatever such a thing is."

Bonara stepped forward, frustration and anger lending him courage. Andar's sword came up slowing him.

"The flat silver object with holes that you found at your father's home. You took it to town. You were asking after me. You must have found it." His voice was pleading, begging for the answer he needed.

Recognition came slowly to Dreanna. "You. You were the old teller of tales? The Friend of the Ancients. It was yours?"

"Yes, yes! Do you still have it?"

"I thought the trail robbers, the men who captured Rothus and I might take it. The first night I buried it."

"No, no! Could you find it still? Do you know where it is? Tell me!" Bonara was losing control again and only Grenfeld's hand on his shoulder prevented him from moving forward.

"Enough of this," said Andar. "I don't know or care what you're talking about. I only know that I've returned with my daughter and your son."

"Rothus? You've found him?" Grenfeld's voice was strained.

"He is alive and well, and I will release him once my daughter, Dajata and I are free. If we don't return before dusk, you *will not* see him again.

"They would kill him?" asked Grenfeld, his voice quiet and controlled.

"Yes."

In the silence Grenfeld stared at Andar. A smile crept to his lips as he turned to Bonara. "Do you hear that Bonara? They will kill my son." He swung back to Andar, levelling his gaze. "Then you will save me the trouble of killing the traitor myself. He attempted to steal away with your daughter. Steal away from his men. My men. I would kill him myself. Now drop your sword and we will go inside and discuss the location of Lord Bonara's key."

Andar raised his sword, motioning the two women behind him. He looked at the guards and the closed gate.

"Druardos, Sandor, knock an arrow," said Grenfeld. "If he doesn't drop his sword by the time I reach the porch, kill his woman. Kill Dajata." Grenfeld turned and strode towards the house.

Andar watched the broad back retreat, Bonara in tow. Closer and closer they moved to the porch. He glanced at the two guards whose eyes shuttled from Grenfeld to Andar. With a frustrated roar, he flung his sword to the ground. The guards herded the three towards the house where Grenfeld stood on the porch.

"I would have killed her," he said looking at Dajata, reaching out to brush her cheek. "I had such plans for you, didn't I?" He looked past her to Dreanna, then back to Andar. "But thanks to you, that has all changed now."

Grenfeld motioned towards the guards as he entered the house. "Bring them inside. Come, Bonara. We have plans to make."

Chapter Two

Bonara's face glowed from the trail fire. His eyes were focused somewhere deep within the flames, far removed from the present as he related details of his search over the years. Grenfeld and his men ringed the fire, Bonnar's words holding everyone, for all saw the power his discovery had over him. He was possessed, the words bursting from him in torrents, for finally he was able to tell others of his fantastic secret.

"It was but an accident of nature that the river should divert itself through the path of one of the tunnels. Fate, that after thousands of years of erosion I should find the exact place where it had been cut in two by the water's course." He looked about him to ensure they understood the miracle of that moment. "That discovery, of the very first vault, changed my life." He paused, letting them wait. "It took me years to explore it, to understand these... people."

"You found the burial vaults of our first ancestors?" The soldier spoke in awe, the very thought of such a discovery astounding.

"No." Bonara went silent as visions of them filled his memory, thoughts of their nature worrying his brow. He shook aside his doubts, caught up once more in the story of his life's search. "I learned that it was not the only storage vault hidden deep within the rock of Zendar. It led me to a second, and then a third and fourth, each containing..." He paused, his eyes going around the circle of spellbound listeners. "each containing former inhabitants of Zendar."

The face of his audience pulled back in nervous surprise, each looking from one to the other as they weighed the credibility of his words. Finally one of Grenfeld's men spoke.

"Lord Bonara, how can we believe such a tale? Why would a group of people choose to live underground in huge caves? It is too-"

"It's true. By the Mother Ship, everything I have told you is true. The caverns hold the remains of Dremords, an earlier civilization that lived here on Zendar. The vaults hold row, upon row, upon row of them encased in tubes or containers. They were sealed, but when I found them, the top of each was open. Those within were dead, all of them."

Bonara lapsed into silence again, his thoughts turned inwards. They waited patiently for him to continue.

"Before we arrived on Zendar, they came in vessels like those spoken of in The History of The Mother Ship and in Legends of The Ancestors. There is nothing they could not do. Those that were here, even before them, could not withstand their knowledge and power. Yes, a long, long time ago, there were others here on Zendar, even before the Dremords. They are gone now."

"What happened to them? Are they too sleeping in these vaults?" asked one of the soldiers.

Bonara gazed at him, his features set. "No, they are there below as well, but they are not sleeping, waiting to be revived. They are dead." He was silent, his eyes downcast as he studied his feet. When he looked up, his eyes were haunted by images.

"The knowledge the Dremords possessed is still beyond my grasp. What I have seen with my eyes defies description; all kinds of things that I cannot explain. Deep within these vaults, in the very air itself, are moving images. Images so real, you feel you could reach out and touch them. Images of floating buildings where they lived, of strange objects that moved them from place to place, of things that sped through the air carrying them to distant destinations." He looked at the ground and an imperceptible shiver shook him. "Images of what they did."

"Tools and weapons and artifacts are stored underground. Stored in caverns so huge, it is impossible to see from one end to another. Full of things waiting to be used again." He went silent as the threat of failure, of never being able to access the knowledge, returned to him. He looked at Andar who sat bound hand and foot just outside the circle. Dreanna and Djata tied together, huddled behind Grenfeld on the other side. Bonara's voice was steady but strained.

"This is the last one. There are no more vaults, except the one beneath your lands. Below you all these years has been the knowledge of an entire civilization. Waiting. Waiting for the right solution that will start the changes that will enable them to awaken safely. In the other vaults, all the others have been awakened through the ages, but none have survived. This is their last chance. I hope to save just one of them. Can you imagine the knowledge, the wisdom he will be able to impart to me?" His eyes glittered in the firelight as passion overcame him. He glared at Andar, his lips drawn back over his teeth, as if possessed by a fever. "You are nothing compared to what can be gained if I am not too late. You should have left when your wife died. It would have been a small sacrifice."

Andar's eyes focused on Bonara as he wrestled with the meaning of what he had said. Bonara's next words drained the blood from his face.

"I thought if you and your wife were to die, the old man and the young ones would move, start over somewhere else. The village. Anywhere. But those two fools in the tavern couldn't even kill a morbid drunk."

"You had Katrena killed to force me to move away? It wasn't an accident?" Andar struggled to his feet and launched himself at Bonara, through the circle of others, ramming him with his shoulder. Andar twisted about, smashing his head into Bonara, using it as a weapon. The merchant scrambled out of the way as others dragged Andar back. They tied him to a tree as he screamed then fastened a cloth about his mouth. He sat numbed, the revelation overpowering him. *It wasn't an accident. It had started so long ago.*

Across from him, Grenfeld gripped his dagger, pressing it against the scabbard in an effort to keep it sheathed. His face had drained of colour, and his eyes bore into Bonara.

Shaken from the attack, Bonara returned to sit by the fire. He glanced cautiously at Andar, but his voice was still strained with excitement.

"It's my hope that some or all of them may still be sealed within the tubes; that they may still be asleep, waiting the slow change that will enable them to survive our climate. If only we can find the key."

Andar's muffled voice carried over the crackling of the fire as he screamed at Bonara. Grenfeld plucked a staff from one of his men, whirled and struck Andar across the side of his head. He raised it again, but Dreanna and Dajata, hands bound, smashed into him, bouncing off his heavy frame. He turned, raising the staff as he struggled for control. His eyes sought Bonara.

"Enough! Enough of your tales, old man. The night is ended. Everyone to your wraps! Tomorrow we start early." He hurled the staff away and stalked out of the firelight.

Andar sat tied to the tree, the gag still in place. Under a clear sky the green mist swirled upwards, disturbed by Bonara's passage as he wound his way between sleeping figures towards Andar. He squatted down in front of him, close, but distant enough to ensure his safety. Andar strained at his bonds.

"I want to tell you that I'm sorry for your loss," Bonara said. "It was a terrible thing that had to be done. It was not easy for me to order that."

Andar jerked and pulled at the ropes that held him.

Bonara eased back a little further. "It was necessary. Although unsuccessful, it started me on a course of action that has led here. You must understand the importance of my quest. Understand that your wife's life was not wasted." He sat back and crossed his knees, settling himself.

"I'm not a fool. The only reason Grenfeld helps me is to gain power for himself. Can you imagine him with the knowledge of the Dremords?" He chuckled. "The fool has no idea of how dangerous they are. He thinks he is going to go down into the vault and pick up some weapon and become the new king of Zendar. He has no idea." Bonara rose, then bent over and whispered to Andar. "If any of them are alive, I will save one. One to keep as my pet. To impart his knowledge to me and only me, in return for his life. The rest need to be destroyed." He straightened up and saw the confused look on Andar's face. He bent down again. "All of Zendar will thank me. I will save them from the Dremords. If you survive, you will thank me for your daughter's life and that of your grandchildren. Remember I said the Dremords came for the resources. Those resources were a race of people much like us." He rose to his feet. "And the Dremords had quite an appetite."

Ahead of Andar, Grenfeld put his arm around Dajata and kissed her. He laughed loudly then dropped back on the trail to circle Andar. His voice was casual, almost friendly, as if he were planning an outing for the two of them.

"You have no idea how much you are going to suffer. I think I will start with your woman first. What would bother you more? To see her used over and over by my men, or do it myself with everyone watching?" Grenfeld slid away as Andar lunged at him, the rope around his neck jerking him to a halt.

"But she has had many men, hasn't she? Wait. A malbar. I'll put her in a cage with a malbar. You'll see her swell and split open like a ripened fruit."

Grenfeld's laughter disappeared, his countenance darkening as he walked back to Bonara to draw more information from the merchant. The knowledge that Bonara had Katrena killed left him in a dangerous, unpredictable state. He fought to keep his strained relationship with the merchant intact. Only when he had what he needed from, would he make him pay.

Andar fought to ignore the constant circle of pain around his neck. More days of walking had made a raw, open ring that never healed. He pulled at the rope that bound his hands. They were checked often, and neither they, nor the noose around his neck, were ever removed.

He didn't know what to think of the information that Bonara had imparted that night. He watched the merchant during the day, trying to assess him. Could the horror of what he said possibly be true? Were his feverish and crazed actions just a game that he played to fool Grenfeld? As he walked, he watched for any sign of Rigersor and Rothus, even though he was sure that they couldn't be near. Grenfeld's contingent of men was well trained and used effectively, a scout always sent ahead, another trailing behind. The rope pulled at his neck and Andar focused on keeping up.

The pace was feverish, for Bonara never let up. He was driven, hurrying them at first light, allowing only the shortest of breaks during the day. Some of his men raced ahead each day to set up camp so that they might travel to the very edge of night. His urgency infected Grenfeld and despite his new found hatred for the man who had Katrena killed, he too began to channel his energy and anger into driving the group at a reckless pace. He spent more time with Bonara, immersed in conversation as they walked, distracted from his prisoners, so that Andar was left alone.

Andar tried again to move near Dajata and Dreanna, but the pull of the rope ended his effort. If the Ancient Ones' tool could carve through the reed trees, he knew he could use it as a weapon. Somehow he had to get it from Dajata's sleeping wrap. So the days passed as they made their way east towards his home.

Rothus lay hidden in the groundcover on the outskirts of his father's camp fighting the guilt for his inability to help Dreanna. The distance to the figures that huddled around the camp fires was great. With the two circles of guards, it was impossible to approach close enough to get a clear shot. One was all he wanted.

Hatred for his father grew every time he watched him approach Dreanna. It had been all Rigersor could do to prevent him from walking into the camp and claiming escape. He knew that he would be suspect and probably killed, but it would be enough to end his father's life. He was sure he could do it. Finally he had listened to reason. Dead he would be of no use, and without his father to keep his men at bay, Dreanna would be easy prey. And if he failed, then what? So they continued to trail the band of travellers, careful not to be detected, watching them at night hoping for an opportunity to act.

Bonara was beside himself, tense and fidgety, wringing his hands and rocking back and forth from foot to foot. They had finally reached a thick reed forest, not a day's march from the smith's homestead. Weary from the forced march, nerves on edge, his tension had affected all as they neared their destination. Now, Grenfeld stood in front of the two survivors who had returned with news of Rothus and Dreanna.

"You are sure this is where you spent the first night after having taken the girl?" he asked.

The men shifted uneasily, looking at each other and about themselves. The lean form of Marno, the older of the two, stiffened as he spoke.

"Yes, Lord Grenfeld. It was here that we stopped. I am sure of it."

Grenfeld stepped close to Marno. "Are you sure it was here?" Grenfeld asked again, his voice cold. "Because if you are mistaken, you will wish you had died fighting the Stomuants."

"I am sure, my Lord," Marno whispered hoarsely.

"Good." Grenfeld was all smiles as he clapped him on the shoulder. "Now tell me, where did you make the fire?"

The soldier walked to a small clearing and pointed to a spot. Grenfeld followed him and kicked lightly at the soil. Under the surface, the darker, charred ashes showed. Relieved, Marno smiled when Grenfeld looked at him. Bonara rushed to Grenfeld, his cheeks flushed with excitement as he pulled at Grenfeld's arm.

"Bring the girl," he said and then turned to Marno. "Where was the girl? Where was she sitting? Where did she sleep?"

Marno looked around, worry again on his brow as he ran a dry tongue over his lips. "I'm not sure, Lord Grenfeld. It has been so long. I think it was over there, by that tree."

"No, it was in this direction," said the second soldier who until now had stood nervously silent. His face paled as Grenfeld's eyes bore into him. "I think it was next to that large reed tree," said the soldier, the confidence in his voice evaporating.

"Yes, yes, Hortos is right. It was there," said Marno.

Everyone turned as Dreanna was brought forward. Her hands were untied and she rubbed her wrists painfully. Grenfeld's face momentarily softened as she approached him, but he steeled himself and spoke to her in slow measured tones, delivering his promise.

"These men tell me that this is where you spent your first night of captivity. I believe it so. You buried the artifact here. Find it for me now." He motioned to two men who forced Andar to his knees and held him in place by the ropes around his neck. A third soldier stood nearby. Dreanna looked down at Andar, a hand at her mouth as she fought back the fear.

"I'll find it father. I know it's here."

Andar forced a smile of encouragement as she was led to the spot the man had indicated. Grenfeld stood waiting.

"Find it!" Bonara demanded, pushing her forward.

Dreanna drew a tremulous breath at the base of the tree. She looked from it to others around her, unsure if it was the right one. She remembered that there had been part of a root that stuck out of the ground. She moved around the tree and found one, but it seemed too large, but then she thought that maybe it had grown. On her knees, she scrapped at the soil near the root. She removed more and more soil, pulling it free. It piled up about her knees, but she found nothing. The fear grew inside as she pulled the soil away, faster and faster. *Nothing*. She moved along the root, clawing desperately, but there was nothing there. Frightened, she looked up.

"It's not here," she stammered.

"It must be here," Bonara cried out. He pushed Dreanna aside and on all fours with his knife dug deeper and deeper. Dreanna looked from him to Grenfeld.

"It should be there," she pleaded. "Something is wrong."

"I'll show you what happens when something goes wrong. I will not play games! Sindago, cut off his head."

The soldier's sword leapt from his scabbard, driven by the anger in Grenfeld's voice. Sindago eyed the Andar's neck and tightened his grip on the hilt. Drenna jumped to her feet, screaming.

"Stop! You-"

The arrow struck Sindago from behind and threw him forward, the sword slipping from his hands. Grenfeld grabbed Dreanna, pulled her in front of him, shouting orders.

"Hurry. After him, before he gets too far! The rest take up your positions. Move." He stood viewing the turmoil. "So, my beloved son isn't dead."

Rothus followed Rigersor, the bow clutched in his hand. They didn't have a plan. He had launched the arrow on instinct when he saw that Andar was about to die. The distance had been great and the shot hurried, but luck and skill had been on his side. Now they ran, putting distance between them and their pursuers. The rubbery, pointed leaves whipped against them as their feet flew over the narrow trail. Shouts of confusion and pursuit faded as they pushed harder. Finally, Rigersor slowed and came to a stop.

"We are far enough from the others. Let us deal with them now. Move down trail and fall. I will attack them from behind."

"We don't know how many are trailing us."

"True, but that does not matter." Drawing his sword, he plunged into the trees as the sounds of pursuit returned.

Rothus ran down the trail, glancing back often. A chorus of shouts arose as his father's men spotted him. Drawing a nervous breath, Rothus fell, careful to keep his bow from under him. His pursuers leapt forward, their prize assured. Over his shoulder, Rothus watched their approach. Rigersor burst through the trees, and the two trailing men crumbled to the ground from his blows. Rothus pushed himself upright and loosed an arrow at the foremost man. As it struck home, the others lurched to a halt. Rigersor attacked the remaining two, one falling before the other became aware of his presence. The last one raised his blade, but the weight and power of the Sleeper ended the attempt before it began. Rothus ran to Rigersor who cleaned the blood from his sword.

"Quickly. Let's return and find out the fate of the others," he said.

"My thoughts as well," replied the Sleeper. Without further comment, Rigersor turned and started down the trail.

Grenfeld released his grip on Dreanna and pushed her away. It had been several moments since the attack and nothing further had occurred. He stalked to where Andar sat, still guarded by the two soldiers.

"So you have taken my son from me too." He stood above Andar, fists clenched. "First Katrena, who should have been mine, and now my son." His hand snaked out grabbing Andar's jaw, forcing his head up. "When my men catch that traitor, the two of you will share the same fate." He released him then slammed his fist against Andar's jaw. Without a sound, Andar slumped to the ground. Grenfeld drew his foot back, aiming a kick at his head, but Dreanna's scream stopped him.

"Stop, stop! It was a mistake. I know where the artifact is. I'm sure. But don't hit him again."

Grenfeld turned a malevolent eye towards her. "No more games, girl. Show me now, or watch him die."

"Yes, yes. It wasn't my fault. This isn't the tree. I remember. The root ran from the tree and pointed towards my village. Towards Bonstag."

Grenfeld stared at the two soldiers who had directed him. Their eyes met his then looked away.

"Get on with it."

"Find it. You must find it." It was Bonara who had been sitting dejectedly by the shallow pit he had dug. Dishevelled, he clambered to his feet and moved towards them.

Dreanna crossed the clearing and approached one of two large trees. She studied the ground beneath it then approached the second one. Here an exposed root grew in the right direction. She knelt, her hands scraping at the soil as she searched. The fear grew inside her again as she probed deeper along the length of the root. *Nothing.* She began again, digging further along it. She felt sick as she pulled the soil free. *Nothing.* Her heart raced and her hands shook. She was sure that this was the tree, the root. Her finger brushed against something, and there it was. She pulled it free and spun on her knees holding it up for all to see.

In a daze, Bonara shuffled towards her. His lips mumbled unintelligible words as he held out a shaking hand. He clutched it, sank to his knees, and bowed his head, sobbing quietly.

Grenfeld studied him, disgusted by the display. He turned and looked down at Andar.

"You escape your fate once more, at least for the moment. His head snapped up and he began shouting orders. "Regroup for a forced march. Scout passage ahead, cover our backs. Two to wait for the party to return with my son." His eyes travelled to Bonara who had risen to his feet and gathered himself. "Come, Bonara. We travel swiftly and should arrive at the smith's home by dusk."

Bonara stood straighter, his chin held high, the mention of Andar's home bringing the fire back to his eyes. "Yes, yes, we must hurry." Bonara wheeled about and set off down the path, the key clutched tightly in his hand.

Grenfeld watched him rush off and turned to the two soldiers who still held Andar. "Guard him well. You four, catch up to the fool before he gets killed. Move." The men grabbed their weapons and hurried off. "Sandor, organize the rest." With a parting glance towards Dreanna, he started down the trail after Bonara.

Beneath the clear waters of the pool, deep within the rock, the subconscious thoughts were angry and confused at their captivity. A single overwhelming obsession for self preservation embodied the nature of the sleeping creatures, as it always had.

Kill, eat, survive. Images swirling. Cold, violent images.

Pale-skinned figures running, resisting. Naive, pale-skinned figures.

Powerful, brutal violence, satisfying the hunger.

Waiting. Waiting for release.

Chapter Three

Doros wound his way through the forest heading towards his home. It was getting late, the sun's waning rays cutting softly through the larger reed trees. Below them, a myriad of head-high reed saplings sought a foothold in the earth before the rains would wash them away. He travelled a different route than the day before, careful not to brush against the leaves, stepping on solid ground so he didn't leave any trace of his presence. He thought he had known the land surrounding his house well before. Now he knew every incline and rock, every fallen tree where he might duck low and hide.

He came to one of three sites that he and Lanos had fashioned to watch the intruders who had taken over their home. To avoid discovery, the sites were far from the pond where the men had been working. At the base of the tree, he listened to ensure that he was alone, then climbed, taking care not to shake the leaves. At the right height Doros unwound the end of the rope from his waist, looped it about the tree trunk, and fastened it to his harness. After checking the grip of his feet on the branch, he leaned back, adjusting the rope for comfort then turned his attention to the emptied pond behind his home. When they had returned home and discovered what the men were doing, they were mystified.

"Grandfather, why are they trying to empty our pond?"

"I have no idea. Could there be something at the bottom of it?"

"I've been swimming in it since I was three. When it's clear, you can see right to the bottom. There is nothing there."

"Then I have no idea why they are doing this. All the more reason to watch them and find out what they are up to."

Doros had been for attacking the men, shooting them from a distance then retreating to safety. Lanos had insisted they do nothing of the kind.

"It will only tell them that we are here. No, we must observe everything. When your father returns we will still have the element of surprise."

Doros had finally agreed that it made sense. A campsite had been set up then they had travelled to the village to gather supplies. Lanos had insisted on avoiding Rakosur for fear that word of them and Andar would travel quickly throughout the village. If they gathered the supplies they needed in the village, so might the invaders of their home. And Roksur liked to talk.

Work on the pond had finished. It had taken the men many days of effort to dig a trench which diverted the creek that filled the pond. Doros had silently cheered when, with the arrival of the rains, the creek had swollen to thrice its size and undone their progress as it overflowed the trench and partially filled the pool again. When the rains had stopped, rocks and boulders had to be found, broken and transported, to reinforce the new path and prevent the emptied pond from filling again.

Doros watched several men who stood guard. He shook his head wondering why they would guard an empty pit. Movement on the far side of the pond drew his attention. Several men stepped out of the forest into the clearing but he didn't recognize them as any of those he had been watching. They were well armed, their chests covered like the council guards with breastplates. One approached those at the pit while the rest waited at the edge of the forest. The guards at the pit sprang to life, one racing back towards the house as the others loosened weapons. When the newcomer reached them, after a short conversation, he signalled to the others who disappeared into the reed trees. Doros shifted impatiently in the tree. Dusk was approaching and he feared it would be dark before he discovered what was happening.

At the forest edge soldiers stepped into the clearing. A short, powerfully built figure and a taller, bearded man followed them. The green mist began to gather at their feet, roiling up to obscure their bodies. Doros jerked, almost upsetting himself, as another figure then a second and a third came into view. He grabbed a tree branch, pulling himself forward. *Was that slight figure Dreanna?* Another taller woman followed her. He held his breath as the blurred image of a man stepped from the trees. Doros was sure that it must be his father. One of the soldiers shoved him and he raised his arms to shrug off the push. Doros saw that his hands were together, as if bound. Heart pounding, Doros stared into the darkening night. All walked towards the house. The tall, cloaked one and the shorter one entered while the others set up camp by the smith shop.

Doros' hands were shaking so much that he couldn't undo the knot that held him in the tree. He drew his knife and cut the rope, scrambling down the tree, forgetful of the need for stealth. All he could think about was getting back to Lanos to tell him that something had gone wrong.

It was several hours later when Bonara stood with a torch, on the embankment at the back of the house gazing at the empty pit. Grenfeld stood beside him. Bonara had been exhausted from the forced march, but a meal and the desire to see the entrance to this last vault had restored his energy. He peered through the dark and the mist at the narrow, deep end of the pit. *Under the rubble will be a dull silver wall, a door set within. The slots will be there to accept the keys. And the tunnel will lead down to room after room filled with...* He stopped, afraid that he might be too late. Grenfeld interrupted the silence.

"How long will it take to clear away the bottom and expose the door?"

"Little time, little time. The funnel-like pit marks the entrance. All the other doors have been just at the end, near the point."

"Good. Now that you have had your look, let's retire. It will be an early start tomorrow." He started down the hill back to the house. Reluctantly Bonara followed.

The Reedsmith of Zendar

The men toiled in the morning sun at the bottom of the pit. Some pried rocks and boulders free, while others dug and scrapped mud away. Bonara plodded restlessly near them, his feet caked in mud, the pouch clutched in his hands as he urged them to work faster. Grenfeld sat upon the embankment, on a boulder, silently studying the scene. His eyes moved back and forth, from the three prisoners who sat below him, to the excavation, to Bonara. He watched him slop through the muck at the bottom of the pit to join him.

"They should have found it by now," Bonara said in frustration.

"Patience my friend. They have barely begun."

"Yes, but that is the worry. The doors have never been deeply buried. They..." Bonara paused, going completely still as he listened. "Do you hear something?" They both listened for a moment.

"I hear nothing."

"Quiet! Be still," he yelled to the men below. Bonara moved higher up the embankment, stopping at the top. "No, no, not now! It can't be. Not so soon!"

"What is it, Bonara?" Grenfeld joined him.

"Can't you hear it? From the house. They were hanging on the porch."

Grenfeld looked in confusion towards the house.

"The crystals! The reed crystals are sounding. The rains are coming!" Without waiting for a reaction from Grenfeld, Bonara raced back to the edge of the pit. "Hurry! Faster! Double wages to the man who discovers the door." He looked at Grenfeld who had returned to his side. "If we don't find it now, we'll have to wait until they stop. I can't wait that long. I can't!"

Below, the men doubled their efforts, hacking at the mixture of earth and stone that clung together. It fell into the water at their feet, splashing their legs and bodies until they were coated in mud. They pulled the muck away from the end, casting the larger chunks of rock onto the banks where they landed with a wet thunk. Heralding the forthcoming rains, a gentle breeze rolled down the embankment and found them.

"Faster. Hurry," yelled Bonara.

Small drops started, spattering the ground. Bonara threw his head back and cursed the sky as they pattered his face. He screamed at the rain.

"Lord Bonara, we've found it!"

Bonara slipped and stumbled down the muddy slope until he stood behind the men once more. Over their shoulders he saw a small patch of silver. "Yes, yes! Hurry!"

The rain was light but steady now as the men worked. It ran from their shoulders, tapping the water and grey mud in the bottom of the pit. It formed small rivulets that snaked down the sides of the pond until the men were standing ankle deep in muddy water. The work continued, mud-slicked hands losing their grasp, curses tainting the air as feet sank into the muck, bodies sliding and falling into the mire. The rain strengthened, the drops growing fat and heavy, until at last all the men donned their face protectors. The water rose to their knees, but now the door was partially exposed. The excitement became infectious and soon Grenfeld was among the soldiers shouting encouragement.

"Enough! That's enough." Bonara's voice was barely audible through the din of the driving rain and rushing water. "Move!"

The men staggered back, thigh deep in water as Bonara fought his way forward. With his body, he sheltered the sack from the rain. Around him the water jumped and danced as he wrestled with the wet knot that kept the keys safe. Carefully he pulled one of them from the bag. The rain hammered his hand and the silver key as he guided it to the closest of the slots that ringed the almost invisible line that was the door. He pushed, but it refused to enter. He withdrew it and moved to the next slot, trying again, meeting with the same result.

"What's wrong?" It was Grenfeld beside him, yelling in his ear to be heard above the torrent of rain.

"Nothing is wrong," Bonara yelled.

On the third attempt, the key slipped into the slot. Bonara withdrew a second key, meeting with success on his first try. In his excitement, he hurried and fumbled the bag. He clutched it, saving it from disappearing in the churning froth that now encircled his waist.

"Hurry, Bonara! The water will soon be over our heads!" With a third key, Bonara reached for one of the two slots that were underwater, blindly searching. He bent lower until his beard kissed the surface. Grenfeld could hear the key scraping against the doorway as Bonara tried to find the slot.

"It's in," he said, struggling upright. He tried the next one at the other submerged slot without success. On the second try, it went in one of the exposed slots. The fifth slipped into the other slot under water. Bonara pulled the last key from the bag and turned to Grenfeld, the rain soaked cowl of his cloak plastered to his face.

"Now watch the power. Watch!" Chest deep in water, he pushed the key home into the final slot then stepped back.

Nothing happened for a moment, then part of the silver wall began to change colour and glow. Ripples appeared as the surface of the metal undulated. Suddenly the wall within the faintly scribed line disappeared and with a surge the water poured into the opening. The water dragged them forward into the doorway. Grenfeld caught the edge of the opening with one hand, and grabbed Bonara around the waist. The level of the water dropped quickly as the water disappeared beyond the opening, leaving them standing knee deep once more.

Grenfeld released Bonara and stared at the vanished door, then back at him. "We'll organize the men and start immediately."

The rain bounced off Bonara's face protector. "We have no need of them. Leave them to guard the prisoners and the entrance."

Grenfeld studied the feverish face then trudged out of the water and up the mud slicked slope.

Bonara tore his eyes from the black opening and followed Grenfeld. *Soon, soon I will know.*

Images faded in and out behind closed eyes;
    Memories within the huge, triangular skulls.
    Splinters of lives, of survival, of violence.
    Thousands of years of hunger.
    Waiting for release.
    Release from the hunger.

Chapter Four

Andar sat leaning against the wall under the porch roof. On either side of him Dreanna and Dajata coughed and sputtered. They sat, hands tied behind their backs, water still running from their bodies as they pulled in air with panting breaths. Although the rains were far from their peak, sitting on the rocky slope with their hands bound, without face protectors, they had barely been able to breathe. They had been dragged to shelter by Grenfeld's and Bonara's men when they had been ordered to get back. Exhausted, their guards stood or sat in silence, grateful to be out of the deluge.

Andar felt Dajata's head on his shoulder, then her face pressed against it as she kissed him. He looked down at her. She gazed up, her face serene despite their peril.

"I love you," she whispered.

He said nothing, knowing his fear and anger would only distort his words. He pressed his head down against hers, holding the pressure like a hug. She had accepted their fate. He couldn't.

He looked up when the men parted to let Grenfeld and Bonara through. Water drained from Grenfeld's head and shoulders as he tore off the face protector. He raked a hand over his hair, squeezing the water from it. Beside him, Bonara's eyes gleamed under the face protector. His gaze moved constantly out into the rains towards the pit.

Grenfeld looked at the three them. "I'll deal with you and your women when I return." His eyes, like Bonara's, gleamed as he spoke.

"Brandos stay here and guard them. You're in charge." He stepped to him, grabbed his wet cloak and pulled him closer. "The men we sent after those who attacked us on the trail did not return. My son could still be out there. Make sure you and the men keep a good watch."

"Yes, Lord Grenfeld. They will be here when you return."

"Good, see to it that they are. Guard them with your life." He looked to others. "The six of you come with me," he yelled above the roar of the rain.

"We have no need of them," yelled Bonara.

Grenfeld eyed him. "You may know what is down there, but I do not. Leave your men here if you wish. Mine will be enough." He slipped the face protector over his head, pulled the hood up, and grabbing the guide rope, stepped once more out into the rain. Bonara motioned to his men to follow him and hurried after Grenfeld.

Brandos looked worriedly at Andar then addressed the men. "Fretin, Mindon, take that end of the porch. Huskar, Restos, the other. Nellos, you'll remain here with the prisoners. I'll guard the front door of the house so that no one approaches that way. Keep your eyes open. If we can still move and work in the rain, they can as well. Remember, the others didn't come back." He looked at the men to make sure his warning was well taken, then glanced down at the three. "Tie their feet together and then to each other."

Two of them gathered some rope and approached Andar who drew his legs in. The tip of Brandos' spear pressed against his neck.

"Don't. I think Grenfeld would rather see you dead than have you escape. I know I would."

Andar's head fell back against the wall and he let his legs relax. They tied the rope around his legs and then around Dreanna's and Dajata's.

"Good," said Brandos. "Keep an eye now." He leaned his spear against the wall and entered the house closing the door behind him.

Huskar looked at Restos. "Keep an eye, he says. I'll bet he keeps an eye in there where it's dry and warm and there's plenty of ale."

"Never mind that," said Huskar. He's right, the others did not return."

"They're probably holed up somewhere warm and dry, waiting this out," said Restos. The two walked to one end of the porch as Fretin and

Minden moved to the other, leaving Nellos eying the three. At the end of the porch, Restos slid to the floor, resting his back against the house. Huskar stood at the roof's edge and peered through the veil of rain.

"Keep a watchful eye?" he said. "There could be an army in front of us and we would never see them." He walked back to where Restos sat, and leaned against the wall.

Beyond the roof's gutter in the rain a blurred vision appeared, faint and obscure. Huskar leaned forward trying to determine if it was something or an image created by the dancing rain. Too late he recognized the shape of a man.

Rothus fought the weight of the bow and of the rain that sought to drag his arm down. With his side pressed against the guide rope, he walked towards the house. As the porch materialized, he pulled the arrow back. Now he could see a man leaning against the wall, staring outwards, straining to see him. He released the arrow high, aiming above the man's head, knowing the rain would drive the arrow downwards.

Seated, Restos heard a dull thud through the din and raised his head. Huskar clawed at the arrow protruding from his chest that had pinned him to the wall. As his weight slowly bent the arrow, blood ran down the length of it to drip from the end. Restos struggled to his feet, groping for his sword as he looked out past the rain and saw the man approaching. The bow was drawn back and he knew he was too late. Nellos, standing beside the three prisoners, wheeled about to see the arrow strike Restos in the side. He watched him slump to the floor.

At the other end of the porch, Rigersor, an apparition from a nightmare, materialized out of the rain. His heavy staff swung at the two, breaking bones and smashing skulls before they knew he was upon them.

Nellos spun around at the sounds, frozen to the spot as he witnessed the carnage.

"Nellos, put away your sword," said Rothus who now stood on the porch, his bow levelled once more.

Nellos turned at the sound of his voice and stared at the tip of the arrow.

"I will kill you. Put the sword down."

The soldier looked at Rothus above the shaking bow, then back to the Sleeper who slowly walked towards him. Without a word, he plunged from the porch, out into the driving rain and disappeared.

"Let him go, Rigersor. He only wants to escape. I don't think we need fear him."

"Rothus!" Dreanna called out as he made his way down the porch to her. The door flew open and Brandos leapt forward, his sword raised. Rothus turned but Brandos pitched forward, a dagger protruding from his back. Framed in the doorway, Doros stood wide-eyed. Behind him Lanos raised his sword at the sight of Rothus.

"You! You took my granddaughter."

"No, Father!" Andar yelled as Rothus stepped back. "Hold your sword!"

Lanos paused, but didn't lower his sword. "This droxeur took Dreanna when you were gone."

Andar laid his hand on Lanos' sword arm. "I know, Father, but things have changed. I'll explain later."

Slowly Lanos lowered his sword. "It is enough, for now, that you say to do so."

Rigersor and Rothus cut the ropes that bound the three. "It's good to see you, my friend," said Andar.

"You as well," replied the Sleeper.

He walked to Lanos who gave him a long hug.

"Colonar," Andar said, his eyes searching his father's.

"He's safe in the village."

Over his father's shoulder, Andar saw Doros staring at the dagger in the back of the man. He released Lanos. "Quickly, everyone inside."

Rigersor ducked under the doorway and entered as Dajata slipped into Andar's arms. She said nothing, but held him tightly as he led her inside. The room reached out and enclosed Andar, a long forgotten friend welcoming him. He led Dajata towards Lanos.

"Father, this is Dajata. She's to be my wife." He left the two and walked to Doros who stood in the center of the room by himself. He knew the conflicting emotions he would be feeling.

"You've done well, Doros. You saved his life." He threw his arm around him and turned to the others. "If any of the things that Bonar has told us are true, we are in danger from these creatures below."

"Creatures?" Lanos said looking up.

"A race of others who lived here on Zendar before us. If they are alive, still sleeping but alive, and if Bonara manages to awaken them... He has told us of the power they possessed." He paused as he remembered Bonara's warning threat. 'They are aggressive and warlike in nature.' "We have to stop Bonara. Stop them. Even if they are all dead, we can't allow Grenfeld or Bonara to get weapons or knowledge from this vault."

"But what can the three of us do against so many?" asked Rothus.

"There are four of us," said Lanos quietly.

"Five," said Andar looking across at Doros. He looked back to Rothus. "But you're right. We can't hope to defeat them by force."

The silence in the great room was suffocating as the rains beat on the roof. Feeble light from the small fire and a single torch barely illuminated the figures as they huddled together.

"Could we not break through the wall they built and let the waters flood the underground vault?" Lanos asked.

"Of course!" said Andar in excitement. "Let the rains do our work for us. It shouldn't take much effort to dislodge a few of the boulders. The force of the water should do the rest."

Dajata's voice filled the silence after the excitement of all had died away. "What if these creatures are not dead? What if they *are* alive? What if Bonara wakes them or he or they close doors to stop the water? How can we know?"

"Dajata's right," said Andar, the disappointment etched into his face. "Perhaps flooding the tunnel won't stop them. We have to know."

"Then what do we do?" asked Lanos.

The rain beat on the roof as everyone avoided the answer.

"Someone has to follow them down and find out."

Andar didn't know who said it. He felt the weight of his journey bear down on him as he realized it still wasn't over. His family was safe. He had found someone. He wanted to stay here, in this house, with this woman. But it wasn't to be. The silence in the room was prophetic, the decision only delayed by it.

The rain beat on the roof as he looked into the hearth where he had sat alone for so long. His eyes explored the great room as he searched for a sense of comfort in the familiar. He looked at Dajata, at his family gathered together, and the burden lifted. He smiled as he accepted what had to be done. For his family. For all of Zendar.

"I'll go into the tunnel and find whether the creatures live or not. If they don't, I'll return and we can flood the tunnel to end Grenfeld and Bonara's lives. If the Dremords are alive and have not been freed, then we flood it and hope it ends their lives as well."

"What if they have been freed?" asked Doros.

Andar shrugged his shoulders. "Then we must spread word of the danger."

The Sleeper smiled when Andar had finished. "And if we do not return?"

Andar looked at Rigersor. "You don't have to go."

"Answer the question."

He hesitated for the briefest moment. "Then the rest will flood the tunnel without us."

The opposition came in a chorus of shouts from everyone. Dreanna and Doros were at his side, pulling at him.

"No, Father, we can't do it," said Dreanna.

"She's right, we can't, said Dorus."

"Let's go to the village. Tell the council. They can do something. They can bring the council guard."

"You just found Dreanna. You can't leave us now," pleaded Doros. "We're back together again."

Andar looked at his children. Dreanna was in tears, holding onto him. He could see the fear in Doros. He raised his eyes and saw Dajata watching them, sad acceptance on her face. She had heard Bonara's stories, seen proof of the threat of those below. She knew that something had to be done. His eyes never left her as he spoke.

"What I have learned about those below is frightening. They are warlike, have conquered others. Something must be done, and quickly.

There's no time to travel to the village. They would not believe such tales. There *is* no other choice." He put his arms around his children and hugged them fiercely then turned to Lanos. "We will need torches. You know the river and pond better than any. Find the best place to break the barrier they have created if it comes to that." Lanos' face was white, but the old man only nodded stiffly and turned away.

"I'll go with you," said Rothus.

"No, you must stay here. If we don't return, I want you by Dreanna's side. You, Dreanna, all of you will need to spread word of that below." Before Doros could argue, Andar turned to him.

"Doros, would you lend me your sword?" Andar smiled at him. "I promise to return it when done."

"I want it back. I want you to bring it back."

"I will," he said placing his hand on his son's shoulder.

Andar walked to Dajata. Her eyes were focused on the floor and didn't acknowledge him when he stood in front of her. Finally, he raised her chin, and as the curtain of hair parted to reveal her face, he saw her again on that first day when he had taken her from her home. He saw the fear in her face, but she put a finger to his mouth before he could speak. She took his hand and pressed something into it. Looking down Andar saw he was holding the artifact still wrapped in the worn cloth.

"Take it with you. I have seen you use it. It is better to use it than hide is away for an eternity. "I know the danger is real. I have heard the stories with you. I know Bonara and Grenfeld must be stopped." And I know you, the kind of man you are, and that is why you must go. I know all this." She spoke quietly, bereft of emotion.

Andar held her hands. "Then know I love you."

She touched his face. "I know that. I love you too," she whispered, kissing him gently before turning away.

Lanos shoved torches and a face protector into Andar's hands then walked and stood together with Doros. Andar looked at his family, nodded to Rigersor who opened the door and the two stepped outside.

Chapter Five

The floor of the tunnel was a shallow, fast flowing river of brown foam that raced along ahead of them into the dark. Flames from the torches danced and flickered, pressing back the darkness as Andar and Rigersor, the rain still running from them, began their descent. Sword in hand, a torch held high, Andar led the way in the narrow passage. Both knew that the light was an alarm but there was no other way.

They moved slowly, carefully shuffling through the water, eyes straining beyond the torch's feeble rays, searching for guards, for the unexpected. The walls were damp, water oozing out of the rough gray stone and running down the walls. The floor started to slope then steepened and the tunnel spiralled downwards into the rock. The walls became dryer the deeper they travelled, the river at their feet dissipating as it slipped into cracks and crevices in the floor. A musty odour replaced the dampness in the air. They increased their speed, confident with the unchanging tunnel which soon ended its corkscrew path, straightened and levelled out.

The tunnel floor was now dry. Andar took a deep breath and started forward, the tracks of the others before him in the dust. Time slipped by, unmeasured in the silence save for the muffled sound of their footsteps. The tunnel walls ran straight and true for a short distance then disappeared. Andar eased forward, holding the torch aloft. They were entering a room so large that the feeble light of the torch could not illuminate it. He turned to the right and continued along the wall. To his left, row upon row of obscure forms became visible as light from the torch bounced off the stone wall. He walked past them until he couldn't resist any longer. Stepping away from the safety of the wall he extended the torch towards them.

Vertical transparent tubes, his height, materialized out of the gloom, dust thick upon each rounded top. Andar stepped closer and peered at the nearest one. Through the clear, amber liquid that filled it, he stared at the bloated, white body of a human-like figure that floated within. Delicate hands on the ends of fleshy arms touched the sides of the tube. Vacant eyes looked back at him, the open mouth seemingly on the verge of speech. Naked, the body hung motionless in the fluid, its bald head touching the rounded top, feet floating above the tube's bottom. It reminded Andar of the dead Suru he had pulled from the water so long ago. He sensed Rigersor beside him.

"I thought they would look different," he said to the Sleeper. Rigersor didn't reply.

"Do we know that this is dead?" asked Rigersor motioning to the thing in the capsule.

Andar turned to see his companion studying the white image. He gazed at the pale figure again. "He must be."

Moving back to the wall, they continued, passing countless tubes, finally entering another room, then another, each filled with identical tubes. In the blackness, they ventured deeper into the vault, the tension building with each step. The torches illuminated another doorway that framed the darkness beyond. They entered silently. Suddenly, glaring light flooded the room, blinding them as they crouched, swords in hand, shielding their eyes. They searched for any sign of attack, but all remained silent as their eyes adjusted to the light which came from the rock walls around them. Andar realized he was holding his breath and exhaled as he looked at Rigersor.

"Perhaps they have reached this thing, what did he call it, the control table?" said Andar. "Maybe he used it to light the room."

The room was immense, filled with rows of long, chest-like containers, the top of each covered in the dust of thousands of years. Andar touched one, finding it cold. He circled it, wiped some of the dust from

The Reedsmith of Zendar

the top, and his hand leapt back when his eyes focused upon the contents.

The horrid image lay still beneath the transparent cover, its quiet presence threatening in its familiarity: his dreams come to life. His heart raced as he gazed upon the angular head. The torch light shone dully on the face, eye sockets cast in deep shadows. Black skin, glazed with indigo streaks, stretched tightly over the heavily boned skull. White teeth, needle sharp, glinted in the light. The face exuded power and brutality, even as it lay motionless. It was all at once threatening and hateful, and the chill of fear Andar felt was real when he moved the torch close and saw the pulsing beat beneath the closed eyelids.

Andar glanced at Rigersor who stood staring at the creature. The Sleeper looked at Andar with troubled eyes.

"It's alive".

"Yes."

"These must be the creatures that the bearded one spoke of."

"Then who are the others?"

Rigersor shrugged his huge shoulders. He looked up from the unearthly face to the rows of other containers, then back to Andar and saw the same worry and fear in his eyes. He nodded his head to proceed. Andar set the torch down and crossed the room to the doorway on the opposite side. They passed through room after room that lighted as they entered, all filled with similar containers. From ahead, Andar recognized the animated voice of Bonara. They crept forward.

"Yes, now you believe me. Now you see what has sustained me for so many years. And it has not been in vain. So many are still sleeping. Waiting."

A calloused hand pulled Andar back behind one of the containers.

"We know that the creatures still live," said Rigersor. We have found what we need to know. Let us return to the surface."

Andar drew his eyes away from the barely visible figure of Bonara. His face was dark, his voice strained. "No, not while Grenfeld and that bastard lives."

"If we flood the tunnel we will end their lives as well as seal the fate of these creatures."

Andar was silent as he wrestled with his emotions. "How do we know that? How do we know that Bonara doesn't have the power or knowledge to seal the tunnel or divert the water? Maybe the water won't damage the containers and whatever controls them. Maybe we need to destroy the...the control table, to smash each of the containers. I think we have to listen until we know what to do."

"Perhaps you are right," Rigersor said. "But, if we take too long-"

"There's a doorway over there. Maybe it will lead to the other side so we can get closer."

Andar moved towards it, darting from one container to another. The room they entered held countless spheres that hung in rows from the ceiling, the closest dark. However, fully half of the spheres glowed, a blue mist twisting and turning inside. The light from them lit up the ceiling with an unhealthy glow. A rhythmic clicking sound emanated from them.

The two moved through the display of light and sound to the next room which contained similar spheres, but here all was silent and in shadows. The next room held rows of containers, each open, exposing the remains of the creatures. They walked past them, nervously viewing the remains of each corpse. Within the first containers the creatures held the same stoic pose, but as they travelled down the rows towards Bonara's voice they saw the change. One of the creatures had its head turned sideways. Several had an arm out of place. Some had managed to grip the edge of the container with a clawed hand. Each had awakened and lived longer. All had long ago dried and shrivelled, lifeless versions of the creatures they had been.

Andar and Rigersor continued through the maze of dead, viewing the effort to change and awaken them. Some died sitting erect, their huge skeletons wrapped in brittle black skin. Others lay crumpled over the side, hanging from their coffin. As they approached the doorway, the last of the containers were free of their burden, bodies lying in grotesque heaps on the floor. One had taken several steps before collapsing.

They were at the door now and Bonara's voice was loud as his feverish monologue continued. Andar and Rigersor flattened on each side of the doorway and peered around the edges.

The Reedsmith of Zendar

Bonara's men stood nervously, their eyes flitting from Bonara to the strange surroundings. Grenfeld's men stood behind them, shifting their feet as they too watched in anxious silence. Bonara hurried from one group of flashing lights to another, touching this, adjusting that. Grenfeld said nothing, but it was obvious he was growing impatient. The tension in the room was palatable.

"It's done! Twenty years of exploring the other vaults has done me service. I've studied the results and seen the changes. They have been too cautious. The answer was so simple." He spun about, away from the panel to face Grenfeld. "All we need is one Dremord to survive. After that we can deal with the rest at our leisure. Think of it, Grenfeld. One lone survivor, owing his life to me! I have much to thank you for. I will not forget the part you played in this venture."

Grenfeld simply stared at him. Bonara spun again, leaning on the table, his hand floating above a glowing button.

"And now, I give you rebirth," he said loudly, raising his head and looking towards the doorway where Andar and Rigersor watched. Bonara's hand paused and Andar knew that he had been seen, but it didn't matter. Bonara jerked stiffly upright, the shock and pain freezing him as the purple blade burst through his stomach. It twisted as Grenfeld withdrew the sword. Bonara pitched forward onto the sloping table - and the button. From behind them the blades of Grenfeld's men flashed and thrust. Bonara's men fell, their screams echoing in the cavern.

"It looks like you were right to stay longer," said Rigersor. When Andar didn't answer he turned and found him, eyes fixed on Grenfeld. "Andar," he whispered again.

Andar came out of his hypnotic stare and turned to Rigersor. His face was drawn and empty.

"Leave Grenfeld to me."

Unoticed, Andar stepped through the doorway and circled the room, moving closer to Grenfeld and away from his men. At the sound of his sword leaving the scabbard, Grenfeld looked up. He held up his arm as his men moved towards Andar. Anger replaced his surprise.

"I should have killed you before, but I wanted the pleasure of making your death a lengthy one. I'll settle for it here and now, with your own sword. Know that when you're dead, I'll do whatever I wish with both your women."

As Andar braced for an attack a soft hissing noise reached them.

In the room behind him a container started to open.

Chapter Six

Andar resisted the urge to look towards the doorway and the sound. Grenfeld's eyes darted to it and back to Andar, indecision creasing his face. The noise from the other room stopped and, as if a signal, Grenfeld lunged low and deep, extending to the limit of his reach. Andar was ready. He caught the blade on his, deflecting it, then his blade raked across Grenfeld's side leaving a thin trail of red. Andar gripped his sword tighter. Grenfeld's escape warned him of his skill.

Andar pushed the memory of the noise out of his mind and concentrated on Grenfeld. He relaxed and let his sword jab, thrust and counter without thought. What he lacked in strength, he made up in agility, dodging and rolling with the quick, powerful strokes Grenfeld delivered. On the dais Grenfeld cursed as he slipped in Bonara's blood. Andar saved himself as he rolled off to the side and escaped a fatal blow. They circled again and again, each looking for an opening to end the conflict as Grenfeld's men silently watched.

From across the room Rigersor viewed the battle. Then his eyes met the pale yellow ones of another who stood large and motionless behind everyone in the far doorway.

Andar sensed that Grenfeld was tiring. The baiting talk had stopped, and the face was red and shinning with sweat. He increased the speed of his attack, his blade jumping left and right, thrusting and slashing, denying him an opportunity to launch an offense. He saw the edges of doubt in Grenfeld's face and pressed harder. Suddenly Grenfeld turned the attack aside and sprang forward, delivering a powerful blow that rang against Andar's weapon, shattering his blade. Grenfeld dropped his sword, knocking Andar to the floor, hands tightening on his throat.

"Thank you for the fine sword, master reedsmith," Grenfeld taunted, bearing down with his weight.

Andar rolled and bucked attempting to break free, but the grip tightened. He hammered at the corded arms as Grenfeld threw his head back, preparing for a final effort. Grenfeld's eyes found the creature watching them from the doorway and the pressure of his grip lessened. Andar sucked in a trickle of air, felt for and drew Grenfeld's dagger. He drove it into Grenfeld's side. Before he could strike again, Grenfeld threw himself sideways. Staggering to his feet, Andar picked up Grenfeld's discarded sword. His sword.

"You will die yet," Grenfeld screamed, pulling the dagger out.

Andar lunged, driving the blade through Grenfeld's chest. The blow jolted his shoulder and wrenched the sword from his hand. Grenfeld tottered then fell heavily to the floor as Andar sank to his knees.

"Andar!"

Through his pain and exhaustion Andar heard his name, but it was not enough to disturb him from his slumped rest. It was over. Grenfeld was dead. He could rest. They were safe.

"Andar!"

The voice was loud and insistent. Wearily he opened his eyes. Grenfeld's body lay still in front of him. He detected movement. Then the horrors of his nightmare towered before him. From under boney ridges, yellow eyes pierced the gloom of the cavern. Below three moist holes in the middle of the triangular black skull, jaws moved experimentally, opening and closing, white teeth flashing in the dark. Black reptilian skin creased and wrinkled as the creature shuffled forward, shifting its weight from clawed foot to clawed foot.

Andar stumbled away from the creature, jumping in surprise when he bumped into Rigersor. Both watched the thing in front of them as it approached Grenfeld's men who stood silent and unmoving. The creature paused at Grenfeld's body. It looked down at the blood that pooled about him then reached out a large hand to encircle the hilt of Andar's sword. It pulled the blade free and examined it, feeling its weight, testing the edge with a taloned finger.

"What do we do?" Rigersor asked tensely.

The Dremord looked at Rigersor as he spoke.

"I don't know," Andar replied, his mouth suddenly dry. He looked to Grenfeld's men who still had not reacted to the creature. "What's wrong with them? Why don't they do something?" Without taking their eyes from the creature the two retreated further.

"We should have attacked it before it became armed," said Andar.

The Dremord ran the side of the blade along its hand. The blood had started to congeal and stuck to its palm. The sword fell to the stone floor. Yellow eyes focused on them as the bloodied hand came to its mouth. The pink and black tongue dabbed at the blood then licked it clean. The eyes closed and a shudder ran through the giant frame.

"Long. Has been so long." The words came slowly, awkward in the huge jaw. It looked at Andar whose eyes were wide with surprise. "Yes, I speak that you understand. I use your thoughts to understand and copy your crude language. But him," he said looking at Rigersor, "is... different." It turned towards Grenfeld's men who neither stared at the creature nor moved. The man closest slowly raised his sword until the tip of the blade rested below his jaw. With a sudden thrust he drove the point upwards. One by one the others followed until all lay dead.

It looked once more at the two who stood silently in shock. The Dremord sank to the floor beside Grenfeld's body. One clawed hand thrust into the stomach, tearing a dripping handful of flesh and organs free. The creature brought it to its mouth and the needle sharp teeth tore at it.

"Andar, the others we saw. That is why they were here. They were to be a source of food. To be eaten when the creatures awoke."

The Dremord looked up. Blood dripped from its jaws as it spoke. "Like we here before you, they... were... before us. They were much like you. Much so. Your crude language is similar." It pushed another handful of flesh into its mouth, all the time studying the two. "But time to free the others." Slowly it rose to its feet, looking longingly at Grenfeld's remains.

"Rigersor, it must be stopped."

The Sleeper moved away from Andar, his sword sliding from its sheath. Andar moved in the opposite direction towards one of the dead soldier's swords, and bending, pulled a sword free. As he stood up a wave of lethargy filled his mind. His arms became sluggish and his feet refused to move.

"Andar, what is wrong?" Rigersor stopped and studied Andar nervously.

"He cannot talk. I control him. More difficult than others. But you," the Dremord said turning to Rigersor, "what manner of creature are you? I cannot read your thoughts and you seem beyond my control."

"Andar! Andar!"

Rigersor saw Andar raise the sword tip. The Sleeper charged, swinging for the creature's head. With surprising speed it ducked under the blade and scooped up the sword it had dropped. It came at Rigersor, wielding the sword with crude strokes. Rigersor backed up.

Andar stirred. His mind cleared and he saw Rigersor deflecting the creature's blows.

"Hurry, Andar! He is not skilled but strong and quick."

The creature paused and turned its head to Andar. Andar's arms went lax and his shoulders sagged. Slowly the sword rose, the point approaching his throat. Rigersor slashed at the creature. The blow caught one of its arms and a scream split the silence of the vault. Enraged, it hacked at Rigersor who fought to counter the blows.

Free once more, Andar started towards the creature. Again, the lethargy numbed him. Rigersor hurled himself forward, flailing at the creature in an effort to keep it distracted. It screamed horribly, attacked Rigersor and drove him back. Andar saw that the creature was learning at a phenomenal rate. It was watching everything that Rigersor did, processing it and using it against him.

"Andar! You must do something. I cannot hold it much longer."

Andar's head was clear again, and it flashed into his mind. His pack and what it held. He saw the creature pause, reading his thought. Andar yelled to Rigersor.

"The Ancient Ones' artifact. It's in my pouch. You..." His mind became muddled and he ceased speaking.

Dropping his sword, Rigersor pulled his dagger and leapt towards the creature grabbing its sword arm and driving the dagger towards its chest.

The lethargy dropped from Andar. He saw Rigersor grapple with the creature, tore his eyes away, and raced to the doorway and his bag. Tired legs baulked at the demand, but the sounds of combat spurred him forward. He reached the doorway, spun around the edge. The bag wasn't there.

The creature grabbed Rigersor's wrist, preventing the blow and Rigersor groaned from the powerful grip of the taloned hand. The jaws screamed and teeth snapped at him. Rigersor refused to drop the dagger, fighting the pain as he held onto the creature's wrist. It forced the Sleeper's arms back, its jaws coming closer and closer. Teeth sank into Rigersor's wrist and in desperation he released the creature's sword arm and gripped its throat. The Dremord dropped the sword, its claws raking the Sleeper's arm, tearing deep gouges in it. It slashed at Rigersor, the blows buffeting him, the talons tearing him apart.

Andar spun about searching for the bag. He saw it lying on the opposite side of the doorway, dove for it and thrust his hand inside. It was at the very bottom wrapped in the cloth. He lurched to his feet, running back into the now silent room.

The creature rose from the bloodied body of Rigersor. Even as Andar raised the artifact, it sensed his presence and turned. The eyes bore into him. Andar saw them shining in the blood splattered face. It walked towards him, holding his eyes, filling his vision. In his hands the silver artifact began to quiver then shake as he fought to raise it. The force that issued from it collided with the numbness that filled his head. He tried to focus on the tingling but all he could attend was the looming presence of the bloodied mouth, the pink tongue, the yellow eyes. Sweat beaded and rolled down his face. He felt he would burst from the pent up energy of the artifact that couldn't be released. The creature was in front of him now, towering over him, Rigersor's blood shinning on its chest and arms. It reached out to take the artifact from him.

It paused when the sound, almost inaudible, filtered into the cavern. It seemed to slowly flood the room, building until it couldn't be ignored by the Dremord. In that moment Andar broke the weakened bonds that held him.

Narrow and brilliant yellow, the beam burst from the artifact striking the creature. Its head flew back from the shock and it screamed. The beam jumped and danced over it as the artifact shook in Andar's hands. Lines of flesh dissolved in the creature. It staggered back, its body now a strange, windowed form, dark red blood oozing and running as the beam dissolved more of it sagging structure. The weakened trunk collapsed, and wide-eyed, Andar followed it down, his whole being focused on the artifact. Severed in two, the head and shoulders crashed towards him onto the stone floor, a clawed hand reaching out and hooking his ankle. The beam swerved to it, severing it at the wrist. Andar stepped back, shaking off the still twitching hand.

He realized that the creature was dead and the beam disappeared as his exhausted mind released control. His arms fell to his sides and he staggered, almost falling as he stumbled towards the silent form of his friend. Andar gasped at the Sleeper's ravaged body. When he could, he looked down again and saw that the rugged face was calm and serene, the silent strength evident even in death. Rigersor's brown eyes stared sightlessly up at him. Andar reached out a trembling hand and closed them.

It was then that the surge of churning water rushed through the doorway, knocking him over and carrying him across the cavern floor.

Chapter Seven

The chest high water swept Andar across the room. It slowed as he was washed by the raised platform, but he couldn't grab the edge and hold on. He grasped something soft that bumped into him, but quickly pushed the body of the dead soldier away. The water rose, its speed increasing as it funnelled through a doorway. He was tumbled through by the foaming torrent. On the other side, the flood water eased its rush then, as it swept past row upon row of containers, it was churned into a maddened frenzy as it sought to circumvent each obstacle. It leaped and plunged and whirled, crazy with power. In it Andar fought for his life. The waves slapped at him, hurling him against the containers. He glanced off their rounded surfaces, was pinned to a clear window, viewing it's still living contents. There was a moment's respite while trapped, then again he was washed down rows of would be coffins, through another doorway, and out into another battleground. The lights dimmed, flickered and went out.

Through the stygian darkness he was hurled and bounced from obstacle to obstacle. He tried to relax and let the water have its way with him, protecting his head with his left hand, holding onto the artifact with his right. The water's surface smoothed as the containers were left below the surface, but now they struck at his legs as he sped by. He journeyed on, swept against a wall then rolled along it by the water's drag. The speed increased and with a rush he was through another doorway, then another and another. Finally the water slowed until he moved at a lazy pace. He bumped a wall, reached out and tried to judge the water's speed with his hand. He realized that he was no longer moving. He bobbed gently in the darkness, the silence complete. Holding onto the stone wall beside him, Andar waited. He wished it over.

As he moved the artifact from one hand to another, its presence became a reality. He held it out of the water, aware of the tingling still present, pointed it upwards, and focused his tired thoughts. It responded instantly, a wide pale yellow beam lighting up the dark. He saw that he was within an arm's reach of the ceiling. There was nothing else. He shone the light into the dark, increasing its strength, and saw the far wall in the distance. There was no sign of the doorway through which he had been washed. Even if he could swim there, and find the doorway, and swim down to it, he would be faced with yet another room, and another, and another. He had no idea where he had come from or how many different rooms he had been swept through. He would never be able to find the entrance. The light vanished and he waited.

Eventually the thought came to him. *What if there is more than one entrance? It would be at the opposite end of the first one, probably near where I have been washed, for wouldn't the water seek out the furthest point?* He looked around. Everything was under water and he cursed himself for his stupidity. *Think!*

It must be in the end wall. He remembered being moved gently along the wall until he had stopped here. *Below. The other entrance must be below. The water would stop here.*

Andar shone the light down into the water but it was far too dirty. The light winked out and he thrust the artifact into the small pouch on his belt. Taking a deep breath, he surged upwards then used his weight to plunge downwards and pull himself to the bottom. He found the doorway on his third attempt. Surfacing for air he rested.

The other entrance, after spiralling downward, had run straight before coming to the first room. If this one did the same then he knew that he would never make it to the air pocket that he hoped to find in the spiral shaft. Once started, there would be no turning back. But there was no choice. To stay meant death. He inhaled several times and then jackknifed his body into the depths.

He found the opening immediately and swam through pulling strongly with his arms. In the murky darkness, he bumped the ceiling, the collision threatening to loosen his precious supply of air. He swam, aware of how exhausted he was. He bumped the wall on the right, corrected his direction, and bumped it again. His lungs started to ache. He realized that he might be in the corkscrew already. Upside down, he clawed and pulled along the ceiling, the burning sensation on his neck and face becoming unbearable. How far would the water have pushed upwards? How much further could he climb?

His arms and shoulders burst free as he drove himself kicking and splashing out of the water. He gasped for breath, fell back and inhaled great lungs full of air. Exhausted, he pulled himself to the water's edge and collapsed in the tunnel.

Andar stood in front of the massive silver door, the pale yellow beam illuminating it. Summoning his strength Andar shone a brilliant beam of light on the door. The light disappeared and he stepped forward to view the small scar that hardly marred its surface. He turned from the door to the stone wall. The beam flared brilliant yellow and a line of solid stone disappeared.

He carved slowly, resting often, the energy required to control the artifact draining him further. He had no idea how deep this entrance might be. The other had been quite near the surface. He hoped for the same.

Time passed and he lay quietly in the dark. He slept and felt somewhat refreshed and cut away more of the stone. He now used the beam at a lower intensity, keeping it wider so that it dissolved the entire end of his small tunnel all at once. It took longer, but did not drain him as much.

Ahead of him he saw that it was no longer rock, but damp compacted soil that he tunnelled through. Encouraged, he brightened the beam and continued, the progress easier. As he worked, Andar sensed a change in the air. Somehow it felt thick. The pressure about him grew, but he pressed on.

Without warning the wall in front of him exploded outwards. He was hurled forward with it, the earth ahead of him scattering. The air pressure shot him from the tunnel out into the daylight and the thundering rain. He crashed into a stand of small reed trees, their supple trunks breaking his fall. Behind him he heard the rush of water slam into the smaller tunnel, sending a gyser of water into the air.

Andar rolled onto his stomach protecting his face from the rain. In his weakened state he lay helpless on the ground as it beat on his back and head, holding him down. He struggled, raised his hand, and the yellow beam spread a protective umbrella of light over him, evaporating the rain and sheltering him. Andar staggered to his feet and took a shaky step towards his home.

The fire flickered in the hearth spilling the glow into Andar's great room. The men and women sat quietly, each suffering from the consequences of their action. Occasionally they spoke in subdued whispers. Dreanna and Rothus sat next to each other, their arms entwined. Tears stained her face as she leaned against him. Lanos sat alone in his chair, his eyes and thoughts lost somewhere on the polished floor boards in front of him. His gnarled hand held a tankard of reed ale, not his first since they had breached the wall and freed the flood waters. Doros poked the fire with a reed, his anger masking the loss of his father. Dajata stood alone by a rear window, her face turned outwards to the rain.

All heard the latch move on the door. It slowly opened to reveal the slim figure of Andar, hair plastered to his head, the face haggard and drawn. Calling his name in unison they rushed to him. Dreanna and Doros reached him first, then Lanos. His children hugged him leaving little room for Lanos who stood silently beside them. Finally Andar released them and smiled grimly at his father.

"It's over, Father. Grenfeld and Bonara are dead. I believe the Dremords are too. The water flooded everything. The lights went out."

Hands shaking, Lanos reached out and held his son tightly then hobbled to his chair by the fire. He sat with his eyes closed, hands lying limp in his lap. Dreanna and Doros hugged him again as his eyes sought Dajata. She had not moved from the window. Andar disengaged from his children and walked towards her. Tears ran down her face as she raised her arms to him. They held each other in a silent embrace for a long time and when he kissed her eyes, they were still wet with tears. Dajata held his face in her hands, staring into his eyes.

"I knew you would come back to me," she whispered.

Andar looked at his family gathered around the hearth, then back to Djata. "It's over now," he said. "We're home."

Epilogue

The fire was only glowing coals as John looked at the faces ringed around him. Susan beamed with joy.

"I knew they would get back together! I just knew it!"

"And just how did you know it?" asked John, smiling at his daughter.

"You could tell," she whispered excitedly so as not to wake up Gordon and Elaine who had fallen asleep in their mother's arms. "They loved each other so much, that nothing could keep them apart." She looked into her father's eyes, her face full of assurance.

"Such a clever little girl," he said, smiling down at her, stroking her cheek.

"Dad, I'm not little any more. I'm just like Dreanna."

"Oh you are, are you?"

"Yes! She was so brave. I'm just like her."

"Good for you. Now help your mother get the others to bed."

"Ahh..."

"Come on now."

Gordon, his oldest, came over to him as Susan joined her mother.

"It was a good story, Dad, except for the mushy parts." He gave John a hug.

"Thanks, son."

"Yeah it was good, Uncle John. I liked Doros."

"Glad you liked it, Mike."

The Reedsmith of Zendar

John sat by the fire watching Gordon and Mike stir the coals with marshmallow sticks, smiling as he recalled some of the day's events. It was a clear night, the stars bright in the sky above the farm field behind his house. He took out the package and unwrapped it as his brother and Susan returned from the house.

"The ladies will be out in a-"

"We're coming," said Donna as the two appeared. Janice eased the door closed.

John looked up as he ran his hands over the object. He handed it to Mark.

"Your turn to hold onto it for a year."

Mark took it, smiling as the tingle began to travel up his arm. He looked up at John. "Ready?"

"Yes sir," John said. "Ladies?"

Everyone nodded as he rose to his feet and stooped to pick up a discarded wooden sword.

Together they began repeating the ceremonial drill that each had been taught since they were old enough to stand.

About the Author

My first book was co-authored with my cousin at age eighteen, written on two old typewriters using carbon paper. An English mystery novel, he wrote one chapter, I wrote the next, usually late on a Friday night. It was a sure fire scheme (one of many) to make us a lot of money. Surprisingly enough, the offers didn't roll in. Go figure. But I guess it was the first feeble start of my writing career. Put that career on hold for 20 years. With my wife and three boys I was busy with a teaching career, writing and directing school plays, building our log home and restoring a classic mustang; for car enthusiasts – a 69 Mach 1. Since then I have continued with a variety of projects. I have taken courses at The Humber School for Writers and Sheridan College, and have continued to, as my site tagline suggests, "write novels that this author would like to read".

Visit at www.danielside.com

Forthcoming

A Change Of Heart

Chapter One

On a July night, the sidewalks were crowded. The rain had stopped, and the air, warm and humid, held the odour of damp concrete as the surfaces dried. The city was just coming alive.

Patrick Corman pulled his taxi in front of the Cherry West bar and scanned the doorway for his fare. He shoved the cab into park, and checked the time. He would give them five. Movement at the bar door caught his attention. Patrick watched two guys exit, gauging their physicality, their dress, anything for a clue that would give him an edge. They spotted the cab, headed towards him, their gait loose but steady. *Drunks*, Patrick thought. *Wonderful, warm big tippers or pain in the ass sons of bitches.* The taller one pulled open the back door and they climbed in.

"Hey guys, where ya going?" Patrick asked, leaning an elbow on the seat back and speaking through the Plexiglas partition.

Mr. Tall studied the identity card fixed to the back of the driver's seat. "Hey, Patrick. Take us to The Hunt Club, 'cause the night has just begun."

"Hunt Club it is," he said as he started the meter then pulled away.

Patrick listened to the conversation from the back seat, feeling them out, trying to determine if they were worth more than cab fare. A couple of beers helped with a sale. He needed more than a few sales in the next couple of days to make up for the shortfall this month. In the mirror he watched them to determine who would be the easiest mark. Mr. Short and Curly was the most enthusiastic, babbling non-stop about their conquests tonight. He was the one.

Up ahead, Patrick saw the line of patrons outside The Hunt Club and cruised by it before pulling over to the curb.

"Hey, you passed it."

"I know guys, but I've got something you might be interested in. Just take a minute."

"Look, we're just interested in beer and some warm pussy," said Mr. Tall. Some other time, eh? We gotta get in that line 'fore it gets any longer. What'd we owe you?"

"Tell you what. Give me a minute of your time and I'll get you in the front door, forget about the line. Either of you guys gamers?"

"Yeah. Why?" asked Short and Curly.

Patrick smiled. "Have you tried Young Soldiers or Alien Storm yet?

"Shit, I wish. They're not out yet. I heard not till Christmas," said Short and Curly. A sly look came over his face. "Unless of course we can find a pirated one."

Okay, reel them in.

"Let's see what we can do," said Patrick as he climbed out of the cab and walked to the rear of the car. His passengers followed and watched as Patrick popped the trunk. The two peered inside. On the trunk floor, beside the gym bag, was a baseball bat and glove.

"What? I thought you were selling videogames, not baseball equipment?" said Mr. Tall.

"That's right." Patrick unzipped the gym bag and pulled out a half dozen games. "Here you go guys. Brand new, still in the wrappers."

"Holy shit. Look, Jimmy," said Short and Curly. He wasn't kidding! His eyes shifted to Patrick. "You sure these are real?"

"The real deal, not copies. Fifty bucks a piece. I can give you two for eighty. Cash only. I don't accept Visa or Mastercard." He smiled. *A little humour between friends.*

The two inspected the games, checking the wrappers and whispering between each other. "We'll give you sixty bucks for the two," said Mr. Tall.

"Nope. Two for ninety. Take it or leave it."

"What the...You said two for eighty."

"Yeah, I did, but time is money, and you're wasting my time. Now its two for ninety, a fucking good deal as both of you know. You can't get them anywhere else for months. As you know." *A little more business-like.* What's it going to be?"

"I told you, you idiot!" said Short and Curly to Mr. Tall. "Give him the money."

Mr. Tall fished out four twenties and a ten and handed it to Patrick.

Patrick folded the money and looked back at them. "Cab fare came to twelve seventy-five."

Short and Curly dug into his pocket and handed Patrick a ten and a five.

"Shall I consider the two and a quarter a tip?"

Short and curly stared at him. "Sure, what the fuck. Hey, what about getting us past those lines?"

Patrick grinned at them. "Sure thing, just give me a second to shut the cab off and I'll be right with you. He walked back to the cab, slipped inside, closing the door as he did. Patrick dropped the transmission into drive and watched the antics of the two in the rear view mirror as he pulled away. Now if he could unload the other eighteen games in the next week, he'd have the month's rent for Jenny. If he couldn't, he'd get the money, one way or the other.

He made his way south as he waited for a call. Searching the streets for prospects. Always looking. Ahead an older couple stood curbside, the man scanning the streets. When he saw Patrick's blue and white cab, he raised his arm. Patrick slowed but cruised by. He didn't need an old couple with suitcases they would like him to carry in. Anyways, he was almost there. Another right off the main drag and he saw the store up ahead.

He parked outside Patel All-Nite Variety and relaxed into the seat as he studied the front door. Through the glass and bars he could see the counter and the man behind it. He was East Indian, probably forty. He left the counter and went in back through a beaded doorway. Patrick slipped out of the cab and was at the door in four steps. The bell rang as he entered. He turned quickly, flipped the open sign to closed, slid the deadbolt home and stepped to the counter as the man returned.

"Yes, may I help you?" the proprietor asked.

"Yeah. You Patel?"

"Yes. Excuse me, but I don't know you."

"No you don't, but you do know a friend of mine who did some work for you. Some electrical, and he asked me to stop by and pick up the cash." Patrick, an arm's length away across the counter watched the man closely for any signs of movement.

"No, I'm not paying him. He does poor work. Very poor. Nothing works."

"Well, my friend says he tested everything before he left, you were happy with what he did, now he wants to get paid."

"No, you-"

Patrick's hand shot out and grabbed a fistful of shirt, pulling the man into the counter. Patel's eyes went wide and he froze.

"My friend has a wife and kids. He needs the money. Now."

"I don't have that much money here." Patrick heard the fear in the man's voice and a trickle of guilt ran through him.

"How much is in the till?" He allowed the man to reach over and open the drawer. "Pull out the twenties and tens."

Patel pulled them out and dropped them on the counter.

"Under the drawer. Let's see what's there."

Patel awkwardly pulled the tray free to expose three fifty dollar bills. He put the tray on the counter and then placed the fifties with the other money. Sweat beaded his face. Patrick studied the money.

"Well that's a start. You're going to need the small bills to make change the rest of the night, so you keep the tens. I'll take the twenties and the fifties." He glanced at Patel's watch. "And I'll take the watch."

Patel looked at the watch, then at Patrick before he removed it with shaking hands. He placed it on the counter. "Please, take it and go," he said weakly.

"Okay. Now, no one's been hurt. That's a good thing, eh? So I let go of your shirt, you just stay cool, I pick up the money and watch and leave. Got it?" Patel nodded slowly. A single drop of sweat hung on the end of his nose. Patrick released his grip, his eyes pinning Patel like a bug to a specimen board. He collected the money and watch. "You want the watch back?" The man looked at him and nodded his head slowly in confusion. Patrick backed away from the counter to the door.

"The next time a guy does an honest day's work for you, don't screw him out of his money. It ain't right. Understand?" Patel nodded again. Patrick turned, slid the deadbolt open, flipped the sign over and slipped outside. The door eased closed behind him with a little bump. Shoving the watch and money into his pocket, he hurried to the car. The engine caught and he accelerated away.

Patrick leaned back in the seat, and cruised slowly down Spadina, waiting for a call, scanning the sidewalks for someone to flag him down. For someone who looked like they might be a gamer. He took a long pull on the bottle of water beside him, wiped his mouth with the back of his hand and checked the time. *7:30. A couple more hours. Still time to unload more games.*

Ahead he saw two figures in the shadow of an alley making an exchange. The anger hit him in the stomach, a hot knife blade of memory. It was all he could do not to floor the cab and drive at the two who were oblivious to just another city taxi. He controlled his breathing and slowed the cab, pulling to the curb. Shutting off the engine, he watched the two as he dug the vial of pills from his pocket and put one of the nitroglycerin tablets under his tongue. He put the vial on the dash, and climbed out of the taxi leaving the door ajar so as to make as little noise as possible. At the back of the car he eased the trunk open and pulled out the baseball bat. Holding the business end of it in his right hand, he held it upright along the back of his arm so that it wasn't obvious. He walked down the sidewalk towards the pair, looking everywhere for some fictitious address. Patrick could feel his heart starting to hammer in his chest, but was helpless to heed its warning. Ahead the two seemed to have concluded their business and they looked towards him. Patrick gave a perplexed look.

"Hey, buddy. You got any idea where the Red Pepper Bar is? I been up and down this Goddamn street a dozen times."

The younger of the two, maybe eighteen, flicked his eyes his way but hurried past without saying anything.

"Hey, thanks for nothing," Patrick said and looked to the second man who was now watching him. He was of average height, thin with long lanky hair. The man stood studying Patrick with wary eyes. "Hey, man. You got any idea where the hell the Red Pepper is?" Patrick was within ten feet of him now. His heart beat like a trip hammer, the adrenaline racing in his body. The man saw the tell-tale signs, sensed the intensity then caught sight of the bat as Patrick let it slide down through his hand until he held it by the grip. By then it was too late. Patrick closed the remaining distance in three steps and had the man by the throat. The bat swung, smashing into the pusher's leg shattering the bones. His scream was caught in his throat, as Patrick leaned his weight into the man's throat, pinning the pusher to the wall.

"Do you want to die, you piece of shit? Do you?"

The man struggled weakly, his cries muted as the pain paralyzed him. He managed to shake his head.

"I'm going to ease up on your throat and let you breathe so that you can empty your pockets. Of everything. Drop it on the ground. If I find anything left in them, I am going to break your other leg. You understand?" The nod this time was quicker, more forceful. "Do it!"

Money and small bags of white powder fell to the ground at their feet. When the pusher stopped, Patrick moved in closer, his face inches from the man. "If I ever, ever see you selling this shit again, the next time I will kill you. You understand?" The man's eyes were wide in terror as he acknowledged the threat. Patrick kicked the money and drugs aside. "Down." With his hand still on the pusher's throat, he guided him down, controlling the cries of pain. Patrick kicked the cell phone towards the man's hand. "I'd call 911 if I were you. It looks like a bad break." Patrick stuck the bat under his armpit, picked up the money and the drugs and walked to the street. Following the curb, he dropped the drugs down a storm drain then walked back to the cab. The discomfort had already started to set in to his chest, heaviness under the breastbone radiating up to his jaw. As he reached the car, the burning sensation intensified. Inside, he pulled the vial from the dash, shook out two pills, placed them under his tongue and leaned back.

He had taken the single tab before he got out of the cab because had known it was going to happen. But the angina had kicked in stronger than in a long time. He was sweating now and his breath had become short and elusive. Two minutes turned into three and still he sat, watching the pusher complete his call as the nausea set in. He had to get the hell out of there before the pusher's cohorts arrived. The tingling in his fingers became more evident as he turned the key in the ignition. He had to get to the nearest hospital or clinic. Vaguely he recalled one on Hedley Street, and pulled the taxi away from the curb.

The pain in the centre of his chest wasn't going away. Sweat trickled down his face as he thumbed the lid off the vial spilling the nitroglycerin pills onto the seat. Awkwardly, almost unable to feel them with his fingers, he pushed two more into his mouth. A driver's horn blared as his cab weaved into the left lane, almost clipping a car. He hunched over the wheel, using it for support as he searched for the clinic he hoped was just ahead.

He almost missed it. It was a plain white brick building, set close to the street like all the others. A small brass sign over the doors read The Living Research Clinic. Patrick pulled up in front and parked. He struggled out of the cab and walked unsteadily to the doors. One slid aside. Through another set and he could see a counter with a receptionist. The second set of doors opened and he staggered through. Pain squeezed his chest making speech almost impossible. "Heart...my heart..." He clutched the counter, holding on until finally the room swam and he passed out.

Patrick woke up in a room with pale yellow walls, the too bright florescent light above him harsh on his eyes. Monitors and machines stood silently around him. One beside him beeped rhythmically, the numbers on the screen changing back and forth as they monitored his pulse and blood pressure. His brown t-shirt had been cut open, electrodes attached to his chest. He reached up with an unsteady hand and adjusted the clear plastic oxygen mask that covered his mouth and nose. There wasn't any pain in his chest, and the tingling in his hands had stopped.

Lifting his arm, he glanced for his watch but it was missing. The clock on the wall read eight fifteen. *Less than half an hour.* He took a deep breath, then another, oxygen flooding his lungs. *That was a bad one. Stupid to attack the pusher.* Movement at his bedside drew his eyes to a white coat. Patrick thought the man had a kind face, a real doctor face, full of care and compassion. Below thinning brown hair, gold rimmed glasses glinted in the light as he smiled.

"Well, Mr. Corman. I don't imagine that was much fun. I'm Doctor Fanco. I think you have probably had more than a few episodes like that."

"Yeah, you're right, doc." His voice was muffled through the oxygen mask. "That one was about the worst of 'em though, except for the heart attack. That wasn't fun either."

The doctor smiled again. "How do you feel now?"

Patrick paused, considering. "You know, not bad."

"We put you on oxygen right away, did a quick blood test and electrocardiogram. Really, it was just the rest and oxygen that have brought you around. And the multiple nitro tablets you must have taken. Just a bad angina episode. No heart attack this time."

Patrick smiled wanly. "Well that's good news, ain't it."

"Yes it is, Mr. Corman." He paused and looked at the chart he was holding. "How long ago was the heart attack?"

"About a year. Yeah, a year this August."

"From the EKG, it looks like quite a bit of damage was done."

"Yeah, so they tell me."

"With that much damage, I assume you are on a waiting list for a transplant."

"Yeah, but they say that it's gonna be hard to find a match, 'cause of my type. Is it okay if I sit up? I feel pretty good now."

"Certainly, but let me elevate the head of the bed. We'll start with that." He held a button until Patrick was sitting upright then looked at the chart again. "I'm going to run another couple of tests to gather a little more information before-"

"Look, doc, no offense, but I'm leavin' now. Like I said, I feel okay, and between you and me, I probably can't afford what you already did, never mind more tests." Patrick pulled off one of the sticky electrodes. It left a pink circular blotch on his pale skin.

"Really, Mr. Corman, I think-"

"Doc," Patrick said patiently as he continued to pull off the electrodes, "if you just tell someone to bring me the bill for what you did, I'll get goin', okay?"

Dr. Fanco was silent as he studied Patrick. "All right, Mr. Corman, I will. However I wish you would allow us to give you further care."

"Well doc, you know how many people died last year waiting for a donor heart? I do. Over eight hundred. So, unless you can give me a new heart today, I don't think there's much you can do for me."

As Fanco left the room, Patrick swung his legs sideways until he was sitting on the edge of the bed. A wave of dizziness swept over him, but he waited it out before he stood and dropped the tangle of wires and electrodes on the mattress.

The night was still warm and sticky when twenty minutes later, Patrick popped the cab's trunk and pulled another brown t-shirt from the gym bag. Ignoring the stares and whispered conversation of a young couple who strolled by on the sidewalk, he slipped the shirt over his stocky, chalk-white frame. He eased the taxi's door shut, dropped the parking ticket on the seat, and started the car. *Christ I'm tired. But no pain. I'll take it.* The doctor had warned him against driving so soon after the attack, but Patrick had shrugged him off with a wry smile and a shake of his head. Like so many people, Fanco had no concept of what some had to do to pay the bills. To stay alive. As Patrick pulled out, he started the meter and picked up the mic.

"Where the hell you been, Corman?" the dispatcher asked.

"Yeah, sorry Bobby. I dropped off this little old biddy who needed help with her groceries, then her frickin' cat gets out the door. By the time I catch the cat, I see my tire's flat. I changed it. When I drop off this fare I'm gonna get it fixed. What a crappy night. Slow too for a Friday. Not much happening."

"All right, Corman, I don't want your life story. Make sure you change the tire back. Don't leave that donut on. You hear me?"

"Yeah, I hear you Bobby. Gotta go. Let my ride off." Patrick hung up the mic. "Fuckin' weasel." He took a deep breath, tried to relax and glanced at his watch. Eight forty-five. The pawn shop was just ahead. He stopped, shut off the meter and took the amount from his pocket to pay for the nonexistent trip. It would help make up for the chunk of time he spent in the clinic. He'd get a receipt for a tire repair from Gary tomorrow. Bobby was a ball breaker. He would expect a receipt, and no driver would pay for the repair out of pocket. Patrick pulled out the watch and money he had taken from the store owner. With the three fifties and the twenties, he had three ten, plus the watch. He dialed a fence he knew. It rang twice.

"Patrick, my man." The voice was that of a baritone, complete with the suggestion of a southern accent. Patrick was convinced he put on the voice as part of his business plan. "How you doin', bro?"

"Hey, Eldridge. I'm good, how're you?"

"Doin' good. So good. What can I do for you?"

"You know anything about watches?"

"You know I know something about everything. You got one you want to unload?"

"Nah, I just need to get an idea of what something like this is worth. It looks like it's worth money, but shit, they all look good today. Might be a knockoff for all I know."

"What kind is it?"

"Says it's a Movado."

"Gold, black face. No numbers on it?"

"Yeah, that's the one."

"Good, ain't I? I told you I know something 'bout everythin'. If it's the real deal, then it's worth 'bout eight hundred. *If* it's the real deal. Sure you don't want to part with it? I'll give you top dollar."

"Nah, thanks, Eldridge, not this time."

"Okay my man, but if you change your mind, you call me back."

"No problem. Thanks." Patrick looked at the watch again. *Eight hundred bucks. Why the hell would you have eight hundred bucks hangin' off your wrist?* He shook his head as he climbed out of the cab.

Inside the pawn shop, the air conditioner churned away noisily at the back of the narrow store. The air was clear, but Patrick shivered from the shock of the cold. A long glass counter ran along the left side chock full of jewelry and electronics. To the right, TVs and computers, a red Ludwig drum set, dozens of ceramic vases and sundry furniture were stacked on wooden platforms. Patrick glanced at the collection beneath the glass of the counter where a bald, heavyset guy stood polishing something. He looked up as Patrick approached, nodded and put down a shiny, brass dog.

"What can I do for you, buddy?" He smiled a grill of yellowed teeth.

Patrick placed the watch on the counter. "I wanna know what you can give me for this."

The man picked up the watch. "Now that's a nice looking watch." He turned it over. "If it's the real thing." He studied it some more. "Hmm, I'm not sure that it is." He looked at Patrick and smiled sympathetically.

Patrick held his gaze. "How long you been here? Fifteen, twenty years? Long as I can remember. So you should know your business, and you better know, for sure, if that is the real deal or not." The man's smile seemed a little less certain.

"Well let me have a closer look at it." He took an eyepiece from his pocket and carefully examined the watch. "Yes, I think I can safely say that this is an authentic Movado."

"Good. What will you give me for it?"

The man knit his brows. "The best I could do would be seventy."

Patrick smiled. "Ten percent's standard. That makes eighty, but I need ninety. You only need to hold it for a week and if he doesn't come back to get it, we both know it'll go quickly for a good price."

The pawnbroker hesitated. "Okay. I'll make out the ticket." As he turned for the back room, Patrick added. "And I don't want it out here in the counter. Hold it back there, just so there's no temptation."

The broker nodded grudgingly in reply.

Dr. Carl Fanco closed the door to his office, sat down behind the desk and stared at the phone. There had been lots of pressure to find a match for the last six months, and now, tonight, that had happened. His hand shook as he reached for the phone. A lot of money had been promised to the one who found the right match. His employer had been getting desperate. The tests weren't conclusive, but from what he had seen, it was as close as they could damn well hope for. He found the number he had never used and punched it in, unconsciously holding his breath, thinking of the reward. When the voice came on the other end of the line, Fanco could hear the excitement and hope in the single word, 'Yes?'

"It's Dr. Fanco, sir. We have a match. He walked in today. A ninety-five per cent match. It couldn't be more perfect. His heart is shot. He needs a transplant, and damn quick."

"What's the name?"

"Corman sir. Patrick Corman. Forty. Except for the heart, otherwise in good shape. The tests-"

"Send the results to me immediately." The line went dead. Fanco stared at the phone in his hand, hung it up and thought about what he would do with the money.

On the other end of the line, Fanco's employer made the phone call immediately. When it was answered, the instructions were curt. "The name's Patrick Corman. He's the one. I want to know everything about him by this time tomorrow. Set the plan in motion, the contingency plan as well." He hung up and breathed a sigh of relief, perhaps the first in a year. Now there was a light at the end of the tunnel.

Proof

Made in the USA
Charleston, SC
28 August 2014